William Hazlitt

**The Life of Napoleon Buonaparte**

Volume 1

William Hazlitt

**The Life of Napoleon Buonaparte**
*Volume 1*

ISBN/EAN: 9783337349837

Printed in Europe, USA, Canada, Australia, Japan

Cover: Foto ©Andreas Hilbeck / pixelio.de

More available books at **www.hansebooks.com**

NAPOLEON CROSSING THE ALPS.

# THE LIFE

OF

# NAPOLEON BUONAPARTE.

BY WILLIAM HAZLITT.

VOLUME I.

PHILADELPHIA:

J. B. LIPPINCOTT & CO.

1875.

# PREFACE

On the work to which the reader is here introduced, HAZLITT was content to rest his claim to distinction as an author; it is his largest work and his last. He lived to complete the LIFE of NAPOLEON, and then laid down his own. He intended to add an Index, which it has been necessary to supply from another hand, for his was stiff and cold before he could accomplish it. He contemplated a Preface, and as the work would wear an unusual appearance without such an introduction, it has been deemed proper to make it the vehicle of a few remarks on the work and its author. HAZLITT rarely wrote till he was urged by necessity: but the LIFE of NAPOLEON was undertaken by choice. He felt that injustice had been done to the character of that extraordinary man, in every attempt that had been hitherto made to describe it. Much time was occupied, and great expense incurred, to obtain ample materials for the present work. Not satisfied with books and written documents, HAZLITT saw and conversed with the persons most likely to afford him information. He resided two years in Paris for this especial purpose; and the work, in consequence, possesses anecdotes and facts which throw quite a new light on many subjects hitherto seen "through a glass darkly." HAZLITT has endeavored, and we think successfully, to trace events to

their spring, in the mighty mind out of whose workings they
arose.   Buonaparte, as the creature of circumstances, is one
thing; as their creator, another; and it is curious to contemplate him under both views.   The author may be accused
of partiality when the very original views he takes are submitted to the judgment of prejudice and preconception.   But
let it be remembered, that wealth and genius have been
lavished to give a false color to many transactions which are
here related in their simple nakedness, and the charge of
partisanship may be retorted on the accuser.   The political
bias of HAZLITT's mind was to popular right and the sovereignty of the people.   When we find this feeling urge its
possessor to accuse his hero of wilfully attempting the subversion of justice, and with a disregard to the social compact,
we may believe him when he praises.   The champions of
things as they were before the Revolution demand of Napoleon that liberality and love of equal right which was unknown in the days they venerate.   They blame Louis XVI.
for those concessions to public opinion which they required
of Napoleon, and which they would have had Charles X. refuse.   They exclaim against those acts of Napoleon which all
regard as tyrannical, but they justify similar deeds in his
legitimate successors.   HAZLITT was not the infatuated
worshipper of an idol, but the champion of an historical
character which he conceives unjustly and wantonly attacked.
He has sacrificed no principle to palliate his hero—he has
rigorously examined and fearlessly blamed where censure
appeared called for—and he has quietly wiped away the stain
from a great picture, when he found that malice or ignorance
had left it there: when faults were in the piece itself he has
not attempted to remove them.   It would be arrogant to say
that the unanimous verdict of posterity will agree with the

decision of the biographer; but we may aver, without fear of contradiction, that the materials from which such a verdict will be drawn are impartially summed up in this work, with an ability which none will doubt. As we have already stated, HAZLITT's fame as an author will mainly depend on the public estimate of this his last labor. Thousands have read and been delighted with his less important works; but here was a subject with which he grappled to the utmost of his strength, a labor of his own seeking, to which he devoted many anxious years, and to which he strove to bring the whole force of his talents, lavish the brilliancy of his genius, and give it the stamp and impress of his powerful mind. How he has succeeded, will be decided by that public to which he has never appealed but with a successful issue.

# CONTENTS OF VOLUME 1

## CHAPTER XII.

## CHAPTER XIII.

## CHAPTER XIV.

## CHAPTER XV.

## CHAPTER XVI.

THE

# LIFE OF NAPOLEON

## CHAPTER I.

FROM HIS BIRTH TO THE PERIOD OF THE SIEGE OF TOULON.

NAPOLEON BUONAPARTE was born at Ajaccio in the island of Corsica, on the fifteenth day of August, 1769. He was the son of Charles Buonaparte, an advocate in the royal court of assize, and of Letitia Ramolino, his wife, a Corsican lady of great beauty, and of a good family, descended from that of Colalto at Naples. He had four brothers, born of the same parents; Joseph (elder than himself), Lucien, Louis, and Jerome; and three sisters, Eliza, Caroline, and Pauline. In the register of his marriage with Josephine Beauharnais, which took place the 9th of March, 1796, the 5th of February, 1768, is given as the date of his birth, and his name is signed NAPOLEONE BUONAPARTE. He was baptised the 21st of July, 1771.*

The ancestors of Buonaparte, on the father's side, came originally from San Miniato in Tuscany: some of the family held the sovereign power at Treviso. In the middle ages they figured as senators in the republics of Florence, Bologna, Sarzana, or as pre-

* It has been pretended that the date of Buonaparte's birth was put forward above a year, in order to make it appear that he was born a French subject, Corsica not having been ceded to France till June, 1768; but the birth of his brother Joseph in January, 1768, makes his birth in February of that year impossible; and the date of August, 1769, is given in the list of pupils at the school of Brienne, at a time when there could be no sufficient motive for falsifying it.

lates of the church of Rome. They were allied to the Medici,
the Orsini, and Lomellini families. While some of them were
engaged in conducting the public affairs of their native cities,
others devoted themselves to literary pursuits at the period of the
revival of learning in Italy. Giuseppe Buonaparte published one
of the earliest regular comedies of that age (1568, or titled " The
Widow," copies of which are still extant in the libraries of Italy,
and in the Royal Library at Paris; where is also preserved " The
History of the Sacking of Rome by the Imperialists under the Constable de Bourbon in 1527," of which Jacopo Buonaparte is the
author. He was a contemporary and an eye-witness, and his nar-
rative is much esteemed.* When Buonaparte marched upon
Rome, literary men, who are ingenious in finding out trifling co-
incidences, remarked, that since the time of Charlemagne this
capital had been twice threatened by great foreign armies, at the
head of one of which was the Constable de Bourbon, and at the
head of the other, a remote descendant of the family of his historian. The manuscript of this work was first printed at Cologne,
in 1756; and the volume contains an elaborate genealogy of the
family of Buonaparte, which is traced very far back. An uncle
of the author, one Nicolo Buonaparte, is mentioned in it as a very
distinguished scholar, and as having founded the class of Juris-
prudence in the University of Pisa. When the French army entered Bologna, in 1796, the Senate had their "Golden Book"
presented to the General-in-Chief, by Counts Marescalchi and
Caprara, in which the names of several of his ancestors were inscribed amongst those of the senators who had done honor to the
state.

In the fifteenth century, a younger branch of the Buonaparte
family, that had been driven from Florence by intestine troubles,
settled first at Sarzana, and then in Corsica. It has also been
stated by an author of some repute (Zopf, in his "Summary of
Universal History") that a scion of the Comnena family, who had
claims on the throne of Constantinople, retired into Corsica in
1462, bearing the name of Calomeros, which, having the same
meaning, was probably Italianised into Buonaparte. This, how-

* This piece has also been attributed to Guicciardini, and is inserted by
him in his History of Italy.

ever, is but a conjecture, though it would be curious to discover
that Napoleon had Eastern blood in his veins.    At the time of his
first campaign in Italy, there was no one left of the Italian branches
of his family, but the Abbot Gregorio Buonaparte, canon of San
Miniato.    He was an old man of great wealth and respectability.
Napoleon, in his way to Leghorn, stopped at San Miniato, and
was entertained with his whole staff at the house of his kinsman.
After supper the conversation turned entirely on a Capuchin friar,
one Father Buonaventura, a member of the family, who had been
beatified a century before ; and the abbot earnestly solicited the
interest of the General-in-chief to procure his canonisation, being
sure that he owed all his good fortune to him.    This proposal,
which occasioned a good deal of laughing and merriment among
the officers, was several times made to Napoleon by Pope Pius VII.
after the Concordat.    The next day, in return for his hospitality
and the interest he took in the family, Buonaparte sent the good
old man a Cross of the order of St. Stephen, which he recollected
he had at his disposal.

The name of Buonaparte was often spelt indiscriminately with
the *u*, or without it, by the different branches of the family : sometimes it has happened, that of two brothers, one has spelt it one
way, and the other the other.    The omission of the letter was
common in very early times.    In the church of St. Francis, belonging to the Minor Friars in the town of San Miniato, on the
right of the principal altar is a tomb with the following inscrip-
tion :

> CLARISSIMO SUÆ ÆTATIS ET PATRIÆ VIRO
> JOANNI JACOBO MOCCII DE BONAPARTE
> QUI OBIIT ANNO MCCCCXXXXI DIE XXV
> SEPTEMBRIS NICOLAUS DE BONAPARTE
> APOSTOLICÆ CAMERÆ CLERICUS FECIT
> GENITORI BENEMERENTI ET POSTERIS.

The name was spelt *Buonaparte* during his first Italian campaigns, which is the reason why I have preferred it in writing this
history.    The Christian name of Napoleon has also been made a
subject of dispute.    It was frequent in the Orsini and Lomellini
families, from whom it was taken by that of Buonaparte : it was

always given to the **second son**. The correct **way** of writing it
is Napoleone. Some pretend **that it is derived from** the Greek,
and signifies *Lion of the Desert;* **others that** it is derived from the
**Latin.** This name is not **to be found in** the Roman calendar.
**From** researches made in the Martyrologies at Rome, at the period
of the establishment of the Concordat, it appears that St. Napoleon was a Greek martyr. Clarke, afterwards Duke **of** Feltré,
(who was proud **of** his Irish extraction,) when sent ambassador to
Florence, busied himself with inquiries into Buonaparte's pedi-
**gree,** to which the latter put a stop by saying, "I am the first of
**my** family;" **and** to **the** Emperor of Austria, who, at the time
**of his marriage with his** daughter, set the heralds at work to trace
his genealogy to the old **Italian nobility, he** answered much in the
same spirit, that "he would rather be **the** son of a peasant than
descended from any **of the** petty tyrants of **Italy."**

Napoleon's great-grandfather had three sons, **Joseph, N**apoleon,
and Lucien. The first of these left only one **son,** whose name
**was Charles:** the second left a daughter, **named** Elizabeth, who
was married to the head of the Ornano family: **the third was a**
priest, and died in 1791, aged eighty years; **he** was archdeacon
of the chapter of Ajaccio. Charles, who thus became the only
representative of his **family,** was the father of Napoleon. **He**
received his education at Rome and Pisa, at which latter place he
took the degree of Doctor of Laws. Shortly after his return to
his native country, **he married. He was but twenty** years of age
**at the** breaking **out of the war of 1768 between France** and Cor-
**sica: he was a staunch friend to Paoli, and a zealous** defender
**of the independence** of his country. The town of Ajaccio having **been occupied** at the commencement of hostilities by French
**troops, he removed** with his family to Corte, in the centre of the
island. **His** young and high-spirited wife, then pregnant with
Napoleon, **followed** Paoli's head-quarters **and the army** of the
Corsican patriots, in the campaign of 1769, across **the mountains,**
and resided a long time on the **summit of Monte Rotondo, in the**
parish of Nioli. But as the term of her pregnancy drew near a
close, she obtained a safe-conduct from Marshal Devaux to return
to her house at Ajaccio. Napoleon was born here on the day of
the **Feast** of the Assumption. His mother had gone to church,

but finding herself taken ill, had hastened back to her room, which she reached just in time, and where the new-born infant came sprawling into the world on an old carpet with huge tawdry figures. It is not unreasonable to suppose, that the harassed life and high-wrought feelings of the mother, previously to his birth, might have had an influence on the temper and future fortunes of the son.

His father, after the unfortunate termination of the contest in which they had been engaged, accompanied Paoli as far as Porto Vecchio, and wished to have embarked with him: but the entreaties of his friends and his fondness for his wife and children prevented him. The French government established Provincial States in Corsica, and continued the magistracy of the twelve nobles, who, like the Burgundian deputies, governed the country. Charles Buonaparte, who was popular in the island, formed part of this magistracy. He was attached as assessor to the tribunal of Ajaccio: which situation gave him great influence with the supreme council of the country. In 1779 the States appointed him deputy for the nobles to Paris. The clergy chose the bishop of Nebbio, and the third estate a Casabianca. The elder Buonaparte took with him on this occasion his two sons, Joseph and Napoleon, the one aged eleven years, the other ten: he placed the former in a boarding-school at Autun; and the latter, through the interest of M. Marbœuf, governor of the Island, entered the military school of Brienne.

Little is known of Buonaparte's early years, except what he himself relates. He says that he was nothing more than an obstinate and inquisitive child :—"In my infancy I was extremely headstrong; nothing overawed me, nothing disconcerted me. I was quarrelsome, mischievous; I was afraid of nobody; I beat one, I scratched another; I made myself formidable to the whole family. My brother Joseph was the one with whom I was oftenest embroiled; he was beaten, bitten, abused; I went to complain before he had time to recover from his confusion. I had need to be on the alert; our mother would have repressed my warlike humor, she would not have put up with my caprices. Her tenderness was joined with severity: she punished, rewarded all alike; the good, the bad, nothing escaped her. My father, a man of

sense, but too fond of pleasure to pay much attention to our infancy, sometimes attempted to excuse our faults: 'Let them
alone,' she replied, 'it is not your business, it is I who must look
after them.' She did, indeed, watch over us with a solicitude unexampled. Every low sentiment, every ungenerous affection was
discarded, discouraged: she suffered nothing but what was grand
and elevated to take root in our youthful understandings. She
abhorred falsehood, was provoked by disobedience: she passed
over none of our faults. I recollect a mischance which befel me
in this way, and the punishment which was inflicted on me. We
had some fig-trees in a vineyard; we used to climb them; we
might meet with a fall, and accidents: she forbade us to go near
them without her knowledge. This prohibition gave me a good
deal of uneasiness: but it had been pronounced, and I attended to
it. One day, however, when I was idle, and at a loss for something to do, I took it in my head to long for some of these figs.
They were ripe; no one saw me, or could know any thing of the
matter: I made my escape, ran to the tree, and gathered the
whole. My appetite being satisfied, I was providing for the future by filling my pockets, when an unlucky vineyard-keeper
came in sight. I was half-dead with fear, and remained fixed on
the branch of the tree, where he had surprised me. He wished
to seize and conduct me before my mother. Despair rendered
me eloquent: I represented my distress, undertook to keep away
from the figs in future, was prodigal of assurances, and he seemed
satisfied. I congratulated myself on having come off so well,
and fancied that the adventure would not transpire; but the
traitor told all. The next day Signora Letitia wanted to go and
gather some figs. I had not left any, there were none to be
found: the keeper came, great reproaches followed, and an exposure; the culprit had to expiate his fault."

When he was between five and six years old, he was placed in
a school with some little girls, the mistress of which was an acquaintance of the family. He was handsome; he was by himself; they all made much of him; but he always had his stockings down about his heels, and in walking out, he never let go
the hand of a charming girl, who was the occasion of many quarrels. His rogues of companions, jealous of his Giacominetta,

connected the two circumstances together, and put them into a
song. He never appeared in the street but they followed him,
repeating the rhymes: *Napoleone di mezzà calzetta fa l' amore à
Giacominetta.** He could not bear being made the sport of this
crew. Sticks, stones, every thing that came in his way he seized
on, and rushed furiously into the midst of the throng. Fortunately, some one always came by to put an end to the affair, and
bring him safe out of it ; but numbers did not intimidate him, he
never stopped to count his adversaries.

Napoleon always spoke in terms of admiration of the courage
and strength of mind which his mother evinced at this period.
" Losses, privations, fatigue," he said, " had no effect upon her :
she endured all, braved all ; she had the head of a man placed
on the body of a woman. But it was very different with the
archdeacon (his uncle) ; he regretted his goats, the Genoese—all,
in short, that he no longer had. He was in other respects an excellent old man. Good, generous, intelligent ; he at a later
period became a father to us, and re-established the affairs of the
family. Sound of mind, but bed-ridden, he suffered no abuse to
escape him. He knew the value, the number of each herd of
cattle ; made them kill one, sell or keep another ; every shepherd
had his task, his instructions. The mills, the cellar, the vineyards, were subjected to the same superintendance. Order,
plenty, reigned every where ; our situation had never been more
prosperous. The good man was rich, but did not like to part
with his money. He strove hard to persuade us that he had saved
nothing. If I asked him for money, ' You know well,' he said, ' that
I have it not ; your father's extravagance has left me nothing.'
At the same time he would authorize me to sell a head of cattle,
a hamper of wine ; it was all a pretence ; but we had discovered
a bag of money, and were piqued at hearing him preaching up
poverty with pieces of gold in his pockets. We were resolved to
play him a trick. Pauline was quite young ; we gave her her lesson : she drew out the bag ; the doubloons rolled out and covered
the floor. We burst out into fits of laughter ; the good old man
was choked with rage and confusion. Mamma came in, scolded,
picked up the pieces of gold, and the archdeacon fell to protesting

* " Napoleon, with his stockings half off, makes love to Giacominetta."

that the money was not his.   We knew what course to follow in
this respect, and took care not to contradict him.   He was taken
ill some time after, and was soon reduced to the last extremity.
We were standing round his bed-side.   We lamented the loss we
were about to sustain, when Fesch was seized with a sudden
zeal, and wanted to plague him with the customary homilies.
The dying man interrupted him : Fesch paid no attention to this,
and the old priest grew impatient.   'Nay, give over,' he cried
out ; 'I have but a few moments to live, and I wish to devote
them to my family.'   He then made us draw near, and gave us
his blessing and advice.   'You are the eldest of the family,' he
said to Joseph : 'but Napoleon is the head of it.   Take care to remember what I say to you.'   He then expired amidst the sobs
and tears which this melancholy sight drew from us.   Left without guide, without support, my mother was obliged to take the
direction of affairs upon herself.   But the task was not above her
strength : she managed every thing, provided for every thing,
with a prudence and sagacity which could neither have been expected from her sex nor from her age.   Ah! what a woman !—
where look for her equal ?"

"I came into the world," says Napoleon, addressing himself to
his fellow-countryman Antommarchi, "in the arms of old Mam-
muccia Caterina.   She was obstinate, captious, continually at
war with all around her.   She was perpetually quarrelling with
my grandmother, of whom she was notwithstanding very fond,
and who had the same regard for her.   They disputed without
ceasing—they had endless wranglings, which afforded us great
amusement.   You grow serious, Doctor ; the portrait hurts you ;
never mind : if your countrywoman was quarrelsome, she was
kind, affectionate ; she walked out with us, took care of us, made
us laugh ; she showed an anxiety for us, the recollection of
which is not yet effaced.   I still remember the tears she shed
when I quitted Corsica.*   That is now forty years ago.   You

* A foster-brother of Buonaparte's, of the name of Ignatio Lorri, entered
the English service, and became master of an English store-ship.  He
landed at some sea-port in France, went in disguise to the French consul,
and said who he was.  The consul took him for an impostor, wrote a long
history to Paris about a man who had presented himself as foster-brother

were not then born : I was young, and did not foresee the glory
that awaited me, still less that we should find ourselves here together ;* but destiny is unchangeable ; one must obey one's star.
Mine was to run through the extremes of life : and I set out to
fulfil the task assigned me.   My father repaired to Versailles,
whither he had been deputed by the Corsican *noblesse*.   I accompanied him ; we passed through Tuscany—I saw Florence
and the Grand Duke.   We at length reached Paris—we had
been recommended to the Queen.   My father was well received,
feasted.   I entered the school at Brienne ; I was delighted.   My
head began to ferment ; I wanted to learn, to know, to distinguish
myself—I devoured the books that came in my way.   Presently
there was no talk in the school except about me.   I was admired
by some, envied by others ; I felt conscious of my strength, and
enjoyed my superiority.   Not that there were even then wanting
some charitably disposed persons who sought to trouble my satisfaction.   I had on my arrival been shown into a hall, where there
was a portrait of the Duke de Choiseul.   The sight of this odious
character, who had sold my country, extorted from me an expression of bitterness : it was a blasphemy, a crime which ought
to obliterate all my other deserts.   I let malevolence take
its course, and only applied more closely than ever to study.   I
perceived by this what human nature was, and made up my mind
on the subject."—The ill-usage we receive from mankind we are
tempted to retort upon them ; and the ball is thus kept up with
great spirit from one generation to another.   Nothing sets in
a clearer point of view the importance of education and early
example.

At the school at Brienne it has been said that his poverty exposed him to mortifications, to which he was forced to submit in
silence but with inward indignation, in the midst of boys more
favored by fortune than himself.   Reports were also spread in-

to the Emperor, and was much surprised when the latter admitted it to be
perfectly true.   It is singular that, during the height of his power, this man
never asked any favor of him, though in their childhood they had been constantly together, and though he knew that, since the elevation of her foster-
son, his mother had been loaded with favors and money.

* At St. Helena.

jurious to the character of his mother and the profession of his
father, which on more than one occasion, drove him beyond
the bounds of patience and discretion. He was alternately
accused of being a son of a Corsican attorney, and next of
Monsieur Marbœuf, the French governor sent over to Corsica,
though the latter only arrived in the island in June, 1769, two
months before the birth of Napoleon. Perhaps to the slights and
repulses he met with at this period, on account of his inferiority
of birth or fortune, we may trace his firmness as to one great
principle of the Revolution—equality of pretension, and his adherence to what he considered as the chief maxim of his reign—
" the career left open to talents." The impressions we receive
from personal suffering or experience last longer and strike deeper than mere theories. The spirit which Napoleon had shown in
vindication of the honor of his parents, procured him many friends
in the school. One day, soon after his arrival, one of the teachers, not attending to the character of the child, had condemned
him to wear a coarse woollen dress, and to dine on his knees at the
door of the refectory. It was a kind of dishonor. Buonaparte felt
it so. The moment of its execution brought on a sudden vomit-
ing and a violent fit of hysterics. The superior, who was passing
by chance, snatched him from the intended punishment, blaming
the teacher for his want of discernment; and Father Patrault, the
mathematical professor, ran up, complaining bitterly that, without
any consideration, they should thus degrade his first mathematician. At the time of entering the school, his strongest feeling
was grief for the subjugation of the independence of his country;
and this kept him in a great measure estranged from his school-
fellows. Almost the only one with whom he was on terms of intimacy, was Fauvelet, brother to De Bourienne, who was afterwards his private secretary during the Consulate. This shy and
reserved humor did not abate as he advanced to maturity, and involved him in many quarrels, of which, though he often came off
with the worst, he never made any complaint; nor could he be
prevailed upon, when appointed in his turn to superintend the
conduct of the other boys, to inform against those who had mis-
behaved. He seldom joined in their sports or exercises; but,
during the hours of recreation, shut himself up with a volume of

Plutarch, or turned over the different works on history in the library.  The want of proper exercise, together with the not giving way to the gaity and flow of animal spirits natural at his time of life, probably stunted his growth.  His body was not pro. portioned to his remarkably fine manly head, cast in the mould of the antique.  The games in which he indulged at this early pe- riod, it was remarked, were images of war: he saw himself sur- rounded with camps, fortifications, armies, and already played the conqueror and hero in little.  In the winter of 1783 the pupils at Brienne had constructed a regular fort with the snow.  Buonaparte took a great share in this important concern: the fort was alter- nately attacked, taken, retaken; and he showed, both in the attack and defence, equal courage, hardihood, and address.  In like manner, afterwards at the school at Paris, when he could snatch a moment's leisure, he was seen leaning on the parapet of fort Thimbrune, which had been constructed for the benefit of the scholars, and with a Vauban, a Cohorn, or Folard in his hand, tracing plans for the assault or defence of this little fortress.

Stubborn and untractable with his equals, he was docile to his superiors, and never rebelled against established authority.  A love of order, a sense of the value of power, whether in himself or others, seems to have been always a first principle in his mind. Diligent, studious, regular, and grave, he became a favorite with the teachers.  Pichegru, who had been brought up in the school on charity, by an old aunt belonging to it, and had been originally intended for the church, was his private tutor and instructor in the four rules of arithmetic.  His chief studies were history and mathematics: the one taught him a knowledge of mankind, as the other put instruments into his hands for mastering them.  Seek. ing neither for relaxation nor amusement, he applied himself closely to those severer branches of study which rested on positive grounds and led to practical results.  Literature and the fine arts had little attraction for his sterner genius; and though at a later period he paid greater attention to them, and took pleasure in the conversation of men distinguished by works of fancy and taste, yet it is to be doubted whether this was not from policy or curios- ity rather than from inclination.  After he grew up, and at the time of his first achievements in Italy, Ossian is known to have

been a favorite with him, which is easily accounted for from its
undefined images of grandeur, the blaze of war and thirst of un-
dying glory that are spread over it! In the campaign of 1814
the victory was bloodily contested between him and Blucher at
the Chateau de Brienne, foot to foot and chamber by chamber, on
the very spot where he was brought up, which must have been a
mortifying reflection to him.   On returning to the place after so
many years, he had an interview with an old woman in the neighborhood, who had formerly sold him milk and fruit, and who had
a difficulty in recognising her youthful acquaintance in the person
of the veteran soldier.   "Did she remember a boy of the name of
Buonaparte?"   "Yes."   "Did he always pay her for what he
had of her?"   "She believed so; perhaps a few *sous* might be
left."   Napoleon presented her with a purse of gold in discharge
of any old-standing debt between them.   Madame de Brienne
used to invite several of the school-boys, and among others Napoleon, to visit her at the Chateau.   It is to her that he is supposed
to have returned the characteristic answer, addressed to some lady
of quality who was complaining of the burning of the Palatinate
by the great Turenne ; "And why not, madam, if it was necessary to his designs?"   This lady afterwards had a house at Au-
teiul, near Paris, where Buonaparte, while Emperor, made a
point of visiting her with the most marked attention and respect.

  Napoleon remained upwards of five years at Brienne, from
March, 1779, till the latter end of 1784.   In 1783 Field-Marshal
the Chevalier Keralio, inspector of the military schools, selected
him to pass the year following to the military school at Paris, to
which three of the best scholars were annually sent from each of
the twelve provincial schools of France.   It is curious as well as
satisfactory to know the opinion at this time entertained of him by
those who were the best qualified to judge.   The manuscript collection which belonged to Marshal Segur, then minister at war,
contains the following remarks, under the article headed SCHOOL
OF BRIENNE : "*State of the king's scholars eligible from their age
to enter into the service or to pass to the school at Paris ; to wit M.
ae Buonaparte (Napoleon), born the 15th of August, 1769, in height
4 feet, 10 inches, 10 lines (5 feet 6½ inches English ;) has finished
his fourth season ; of a good constitution, health excellent ; charac-*

*ter mild, honest, and grateful; conduct exemplary; has always distinguished himself by his application to the mathematics; understands history and geography tolerably well; is indifferently skilled in merely ornamental studies, or in Latin, in which he has only finished his fourth course; would make an excellent sailor; deserves to be passed on to the school at Paris.*" His old master Leguille, professor of history at Paris, boasted, that in a list of the different scholars, he had predicted his pupil's subsequent career. In fact, to the name of Buonaparte the following note is added: "*A Corsican by birth and character—he will do something great, if circumstances favor him.*" Monge was his instructor in geometry, who also entertained a high opinion of him. M. Bauer, his German master, was the only one who saw nothing in him, and was surprised at being told he was undergoing his examination for the artillery. Buonaparte was not quite a year at Paris, where his principal associates were Messrs. Lauriston and Dupont. In the month of August, 1785, he was examined by the celebrated mathematician La Place, and obtained the brevet of a second-lieutenant of artillery in the regiment of La Fère: he was then sixteen years of age. He received this appointment with transports of joy. The height of his ambition then bounded itself to wearing an epaulet with puffs on each shoulder: a colonel of artillery appeared to him the *ne plus ultra* of human grandeur! Phelippeaux, Pecaduc, and Demasis, passed at the same examination with him: they all three emigrated at the commencement of the Revolution. The first defended St. Jean d'Acre in 1799, where he displayed much talent, and where he fell; the second was a Breton, and attained the rank of major in the Austrian service; the third, who returned to France during the Consulate, was appointed administrator of the crown-moveables, and chamberlain. It was in the beginning of this year he lost his father (February 24, 1785).

The regiment of La Fère was stationed at Valence in Dauphiny, where Napoleon kept garrison for the first time. He was well received at the house of a Madame du Colombier, and conceived a tender attachment for her daughter, a girl of his own age; but it came to nothing more than their walking out in a morning and eating cherries together. The society he met with here, and the manners to which he became accustomed, he con-

sidered as having been of great service to him in after-life.   Some
disturbances having broken out in the city of Lyons, he was ordered thither with his battalion.*   His regiment afterwards passed
to Douay in Flanders, and to Auxonne in Burgundy.   In 1791
Napoleon was made a captain in the regiment of artillery of Grenoble, then in garrison at Valence, whither he returned.   The
revolutionary ideas now began to prevail very generally.   Several of the officers emigrated.   Gouvion, Vaubois, Galbo Dufour,
and Napoleon, were the four captains of the regiment who retained the confidence and good-will of the soldiers, and kept them
within the bounds of discipline.   The regiment of La Fère, in
which Buonaparte commènced his military career, was afterwards
broken by him for scandalous behavior to the inhabitants of
Turin.   He accordingly had them marched to Paris, assembled
them on the parade, ordered their colors to be taken from them,
and lodged in the church of the Invalids, covered with black.
He disposed of the officers who had behaved less shamefully than
the rest, in other regiments.   Some months after, he formed
the regiment again under different officers ; and the colors were
taken from the church with great pomp by a number of colonels,
each tearing off a piece, which they burnt, and then new ones
were given in their stead.

   When at Lyons with his regiment in 1786, our young lieutenant of artillery gained a gold medal from the college on the
following theme: " *What are the sentiments most proper to be
cultivated, in order to render men happy ?*"   When seated on the
throne many years afterwards, he mentioned the circumstance to
Talleyrand, who sent off a courier to Lyons to procure the essay,
which he easily obtained from knowing the subject, and as the
author's name was unknown.   One day soon after, when they

---

* While here, he narrowly escaped being drowned in the Saone: the
cramp seized him while swimming, and after repeated ineffectual struggles,
he sank.  He experienced at the moment all the sensations of dying, and
lost his recollection ; but after he had sunk, the current drifted him against
a sand-bank, on the edge of which it threw him, where he lay senseless for
some time, and was restored to life by the aid of some of his companions,
who discovered him there by accident.  Previously to this they had given
him up for lost, as they saw him sink, and the current of the river had carried him to a considerable distance.

were alone together, Talleyrand took the manuscript out of his pocket, and thinking to please and pay his court to the Emperor, put it in his hands, and asked if he knew it ?  He immediately recognized the writing, and threw it into the fire, where it was consumed in spite of Talleyrand's efforts to save it, who was greatly mortified, as he had not taken the precaution of causing a copy to be made previously to showing it to the author.  Buonaparte, on the contrary, was much pleased, as the style of the work was highly romantic and extravagant, abounding in sentiments of liberty suggested by the warmth of a fervid imagination, at a moment when youth and the rage of the times had inflamed his mind, but too exalted (according to his own account of the matter) ever to be put in practice.  At the same period, or when he was about seventeen, he composed a short *History of Corsica*, which he submitted to the Abbé Raynal, who praised and urged him to publish it, saying that it would do him much credit, and render great service to the cause then in agitation.  Buonaparte afterwards expressed his satisfaction that he did not follow this advice, as the work was written entirely in the spirit of the day, at a time when the zeal for republicanism was at its height, and contained the strongest arguments in favor of it.  It likewise contained many violent things on the subjugation of Corsica by France, a feeling of resentment against which had been early instilled into his mind, and no doubt added its gall to his love of liberty.  This production he also afterwards lost.  It appears that at this period, and long after, Buonaparte was the ardent defender of liberty in its most unfettered forms.  He professed himself a republican during all the first years of the Revolution ; he witnessed with eager enthusiasm the great national festivals celebrating the triumphs over the Coalition : he retained the same principles (to all outward appearance) in taking the command of the Army of Italy, and the same spirit shone with undiminished force and brilliancy through the proclamations that he issued during all his first campaigns.  It would have been strange if, in the circumstances and at his time of life, he had felt otherwise ; but the feeling was merely common to him with others, an impression from without, or the impulse of warm youthful blood, not a conviction profoundly engraven on his understanding.

or the result of the powerful and characteristic bent of the genius
of the man.

In 1790 Buonaparte, who was then in garrison at Auxonne,
agreed with M. Joly, a bookseller at Dôle, to come over to see
him, to treat for an impression of the History of Corsica. He,
in fact, came, and found Buonaparte at the *Pavilion*, lodging in a
chamber with bare walls, the only furniture in which was an indifferent bed without curtains, two chairs, and a table standing in
the recess of a window, covered with books and papers: his
brother (Louis) slept on a coarse mattress in an adjoining room.
They agreed about the expense of the impression; but Buonaparte was expecting every moment an order to leave Auxonne,
and nothing was finally settled. The order arrived a few days
after, and the work was never printed. It was odd enough that
the clerical ornaments of the almoner of the regiment, whose
office had been just suppressed, were left in his charge. He
showed these to M. Joly, and spoke of the ceremonies of religion
with respect. " If you have not heard mass," said he, " I can
repeat it to you." This M. Joly had just before printed his
*Letter to Monsieur Matteo Buttafoco*, deputy from Corsica to the
National Assembly, who had highly displeased Buonaparte and
the Corsican patriots, by his want of civism. The author had re-
vised the proofs with his own hand, for which purpose he used to
go over on foot to Dôle, setting out from Auxonne at four in the
morning: after looking over the proofs, he partook of an extremely frugal breakfast with his bookseller, and immediately prepared to return to his garrison, where he arrived before noon,
having walked above twenty miles in the course of the morning.
This little pamphlet is written with great point and spirit, in a
strain of bitter irony and unsparing invective. It concludes with
an apostrophe to Lameth, Robespierre, Petion, Volney, Mirabeau,
Barnave, Bailly, La Fayette, whom the writer places in the same
rank of patriots (and there was no reason at this time why he
should not, since they all made the same professions,) and considers M. Buttafoco as unworthy to sit in the same assembly with
them. During some part of the time Buonaparte was quartered
here, he lodged at the nouse of a barber, to whose wife he did not
pay the customary degree of attention. When he passed through

Auxonne on his way to Marengo, he called at the shop-door to ask if she recollected such a person.  "Yes," was the answer, " and a very disagreeable inmate he was ; he was always either shut up in his room, or if he passed through the shop to walk out, he never stopped to speak to any one."  "Ah," he said, ' if I had employed my time then as you would have wished me, I should not now be going to fight a great battle."  On his return he stopped again, calling out, "*Nous revoila!*" in bad French, and with great good-humor, as if to efface all former impressions ; and the ungallant lieutenant was forgotten in the victorious general.

The Revolution had commenced in 1789, while he was with his regiment at Auxonne, and he has left a lively picture of his feelings and of the state of parties at this period, in an account of an excursion which he made in the neighboring country.  He went to sup at Nuits with an old acquaintance, Gassendi, then a captain in the same regiment, and lately married to the daughter of the physician of the place.  The young traveller soon perceived a difference of political opinion between the father and the son-in-law.  Gassendi, who bore the king's commission, was an aristocrat, as became him, and the physician a warm patriot.  The latter found a powerful auxiliary in the new guest, and was so delighted, that he was up the next morning by break of day, to pay him a visit of acknowledgment and sympathy.  The appearance of a young artillery-officer, of a sound logic and a voluble tongue, was an important reinforcement for the place.  It was easy for our traveller to see that he created a sensation.  It was on a Sunday : the town's-people pulled off their hats to him from the end of the street.  This triumph, notwithstanding, was not without its alloy.  He was invited to sup at the house of a Madame Marey, which was the resort of the aristocracy of the district, though the mistress was only the wife of a wine-merchant, but she possessed a large fortune and elegant manners.  She was the duchess of the quarter, and here were to be found all the gentry of the neighborhood.  The young officer had got into a hornet's nest.  He was obliged to break a great number of lances.  The odds were against him.  In the thickest of the battle the mayor was announced.  "I thought," said Napoleon, "it was a succor which Heaven had sent me in a moment of extremity; out he proved the worst of all. I see him still, this inauspicious personage, dressed out in his fine Sunday's clothes, and proud of his rich crimson coat; he was a very wretch. Luckily the generosity of the mistress of the house, perhaps a secret similarity of opinion, saved me. She turned aside with great presence of mind the blows that were intended to annihilate me, and was the welcome shield behind which I escaped unhurt. I have always retained a grateful sense of the service she was of to me in this kind of fool-hardy enterprise. The same diversity of opinions at that time was to be found all over France. In the drawing-rooms, in the streets, on the highways, at the inns, people's minds were ready to kindle into a flame, and nothing was more easy than to deceive one's self as to the strength of parties and of opinion, according to the situation in which one was placed. Thus, for instance, a patriot was very liable to be discouraged, if he appeared in the drawing-rooms or in a group of officers, so greatly was he in the minority; but no sooner did he get into the street, or among the soldiers, than he felt himself to be in the midst of the entire nation. The sentiments of the time were not, however, slow in gaining ground even among the superior officers, especially after the famous oath *To the nation, the law, and the king.* Till then, if I had received the order to point my guns against the people, I have little doubt that habit, prejudice, education, the name of the king, would have led me to obey: but the civic oath once taken, it was all over; I should no longer have acknowledged any authority but that of the nation. My natural inclinations were then reconciled with my duty, and fell in wonderfully with all the metaphysics of the Assembly.* Still it must be confessed, the officers on the patriotic side amounted only to a small number, yet with the aid of the soldiers they managed the regiment and gave the law. Those who were of the opposite party were often obliged to come to us for assistance in moments of exigency. I remember having snatched from the fury of the mob one of our own mess, whose crime had been that of singing from the windows of our dining-

---

* The following expression has been attributed to Buonaparte: "Had I b en a general officer, I might have adhered to the court party; a sub-lieutenant, I sided with the Revolution."

room the well known song, ' *O Richard! O my king!*' I little thought then that one day this air would be proscribed on my account."

There is a letter of Buonaparte's, dated June, 1789, addressed to Paoli (then in England) on the subject of his History of Corsica, in which he broods over the wrongs and oppressions of his country, and seems to found the only hope of relief on the liberal turn which things were then taking. Not long after, Mirabeau proposed the recal of the exiled patriots, and spoke of this measure as the least atonement he could make for the share he had formerly had in the unjust and forcible annexation of that island to France. Paoli had resided for the last twenty years in England, where we find him described in Boswell's Life of Johnson as mingling in the literary society of the day. But on hearing of this decree, he immediately quitted London for Paris, was presented to the Constituent Assembly by La Fayette, and was received in the French capital with all the honors which the love of liberty could pay to one of its most devoted and heroic defenders. On his return to Corsica, in 1790, he was every where hailed with shouts of enthusiasm, and was appointed lieutenant-general in the French service, and commandant of the twenty-third military division. In 1792 Napoleon oatained leave of absence from his regiment, and passed six months in Corsica. He took the earliest opportunity of seeking out Paoli, who received him in a very friendly manner, and did all in his power to detain him and keep him at a distance from the disturbances with which France was then threatened. Meanwhile, his young friend was appointed to the temporary command of a battalion of National Guards, levied in Corsica to maintain the public tranquillity. The island was at this time torn in pieces by the two contending factions, who favored or were hostile to the union of Corsica with France. Ajaccio, the birth-place of Napoleon, was the head quarters of the opposition party ; and such was the ferment, that he was obliged, at the head of his troop, to employ force against the national guard of the town. The tumult, which he succeeded in quieting, took place the day after Good Friday in this year. Peraldi, one of the chiefs of the mal-contents, and an old enemy of his family (which is provocation enough in a country where hatred is hereditary,)

accused him to the government of having caused the disturbance
which he had been the means of suppressing. He was under the
necessity of going to Paris, in order to acquit himself of this injurious imputation. He was there on the 20th of June and on
the 10th of August, 1792, and was an eye-witness of the events
of both these days.

In Las Cases's account (which is not free from mistakes) he is
made to apply the epithet "hideous" to the latter epoch, and to
speak of a "hideous group of men that he met, carrying a head
upon a pike," in a tone which is neither consonant with his feelings at the time, nor with a sober estimate of the circumstances
on reflection. Be it so, that this group of men were hideous;
they did not proceed out of the Revolution, but out of the ancient
monarchy: their squalidness and frantic gestures were the counterpart of the finery and haughty airs of the old court. The
state of degradation of the French populace at the time of the
Revolution was not an argument against it, but the strongest argument for it. They wished to better their condition, to get rid of
some part of their "hideousness" (moral and physical)—so much
light, at least, had broken in upon them—and because this was
denied them, they naturally flew out into rage and madness.
Whose was the fault? If a regiment of soldiers in smart uni-
forms had been ordered by a martinet officer in cold blood, and
without any distortion of features, to fire upon this group of wretched fanatics, there would have been nothing "hideous" in it—so
much do we judge by rule and appearances, and so little by reason! Did these men parade the streets with this tragic apparatus
for nothing? Did they challenge impunity for nothing? Was
the voice of justice and humanity stifled? No! It had now for
the first time called so loud, that it had reached the lowest depths
of misery, ignorance, and depravity, and dragged from their dens
and lurking-places men whose aspect almost scared the face of
day, and who having been regarded as wild beasts, did not all at
once belie their character. *Ecquid sentitis in quanto contemptu
vivatis? Lucis vobis hujus partem, si liceat, adimant. Quod spi-
ratis, quod vocem mittitis, quod formas hominum habetis indignantur!*
Is it wonderful that 'n throwing off this ignominy, and in trying
to recover this form, they were guilty of some extravagances and

convulsive movements? This genteel horror, as well as callous indifference, is exceedingly misplaced, and is the source of almost all the mischief. The mind is disgusted with an object, conceives a hatred and prejudice against it, and proceeds to act upon this feeling without waiting to consider whether its anger ought not to be rather directed against the system that produced it, and which is not entitled to the smallest partiality or favor in such an examination. There is a kind of *toilette* or drawing-room politics, which reduces the whole principle of civil government to a question of personal appearance and outward accomplishments. The partizans of this school (and it is a pretty large one, consisting of all the vain, the superficial, and the selfish) tell you plainly that "they hate the smell of the people, the sight of the people, the touch of the people, their language, their occupations, their manners"—as if this was a matter of private taste and fancy, and because the higher classes are better off than they, that alone gave them a right to treat the others as they pleased, and make them ten times more wretched than they are. It is true, the people are coarsely dressed—is that a reason they should be stripped naked? They are ill-fed—is that a reason they should be starved? Their language is rude—is that a reason they should not utter their complaints? They seek to redress their wrongs by rash and violent means—is that a reason they should submit to everlasting oppression? This is the language of spleen and passion, which only seeks for an object to vent themselves upon, at whatever price, not of truth or reason, which aims at the public good. At this rate, the worse the government, the more sacred and inviolable it ought to be; for it has only to render the people brutish, degraded, and disgusting, in order to bereave them of every chance of deliverance, and of the common claims of humanity and compassion. The cowardice and foppery of mankind make them ashamed to take part with the people, lest they should be thought to belong to them; and they would sooner be seen in the ranks of their oppressors, who have so many more advantages—fashion, wealth, power, and whatever flatters imagination and prejudice on their side. But "the whole need not a physician;" it is the wants, the ignorance, and corruption of the lower classes that demonstrate the abuses of a government, and call loudly for reform:

and the family physician would not be more excusable who refused to enter a sick room or to administer to the cure of a patient
in the paroxysms of a fever, than the state physician who gives up
the cause of the people from affecting to be disgusted with their
appearance, or shocked at their excesses!*

Buonaparte returned to Corsica in the month of September,
1792, deeply impressed with the mighty changes he had witnessed and that were daily taking place, and his mind fully made
up as to the side he should espouse. A squadron under the orders of vice-admiral Truguet, entrusted with an attack on Sardinia, arrived at Ajaccio in December, 1792. The forces stationed in Corsica were put in motion; and in January, 1793,
Buonaparte, at the head of two battalions of the National Guard,
was specially charged to make a diversion on the north of Sardinia, while Truguet directed his operations against Cagliari.
The expedition not having succeeded (owing to a total want of
discipline and management) he brought his troop safely back to
Bonifacio. This was his first military enterprise, and gained him
testimonials of the satisfaction of the soldiers, and a local reputation. Of the entire hold which his professional studies had taken
of his mind, and of the unremitting assiduity with which he made
every occasion subservient to this grand object, the following
anecdote furnishes rather a whimsical example. "It was in 1793
I had obtained a furlough, and had come to spend it at Ajaccio.
I was as yet only a captain: I foresaw that the war would be long
and sanguinary: I prepared myself for it. I had fixed my study
in the quietest part of the house; I had, in fact, got on the roof;

* The passage in Las Cases gives a striking account of the violent fermentation of the public mind in the coffee-houses and streets, of the suspicious and watchful looks with which a stranger was viewed, and of the
circumstance of well-dressed women prowling about and insulting the dead
bodies of the Swiss in the garden of the Thuilleries. Buonaparte was
struck with the number of these, neither from the smallness of the space,
nor from the novelty of the sight, but his imagination was overloaded and
oppressed from there being no other interest to carry off and absorb the
natural horror of the scene. The dead bodies were many, because they
were there without his knowledge or connivance: had they served to swell
his triumphs, or to furnish proofs of his power and skill, they would have
seemed too few

I saw no one, seldom went out, but studied hard.   One Sunday morning, as I was crossing the pier, I met Barberi, who complained that he never saw me, and proposed an excursion of pleasure.   I consented, on condition that it should be on the water.   He made a signal to the sailors on board a vessel of which he was a proprietor ; they came, and we set out.   I wanted to measure the extent of the gulf, and made them direct their course to the Recanto.   I placed myself at the stern, undid my ball of packthread, and obtained the result which I wished for.   Arrived at Costa, we ascended it ; the position was magnificent ; it is the same that the English afterwards surmounted with a redoubt ; it commanded Ajaccio.   I was desirous to examine it : Barberi, who took little interest in researches of this kind, pressed me to have done ; I strove to divert him and gain time, but appetite made him deaf.   If I spoke to him of the width of the bay, he replied, that he had not yet breakfasted : if of the church-steeple, of such or such a house which I could reach with my bomb-shells, ' Good,' he said ; ' but I am in haste, and an excellent breakfast awaits me ; let us go by all means !'   We did so, but his friends were tired of waiting for him ; so that on his arrival he found neither guests nor banquet.   He resolved to be more cautious in future, and to mind the hour when he went on a reconnoitring party."

Shortly after this, Paoli, against whom an accusation had been already preferred by the senate, threw off the mask and revolted. Previously to declaring himself openly, he communicated his design to his young *Protégé*, of whom he entertained a very high opinion, and to whom he used frequently to say, patting him on the head, " You do not belong to modern times ; you are one of Plutarch's men !"   But all the persuasions and flatteries of this hasty and ardent-minded old man did not move him a jot.   Napoleon allowed that France was in an alarming state, but reminded him that nothing that is violent can last long ; and that as he had an immense influence over the inhabitants, and was master of the strong-places and of the troops, he ought to exert himself to maintain tranquillity in Corsica, and let the fury of the moment pass away in France ; that the island ought not to be severed from its natural connexion on account of a temporary inconvenience ; that it had every thing to lose in such a conflict ; that it belonged geo-

graphically either to France or Italy ; that it never could be English ; and that as Italy was not a single undivided power, Corsica
ought always to remain in the possession of the French. The old
general had no answer to make to all this, but he persisted in his
intention of annexing Corsica to the crown of England. Paoli
had an old grudge against France, as the oppressor of his country ; and however the situation of things might be altered, was
ready to seize the first opportunity to pick a personal quarrel with
her. Because the French government had formerly trampled on
the independence of Corsica, he thought that the best way to retaliate upon her and secure his favorite object, was to turn against
France at the moment when, having thrown off her ancient yoke,
she was struggling for her own, and consequently for the liberties
of mankind. The defeated patriot of 1769 did not or would not
understand that the cause which had been the ruling passion of
his life, had taken a more enlarged and general ground ; that the
part which he had urged Corsica to act against France, France
had now to sustain against Europe ; he was one of those who
looked at politics as made up chiefly of local and party differences, as it affected an irritable set of nerves, or piqued his habitual prejudices, and could not reach to contemplate it from a higher
point of view in its general principles or more distant consequences. Paoli was at length compelled to take refuge once more in
England, where he died in 1807, having been several years pen-
sioned by the king, and has a monument erected to him in West-
minster Abbey.—This was the first occasion on which Buonaparte
proved himself worthy of the praises which his late friend and
patron lavished upon him, or displayed that decided superiority
of character which, disentangling itself from petty and local ties,
marches boldly on to the grand and future. He saw that Corsica
was no longer the scene on which the love of freedom or military
prowess could take their loftiest stand. The great drama which
Paoli had rehearsed in his younger days in an obscure corner (to
which he still wished to confine it) had got " a kingdom for a stage,
and nations to behold the swelling act." Thither the keen glance,
the towering spirit of his new associate directed itself: not assuredly that he was aware, or probably even ambitious of the fortune
that was in store for him ; but he was naturally attracted to

the scene, where his latent capacities had the fairest opportunity of unfolding themselves, and where the passing events were of an interest and magnitude to answer his utmost wishes. It is the distinguishing property of a great mind that it attaches itself to great objects, to the larger masses and powerful impulses of things, expands and gathers strength with them, and in the end becomes the governing spirit that directs and wields them to its purposes!

Napoleon quitted the convent of Rostino, where he held this conference with Paoli, two hours afterwards. He got as far as Bocognano, where he was overtaken by the mountaineers, and made his escape from them by a stratagem. His friend Barberi also gave him shelter. Paoli sent him word, that if he and his brothers did not instantly return back, he would seize their flocks, their vineyards, and lay waste every thing belonging to them. A refusal was given, and the threat was immediately put in execution. Affairs daily grew worse for the French party. Corte openly revolted; bodies of insurgents from all quarters advanced on Ajaccio, where there were no troops of the line or means of resistance proportioned to the danger. The Buonaparte family retired from the impending storm to Nice, and afterwards to Marseilles. Their property was confiscated: their house at Ajaccio, after being pillaged, was used as a barrack by a battalion of English troops. The serious mischiefs which Paoli had inflicted on the son of his old friend, did not produce rancor or ill-will on either side. Napoleon still esteemed him, and regretted their separation; and Paoli watched the progress of his rising fame and fortune with the fond anxiety of a parent, and received the intelligence of his victories with such extravagant demonstrations of joy as to give offence in England where he was. Napoleon had thoughts of recalling him, that he might witness the splendor with which he was surrounded, when he was prevented by his death. Friendship and good-will are often neither conciliated by benefits nor effaced by injuries, but seem to depend on a certain congeniality of temper or original predilection of mind.*

---

* Napoleon had occasion to send a peasant, dressed as a beggar, across the country with letters to his friends. The messenger was stripped and examined at every post; they could make nothing of him. He was brought

Napoleon, on reaching Nice, was preparing to join his regiment at Avignon, when General Dujear, who commanded the artillery of the Army of Italy, required his services, and employed him in several delicate commissions. Not long after, Marseilles revolted against the revolutionary government. The Marseilles troops took possession of Avignon; the communications of the Army of Italy were cut off; there was a want of ammunition, a convoy of powder having been intercepted; and the general-in-chief found himself considerably at a loss what to do. In these circumstances General Dujear, dispatched Napoleon to the Marseillois insurgents, to endeavor to induce them to let the convoys pass, and at the same time to take all necessary measures to hasten and secure their passage. He went to Marseilles and Avignon, had interviews with the leaders of the insurgent troops, satisfied them that it was for their interest not to provoke the resentment of the army of Italy, and got the convoys forwarded. In the meantime Toulon had surrendered to the English and Spanish fleets. Napoleon, now a lieutenant-colonel (*chef de bataillon*), was immediately ordered on service to the siege of this place, on the recommendation of the Committee of artillery. He joined the besieging army on the 12th of September, 1793.

During his stay at Marseilles, when sent to the heads of the insurrection, he had an opportunity of closely observing the weakness and want of combination in their means of resistance to the Convention. In his way back he supped at an inn at Beaucaire, in company with a merchant from Nismes and another from Montpelier, when the conversation turned on this subject, and on the politics of the south of France. On his return to Avignon, having a little leisure on his hands, he drew up a short pamphlet, retailing the arguments of the different speakers, which was published under the title of "The Supper of Beaucaire."* The dialogue is managed with great spirit, shrewdness, and *naiveté*. The object of the writer is to open the eyes of the disaffected to the inefficiency as well as unseasonableness of their efforts, and

---

before Paoli. He was searched to the last rag. "Has he nothing else about him?" "Nothing but a small gourd." "Open it," said Paoli. They did so, and the dispatches were found in it.

 * Le Souper de Beaucaire. See Appendix, No. I.

to prove that the only result of their perseverance would be to fur
nish a pretext to "the men of blood of the day" to send more persons to the scaffold.  It is to be remarked, that Buonaparte evinced from the first the same horror of the shedding of blood in civil
quarrels.  The counsels that he gave to others, or adopted himself
on that head, almost always inclined to the timid and prudential
side.  There is a natural cowardice as well as a heavy responsibility attached to the consideration in ordinary cases, which only
strong enthusiasm or studied cruelty can overcome, and for disregarding which the calculations of mere policy are hardly a sufficient warrant.  The occasion too that he had to shut his eyes
and brace his nerves to the prodigal waste of human life in war
and in the field of battle, perhaps exhausted all his stock of fortitude in his professional capacity, and left the statesman hesitating, cautious, and almost pusillanimous.

It was at this period of his life, or the year following, that
Buonaparte fell in love with Mademoiselle Desirée Clary, the
daughter of a merchant at Marseilles.  The courtship, by his own
account, had proceeded so far, that a marriage was in treaty, but
was broken off in consequence of his being suddenly called away
by the pressure of affairs, and was never afterwards renewed.  In
1794 his brother Joseph married her sister; and some years after,
Bernadotte married this young lady, with Napoleon's approbation.
It was to please her, and make her a queen, that he principally
consented to Bernadotte's succeeding to the throne of Sweden.
Thus, to the indulgence of an early romantic sentiment, by putting
power into the hands of a capricious and dangerous rival, he possibly owed the loss of his own crown and life.

# CHAPTER II.

### SOME ACCOUNT OF CORSICA.

In order to throw a clearer light on some of the transactions mentioned in the preceding chapter, it will be proper to give a brief sketch of the history of Corsica, which is also entitled to this distinction as having been the birth-place of Napoleon.

Little certain is known of Corsica in early times. Philippini, the author of the oldest chronicle of that island, lived in the fifteenth century, and was archdeacon of Aleria. Towards the end of the last century, Lampridi (a man of talent and learning) published a very voluminous history of the revolutions of this country at Rome. Many other accounts have since appeared. The public attention was kept alive during a great part of the eighteenth century by the unequal but daring struggle maintained by the inhabitants, in order to resist oppression and throw off a foreign yoke.

The Arabs of Africa were long masters of Corsica. The arms of this kingdom are still a Death's head, with a bandage over the eyes, on a white ground. The Corsicans distinguished themselves at the battle of Ostia (in 1520), where the Saracens were defeated, and compelled to relinquish their views on Rome. Some persons are of opinion that these arms were given them by Pope Leo X., in acknowledgment of the valor they displayed on that occasion.

Corsica formed part of the inheritance of the Countess Matilda. The Colonnas of Rome pretend, that in the ninth century one of their ancestors conquered this island from the Saracens, and reigned as king there. The Colonnas of Itria and Cinerca have been acknowledged by the Colonnas of Rome, and genealogists have traced the relationship; but the historical fact of the sovereignty of a branch of the Colonna family in Corsica remains at this day doubtful. It appears, however, certain that Corsica at one time formed the twelfth kingdom acknowledged in Europe; a title which these islanders were proud of, and would never renounce. It was in virtue of this title that the Doge of Genoa wore the regal crown. At the most enthusiastic moments of their zeal for liberty, they reconciled these opposite notions by declaring the Holy Virgin their queen. Traces of the same expedient appear even in the deliberations of several councils, amongst others, of that held at the convent of La Vinsolasca.

Corsica, like the rest of Italy, was subjected to the feudal system; every village had its lord: but the emancipation of the common people was effected there fifty years earlier than the general movement which took place in Italy for the same purpose in the eleventh century. There are still to be seen on the top of steep rocks the ruins of castles, which tradition represents as the refuge of the lords in the war of the Communes during the twelfth, thirteenth, fourteenth, and fifteenth centuries. The Liamone party, as it was called, and especially the province of La Rocca, had, at this period, the principal direction of the affairs of the island. But in the sixteenth, seventeenth. and eighteenth centuries, the *pieves* (parishes) of the lands of the Communes, or of La Castagnichia, were, in their turn, preponderant in the councils and assemblies of the nation.

Pisa was the nearest continental city to Corsica. The Pisans began to trade with that island, established factories there, extended their influence gradually, and at length subjected the whole island to their government. Their administration was, however, mild, and suited to the wishes and opinions of the natives, who served them with zeal in their wars against Florence. Their enormous power ended with the battle of La Maloria; and the greatness of Genoa, to which state the commerce of Pisa devolved, arose out of the ruins of the latter city. The Genoese established themselves in Corsica. This was the beginning of the misfortunes of that country, which thenceforth constantly increased. The senate of Genoa, not having found the way to gain the affection of the inhabitants, endeavored to weaken and divide them, and to keep them in poverty and ignorance. The picture which the Corsican writers have left of the tyranny of the oligarchy of Genoa is one of the most revolting that the history of the world affords; and the antipathy and animosity of these islanders towards the Genoese are also nearly unexampled. Such are the lessons we meet in every page of history: yet persons are not wanting who would persuade us that the words *tyrant* and *tyranny* are without any counterpart in nature, the mere invention of modern sophists and innovators !*

France, although so near Corsica, had never pretended to the government of the island. It has, indeed, been asserted that Charles Martel sent one of his lieutenants thither against the Saracens: but this is without any authority. Henry II. sent an army into Corsica, under the command of the Marshal de Thermes, the famous San Pietro Ornano, and one of the Orsini, but they remained only a short time there. Old Andrew Doria, when eighty-five years of age, reconquered the island, and restored it to his country. Spain, divided into several kingdoms, and wholly occupied by her wars with the Moors, entertained no views on Corsica until a very late period, and was then diverted from them by her wars in Sicily.

The *pieves* of Rostino, Ampugnano, Orezza, and La Penta, were the first that rose, in the beginning of the last century, against the government of the senate of Genoa; the *pieves* of Castagnichia and all the other districts of the island, by degrees, followed their example. This war, which began in 1729, ended in 1769, in the annexation of Corsica to the French monarchy, the contest having lasted forty years. The Genoese levied Swiss mercenaries, and several times had recourse to the greater powers, taking auxiliary troops into their pay. Thus the Emperor of Germany sent first Baron Wachtendorf and afterwards the Prince of Wurtemberg into Corsica, as Louis XV. sent Count Boissieux, and afterwards Marshal Maillebois. Wachtendorf and Boissieux were beaten; the Prince of Wurtemberg and Maillebois both succeeded in subduing the country; but they left the fire under the embers, and immediately after their departure, the war broke out again and raged with redoubled fury. Old Giafferi, the Canon

---

* It is a circumstance somewhat characteristic of the times, that the court-censor lately struck these words out of an entire tragedy, as offensive to "ears polite," and as implying an unjust imputation on the immaculate purity and benignant sway of all established authority.

Orticone (a man of address and eloquence), Hyacinth Paoli, Cianaldi, and Gafforio were placed by turns at the head of affairs, which they conducted with various degrees of good fortune, but always honorably, and under the guidance of the noblest sentiments. The sovereignty of the country resided in a council, composed of the deputies of the *pieves*, which decided on war and peace, and decreed the taxes and levies of militia. There were no hired troops, but the names of all the inhabitants capable of bearing arms were inscribed in three muster-rolls in each district, and they marched against the enemy at the call of their leaders. Arms, ammunition, and subsistence were provided by each individual.

It may seem difficult at first sight to comprehend the policy of Genoa. Why, it may be asked, so much perseverance in so unprofitable a struggle? She should either have given up Corsica, or else satisfied the inhabitants. Such was the dictate of common sense as well as of humanity. Had she, for instance, inserted the names of the principal inhabitants in her *Golden Book*, and tried the contrary system to that which had proved so ruinous, and which she had never been able quietly to establish, she would have ensured the good-will of the Corsicans, and rendered the connexion useful to herself. But this does not appear to have been the object. It had often been urged to the senate: "The militia of Corsica are more able to possess themselves of Genoa than you are to conquer their mountains. Acquire the confidence of these islanders by a just government, flatter their ambition and haughty spirit of independence; you will thereby obtain a nursery of good seamen, who will be serviceable in guarding your capital, and establish factories of great value to your commerce." The proud oligarchy replied: "We cannot treat the Corsicans more favorably than the people of the two *Rivieras*. Is the *Golden Book* then to be principally filled with the names of provincial families? This would be a total subversion of our Constitution; it is proposing that we should abandon the inheritance left us by our forefathers. The Corsicans are not formidable: all their successes are owing to our neglect. By pursuing more prudent and vigorous measures, it will be easy for us to subdue this handful of rebels, who are without arms, discipline, or con cert." So much easier is it always to persist in our errors than to retract them. The reasoning of Genoa with regard to Corsica might find numberless parallels. It is a stooping from our dignity to redress the wrongs we may have done, and thus to admit that we have any wrongs to redress. The behavior of governments to their dependencies would be indeed in many cases a riddle, if states, any more than individuals, were influenced by right reason, and did not suffer their passions, their prejudices, and idle humors constantly to prevail not only over justice but policy. The habit of treating others ill seems by degrees to confer the right: there is no hatred equal to that we feel towards those we have injured; and the conscious incapacity to govern finds obvious relief in the resolution to oppress. A word spoken in season, a trifling concession made in the spirit of conciliation, would perhaps heal all differences, and put a stop to wide-spread mischiefs: but we reject every such expedient, as if moderation were weakness, and obstinacy wisdom; or as if by entailing misery, ignorance, and oppression on a whole nation, it would appear that their degradation and sufferings were in the inevitable order of Providence, and not the effect of our caprice and mismanagement. The parent state plays the part of a step-mother to her less-favored children, and is not unwilling by taunts and cruelty to drive them to despair, that she may thus have a pretext for confirming the abuses of power into a system, and a vindication of her original prediction of their being incorrigible to mild and rational treatment. Pride is the master-key of the human breast; and of all the rights claimed by governments over their subjects, the *right of injustice* is the most precious in their eyes, and the one they are the least disposed to part with. It is on this principle that we lost America, and that we still keep Ireland in a state of vassalage.

The Corsicans in all their councils, of which they sometimes held several in a year, published manifestos, wherein they enumerated their ancient and more recent complaints against their oppressors. Their object was to rouse the patriotism of the nation, and also to interest Europe in their behalf. Several of these manifestos, drawn up by Orticone, are full of energy, sound reasoning, and a lofty enthusiasm.

Theodore, king of Corsica, excited a great interest towards the middle of the last century in Europe, and particularly in England, where he was reduced to the utmost distress, and was confined in gaol for debt for a length of time. His story has not been generally understood.- He was not a dethroned prince according to the popular belief concerning him, which made him an object of extreme curiosity and attention. The Baron Nieuhoff was by birth a Westphalian. He landed on the coast of Aleria in Corsica, with four transports at his disposal, laden with musquets, powder, shoes, and other articles useful in war. The expences of the armament had been defrayed by private individuals or Dutch speculators. This unexpected succor, arriving at a moment of the greatest need, appeared to have descended from heaven. The chiefs on this proclaimed the German baron king, describing him to the people as a great European potentate, whose appearance was a pledge of the powerful assistance they should soon receive. The artifice had the effect it was intended to produce ; it operated on the multitude for a while, till at length it was worn out, and Baron Nieuhoff returned to the Continent. He afterwards, at different intervals, revisited the shores of the island with important succors, with which he was supplied by the Court of Sardinia and the Bey of Tunis. This is a romantic episode in that memorable war, and shows the readiness of the leading characters of the country to avail themselves of every resource or advantage that presented itself.

In 1755 Pascal Paoli was declared first magistrate and general of Corsica. He was the son of Hyacinth Paoli, had been brought up at Naples, and was a captain in the service of the king Don Carlos. The *pieve* of Rostino appointed him their deputy to the council of Alesani. His family was very popular. He himself was tall, young, handsome, learned, eloquent. The council was divided into two parties : one of them, that of the most zealous patriots and most hostile to any accommodation, proclaimed him their chief. The Moderates set up Matras, the deputy for Fiumorbo, in opposition to him. The two parties came to action : Paoli was defeated, and obliged to shut himself up in the convent of Alesani. His case seemed desperate : his rival's troops surrounded him. But as soon as the news reached the *pi*

Communes, all the peaks of the mountains blazed with fires; the caverns and forests echoed with the mournful sound of the horn, the signal of civil war. Matras wished to anticipate the insurgents; and endeavored to take the convent by assault. With his natural impetuosity, he rushed on foremost, and fell mortally wounded. Both parties thenceforth submitted to Paoli. In the course of a few months the council of Alesani was recognised by all the *pieves*. Paoli displayed much talent; he reconciled the different factions, governed on a regular plan, erected schools and a University, gained the friendship of Algiers and the Barbary pirates, built a navy of light vessels, kept agents in the towns on the sea-coast, and made himself beloved by the inhabitants. In a naval expedition he possessed himself of Capraia, and drove out the Genoese, who were even apprehensive that the Corsican rovers would land in the *Riviera*.\* He did all that it was possible to do under the circumstances of the time, and with the nation that he ruled; and was on the point of making himself master of the five ports of the island, when the senate of Genoa, seriously alarmed, had recourse for the third time to France. In 1764 French troops occupied the maritime towns, which under their control continued to acknowledge the authority of the Senate.

These French garrisons took no decided part. The officers were in general favorably disposed towards the islanders, who were encouraged by the circumstance, and waited impatiently for the departure of the troops to break out into open rebellion against the Genoese. But the Duke de Choiseul about this time conceived the project of annexing Corsica to France, as a natural dependency of Provence, and also as calculated to protect the commerce of the Levant, and facilitate any subsequent operations in Italy. After considerable hesitation, the Senate consented; and Spinola, their ambassador at Paris, signed a treaty, by which it was made over to France by a diplomatic subterfuge: it being agreed, that the king of France should take and keep possession of Corsica, till the Republic should be in a situation to reimburse him the expense of sending an army of 30,000 men to subdue the island, and of maintaining garrisons there for several years, which

---

\* The sea-coast of Genoa, a long, narrow slip between the Mediterranean and the Alps

it was to be foreseen they neither could nor would repay. This
equivocal mode of proceeding at once saved the Genoese the reproaches of Italy for having sold Corsica to a foreign power, and
furnished the French minister with a pretext for retracting, in
case the English should object to the new arrangement, for Louis
XV. was averse to a war with England: but England, at this
time uneasy at the disposition to revolt which manifested itself in
the American colonies, had no desire to interfere on a feeling of
pure disinterested generosity, the example of which might be
turned against herself. When France became republican, then
it became an object to detach Corsica from her at any rate. But
that was a widely different question.

The Duke de Choiseul made splendid overtures to Paoli to induce him to persuade the Corsicans to declare themselves a province of France. He rejected all these offers with disdain. He
convoked the council, and laid before them the critical state of
affairs. A youth of twenty, deputed to the council, (Charles
Buonaparte, the father of Napoleon,) decided its resolution by a
speech imbued with the noblest sentiments of antiquity. There
was but one cry—"Liberty or Death!" The conduct of the
French government, that after pretending to act as a mediator,
now came forward as a party concerned, and did not blush to bar-
gain for the transfer of Corsica, as if they were no better than a
herd of slaves, excited the strongest reprobation. Some, indeed, gave
a different turn to the affair: they said, "Their ancestors had resisted the tyranny of the oligarchy of Genoa: they were now freed
from it forever. If Giafferi, Hyacinth Paoli, Gafforio, Orticone,
and the other lofty-minded men who had fallen in defence of their
rights, could now see their country united to the finest monarchy
in Europe, they would feel satisfied, and no longer regret the blood
they had shed for her independence. By accepting the protection
of Louis, they would secure all the privileges of French subjects,
and have the commerce of the ports of Europe thrown open to
them." But these arguments and excuses had little effect: the
people and their leaders were alike deaf to them. " We are invincible in our mountains," they said: " there let us remain, and
laugh at our enemies. They talk of the advantages we should
obtain by submission: we have no ambition for them. We wish

to remain poor, but free ; our own masters, governed by our own laws and customs, and not the sport of a clerk from Versailles. They talk of the privileges to which we might be admitted—the privilege of becoming vassals to a despot. *As wills the king, so wills the law*; such is the maxim of the French monarchy. What security then is it likely to afford against the caprice and rapacity of a subaltern ?" And the cry of " Liberty or Death" rang through the valleys of Corsica, and was echoed from her mountain-tops.

The priests and monks joined in sounding the alarm. The mass of the people, especially those who dwelt in the mountains, had no notion of the power of France. They thought a few straggling regiments which they had seen, comprised the whole of the French armies. The public in France were by no means inclined to a war with Corsica. " What had they to do with Corsica ? Had it never existed till now ? Why then was it now thought of for the first time ?" Besides, there seemed to be something not only useless but cowardly in directing the power of a great nation against a handful of poor but spirited mountaineers. The expedition under Chauvelin, with 12,000 men, also failed ; and his troops, after their defeat at Borgo, were glad to retire into the fortresses, having no communication with each other but by sea. The Corsicans believed their deliverance accomplished. The English cabinet did no more than give in a feeble remonstrance at the court of Versailles,—(oh ! impotent to save, powerful to destroy !)—and acquiesced in an evasive reply. But clubs were formed in London that sent arms and money, and a correspondence was kept up with Sardinia and other parts of Italy. Even Louis XV. was in some sort friendly, and showed no haste to set this new crown on his head, until it was represented to him how pleased the French philosophers would be to see the *Grand Monarque* foiled, and compelled to retreat before a free people. This, it was urged, would materially affect royal authority, since independence had its fanatics, who would see miracles in the success of so unequal a contest. There was no longer room for deliberation. The dread of opinion is the spring that has moved the politics of Europe and settled the question of peace or war for the last sixty years. Marshal De Vaux set sail for Corsica in 1768 with 30,000 men : the ports of the island were inundated with troops.   The Corsicans made a brave, but ineffectual resistance. They could not raise more than 20,000 disposable troops, besides those which were necessary to keep the enemy's garrisons in check.   The passage of the Golo was manfully disputed by the patriots.   Not having had time to cut down the bridge, which was of stone, they made use of the bodies of their dead to form a rampart.   Paoli, driven to the southward of the island, embarked in an English ship at Porto Vecchio, landed at Leghorn, crossed the Continent and repaired to London.   He was every where received with tokens of respect and admiration, both by the people and their princes.   The quarrel in which he had been engaged, and to which he had fallen a sacrifice, was not then generally understood to have more than a personal or local application.   The stream of liberty was like the crystal spring, making its way through the clefts of rocks or among wild flowers, the object of curiosity and pity ; and had not then, as afterwards, swollen into a torrent, burst through all obstacles that contained it, and swept away states and kingdoms in its furious course, filling the world with wonder and dread.

It was not to be looked for that the Corsicans should resist the numbers sent against them.   Yet at one time Marshal de Vaux had very imprudently dispersed his troops, thinking the country subdued, though, in fact, none but old men, women, and children remained in the villages, and none but useless musquets had been given up in disarming the inhabitants.   All the brave men, inured to arms by forty years' civil war, were wandering in the woods and caverns or on the tops of the mountains.   Corsica is so difficult and dangerous a country, that a San Pietro Ornano under such circumstances might have fallen on the French army separately, and have cut them in pieces.   But Paoli had not the military tact, promptitude, or vigor for executing so bold an enterprise.   Four or five hundred persons followed him in his retreat, and emigrated :  a great number abandoned their villages and houses, and kept up a pretty harassing warfare for a long time against their invaders.   Five years after (in 1774) some of the refugees returned home, and raised an insurrection in Nioli, a piece among the peaks of the highest mountains.   The Count de

Narbonne-Frizzlar and his *marechal de camp*, Sionville, disgraced
themselves, and made the French name odious by the cruelties
they committed on this occasion, burning the dwellings, cutting
down the olive and chestnut-trees, and pulling up the vines belonging not only to the patriots themselves (or *banditti*, as they
were termed) but to their kinsmen to the third degree. The inhabitants were struck with terror by this treatment, but harbored
a deep and lasting resentment.

The views of the court of Versailles were, however, upon the
whole moderate. The Corsicans were allowed provincial states,
the magistracy of the twelve nobles (an ancient Pisan institution),
and a direct appeal to the throne, representing the grievances of
which they had to complain, once a year. Schools were opened ;
encouragement was given to commerce and agriculture ; the
taxes were not burdensome ; and it was in Corsica that the
French economists first made the experiment of taxation in kind.
In the course of twenty years the island was considerably improved ; but all these advantages produced no effect on the sentiments of the people, who in their hearts were any thing but
French at the period of the Revolution. We are not thankful for
benefits conferred against our will. A French infantry-officer,
who was crossing the mountains, entered into conversation with a
shepherd on the ingratitude of his countrymen. " In your Paoli's
time, you paid double what you pay now." " True, signor ; but
then we gave it, and now you take it !" The native wit of these
islanders appears on most occasions, and was at this time sharpened by political animosities. One of their repartees may serve as
a specimen for many others. Some officers of rank travelling in
Nioli were observing one evening to their host, one of the poorest inhabitants of the place, " What a difference there is between
us Frenchmen and you Corsicans ; see how we are clothed and
maintained !" The peasant rose ; and looking at them atten-
tively, asked each of them his name. One turned out to be a
marquis, another a baron, and a third a chevalier. " Pshaw !"
said the peasant, " I should like very well to be dressed as you
are, I own ; but pray, are all Frenchmen marquises, barons, and
chevaliers ?"

The Revolution produced a great alteration in the disposition of

hese people: they became reconciled to the French in 1790.
Paoli then left England, where he had been living on a pension
allowed him by the King, passed through Paris, where he was received in the most flattering manner, and returned to his own
country after an absence of above twenty years. The whole
island flocked to see him: his arrival occasioned a general rejoicing. He was invested with the chief power in the island,
civil and military, and became once more exceedingly popular.
He was, however, frequently astonished at the little attention he
obtained in private conferences. Many of those very persons
who had followed him into England, where they had spent their
whole time in uttering curses against France, were now the most
refractory to his authority. A new era had arrived, and he did
not perceive it. He began to waver in his opinion of the Revolution after the well-known 10th of August. The death of Louis
XVI. completed his dissatisfaction. He was denounced by the
popular societies of Provence; and the National Convention summoned him to its bar. This was an invitation to lay down his
head upon the scaffold. He was near eighty years of age. He
had but one resource, which was to appeal to his countrymen,
and prevail on them to revolt against the Convention. The banner of the Death's-head was in an instant hoisted on every steeple,
and Corsica ceased to belong to the Republic. After the evacuation of Toulon by the English, Admiral Hood landed 12,000 men,
under the orders of Nelson, at San Fiorenzo. Paoli joined them
with 6,000 more, and they surrounded Bastia, which fell after a
siege of four months, and an obstinate resistance by La Combe St.
Michel and Gentili. General Dundas, encamped with 4,000 men
at San Fiorenzo, refused to take part in the siege without the
special orders of his government.

In the month of June, 1794, the Council, with Paoli at its
head, proposed that the crown of Corsica should be offered to the
King of England. A deputation, consisting of Galeazzi, Filippo
of Vescovato, Negroni of Bastia, and Cesari Rocca of La Rocca,
proceeded to London for this purpose; and the King accepted the
offer. Sir Gilbert Elliot was appointed viceroy, with young Colonna and Pozzo di Borgo (since ambassador from Russia to
France) under him. They soon quarrelled with Paoli, who de-

clared in a pique, "This is my kingdom : I carried on war against the King of France for two years ; I expelled the republicans ; if you violate the privileges and rights of the people, I can more easily expel you than I did them." He had expected to be chosen governor ; and was extremely disappointed and chagrined to find others placed in authority over him. His views suited the policy of neither party; and he became by turns the outcast of both. He was willing to make Corsica the focus of contention and independence on a small scale, though he would not allow France to be so on a large one. Persons of this stamp are surprised that they cannot get all the rest of the world to agree with them, though they are determined to see every object from their own narrow and pragmatical point of view. Shortly after, he received a friendly letter from the King of England, begging him to go and spend the remainder of his days in a country where he was respected and had been happy. This invitation was considered as a command : after some hesitation, he submitted to necessity, and went to London, where he died in 1807. It has been said that he afterwards regretted the part he had taken on this occasion. By his will he left a considerable sum to establish a University at Corte.

The Corsicans very soon grew discontented with their new masters. Their language, their manners, their religion, and mode of living were equally strange to them. This was the first time since the origin of Christianity that their territory had been profaned by what they regarded with abhorrence as an heretical worship. In the mean time, Napoleon entered Milan, and took possession of Leghorn, where he collected all the Corsican refugees under the command of Gentili. At a grand entertainment at Ajaccio, young Colonna was accused, though unjustly, of having insulted the bust of Paoli. The mere rumor was sufficient to provoke hostilities ; the viceroy was hemmed in, and his two favorite advisers with difficulty escaped and reached the seacoast in disguise and by cross-roads. In October, 1796, Gentili, with his refugees, made good his landing, in spite of the vigilance of the English cruisers. They called for a general rising of the people : the summits of the mountains were covered with fires during the night, and the hoarse sound of the horn, the signal of insurrection, was heard in the valleys. The republican party seized upon Bastia and on the different fortresses. The English hastily embarked, leaving a number of prisoners. The King of England wore the crown of Corsica two years, a distinction which cost the British treasury five millions sterling. Corsica, from this time, formed the twenty-third military division of the Republic. General Vaubois was entrusted with the command of it. In the beginning of 1798, a partial insurrection broke out on a religious account in Fiumorbo, at the head of which General Giafferi was persuaded by his confessor to place himself. He was ninety years of age. He was taken prisoner, and given up to a military commission to be shot. His tragical end was deeply lamented by his fellow citizens and old companions in arms. He was the son of the famous Giafferi, who had commanded for thirty years in the war of independence. His name and age ought alike to have saved him.

Corsica is situated at the distance of twenty leagues from the coast of Tuscany, forty from that of Provence, and sixty from that of Spain. The surface of the island is fifteen hundred square miles in extent; it contains four maritime towns, Bastia, Ajaccio, Calvi, and Bonifacio; sixty-three *pieves* (or parishes), four hundred and fifty hamlets, and three fine harbors, capable of holding the largest fleets, namely, San Fiorenzo, Ajaccio, and Porto-Vecchio. A chain of lofty mountains runs through the island from the north-west to the south-east; the highest peaks of the range are covered with perpetual snow. The three principal rivers are the Golo, the Liamone, and the Tavignano. Rivers and torrents rush from the highest mountains, and fall into the sea in all directions; towards their mouths are small verdant spots, five or six miles in circuit. The coast on the side of Italy, from Bastia to Aleria, is a level sixty miles in length, and from ten to twelve in breadth. The isle is woody, and the valleys filled with olives, mulberry, orange, lemon, and other fruit-trees. The sides of the mountains are clothed with chestnut-trees of the largest species, with villages of the most romantic appearance peeping out and forming a kind of natural fortifications. On the tops of the hills are forests of pine, fir, and ever-green oaks. The pine-trees are equal in size to those of Russia, but less durable lasting only three or four years when made into masts for vessels. Oil, wine, silk, and timber are the four staple commodities of the island, that are proper for exportation. San Fiorenzo ought to be the capital. Corsica possesses a beautiful climate in the winter-months; but in the heat of summer it grows dry, and there is a want of water, which drives the inhabitants into the recesses of the hills, whence they descend again in winter either to graze their flocks or to cultivate the plains. The population is not a hundred and eighty thousand, though it might be five hundred thousand.

This is one instance, among so many others that history and geography afford, to show that the earth is not full, or that population is not necessarily and wisely kept back by its having reached the utmost possible limits of the means of subsistence, but that various political and accidental causes constantly conspire to depress it much below the level of the means of subsistence or natural resources of the country. Not only is it untrue that population and the means of subsistence have (according to a very prevalent hypothesis, and as a general and invariable rule) attained their *maximum*, beyond which every advance is to be deprecated as the most serious evil, but it is clear in most instances, both that the earth by care and management, might be made to produce a much greater quantity of food than it actually does, and that its produce might be distributed in such a manner as to maintain a much greater number of persons in equal ease and plenty. That it does not do so is not the fault of the earth, but the fault or (as some will have it) the excellence of human institutions. There is surely some neglect, waste or misapplication of obvious advantages in the best ordered communities, and much more so in the worst. Nay farther, the same causes which keep population down below its natural or necessary limits, such as ignorance, barbarism, oppression &c. also tend to render the scanty remains of it degraded and miserable. Where there are few inhabitants, those few are uniformly ill off. Good government, arts, industry, and civilization at the same time favor the population, and diffuse comfort and abundance among them. The contrary doctrine is a paradox founded neither on facts nor reasoning, but which has gained converts, because it serves as a screen for the abuses of power, and to shift the responsibility of a number of evils existing in the world from the shoulders of individuals on the order of Providence or on the mass of the people.— Before the invasion of Corsica by the Saracens, it appears that all the sea-shore was peopled. Aleria and Mariana, two Roman colonies, were great cities of sixty thousand souls ; but the incursions of the Mussulmans in the seventh and eighth centuries, and afterwards those of the Barbary powers, drove the whole population into the mountains. Hence the plains became uninhabited, and in process of time unhealthy. If the plain of Lombardy were suffered, through mismanagement or oppressive exactions or foreign wars, to go into neglect, it would become, like the Campagna of Rome, instead of a fruitful and populous country, a pestilential marsh, and we should hear complaints of the niggardliness of nature, and of the impossibility of remedying it by human art or contrivance.*

The Corsicans retain some traces of Eastern manners, as well as of barbarous life. For example, the father of the family and the sons sit at table, while the wife and daughters wait upon them, or eat their meal in one corner of the room standing. When they go a journey, the husband rides on before, well armed and mounted, and the wife follows on foot, carrying one or two of her children. Boys at twelve years of age learn the use of the gun, and go armed like men. You are in constant danger of being stopped on the high-roads by straggling banditti. Troops of these enter the towns and country-houses, and carry off the most respectable individuals, who, on paying a certain ransom, are suffered to return home, and are glad to hush the matter up. The priests even, in some remote districts, officiate at the altar armed, and are often compelled to give absolution to assassins,

* Young, in his Travels through France, says, "We passed three rivers, the waters of which might be applied to irrigation, yet no use made of them. The Duke de Bouillon has vast possessions in these lands. A *grand seigneur* will at any time, and in any country, explain the reason of improvable land being left waste." Yet Arthur Young was no enthusiast, but a plain, practical man. But this was forty years ago, before common sense and liberal feeling were overlaid and buried under a heap of paradoxes and counter-paradoxes.

under pain of becoming themselves their victims. The state of Corsica presents the image of war in time of peace. The natives approach to the wildness of the savage or animal tribes. Hunted down, exposed to the incursions and ravages of different neighboring states for centuries, their natural fierceness has been exasperated by danger and ill-usage: jealousy, distrust, hatred, sudden shifts, want and sloth are become familiar to them. They plant themselves on the top of a rock for security against the fancied foe, instead of cultivating the field beneath as a precaution against hunger; the necessity of snatching a precarious subsistence by chance or violence takes away the industry or patience required to improve their condition; the hoarse sound of the horn lingering in the ear of memory keeps alive their courage and their fears; and to inflict or revenge injuries is considered as the first duty they owe to their country. Feuds between families are handed down with unabated rancor from one generation to another; and a bride reckons as the most valuable part of her dowry the number of her kindred, who are bound to take up and avenge her quarrel. How far this picturesque and dramatic situation of things may have its charms either for the inhabitants themselves, or in the eyes of the poet or romance-writer, is another question; but there is nothing in the considerations of philosophy or the laws of statistics, to prevent them from exchanging it for one of greater security, numbers, and plenty, whenever they choose.

The most effectual means for accomplishing such an object, as laid down by Napoleon, are—1. A good code of rural laws, to protect agriculture against the inroads of the cattle, and to destroy the goats. 2. The draining of the marshes, so as to recal the inhabitants by degrees to the sea-coast. 3. Premiums for the encouragement of planting and the grafting of olive and mulberry trees, which ought to be double for plantations by the sea-side. 4. A just but severe police, and a general and absolute disarming, as well with respect to great as small arms, such as stilettoes and poniards. 5. Two hundred places, exclusively reserved for young Corsicans in the military and veterinary schools, and schools of agriculture, arts, and commerce in France. 6. A regular exportation of timber for the use of the navy, and consequently the foundation of towns by the sea-side and at the entrance of the forests, since it ought to be the constant aim of government to draw the population into the plains, if it intends to aid the advances of civilization.

Buonaparte, when a boy, used to have frequent disputes with his uncle, the Archdeacon of Ajaccio, about the mischief done by his goats, (which procured him the appellation of *an innovator* from the old man,) and he does not appear to have forgotten his former grudge against them. He brooded up to the period of manhood on the vexations and debasement of his country, (as is evident from his letter to Paoli, dated June, 1789,*) so that his first revolutionary ardor was engrafted on his resentment of the wrongs or insults suffered by Corsica from the old French government and on the hope of her emancipation. He retained to the last a vivid recollection of the scene of his early childhood, and spoke of its valleys, its precipices, its torrents, its glowing sky, and keen passions with all the enthusiasm of a lover. Those objects excite the deepest regret which give scope to the imagination, not those which satisfy it. His attachment to Corsica must have been strong, since he fancied at one time it might afford him a final refuge from his enemies. He repelled with indignation the sarcasm thrown out by some writer, that "the French had sought an emperor among a people whom the Romans had refused to receive as slaves." This, which was meant for a satire, was in fact a compliment. Their unwillingness to serve did not make them unfit to rule. Yet the French themselves sometimes affect to throw the blame of Buonaparte's ambition and of all their misfortunes (which they say he brought upon them) on the original sin of his not being born in France.†

* See Appendix, No. 2.

† The particulars of the foregoing account are chiefly taken from his Memoirs, and may therefore be considered as in all likelihood comprising the substance of his *History of Corsica*, which has been lost.

# CHAPTER III.

Buonaparte was not quite twenty years old, when the French Revolution broke out in 1789. From the time of his being employed at the siege of Toulon and in the war of Italy which followed, he may be considered as its sword-arm. From that time, its fate became in a manner bound up with his. It awaited his appearance to triumph and to perish with him. It will be therefore not improper in this place to give some account of its origin and progress up to that period.

The French Revolution might be described as a remote but inevitable result of the invention of the art of printing. The gift of speech, or the communication of thought by words, is that which distinguishes man from other animals. But this faculty is limited and imperfect without the intervention of books, which render the knowledge possessed by every one in the community accessible to all. There is no doubt, then, that the press (as it has existed in modern times) is the great organ of intellectual improvement and civilization.* It was impossible in this point of view, that those institutions, which are founded in a state of society and manners long anterior to this second breathing of understanding into the life of man, should remain on the same proud footing after it, with all their disproportions and defects. Many of these, indeed, must be softened by the lapse of time and influ-

---

* The free states of antiquity, or the republics in the middle ages, were single cities, where the spirit of liberty and independence was called forth, and strengthened by personal intercourse and communication. The towns in different parts of Europe, on the same principle, obtained several immunities before the *villains* or country people thought of throwing off their yoke. In Spain the cities are ripe for a revolution, while the peasantry are averse to any change

ence of opinion, and give way of their own accord: but others are too deeply rooted in the passions and interests of men to be wrenched asunder without violence, or by the mutual consent of the parties concerned; and it is this which makes revolutions necessary, with their train of lasting good and present evil. When a government, like an old-fashioned building, has become crazy and rotten, stops the way of improvement, and only serves to collect diseases and corruption, and the proprietors refuse to come to any compromise, the community proceed in this as in some other cases; they set summarily to work—"they pull down the house, they abate the nuisance." All other things had changed: why then should governments remain the same, an excrescence and an incumbrance on the state? It is only because they have most power and most interest to continue their abuses. This circumstance is a reason why it is doubly incumbent on those who are aggrieved by them to get rid of them; and makes the shock the greater, when opinion at last becomes a match for arbitrary power.

The feudal system was in full vigor almost up to the period of the discovery of printing. Much had been done since that time: but it was the object of the French Revolution to get rid at one blow of the frame-work and of the last relics of that system. Before the diffusion of knowledge and inquiry, governments were for the most part the growth of brute force or of barbarous superstition. Power was in the hands of a few, who used it only to gratify their own pride, cruelty, or avarice, and who took every means to extend and cement it by fear and favor. The lords of the earth, disdaining to rule by the choice or for the benefit of the mass of the community, whom they regarded and treated as no better than a herd of cattle, derived their title from the skies, pretending to be accountable for the exercise or abuse of their authority to God only—the throne rested on the altar, and every species of atrocity or wanton insult having power on its side, received the sanction of religion, which it was thenceforth impiety and rebellion against the will of Heaven to impugn. This state of things continued and grew worse and worse, while knowledge and power were confined within mere local and personal limits. Each petty sovereign shut himself up in his castle

or fortress, and scattered havoc and dismay over the unresisting
country around him. In an age of ignorance and barbarism,
when force and interest decided everything, and reason had no
means of making itself heard, what was to prevent this, or act as
a check upon it? The lord himself had no other measure of
right than his own will : his pride and passions would blind him
to every consideration of conscience or humanity ; he would regard every act of disobedience as a crime of the deepest die, and
to give unbridled sway to his lawless humors, would become the
ruling passion and sole study of his life. How would it stand
with those within the immediate circle of his influence or his vengeance? Fear would make them cringe, and lick the feet of
their haughty and capricious oppressor: the hope of reward or
the dread of punishment would stifle the sense of justice or pity ;
despair of success would make them cowards, habit would confirm them into slaves, and they would look up with bigoted devotion (the boasted *loyalty* of the good old times) to the right of
the strongest as the only law. A king would only be the head of
a confederation of such petty despots, and the happiness or rights
of the people would be equally disregarded by them both. Religion, instead of curbing this state of rapine and licentiousness,
became an accomplice and a party in the crime ; gave absolution
and plenary indulgence for all sorts of enormities ; granting the
forgiveness of Heaven in return for a rich jewel or fat abbey-
lands, and setting up a regular (and what in the end proved an
intolerable) traffic in violence, cruelty, and lust. As to the
restraints of law, there was none but what resided in the breast
of the *Grand Seigneur*, who hung up in his court-yard, without
judge or jury, any one who dared to utter the slightest murmur
against the most flagrant wrong. Such must be the consequence,
as long as there was no common standard or impartial judge to
appeal to ; and this could only be found in public opinion, the offspring of books. As long as any unjust claim or transaction was
confined to the knowledge of the parties concerned, the tyrant and
the slave, which is the case in all unlettered states of society,
*might* must prevail over *right ;* for the strongest would bully, and
the weakest must submit, even in his own defence, and persuade
himself that he was in the wrong, even in his own despite: but

the instant the world (that dread jury) are impannelled, and
called to look on and be umpires in the scene, so that nothing is
done by connivance or in a corner, then reason mounts the judg-
ment-seat in lieu of passion or interest, and opinion becomes law,
instead of arbitrary will ; and farewell feudal lord and sovereign
king !

From the moment that the press opens the eyes of the community beyond the actual sphere in which each moves, there is
from that time inevitably formed the germ of a body of opinion
directly at variance with the selfish and servile code that before
reigned paramount, and approximating more and more to the
manly and disinterested standard of truth and justice. Hitherto
force, fraud, and fear decided every question of individual right
or general reasoning ; the possessor of rank and influence, in
answer to any censure or objection to his conduct, appealed to
God and to his sword :—now a new principle is brought into play
which had never been so much as dreamt of, and before which he
must make good his pretensions, or it will shatter his strongholds
of pride and prejudice to atoms, as the pent-up air shatters whatever resists its expansive force. This power is public opinion,
exercised upon men, things, and general principles, and to which
mere physical power must conform, or it will crumble it to
powder. Books alone teach us to judge of truth and good in the
abstract : without a knowledge of things at a distance from us,
we judge like savages or animals from our senses and appetites
only ; but by the aid of books and of an intercourse with the
world of ideas, we are purified, raised, ennobled from savages
into intellectual and rational beings. Our impressions of what is
near to us are false, of what is distant feeble ; but the last ga'n-
ing strength from being united in public opinion, and expressed
by the public voice, are like the congregated roar of many
waters, and quail the hearts of princes. Who but the tyrant
does not hate the tyrant ? Who but the slave does not despise
the slave ? The first of these looks upon himself as a God, upon
his vassal as a clod of the earth, and forces him to be of the same
opinion : the philosopher looks upon them both as men, and in-
structs the world to do so. While they had to settle their pretensions by themselves, and in the night of ignorance, it is no won-

der no good was done; while pride intoxicated the one, and fear
stupefied the other. But let them be brought out of that dark
cave of despotism and superstition, and let a thousand other persons who have no interest but that of truth and justice, be called
on to determine between them, and the plea of the lordly oppressor to make a beast of burden of his fellow-man becomes as
ridiculous as it is odious. All that the light of philosophy, the
glow of patriotism, all that the brain wasted in midnight study,
the blood poured out upon the scaffold or in the field of battle
can do or have done, is to take this question in all cases from
before the first gross, blind and iniquitous tribunal, where power
insults over weakness, and place it before the last more just, disinterested, and in the end more formidable one, where each individual is tried by his peers, and according to rules and principles which have received the common examination and the common consent. A public sense is thus formed, free from slavish
awe or the traditional assumption of insolent superiority, which
the more it is exercised becomes the more enlightened and
enlarged, and more and more requires equal rights and equal
laws. This new sense acquired by the people, this new organ
of opinion and feeling, is like bringing a battering-train to bear
upon some old Gothic castle, long the den of rapine and crime,
and must finally prevail against all absurd and antiquated institutions, unless it is violently suppressed, and this engine of political
reform turned by bribery and terror against itself. Who in
reading history, where the characters are laid open and the circumstances fairly stated, and where he himself has no false bias
to mislead him, does not take part with the oppressed against the
oppressor? Who is there that admires Nero at the distance of
two thousand years? Did not the *Tartuffe* in a manner hoot
religious hypocrisy out of France; and was it not on this account
constantly denounced by the clergy? What do those, who read
the annals of the Inquisition, think of that dread tribunal? And
what has softened its horrors but those annals being read? What
figure does the massacre of St. Bartholomew make in the eyes
of posterity? But books anticipate and conform the decision of
the public, of individuals, and even of the actors in such scenes,
to that lofty and irrevocable standard, mould and fashion the heart

and inmost thoughts upon it, so that something manly, liberal, and generous grows out of the fever of passion and the palsy of base fear; and this is what is meant by the progress of modern civilization and modern philosophy. An individual in a barbarous age and country throws another who has displeased him (without other warrant than his will) into a dungeon, where he pines for years, and then dies; and perhaps only the mouldering bones of the victim, discovered long after, disclose his fate: or if known at the time, the confessor gives absolution, and the few who are let into the secret are intimidated from giving vent to their feelings, and hardly dare disapprove in silence. Let this act of violence be repeated afterwards in story, and there is not an individual in the whole nation whose bosom does not swell with pity, or whose blood does not curdle within him at the recital of so foul a wrong. Why then should there be an individual in a nation privileged to do what no other individual in the nation can be found to approve? But he has the power, and will not part with it in spite of public opinion. Then that public opinion must become active, and break the moulds of prescription in which his right derived from his ancestors is cast, and this will be a revolution. Is that a state of things to regret or bring back, the bare mention of which makes one shudder? But the form, the shadow of it only was left: then why keep up that form, or cling to a shadow of injustice, which is no less odious than contemptible, except to make an improper use of it?

Let all the wrongs, public and private, produced in France by arbitrary power and exclusive privileges for a thousand years be collected in a volume, and let this volume be read by all who have hearts to feel or capacity to understand, and the strong, stifling sense of oppression and kindling burst of indignation that would follow will be that impulse of public opinion that led to the French Revolution. Let all the victims that have perished under the mild, paternal sway of the ancient *régime*, in dungeons, and in agony, without a trial, without an accusation, without witnesses, be assembled together, and their chains struck off, and the shout of jubilee and exultation they would make, or that nature would make at the sight, will be the shout that was heard when he Bastille fell! The dead pause that ensued among the gods .

of the earth, the rankling malice, the panic-fear, when they saw
law and justice raised to an equality with their sovereign will,
and mankind no longer doomed to be their sport, was that of fiends
robbed of their prey : their struggles, their arts, their unyielding
perseverance, and their final triumph was that of fiends when it
is restored to them !

It has been sometimes pretended as if the French Revolution
burst out like a volcano, without any previous warning, only to
alarm and destroy—or was one of those comet-like appearances,
the approach of which no one can tell till the shock and conflagration are felt. What is the real state of the case ? There was
not one of those abuses and grievances which the rough grasp of
the Revolution shook to air, that had not been the butt of ridicule, the theme of indignant invective, the subject of serious reprobation for near a century. They had been held up without ceasing and without answer to the derision of the gay, the scorn of the
wise, the sorrow of the good. The most witty, the most eloquent,
the most profound writers were unanimous in their wish to remove or reform these abuses, and the most dispassionate and
well-informed part of the community joined in the sentiment ; it
was only the self-interested or the grossly ignorant who clung
to them. Every public and private complaint had been subjected
to the touchstone of inquiry and argument ; the page of history, of
fiction, of the drama, of philosophy had been laid open, and their
contents poured into the public ear, which turned away disgusted
from the arts of sophistry or the menace of authority. It was this
operation of opinion, enlarging its circle, and uniting nearly all
the talents, the patriotism, and the independence of the country in
its service, that brought about the events which followed. Nothing else did or could. It was not a dearth of provisions, the loss
of the queen's jewels, that could overturn all the institutions and
usages of a great kingdom—it was not the Revolution that produced the change in the face of society, but the change in the
texture of society that produced the Revolution, and brought its
outward appearance into a nearer correspondence with its inward
sentiments. There is no other way of accounting for so great
and sudden a transition. Power, prejudice, interest, custom, ignorance, sloth, and cowardice were against it : what then remained

to counterbalance this weight, and to overturn all obstacles, but reason and conviction which were for it ? *Magna est veritas, et prevalebit.* A king was no longer thought to be an image of the Divinity; a lord to be of a different species from other men; a priest to carry an immediate passport to heaven in his pocket. On what possible plea or excuse then, when the ground of opinion on which they rested was gone, attempt to keep up the same exclusive and exorbitant pretensions, without any equivalent to the community in the awe and veneration they felt for them ? Why should a nobleman be permitted to spit in your face, to rob you of an estate, or to debauch your wife or daughter with impunity, when it was no longer deemed an honor for him to do so ? If manners had undergone a considerable change in this respect, so that the right was rarely exercised, why not abrogate the insult implied in the very forbearance from the injury, alike intolerable to the free-born spirit of man ? Why suspend the blow over your head, if it was not meant to descend upon it ? Or why hold up claims in idle mockery, which good sense and reason alike disowned, as if there were really a distinction in the two classes of society, and the one were rightful lords over the other, instead of being by nature all equal ? But the evil did not stop here ; for it was never yet known that men wished to retain the semblance of a wrong, unless they aimed at profiting as far as in them lay by the practice of it. While the king wore the anointed crown that was supposed to be let down in a golden chain from heaven on his head, while the lord dyed his sword in blood, while the priest worked fancied miracles with a crucifix and beads, they did well to claim to be masters of the world, and to trample in triple phalanx on mankind : but why they should expect us to allow this claim in mere courtesy and good-will, when it is no longer *backed* by fraud or force, is difficult to comprehend.

What is a legitimate government? It is a government that professedly derives its title from the grace of God and its ancestors, that sets the choice or the good of the governed equally at defiance, and that is amenable for the use it makes of its power only to its own caprice, pride, or malice. It is an outrage and a burlesque on every principle of common sense or liberty. It puts the means for the end : mistakes a trust for a property, considers

the honors and offices of the state as its natural inheritance, and
the law as an unjust encroachment on its arbitrary will. What
motive can there be for tolerating such a government a single
instant, except from sheer necessity or blindfold ignorance? Or
what chance of modifying it so as to answer any good purpose,
without a total subversion of all its institutions, principles, or prejudices? The kings of France, tamed by opinion, conforming to
the manners of the time, no longer stabbed a faithful counsellor
in the presence-chamber, or strangled a competitor for the throne
in a dungeon, or laid waste a country or fired a city for a whim:
but they still made peace or war as they pleased, or hung the
wealth of a province in a mistress's ear, or lost a battle by the
promotion of a favorite, or ruined a treasury by the incapacity of
a minister of high birth and connexions. The noble no longer,
as in days of yore, hung up his vassal at his door for a disre-
spectful word, or look (which was called the *haute justice,*) or issued with a numerous retinue from his lofty portcullis to carry
fire and sword into the neighboring country; but he too labored
in his vocation, and in the proud voluptuous city drained the last
pittance from the toil-worn peasant by taxes, grants, and exactions, to waste it on his own vanity, luxury, and vices. If he
had a quarrel with an inferior or with a rival less favored than
himself, the king would issue his *lettre-de-cachet,* and give the refractory and unsuspecting offender a lodging for life in what Mr.
Burke is pleased to call the *" king's castle!"* Had opinion put a
stop to this crying abuse, had it rendered this odious privilege of
royalty merely nominal? "In the mild reign of Louis XV.
alone," according to Blackstone, "there were no less than 15,000
*lettres-de-cachet* issued." Some persons will think this fact alone
sufficient to account for and to justify the overturning of the
government in the reign of his successor. The priests no longer
tied their victim to the stake or devoted him to the assassin's
poniard as of old; they thought it enough if they could wallow
in the fat of the land, pander to the vices of the rich and the
abuses of power, to which they looked for the continuance of
wealth and influence, and fly-blow every liberal argument and
persecute every liberal writer, from whom they dreaded their loss.
From the moment that the ancient *régime* ceased to be supported

by that system of faith and manners in which it had originated, the whole order of the state became warped and disunited, a wretched jumble of claims that were neither enforced nor relinquished. There was ill-blood sown between the government and the people ; heart-burning, jealousy, and want of confidence between the different members of the community. Every advance in civilization was regarded by one party with dislike and distrust, while by the other every privilege held by ancient tenure was censured as the offspring of pride and prejudice. The court was like a decayed beauty, that viewed her youthful rival's charms with scorn and apprehension. The nation, in the language of the day, *had hitherto been nothing, was every thing, and wanted to be something.* The great mass of society felt itself as a degraded *caste,* and was determined to wipe out the stigma with which every one of its opinions, sentiments and pretensions was branded. This was a thing no longer to be endured and must be got rid of at any rate. The States-General of 1789 met under different auspices from what they did in 1614, when the president of the nobles reviled the *Tiers Etat,* and was echoed by the King with greater acerbity of language for begging to be looked upon in the light of "a younger brother of the family !"* From the same want of unity and concert in the parts of the system, magnificent roads were built by the *corvées* or forced labor of the peasants, leading no where, and without a traveller upon them, to gratify the caprice and ostentation of the lords of the manor. Great and expensive works were undertaken by royal liberality, and laid aside by royal caprice or ministerial incapacity. The resources of the country, clogged by the remains of feudal tenures, by the ravages of the game-laws, and the sloth and depression resulting from partial laws, were found inadequate to keep pace with the expenses of the court, conducted on a scale of modern dissipation and extravagance. All this was known, and had been repeated a thousand times, till it became a kind of burning-shame at the door. Such a state of things was ripe for change. After Pascal's *Provincial Letters,* the treatises of the Economists, and the clouds of Memoirs of the courts of Louis XIV. and XV., after the wit of Voltaire and the eloquence of Rousseau had exhausted

* See Appendix No. 3.

every topic, light or serious, connected with the prevailing order of things, the old French government became effete in all its branches, and fell to the ground as a useless incumbrance, almost without a struggle, and without one feeling of regret in one worthy and well-informed mind.*

Nor was this all. England had long set the example, and had long been looked up to for the opinions of her writers and the freedom of her institutions by those who wished to serve the cause of their country or of mankind. Nor had she been backward to encourage this disposition, but had been in the constant practice of "insulting the slavery of the rest of Europe by the loudness of her boasts of freedom." The spirit of the reigning government and laws was founded on one regicide, that of Charles I., on the glorious Revolution of 1688 under King William, and on the suc-

* The subjoined passage, taken from Arthur Young's Travels in France in the year 1787, will show how little the French Revolution could be characterized as a merely fortuitous or unexpected event

"Dined to-day (Sept. 17) with a party whose conversation was entirely political. One opinion pervaded the whole company, that they are on the eve of some great revolution in the government; that every thing points to it: the confusion in the finances great, with a *deficit* impossible to provide for without the States-General of the kingdom, yet no ideas formed of what would be the consequence of their meeting; no minister existing, or to be looked to in or out of power, with such decisive talents as to promise any other remedy than palliative ones; a prince on a throne with excellent dispositions, but without the resources of a mind that could govern in such a moment without ministers; a court buried in pleasure and dissipation, and adding to the distress, instead of endeavoring to be placed in a more independent situation; a great ferment amongst all ranks of men, who are eager for some change, without knowing what to look to or to hope for; and a strong leaven of liberty, increasing every hour since the American Revolution; altogether form a combination of circumstances that promise ere long to ferment into motion, if some master-hand, of very superior talents, and inflexible courage, is not found at the helm to guide events, instead of being driven by them. It is very remarkable that such conversation never occurs, but a bankruptcy is the topic. All agree that the States of the kingdom cannot assemble without more liberty being the consequence: but I meet with so few men that have any just ideas of freedom, that I question much the species of this new liberty that is to arise. They know not how to value the privileges of THE PEOPLE. As to the nobility and clergy, if a revolution added any thing to their scale, I think it would do more mischief than good."—Vol. i. p. 138.

cession of the present family to the throne, in spite of two rebellions to restore the legitimate Pretender, and to re-establish
popery and slavery. The Reformation was the great event in
modern times (aided and promoted by the invention of printing)
that striking at the encroachments of the papal power (the nurs-
ing mother of ignorance and blind submission) shook all arbitrary,
self-constituted power to its centre, and destroyed the illusions
both of spiritual and secular authority, by bringing them to the
test of reason and conscience. The tiara and the crown lost their
magnetic charm together. The domineering, supercilious pretensions of infallible orthodoxy and bloated power were insepara-
bly linked together, and both gave way or recoiled under the
shock and encounter of the common nature and the common
understanding of man. The first step to emancipate the bodies
of the enslaved people, was to enfranchise their minds ; and the
foundation of the political rights and independence of states was
laid in the ruins of that monstrous superstition, that reared its
head to the skies, and ground both princes and people to powder.*
The first blows that staggered this mighty fabric were given, and
the first crash was heard abroad ; but England echoed it back
with " her island voice," and from that time the triumph of truth
and reason over pride and hypocrisy was secure, though remote
and arduous. The principle of religious toleration became the
counterpart and firm ally of civil liberty in England : the habit of
refusing to subscribe to bigoted dogmas for conscience-sake and in
matters of faith, was the germ and root of that manly independence
of spirit and resistance to the encroachments or exactions of arbitrary power, which is so marked a feature in English history.
There is something in the plain, grave, straight-forward, sturdy cha
racter of the English people that makes them ready to assert their
rights and grapple with the iron hand of power ; and from the rigid
discipline and simple forms of the Puritanic faith, engrafted on the
Protestant, there was an obvious tendency to republicanism.

The Reformation had laid open the translation of the Bible to
the meanest peasant, the effects of which were distinctly visible,
both in our government and literature. The model of the Jewish
theocracy was thus placed perpetually before the eyes of the

* See Cardinal Wolsey's advice to Thomas Cromwell. Appendix, No. 4.

4*

political and religious enthusiast, who longed to reduce it to
practice in the *English Commonwealth*. This mixture of faith
and zeal gave a degree of sanctity and elevation to their political
tenets ; and the parliament-soldiers marched to the field of battle
with the same fervor of feeling and heroic self-devotion that they
would to take possession of the crown of martyrdom. Meanwhile,
the Stuarts, either from regretting the privileges of their Scottish
ancestors, or from their intermarriages with foreign princesses,
imbibed more and more a spirit of absolute authority and implicit
faith, that, coming into contact with the stern and reckless impulse derived more or less remotely from the Reformation, caused
their ruin, first in the beheading of Charles I., and afterwards (for
kings are superior to warning and experience) in the expulsion of
his son, James II., from his throne and kingdom, for persisting in
the attempt to bring back Popery and arbitrary sway. The Revolution of 1688 gave the death's wound to the doctrine of hereditary right, and fixed the sovereign power on a popular basis in
practice. Mr. Locke's *Treatise on Government* (written at the
desire of King William) settled the same question in theory forever, and has been the text-book of all lovers of liberty and friends
of their country ever since. This example, set by the English
people and confirmed by English philosophers, was the glass in
which France (if she knew her own dignity and interest) was
to dress herself. There was an honest simplicity and severity
in our style of civil architecture (whether we chose to add or to
retrench) that acted as a foil to the Gothic redundancy and disproportioned frippery of our continental neighbors. The French
wits and politicians laughed at Sir Robert Filmer and his patri-
archal scheme, and held up the energy and firmness of the English nation as an example to their own. It is true the French
government levied troops and money, and instigated and aided
two rebellions (in 1715 and 1745) against the reigning family,
bestowing on them every epithet of abuse and obloquy, as rebels,
heretics, usurpers, upstarts, which the legitimate vocabulary
affords ;* at the same time that the English press teemed with
libels on the *Grand Monarque ;* and not a newspaper, not a print,
not a ballad, but was filled with sarcastic allusions to the wooden

* See Appendix, No. 5.

shoes and *soupe-maigre* of the French under a debasing *régime*, which they were urged by every species of taunt and argument to throw off and shew themselves men. In short, the chief quarrel which the English had with the French was supposed (up to the period of which we have been speaking) to be that which freemen must ever have with slaves. When his Majesty George III. came to the crown, the claim of the Stuarts was either completely set aside, or in a state of *abeyance ;* the phantom of Divine Right, which had, during two reigns, haunted the august monarchs of the House of Hanover, had, however, no sooner vanished than another apparition arose in its stead, the dread of popular government. Hitherto the principles which had seated his Majesty's family on the throne were the favorite theme alike of patriots and courtiers; now, the alarm from an hereditary Pretender being over, it was high time to exchange them for the principles that were to keep them there, and to prevent the dangerous precedent which had been set from spreading farther, or from being turned against those who had thus far only profited by it. As there was an unlucky flaw in the original title-deed, it was natural to make this good by every extension of influence and prerogative. It was a delicate point, either to do without the choice of the people, looking back to past vicissitudes, or to admit them into a copartnery in the concern, looking forward to possible contingencies ; and on this point the courtiers and the patriots, the crown and the people, from that time forward split, and it remained the bone of contention between the two parties, the source of endless heartburnings, rancor, and jealousies, that "spread like a thick scurf'" over the state, during the greater part of the last reign. Almost immediately after its commencement, the right of the people to choose their representatives in parliament was grossly tampered with, and this was enough to shew the temper and spirit of the new cabinet. Then the American war broke out, and soon after its disastrous conclusion, the French Revolution—dreadful blows, following hard upon each other, to the deliberate design (if any such had been formed) to retrograde upon the steps of the Stuarts, now that there was no farther apprehension from their persons, and which unhinged the reason, though they could not quell the resolution of the reigning monarch. The cause of American independence had succeeded ; it became doubly urgent to stifle the flame of liberty which had spread from thence to France, and might consume every neighboring government in its dazzling blaze. Great was the disappointment, and foul the stain, when England declared herself against France, thus seeking to extinguish the light it had kindled once more in the night of slavery, and heading the league of kings against the people, thenceforth never to turn back till it had finally accomplished its unrelenting purpose!

What had England to do with the quarrel? Was her religion Catholic? She had been stigmatized for above two centuries, and almost shut out of the pale of Christendom as a heretic. Was her crown despotic? Her king reigned, in contempt of an exiled Pretender and of hereditary right, as the king of a free people. Did her nobles form a privileged class, above the law? God forbid. Were her clergy armed with a power to bind and to unloose, in heaven and on earth? It was long since they had been stripped of any such power or pretension. What then was the crime which drew down on France the vengeance not only of the despots of the Continent, but the last enmity and implacable hatred of a free nation and of a constitutional king? She had dared to aspire to the blessings of the English Constitution. Was there treason, was there danger in this? Yes ; for if they made a step in advance from slavery to freedom, it was thought that we might be tempted to keep the start which we had always maintained in the race of freedom, and become *too free!* To this illiberal, mean, and envious policy we were not merely to sacrifice the peace and happiness of the world, but were to abjure and reverse and load with opprobrium every sentiment and maxim on which our own freedom and pre-eminence rested. Those who have deprived us of the natural language of liberty, and changed it to the fretful whine of the hunting-tigers of Legitimacy have much to answer for. The dilemma was not a common one. It was judged best to wait, to watch, and to improve opportunity ; to regard " with jealous leer malign" the first attempts of liberty, to irritate by coldness and mistrust, to goad a people at all times too prone to excitement into frenzy, in order that they might be led back manacled to their prison-house, and to rouse the national prejudices of John Bull against the French, as if this were the old vulgar quarrel, instead of being the great cause of mankind. The two noblest impulses of our nature, the love of country and the love of kind, were to be set in hostile array, and armed with inextinguishable fury against each other. It was a prostitution of names and things worthy of the end which it was meant to serve, and of those who planned and executed it! As this was a nice point to manage, the blow was not struck on our parts till the French king's head fell on the scaffold for being secretly in league and correspondence with the other coalesced monarchs; but the storm had been long gathering. This was a great and mortifying change for Old England—from the champion of liberty to its ungenerous foe; from the exiler and beheader of its own kings to the avenger of those of others. Mr. Burke was employed gradually to prepare the public mind for such a change, by sounding the alarm to power and discrediting the popular cause. The loud asserter of American independence appeared first the cautious calumniator, and afterwards, inflamed by opposition and encouraged by patronage, the infuriated denouncer of the French Revolution. He who had talked familiarly of kings as "lovers of low company," now qualified the people as "a swinish multitude." He who had so bespattered the late King that poor Goldsmith was obliged to leave the room, now had occasion to speak of him with proud humility as "his kind and gracious benefactor." Literary jealousy came in aid of royal bounty. He had always entertained a pique against Rousseau, whom he had known formerly when in England, and could not bear to see a great kingdom overturned by his genius, when all that he himself had been able to effect was a reform in *the turnspit of the king's kitchen.* Without the help of his powerful pen, perhaps the necessary change in the tone of politics could not have been accomplished effectually or without violence. Liberty had hitherto been the watch-word of Englishmen, and all their stock of enthusiasm was called forth by the mention of resistance to oppression, real or supposed. Such had been our theory; such (when occasion offered) was our practice. Mr. Burke strewed the flowers of his rhetoric over the rotten carcase of corruption; by his tropes and figures so dazzled both the ignorant and the learned, that they

could not distinguish the shades between liberty and licentiousness, between anarchy and despotism; gave a romantic and novel
air to the whole question; proved that slavery was a very chivalrous and liberal sentiment, that reason and prejudice were at bottom very much akin, that the Queen of France was a very beautiful vision, and that there was nothing so vile and sordid as useful knowledge and practical improvement. A crazy, obsolete
government was metamorphosed into an object of fancied awe and
veneration, like a mouldering Gothic ruin, which, however de-
lightful to look at or read of, is not at all pleasant to live under.
Thus the poetry and imagination of the thing were thrown into
the scale of old-fashioned barbarism and musty tradition, and
turned the balance. A falser mode of judging could not be
found; for things strike the imagination from privation, contrast, and suffering, which are proportionably intolerable in
reality.* It excites a pleasing interest to witness the representation of a tragedy; but who would, for this reason, wish to
be a real actor in it? The *good old times* are good only because they are gone, or because they afford a picturesque contrast
to modern ones; and to wish to bring them back, is neither to ap-

---

* If this is not a complete account of imagination, it is, at least, true that
it either produces its effects in this way, or aims at aggrandizing some one
object, person, or thing at the expense of all others. It fixes upon the first
impression that offers, and endeavors, by every art of sophistry, prejudice,
and passion, to make this as strong as possible, let the consequence be what
it will. Reason, on the contrary, conquers by dividing; and, instead of
exaggerating and excluding, aims at universality, connection, and proportion
in all its determinations. As we know a few things, the imagination seizes
upon some one of them, and pampers and exalts it in preference to all the
rest, which are made subservient to it; as we enlarge our inquiries, a va-
riety of new objects dispels our first prejudices, and reason is appealed to to
adjust their precedence and reduce them to their relative value. The tendency of the human understanding is from the *concrete* to the *abstract*, in institutions, in religion, in literature, in life, and manners, in all cases in
which the experience and reflection of civil society can be supposed to receive a gradual enlargement; and this marked and unavoidable tendency
points, for the most part, to the greatest quantity of truth, and, I should
hope, of good. At least I am sure that no good can be done by transposing
the different stages of its progress, and forcing upon any one age or country
those institutions, views, or feelings, which are not natural to it.

preciate the old or the new. This served, however, to produce a diversion, and to silence the clamor, that might otherwise have arisen. The mob of readers stared without knowing what to think, and the King presented the work to his friends (bound in morocco) as " a book that every gentleman ought to read." From that time the French Revolution was accounted vulgar; and for a man to appear at court, it was necessary that he should be understood to set his face against modern reasoning and philosophy, and to have discarded Rousseau and Voltaire from his library. No one could have performed this feat but the celebrated author of *The Sublime and Beautiful*, with his metaphysical subtlety and poetical flights. Mr. Pitt has been hailed by his flatterers as " the pilot that weathered the storm;" but it was Mr. Burke who, at this giddy, maddening period, stood at the prow of the vessel of the state, and with his glittering, pointed spear *harpooned* the Leviathan of the French Revolution, which darted into its wild career, tinging its onward track with purple gore. The answers to this work were numerous and respectable; but they evaded the recondite meaning that lurked in it, and in the colors of style no one could pretend to vie with him. The *Vindiciæ Gallicæ*, by Sir James Macintosh, was stately and elaborate. Paine's *Rights of Man* was the only really powerful reply, and indeed so powerful and explicit, that the Government undertook to quash it by an *ex-officio* information, and by a declaration of war against France, to still the ferment and excite an odium against its admirers, as taking part with a foreign enemy against their prince and country. The contest now raged with all the fury and inveteracy of a civil war. It was, in fact, a civil war between France and Europe, or rather a *servile* war, of which France was the seat, and the sole object of which was to decide by a deadly strife, by the *bellum internecinum*, whether mankind should make good their presumptuous claims to be free, or should be dragged back to their ancient bondage with stripes and taunts. The latter event took place, and the strife ceased as a matter of course.

The French writers who have treated of the rise and progress of the Revolution have been prevented by various causes from doing full justice to the truth of the question. It does not appear from their accounts that such a person as George III. ever existed. If we were to suppose a King, who concentrated in him-self all the instincts and prejudices of royalty. whose perceptions, naturally obtuse and limited, were rendered acute and uncon-trolable by disease and passion, who held with a convulsive grasp the crown that had been just snatched from the head of a legiti-mate Pretender, and that he now fancied in danger of being torn from his own by a lawless rabble, whose reputation for private virtue and religious scruples softened every stretch of prerogative, and who, by dint of selfish fear and cunning, and by deafness to all remonstrance, turned the whole strength, moral and physical, of a great people, equally formidable from their courage, their obstinacy, their resources, and their insular situation, against the cause of popular freedom, the consequences must be as baneful as they were incalculable in preventing the good or in turning it to evil ; but no such character is drawn, nor any such consequences traced in the pages of the French historian, which we might thence suppose to be purely chimerical. No more notice is taken of this part of the subject (except in casual allusions and momen-tary ebullitions of spleen) than if England had never laid out a single guinea in whetting the secret dagger, or in hiring foreign bayonets to restore the old government—had never mouthed out a single speech from the throne, declaring France to be incapable of maintaining the usual relations of peace and amity—or never, by trying her patience to the utmost by every species of con-tumely and scorn, done all in its power to render her desperate and furious in her resistance to such unprincipled and continued aggression.—Neither in these circumscribed pages are the Emi-grants seen to hover on the frontiers, like harpies waiting for their prey, and ready to pollute what they could not enjoy, en-couraging hostile bands to spread desolation, havoc, and dismay through their devoted country, defeated, driven back, returning to the charge, unable to regain or to relinquish their unnatural pre-tensions, and intent only on robbing the people of Liberty, "their three hours' bride," and leading them back again at all hazards, like felons and renegades, to that galling and disgraceful bondage, under which they had groaned for centuries, and from which there would in future be no hope of escape. A manifesto, signed by princes and generals-in-chief, gave Paris up to slaughter and pillage, and the palace of the Thuilleries was beset and insulted: the news came that Verdun was taken, the last place interposed between the Allies and the execution of their threat, and the prisons floated with blood. A plan for dismembering France and signalizing another Poland was divulged, and Louis XVI. was led to the scaffold. There was certainly something in this state of things to work up the feelings of manhood and independence to a pitch of frenzy—"to make mad the thinking and appal the free" —not merely in the immediate view of the physical calamities and evils held out as the punishment of their having broke their chains, but in that still more intolerable and irritating tone of authority, that barefaced assumption of right and superiority over a whole people as the property and sport of a few antiquated *petits-maîtres,* in the bold and fixed determination to blot out the light of reason and to stop the breath of liberty, and to bring back (at the point of the sword) that night of darkness and slavery that should know no dawn. It was this insult, this outrage to the image of man's nature, that produced and called aloud for retaliation and defiance to the *outrance*—that cried to "strike and spare not"— that made the eye start and the brain split—that filled every faculty with fear, with shame, and hate—that made the fountain of their tears run blood, and the glow of passion sear the heart. This is the true version of the horrors and excesses of that period. It was the pressure from without that caused the irregularities and conflicts within, and retorted the boasted schemes of vengeance and cruelty on the heads of the aggressors. It is in vain to mince the question, or to give a cool and critical account of it. Such an account would be wide of the feelings of the moment, and would neither explain the excesses nor the provocation. All was wild and hurried, and in the extremes of right or wrong : there was no time for reflection nor power of choice, and it was necessary either to inflict or to endure the last injury and degradation. The poet says, "to do a great right, do a little wrong." Here, to do the greatest right, much wrong was done. In contending for all that was great and excellent in human nature against all that was corrupt and profligate, some allowance was to be made for the goodness of the cause, the excitement of the moment, the extreme insolence of power, and the want of confidence and consequent rashness and violence of the multitude in striving against it, who have always been and seem destined always to be its prey, like the poor bird fluttering and agitated under the outstretched jaws and fascinating gaze of its mortal foe!

Nothing of all this, however glaring, appears in the most approved and candid French accounts, whether from the apprehended restrictions on the public press, or from the habitual propensity of the French to see every thing through a French medium. Their description of the Revolution resembles " a phantasma or a hideous dream," that has no flesh or blood in it. The scene is Paris—the whole (or nearly so) passes in the Palais Royal—the tree of liberty is planted—up gets an orator and makes a flaming speech, or another hawks about a pamphlet or a new Constitution. Upon this a number of persons rush forward, make extravagant gesticulations, and the foremost are led off to the scaffold. Thus you see nothing but a succession of hair-brained leaders and sanguinary factions, chasing one another round the arena, tripping up one another's heels, cutting one another's throats, doing nothing for the people, and ready in every pause of mischief to deliver up the cause of Liberty to the Allies. The scene is at once monstrous and farcical. The actors in it are like tragic puppets, without dignity of deportment, or any motives for their extravagance. The Italian poet, Monti, has given much the same description in his *Basseviglia*, where he represents the chief characters of the Revolution as running up and down before the gates of the Thuilleries, brandishing daggers, twining serpents round their necks, hurling fire-brands in the height of their delirium and distraction; to explain all which allegorical mummery, he paints the fury of Intestine Discord hovering in the air and goading them on with whips of scorpions to their mutual destruction; instead of which he ought to have painted the Allied Powers, with their frowning battery of artillery and proclamations in the background. The horrors then of the French Revolution did not arise out of the Revolution, but from the dread of the Coalition formed against it. To those who insist (either wilfully or from blind prejudice) that all revolutions are a scene of confusion and violence, and that this is their very end and essence. it may be

proper to remark, that the American Revolution was accompanied
with no such excesses; that the English Revolution of 1688 was
accomplished without a reign of terror, though it entailed a civil
war and two rebellions on the kingdom; that the Low Countries
revolted against, and, after a long and dreadful struggle, shook
off the tyranny of Spain, yet no third party interfering between
the people and the old government, all the cruelties and atrocities
were on the side of the Duke of Alva; and that of late the Spanish Constitution was twice established without blood, though it
seemed to require that cement, and fell to the ground again, being
at once assailed by external and internal foes. When a house is
beset by robbers, you know pretty well what course to follow,
and how to calculate on your means of resistance; but if you find
those within the house in league with those without, the ordinary
rules of prudence and safety must be dispensed with, for there is
no defence against treachery. Another circumstance which is to
be taken into the account, and which is not, of course, brought
forward in a very prominent light by their own writers, is, that
the French were very hardly dealt with in this case, which was
an *experimentum crucis* upon the national character. They are
a people extremely susceptible of provocation. Like women,
forced out of their natural character, they become furies. Naturally light and quick, good sense and good temper are their unde-
niable and enviable characteristics; but if events occur to stagger
or supersede these habitual qualities, there then seems no end of the
extravagances of opinion, or cruelties in practice, of which they are
capable, as it were, from the mere impression of novelty and contrast. They are the creatures of impulse, whether good or bad.
Their very thoughtlessness and indifference prevent them from
being shocked at the irregularities which the passion of the moment leads them to commit; and from the nicest sense of the
ridiculous and the justest *tact* in common things, there is no absurdity of speculation, no disgusting rodomontade or wildness of
abstraction, into which they will not run when once thrown off
their guard. They excel in the trifling and familiar, and have
not strength of character or solidity of judgment to cope with
great questions or trying occasions. When they attempt the
grand and striking, they fail from too much presumption and from

too much fickleness.  In a word, from that eternal smile on the
cheek to a massacre, there is but one step : for those who are delighted with every thing, will be shocked at nothing.  Vanity
strives in general to please and make itself amiable ; but if it is
the fashion to do mischief, it will take the lead in mischief, and is,
therefore, a dangerous principle in times of crisis and convulsion.
A revolution was the Ulysses' bow of the French philosophers and
politicians.  They might, perhaps, have left it to others ; but having made the attempt, they demanded every kind of indulgence
and encouragement in the prosecution of it, like children when
they first begin to walk.  Extremes in all cases meet.  The
abuses and corruptions of the old political system were so numerous and intricate, that they led to the most visionary and air-
drawn principles of government as the only alternative ; and the
overgrown absurdities and mummery of the Catholic Church had
risen to such a height, that they obscured religion itself, and both
were overturned together.  The scepticism and indifference which
succeeded, did not afford the best medium of resistance to power
or prejudice.  Perhaps a reformation in religion ought always to
precede a revolution in the government.  Catholics may make
good subjects, but bad rebels.  They are so used to the trammels
of authority, that they do not immediately know how to do without them ; or, like manumitted slaves, only feel assured of their
liberty in committing some Saturnalian license.  A revolution, to
give it stability and soundness, should first be conducted down to
a Protestant ground.

It has been the fashion to speak of the horrors of the French
Revolution as if they were an anomaly in the history of man,
and blotted out the memory of all other cruelties on record.  Let
us turn to another example in the annals of the same people, but
at a different period, when monarchy and monkish sway were in
their " high and palmy state," not shorn of their beams or cur-
tailed of their influence by modern discoveries or degeneracy of
manners.  The *reign of terror*, while it lasted, cost the lives of
between three and four thousand individuals in the course of less
than two years in Paris alone.  The massacre of St. Bartholomew cost the lives of seventy thousand Protestants in eight days
throughout all France.  The following is Sully's account of it,

who was partly an eye-witness, and narrowly escaped falling a victim to it.

"If I sought to augment the horror which has been generally conceived against a transaction so barbarous as was that of the 24th of August, 1572, too well known by the name of St. Bartholomew, I should enlarge in this place on the number, the quality, the virtues, and the talents of those who were inhumanly massacred on this dreadful day, as well in Paris as throughout the rest of the kingdom. I should recapitulate at least a part of the insults, the ignominious treatment, and the odious refinement in cruelty, which sought while in the act of consigning to death, to inflict a thousand stabs as painful as death itself on its unhappy victims. I have still in my possession documents containing the proofs of the pressing instances which the court of France made to the neighboring courts, to follow up its example against the Reformers; or at least to refuse all asylum to those unfortunate people. But I prefer the honor of the nation to the malicious pleasure which some persons might derive from a detail, in which they would find the names of those who forgot humanity so far as to imbrue their hands in the blood of their fellow citizens and of their own kindred. I would willingly bury forever, if it were possible, the memory of a day, for which the Divine vengeance has visited France with twenty-six years of disasters, carnage, and dismay; for one cannot help judging in this manner, when one reflects on all that has happened since that fatal moment to the peace of 1598. It is even with regret that I dwell on what regards the prince who is the subject of these Memoirs, and on what touches myself in the transaction.

"I had gone to bed betimes the evening before. I found myself awakened about three hours after midnight by the tolling of the bells, and the confused cries of the populace. St. Julien, my tutor, rushed out hastily with my valet-de-chambre to learn the cause, and I have never since heard speak of these two persons, who were, without doubt, sacrificed among the first to the fury of the mob.* I was left alone to dress myself in my bed-room, into

* The upper classes of that day made no complaints of the *fury of this mob*, which did their work for them. Mr. Macculloch, in his Essay on Wages, strenuously recommends it to governments to educate the poor, in

which, a few moments after, I saw the master of the house enter, pale and terrified. He was of the reformed religion, and having heard what was in agitation, had come to the resolution of going to mass to save his life and to protect his property from pillage: he came to advise me to the same, and to take me with him. I did not think fit to accompany him. I resolved to try to reach the College of Burgundy where I prosecuted my studies, notwithstanding the distance from the house where I lodged, which rendered my design sufficiently hazardous. I dressed myself in my scholar's gown, and taking a large prayer-book under my arm, I went down stairs.* I was seized with horror as I entered the street, to see the infuriated populace, who thronged from all parts, and forced open the houses, crying out, " *Kill, kill, massacre the Huguenots!*" and the blood which I saw spilt before my eyes redoubled my fright. I fell into the hands of a *corps de garde*, who detained me. I was questioned: they were beginning to maltreat me, when the book which I carried was perceived luckily for me, and served me for a safe-conduct. I fell twice after into the same danger, from which I escaped by the same good fortune. At length I arrived at the College of Burgundy. Here I encountered a still greater risk. The porter having twice refused me entrance, I remained in the middle of the street at the mercy of an enraged multitude, whose number continually increased, and who sought eagerly for their prey, when I bethought me of asking for the principal of the college, whose name was La Faye, a man of worth, and who loved me tenderly. The porter, prevailed upon by some trifling piece of money which I had put into his hand, agreed to go in quest of him. This good man made me go with him to his room, where two inhuman priests, whom I heard speaking of the *Sicilian Vespers*, attempted to snatch me out of his hands, with a view to tear me in pieces, saying that the order was to kill even infants at the breast. All that he could do was to convey me with the greatest

order to put an end to the fear of mobs, as if they never wanted their assistance. They are not so hard upon their old friends; and sometimes require other less exact and more expeditious tools to work with than political economists.

* Young Sully was at that time not quite thirteen years of age.

secresy to a remote closet, where he locked me in. I remained there three whole days, uncertain of my fate, and receiving no assistance, except through a domestic of this charitable man, who came from time to time to bring me food. At the end of this period, the prohibition to kill and pillage having at length been published, I was brought out of my cell, and almost at the same moment I saw Ferriere and La Vieville, two archers of the Guard, dependants of my father, enter the college. They came to learn what was become of me, and were armed, no doubt to take me away by force wherever they might find me. They informed my father of my adventure, from whom I received a letter eight days after. He there said how much he had been alarmed on my account, that his advice was nevertheless that I should remain in Paris, since it was not in the choice of the prince whom I served to leave it; but that in order not to run any imminent risk, I must resolve to do what this prince himself had done, that is to say, go to mass.

"The King of Navarre (Henry IV.) had in fact found this the only way to save his life. He was awakened with the Prince of Condé, two hours before day, by a multitude of archers of the Guard, who abruptly entered the chamber in the Louvre where they slept, and in an insolent manner ordered them to dress themselves, and go with them to the King (Charles IX.) They were forbidden to take their swords; and as they went out, they saw a party of their gentlemen massacred before their eyes, without any remorse. Charles was waiting for them, and received them with eyes and a visage inflamed with rage. He commanded them with oaths and blasphemies, which were familiar to him, to quit the religion which they had only taken up, he said, to serve as a pretext for their rebellion. The condition to which they had reduced these princes, not having hindered them from expressing the reluctance they felt to obey this mandate, the anger of the King became excessive. He told them, in an altered tone, full of passion, that he would no longer suffer himself to be contradicted in his will by his subjects; that they ought to teach others by their example to revere him, as being the image of God, and to be no longer enemies to the images of his mother (the Virgin Mary). He concluded, by declaring that if from this day they did not go to mass, he was determined to have them treated as

guilty of high treason against the divine and human majesty."[*]
—*Memoirs of Sully*, book i. p. 49.

We here see what kings were, and what they thought of them-

[*] **Pope Pius V.** pretended to be scandalized by this massacre; but **Gregory XII.,** who succeeded him, had thanks publicly returned to God for it at Rome, and sent a legate to Paris to congratulate Charles IX. on it, and to encourage him to go on. Let those who are enamored of the good old times, and imagine all evil began with the French Revolution, read Sully. The progress of the story is choked up with mangled carcases: the page is slippery with blood. The perusal is revolting to modern readers. Take the following as a specimen:—

"The church (of Mas de Verdun, in Armagnac) into which the enemy fled, was large, strongly built, and well supplied with provisions, as it was the ordinary rendezvous of the peasants, and there was a great number of them there at this very time. The King of Navarre undertook to force open the church; and for this purpose sent for soldiers and workmen from Montauban, Leictoure, and other neighboring towns; not doubting that Beaumont, Miranda, and the other Catholic towns would speedily send powerful succors to the besieged, if he gave them time. In the meanwhile, we set to work to undermine the church, with the assistance of our servants. The side of the choir fell to my share; in twelve hours I had made an opening, though the wall was very thick, and built of an extremely hard kind of stone. Afterwards, by means of a scaffolding raised to the height of the breach, I succeeded in throwing a quantity of grenades into the church. The besieged were in want of water, and moistened their flour with wine; and what inconvenienced them still worse, was that they had neither surgeons nor bandages, nor remedies for the wounds caused by the grenades, which we began to throw in from all parts. They accordingly came to terms, seeing a powerful reinforcement coming up from Montauban to the King of Navarre. This prince contented himself with giving orders that they should hang seven or eight of the most mutinous: but he was obliged to abandon them all to the fury of the inhabitants of Montauban, who dragged them by force from us, and poinarded them without remorse. We learnt the motive which actuated them from the reproaches they heaped on these wretches, who had made six women, whom they had carried off, serve the purposes of the most infamous debauch; and had then devoted them to death by filling them with powder, to which they set fire and blew them to pieces, a horrible excess of brutality and cruelty."—Ibid. p. 80.

We have certainly improved a little since this time, but the power of kings, priests, and nobles has been proportionably on the wane; and the reason is, that as general knowledge and civilization advance, the influence and advantages of the privileged few necessarily decrease. These two present an everlasting counterpoise to each other, which is as true as that if you enlarge one half of a right angle, you diminish the other half. Sol-

selves, little more than two centuries ago—the spirit that actuated them while they had the power, and the pretensions which,
pampered by ignorance and the freedom from all control, made
them fancy themselves idols set up for the worship and wonder
of mankind, and which were never formally set aside till the
period of the French Revolution. Such was their government,
such their religion, and such their law; such they were, and
such they would fain continue, if the world would have let them.
It was to reduce this power, and to abrogate the forms in which
it still resided like a public plague, constantly tainting and
thwarting that influence of manners and opinions which sat as a
suppliant on the lowest step of an absolute throne, and alone
tamed its will and "checked its pride," that the French Revolution was commenced; as it was to the infatuated determination to
restore and revive those unjustifiable forms and pretensions, that
its principal mischiefs were owing. Some of that baseness and
fierceness and want of intelligence which they had for so many
centuries fostered, had no doubt its share in the endeavor to overturn them. The struggle was a long and arduous one; but it
was worth the price of blood and gold it cost, for it was a struggle whether half a dozen individuals should be more, and all
the rest of the species (with the exception of a given number,
to whom they granted letters-patent of gentility) less than men.
Did the success depend on the goodness of a cause, the result
would have been different; but the selfish passions are the
strongest, and in proportion as an object is pernicious, that is,
advantageous to a few at the expense of the many, is the zeal,
union, and perseverance manifested in its defence. The love of
power is an instinct—humanity and justice are idle names.
What tyrant or slave ever came over to the cause of the people?
Among the latter, how many have been found faithful? One, or
two, or three. But the wounds inflicted on either side were
nearly fatal; nor is it to be expected, that the scars should ever
wear out!

diers, priests, books in turn govern the world; and the last do it best, because they have no pretence to do it at all but by making the public good
their law and rule.

# CHAPTER IV.

### BREAKING OUT OF THE FRENCH REVOLUTION.

Louis XVI. succeeded to the throne of France in 1774; and soon after married Maria Antoinette, a daughter of the house of Austria. She was young, beautiful, and thoughtless. In her the pride of birth was strengthened and rendered impatient of the least restraint by the pride of sex and beauty; and all three together were instrumental in hastening the downfal of the monarchy. Devoted to the licentious pleasures of a court, she looked both from education and habit on the homely comforts of the people with disgust or indifference; and regarded the distress and poverty which stood in the way of her dissipation with incredulity or loathing.* Louis XVI. himself, though a man of good intentions, and free, in a remarkable degree, from the common vices of his situation, had not firmness of mind to resist the passions and importunity of others; and in addition to the extravagance, petulance, and extreme counsels of the Queen, fell a victim to the intrigues and officious interference of those about him, who had neither the wisdom nor spirit to avert those dangers and calami-

* Mr. Burke has passed a splendid and well-known eulogium on the beauty and accomplishments of the late Queen of France, and it was in part the impression which her youthful charms had left in his mind, that threw the casting-weight of his talents and eloquence into the scale of opposition to the French Revolution. I have heard another very competent judge (Mr. Northcote) describe her entering a small ante-room (where he stood) with her large hoop sideways, and gliding by him from one end to the other with a grace and lightness as if borne on a cloud. It was possibly to " this air with which she trod or rather disdained the earth," as if descended from some higher sphere, that she owed the indignity of being conducted to a scaffold. Personal grace and beauty cannot save their possessors from the fury of the multitude, more than from the raging elements, though they may inspire that pride and self-opinion which expose them to it.

ties which they **had provoked** by their **rashness,** presumption, and obstinacy.

The want of economy in the court, or a mal-administration of the finances, first occasioned pecuniary difficulties to the **Government,** for which a remedy **was** in vain sought **by a succession of ministers,** Necker, Calonne, Maupeou, and **by the parliament.** Considerable embarrassment and uneasiness **began to be felt** throughout the kingdom, **when in** 1787 the King undertook to con-voke the States-General, as **alone competent to** meet the emergen-cy, and to confer on other topics of the highest consequence, which were at this time agitated with general anxiety and interest.  The necessity of raising the supplies to defray the expences of govern-ment was indeed **only** made the handle to introduce and enforce other more important and widely-extended plans of reform.  For **some time past,** the public mind had been growing critical **and** fastidious with **the** progress of civilization and letters : the mon-archy, as **it existed at** the period " with **all its imperfections on** its head" had been weighed in the balance of reason and opinion, and found wanting ; and a favorable opportunity was only required, and the first that presented itself was eagerly seized to put in practice what had been already resolved upon in theory by the wits, philosophers, and philanthropists of the eighteenth century. From the first calling together the general council of the nation to deliberate and determine for the public good, in the then pre-vailing ferment of the popular feeling and with the predisposing causes, not a measure of finance was to be looked to, but a revolu-tion **became inevitable.**   All the *cahiérs*, or instructions given to the deputies **by the great mass of** their constituents, show that the kingdom **at large was ripe** for a material change in its civil and political **institutions ; and for the most part,** point out the individ-ual grievances **which** were afterwards **done away.**

The **States-General met at** Versailles on **the 5th of** May, 1789. **They** consisted of the representatives of the nobility, of the cler-gy, **and** of the *Tiers Etat* or people in general, the number of the last having been doubled in order to equal that of the other two. They heard mass the evening before **at the church of St.** Louis, in the same dresses, and with the same forms and order of prece-dence as in 1614, the last time they had ever been assembled.

The King opened the sitting with a speech which gave little satisfaction, as it dwelt chiefly on the liquidation of the debt, and the
unsettled state of the public mind, and did not go into those general
measures, on which the views of the assembly were bent, and from
which alone relief was expected. The first question which divided opinion and led to a conflict was that regarding the vote by
head or by order. By the first mode, that of counting voices, the
commons would be numerically on a par with the privileged classes; by the latter, their opponents would always have the advantage of two to one. In order to keep this advantage, and prevent
that reform of abuses which the third estate was supposed to have
principally at heart, the court did all it could to separate the different orders, first by adhering to etiquette, afterwards by means
of intrigue, and in the end by force. On the day following the
meeting, the deputies of the three estates were called upon to
verify their powers, which the nobles and clergy wished to do
apart; but the commons refused to take any steps towards this
object, except conjointly, or as a general legislative body. This
led to various overtures and discussions, which lasted for several
weeks. The court offered its mediation; but the nobles giving a
peremptory refusal to come to any compromise, at the motion of
the Abbé Siéyes, the third estate, after in vain inviting the two
others to join them, constituted themselves into a National Assembly. This was the first act of the Revolution, or the first occasion on which a part of a given body of individuals took upon
them to decide for the rest, from the urgency and magnitude of
the case, without the consent of their coadjutors, and contrary to
established rules. It was a stroke of state-necessity to be defended
not by the forms but by the essence of justice, and by the great
ends of human society. The usurpation of a discretionary and illegal power was clear, but nothing could be done without it, every
thing with it. Yet so strong and natural is the prejudice against
every appearance of what is violent and arbitrary, that serious attempts were made to reconcile the letter with the spirit of justice in
this instance, and to prove that the *Tiers Etat* being the representatives of the nation and the nation being every thing, the nobility
and clergy were included in it, and had nothing to complain of.[4]

* See the Abbe Siéyes's pamphlet entitled " *Qu'est ce que le Tiers Etat ?*"

It is not worth while to answer this sophistry at the present day. The truth is, that the *third estate* erected themselves from parties concerned into framers of the law and judges of the reason of the case, and must themselves be judged not by precedent and tradition, but by posterity, to whom, from the scale on which they acted, the benefit or the injury of their departure from common and worn-out forms will reach. Acts that supersede old-established rules and create a new era in human affairs, are to be approved or condemned by what comes after, not by what has gone before them.

This first independent and spirited step on the part of the commons produced a reaction on the part of the court. They shut up the place of sitting. The King had been prevailed on to consent to hostile measures against the popular side, during an excursion to Marly with the Queen and princes of the blood. Bailly (afterwards mayor of Paris) had been chosen president of the new National Assembly ; and arriving with other members, and finding the doors of the hall shut against them, they repaired to the *Jeu de Paumes* (the tennis-court) at Versailles, followed by the people and soldiers in crowds, and there enclosed by bare walls, with heads uncovered, and a strong and spontaneous burst of enthusiasm, made a solemn vow, with the exception of only one person present, never to separate till they had given France a Constitution. This memorable and decisive event took place on the 20th of June. On the 23d the King came to the church of St. Louis, whither they had been compelled to remove, and where they were joined by a considerable number of the clergy —addressed them in a tone of authority and reprimand, treated them as simply the *Tiers Etat*, pointed out certain partial reforms which he approved, and which he enjoined them to effect in conjunction with the other orders, or threatened to dissolve them and take the whole management of the government upon himself, and ended with a command that they should separate. The nobles and the clergy obeyed : the deputies of the people remained firm, immoveable, silent. Mirabeau then started from his seat and appealed to the Assembly in that mixed style of the academician and the demagogue which characterized his eloquence. The words are worth repeating here, both as a sample of the unqualified tone of the period, and on account of the fierce

and personal attack on the King, whom he stigmatizes by a sort
of nickname. " Gentlemen, I acknowledge that what you have
just heard might be a pledge of the welfare of the country, if the
offers of despotism were not always dangerous. What is the
meaning of this insolent dictation, the array of arms, the violation
of the national temple, merely to command you to be happy?
Who gives you this command? your *Mandatory* (deputy). Who
imposes his imperious laws? your *Mandatory*, he who ought to
receive them from you; from us, Gentlemen, who are invested
with an inviolable political priesthood; from us, in short, to whom
(and to whom alone) twenty-five millions of men look up for a
happiness ensured by its being agreed upon, given, and received
by all. But the freedom of your deliberations is suspended: a
military force surrounds the Assembly! Where are the enemies of the nation, that this outrage should be attempted? Is
Catiline at our gates? I demand, that in asserting the claims
of your insulted dignity, of your legislative power, you arm yourselves with the sanctity of your oath: it does not permit us to
separate till we have achieved the Constitution." From this unbridled effusion of bombast, affectation, and real passion, two
things are evident; first, that the designs of the court were already looked upon as altogether hostile and alien to the patriotic
side; secondly, that the Assembly, from the beginning, felt in
themselves the strong and undoubted conviction of their being
called to the task of removing the abuses of power, and regenera-
ting the hopes of a mighty people. The die was cast, the lists
were marked out in the opinions and sentiments of the two parties towards each other. The grand-master of the ceremonies on
this occasion, seeing that the Assembly did not break up, reminded them of the command of the King. " Go tell your master," cried Mirabeau, " that we are here by order of the people;
and that we shall not retire but at the point of the bayonet."
This was at once an invitation to violence, and a defiance of authority. Siéyes added, with his customary coolness, " You are
to-day in the same situation that you were yesterday; let us deliberate!" The Assembly immediately confirmed its former
resolutions; and at the instance of Mirabeau, decreed the inviolability of its members. Such was at one time the brilliant, dar-

ing, and forward zeal of a man, who not long after sold himself
to the court: so little has flashy eloquence or bold pretension to
do with steadiness of principle! Indeed, the Revolution, of which
he was one of the most prominent leaders, presented too many
characters of this kind—dazzling, ardent, wavering, corrupt—a
succession of momentary fires, made of light and worthless materials, soon kindled and soon exhausted, and requiring some new
fuel to repair them: nothing deep, internal, relying on its own
resources—"outliving fortunes outward with a mind that doth
renew swifter than blood decays"—but a flame rash and violent,
fanned by circumstances, kept alive by vanity, smothered by sordid interest, and wandering from object to object in search of the
most contemptible and contradictory excitement! We may also
remark, in the debates and proceedings of this early period, the
fevered and anxious state of the public mind, while galling and intolerable abuses, called in question for the first time and defended
with blind confidence, were exposed in the most naked and flagrant point of view; and the drapery of forms and circumstances
was torn from rank and power with sarcastic petulance, or a
ruthless logic.

The resistance of the Assembly alarmed the court, who did
not, however, as yet dare to proceed against it. Necker, who
had disapproved of the royal interference, and whose dismission
had been determined on in the morning, was the same night
entreated both by the King and Queen to stay. On the next
meeting of the Assembly, a large portion of the clergy again
repaired to their place of sitting; and four days after, forty
members of the *noblesse* joined them, with the Duke of Orleans
at their head. The conduct of this nobleman, all through the
Revolution, was in my opinion uncalled for, indecent, and profli
gate, and his fate not unmerited. Persons situated as he was
cannot take a decided part one way or the other, without doing
violence either to the dictates of reason and justice, or to all their
natural sentiments, unless they are characters of that heroic
stamp as to be raised above suspicion or temptation: the only
way for all others is to stand aloof from a struggle in which they
have no alternative but to commit a parricide on their country or
their friends, and to await the issue in silence and at a distance.

The people should not ask the aid of their lordly taskmasters to
shake off their chains; nor can they ever expect to have it cordial
and entire.   No confidence can be placed in those excesses of
public principle, which are founded on the sacrifice of every private affection, and of habitual self-esteem!   The court, soon after
this reinforcement to the popular party, came forward of its own
accord to request the attendance of the dissentient orders, which
took place on the 27th of June; and after some petty ebullitions
of jealousy and contests for precedence, the Assembly became
general, and all distinctions were lost.   The King's secret advisers were, however, by no means reconciled to this new triumph
over ancient privilege and existing authority; and meditated a
reprisal by removing the Assembly farther from Paris, and there
dissolving, if it could not overawe them.   For this purpose the
troops were collected from all parts; Versailles (where the
Assembly sat) was like a camp; Paris looked as if it were in a
state of siege.   These extensive military preparations, the trains
of artillery arriving every hour from the frontier, with the presence of the foreign regiments, occasioned great suspicion and
alarm; and on the motion of Mirabeau, the Assembly sent an
address to the King, respectfully urging him to remove the troops
from the neighborhood of the capital: but this he declined doing,
hinting at the same time that they might retire, if they chose, to
Noyon or Soissons, thus placing themselves at the disposal
of the crown, and depriving themselves of the aid of the people.

Paris was in a state of extreme agitation.   This immense city
was unanimous in its devotedness to the Assembly.   A capital
is at all times, and Paris was then more particularly, the natural
*focus* of a revolution.   To this many causes contribute.   The
actual presence of the monarch dissipates the illusions of loyalty;
and he is no longer (as in the distant province or petty village)
an abstraction of power and majesty, another name for all that is
great and exalted, but a common mortal, one man among a million of men, perhaps one of the meanest of his race.   Pageants
and spectacles may impose on the crowd; but a weak or haughty
look undoes the effect, and leads to disadvantageous reflections on
the title to, or the good resulting from all this display of pomp
and magnificence.   From being the seat of the court, its vices

are better known, its meannesses are more talked of.* In the number and distraction of passing objects and interests, the present occupies the mind alone—the chain of antiquity is broken, and custom loses its force. Men become " flies of a summer." Opinion has here many ears, many tongues, and many hands to work with. The slightest whisper is rumored abroad, and the roar of the multitude breaks down the prison or the palace gates. They are seldom brought to act together but in extreme cases ; nor is it extraordinary that, in such cases, the conduct of the people is violent, from the consciousness of transient power, its impatience of opposition, its unwieldy bulk and loose texture, which cannot be kept within nice bounds or stop at half-measure.— Nothing could be more critical or striking than the situation of Paris at this moment. Every thing betokened some great and decisive change. Foreign bayonets threatened the inhabitants from without, famine within. The capitalists dreaded a bankruptcy ; the enlightened and patriotic the return of absolute power ; the common people threw all the blame on the privileged classes. The press inflamed the public mind with innumerable pamphlets and invectives against the government, and the journals regularly reported the proceedings and debates of the Assembly. Everywhere in the open air, particularly in the Palais-Royal, groups were formed, where they read and harangued by turns. It was in consequence of a proposal made by one of the speakers in the Palais-Royal, that the prison of the Abbaye was forced open and some grenadiers of the French Guards, who had been confined for refusing to fire upon the people, were set at liberty and led out in triumph.

Paris was in this state of excitement and apprehension when the court, having first stationed a number of troops at Versailles, at Sevres, at the Champ-de-Mars, and at St. Denis, commenced offensive measures by the complete change of all the ministers and by the banishment of Necker. The latter, on Saturday the 11th of July, while he was at dinner received a note from the

---

* It was observed, that almost all the greatest cruelties of the *reign of terror* were resolved on by committees of persons who had been in the immediate employment of the great, and had suffered by their caprice and insolence.

King, enjoining him to quit the kingdom without a moment's delay. He calmly finished his dinner, without saying a word of
the order he had received, and immediately after got into his carriage with his wife and took the road to Brussels. The next
morning the news of his disgrace reached Paris. The whole city
was in a tumult: above ten thousand persons were, in a short
time, collected in the garden of the Palais-Royal. A young man
of the name of Camille Desmoulins, one of the habitual and most
enthusiastic haranguers of the crowd, mounted on a table, and
cried out, that " there was not a moment to lose ; that the dismission of Necker was the signal for the St. Bartholomew of liberty ;
that the Swiss and German regiments would presently issue from
the Champ-de-Mars to massacre the citizens ; and that they had
but one resource left, which was to resort to arms." And the
crowd, tearing each a green leaf, the color of hope, from the
chestnut-trees in the garden, which were nearly laid bare, and
wearing it as a badge, traversed the streets of Paris, with the
busts of Necker and of the Duke of Orleans (who was also said
to be arrested) covered with crape and borne in solemn pomp.
They had proceeded in this manner as far as the Place Vendôme,
when they were met by a party of the Royal Allemand, whom
they put to flight by pelting them with stones ; but at the Place
Louis XV. they were assailed by the dragoons of the Prince of
Lambesc ; the bearer of one of the busts, and a private of the
French Guards were killed ; the mob fled into the Garden of the
Thuilleries, whither the Prince followed them at the head of his
dragoons, and attacked a number of persons who knew nothing
of what was passing, and were walking quietly in the Gardens.
In the scuffle, an old man was wounded ; the confusion as well
as the resentment of the people became general ; and there was
but one cry, To arms, to be heard throughout the Thuilleries, the
Palais-Royal, in the city, and in the suburbs.

The French Guards had been ordered to their quarters in the
Chaussée-d'Antin, where sixty of Lambesc's dragoons were posted
opposite to watch them. A dispute arose, and it was with much
difficulty they were prevented from coming to blows. But when
the former learned that one of their comrades had been slain,
their indignation could no longer be restrained ; they rushed out,

killed two of the foreign soldiers, wounded three others, and the rest were forced to fly. They then proceeded to the Place Louis XV., where they stationed themselves between the people and the troops, and guarded this position the whole of the night. The soldiers in the Champ-de-Mars were then ordered to attack them, but refused to fire, and were remanded back to their quarters. The defection of the French Guards, with the repugnance of the other troops to march against the capital, put a stop for the present to the projects of the court. In the mean time, the populace had assembled at the Hôtel-de-Ville, and loudly demanded the sounding of the tocsin and the arming of the citizens. Several highly respectable individuals also met here, and did much good in repressing a spirit of violence and mischief. They could not, however, effect every thing. A number of disorderly people and of workmen out of employ, without food or place of abode, set fire to the barriers, infested the streets, and pillaged several houses in the night between the 12th and 13th.

The departure of Necker, which had excited such a sensation in the capital, produced as deep an impression at Versailles and on the Assembly, who manifested surprise and indignation, but not dejection. Lally Tollendal pronounced a formal eulogium on the exiled minister. After one or two displays of theatrical vehemence, which is inseparable from French enthusiasm and eloquence* (would that the whole were not so soon forgotten like a a play!) they dispatched a deputation to the King, informing him of the situation and troubles of Paris, and praying him to dismiss the troops and entrust the defence of the capital to the city militia. The deputation received an answer which amounted to a repulse. The Assembly now perceived that the designs of the court-party were irrevocably fixed, and that it had only itself to rely upon. It instantly voted the responsibility of the ministers and of all the advisers of the crown, *of whatsoever rank or degree.* This last clause was pointed at the Queen, whose influence was greatly dreaded. They then, from an apprehension that the doors might be closed during the night in order to dissolve the Assembly, de-

---

* Such as appealing to their own "*illustrious* decrees," swearing by "the *celebrated* day of the 20th of June," &c. This forestalling and regrating of fame and immortality seems almost peculiar to the French.

clared their sittings permanent.  A vice-president was chosen, to
lessen the fatigue of the Archbishop of Vienne.  The choice fell
upon La Fayette.  In this manner a part of the Assembly sat up
all night.  It passed without deliberation, the deputies remaining
on their seats, silent, but calm and serene.  What thoughts must
have revolved through the minds of those present on this occasion !  Patriotism and philosophy had here taken up their sanctu-
ary.  If we consider their situation ; the hopes that filled their
breasts ; the trials they had to encounter ; the future destiny of
their country, of the world, which hung on their decision as in a
balance ; the bitter wrongs they were about to sweep away ; the
good they had it in their power to accomplish—the countenances
of the Assembly must have been majestic, and radiant with the
light that through them was about to dawn on ages yet unborn.
They might foresee a struggle, the last convulsive efforts of pride
and power to keep the world in its wonted subjection—but that
was nothing—their final triumph over all opposition was assured
in the eternal principles of justice and in their own unshaken devotedness to the great cause of mankind !  If the result did not
altogether correspond to the intentions of those firm and enlightened patriots who so nobly planned it, the fault was not in them
but in others.

At Paris the insurrection had taken a more decided turn.
Early in the morning, the people assembled in large bodies at the
Hôtel-de-Ville ; the tocsin sounded from all the churches ; the
drums beat to summon the citizens together, who formed themselves into different bands of volunteers.  All that they wanted
was arms.  These, except a few at the gunsmiths' shops, were
not to be had.  They then applied to M. de Flesselles, a provost
of the city, who amused them with fair words.  " My children,"
he said, " I am your father !"  This paternal style seems to have
been the order of the day.  A committee sat at the Hôtel-de-Ville
to take measures for the public safety.  Meanwhile a granary
had been broken open ; the *Garde-Meuble* had been ransacked
for old arms ; the armorers' shops were plundered ; all was a
scene of confusion, and the utmost dismay every where prevailed.
But no private mischie was done.  It was a moment of popular
frenzy, but one in which the public danger and the public good

overruled every other consideration.    The grain which had been
seized, the carts loaded with provisions, with plate or furniture,
and stopped at the barriers, were all taken to the Grève as a public
depôt.    The crowd incessantly repeated the cry for arms, and
were pacified by an assurance that thirty thousand muskets
would speedily arrive from Charleville.    The Duke d'Aumont
was invited to take the command of the popular troops : and on
his hesitating, the Marquis of Salle was nominated in his stead.
The green cockade was exchanged for one of red and blue,
the colors of the city.    A quantity of powder was discovered, as
it was about to be conveyed beyond the barriers ; and the cases
of fire-arms promised from Charleville turned out, on inspection,
to be filled with old rags and logs of wood.    The rage and impatience of the multitude now become extreme.    Such perverse
trifling and barefaced duplicity would be unaccountable anywhere else ; but in France they pay with promises ; and the provost, availing himself of the credulity of his audience, promised
them still more arms at the Chartreux.    To prevent a repetition
of the excesses of the mob, Paris was illuminated at night, and
a patrol paraded the streets.

The following day, the people being deceived as to the convoy
of arms that was to arrive from Charleville, and having been
equally disappointed in those at the Chartreux, broke into the
Hospital of Invalids, in spite of the troops stationed in the neighborhood, and carried off a prodigious number of stands of arms
concealed in the cellars.    An alarm had been spread in the night
that the regiment quartered at St. Denis was on its way to Paris,
and that the cannon of the Bastille had been pointed in the direction of the street of St. Antoine.    This information, the dread
which this fortress inspired, the recollection of the horrors which
had been perpetrated there, its very name, which appalled all
hearts and made the blood run cold, the necessity of wresting it
from the hands of its old and feeble possessors, drew the attention of the multitude to this hated spot.    From nine in the morning of the memorable 14th of July till two, Paris from one end to
the other rang with the same watch-word : " *To the Bastille !
To the Bastille !*"    The inhabitants poured there in throngs from
all quarters, armed with different weapons ; the crowd that

already surrounded it was considerable; the sentinels were at
their posts, and the drawbridges raised as in war-time.

A deputy from the district of St. Louis de la Culture, Thuriot
de la Rosiere, then asked to speak with the Governor, M. Delaunay. Being admitted into his presence, he required that the
direction of the cannon should be changed. Three guns were
pointed against the entrance, though the Governor pretended that
every thing remained in the state in which it had always been.
About forty Swiss and eighty Invalids garrisoned the place, from
whom he obtained a promise not to fire on the people, unless they
were themselves attacked. His companions began to be uneasy,
and called loudly for him. To satisfy them, he showed himself
on the ramparts, from whence he could see an immense multitude
flocking from all parts, and the Fauxbourg St. Antoine advancing
as it were in a mass. He then returned to his friends, and gave
them what tidings he had collected.

But the crowd, not satisfied, demanded the surrender of the fortress. From time to time the angry cry was repeated : " *Down
with the Bastille !*" Two men, more determined than the rest,
pressed forward, attacked a guard-house, and attempted to break
down the chains of the bridge with the blows of an axe. The
soldiers called out to them to fall back, threatening to fire if they
did not. But they repeated their blows, shattered the chains, and
lowered the drawbridge, over which they rushed with the crowd.
They threw themselves upon the second bridge, in the hopes of
making themselves masters of it in the same manner, when the
garrison fired and dispersed them for a few minutes. They soon,
however, returned to the charge ; and for several hours, during a
murderous discharge of musketry, and amidst heaps of the
wounded and dying, renewed the attack with unabated courage
and obstinacy, led on by two brave men, Elie and Hulia, their
rage and desperation being inflamed to a pitch of madness by the
scene of havoc around them. Several deputations arrived from
the Hôtel-de-Ville to offer terms of accommodation ; but in the
noise and fury of the moment they could not make themselves
heard, and the storming continued as before.*

* It has been said (I know not how truly) that Thomas Clarkson, the

The assault had been carried on in this manner with inextinguishable rage and great loss of blood to the besiegers, though with little progress made for above four hours, when the arrival of the French Guards with cannon altered the face of things. The garrison urged the Governor to surrender. The wretched Delaunay, dreading the fate which awaited him, wanted to blow up the place and bury himself under the ruins, and was advancing for this purpose with a lighted match in his hand towards the powder magazine,. but was prevented by the soldiers, who planted the white flag on the platform, and reversed their arms in token of submission. This was not enough for those without. They demanded with loud and reiterated cries to have the drawbridges let down ; and on an assurance being given that no harm was intended, the bridges were lowered and the assailants tumultuously rushed in. The endeavors of their leaders could not save the Governor or a number of the soldiers, who were seized on by the infuriated multitude, and put to death for having fired on their fellow-citizens. Thus fell the Bastille ; and the shout that accompanied its downfall was echoed through Europe, and men rejoiced that " the grass grew where the Bastille stood !" Earth was lightened of a load that oppressed it, nor did this ghastly object any longer startle the sight, like an ugly spider lying in wait for its accustomed prey, and brooding in sullen silence over the wrongs which it had the will, though not the power to inflict.*

author of the Abolition of the Slave Trade, was one of those most actively employed on this occasion.

\* The Bastille was taken about a quarter before six o'clock in the evening (Tuesday the 14th of July), after a four hours' attack. Only one cannon was fired from the fortress, and only one person was killed among the besieged. The garrison consisted of 82 Invalids, 2 cannoneers, and 32 Swiss. Of the assailants, 83 were killed on the spot, 60 were wounded, of whom 15 died of their wounds, and 13 were disabled. A great many barrels of gunpowder had been conveyed here from the arsenal, in the night between the 12th and 13th. Delaunay the Governor was killed on the steps of the Hôtel-de-Ville, as also Delosme the Mayor. Only seven prisoners were found in the Bastille; four of these, Pujade, Bechade, La Roche, and La Caurege, were for forgery. M. de Solages was put in in 1782, at the desire of his father, since which time every communication from without was carefully withheld from him. He did not know the smallest event that had taken place in all that time, and was told by the turnkey when he heard the firing

The stormers of the Bastille arrived at the Place de Grève, rending the air with shouts of victory. They marched on to the great hall of the Hôtel-de-Ville, in all the terrific and unusual pomp of a popular triumph. Such of them as had displayed most courage of the cannon, that it was owing to a riot about the price of bread. M. Tavernier, a bastard son of Paris Duverney, had been confined ever since the 4th of August, 1759. The last prisoner was a Mr. White, who went mad, and it could never be discovered who or what he was · by the name he must have been English. When Lord Albemarle was ambassador at Paris, in the year 1753, he by mere accident caught a sight of the list of persons confined in the Bastille, lying on the table of the French minister, with the name of Gordon at their head. Being struck with the circumstance, he inquired into the meaning of it; but the French Minister could give no account of it; and on the prisoner himself being released and sent for, he could only state that he had been confined there thirty years, but had not the slightest knowledge or suspicion of the cause for which he had been arrested. Nor is this wonderful, when we consider that *lettres de cachet* were sold, with blanks left for the names to be filled up at the pleasure or malice of the purchasers. Is this a system of government, to defend or restore which to the utmost Englishmen arm, bleed, and spend millions? If it was only to prevent the recurrence of one such instance (with the feeling in society at once shrinking from and tamely acquiescing in it), the Revolution was well purchased. When the crowd gained possession of this loathsome spot, they eagerly poured into every corner and turning of it, went down into the lowest dungeons with a breathless curiosity and horror, knocking with sledge-hammers at their triple portals, and breaking down and destroying every thing in their way. The stones and devices on the battlements were torn off and thrown into the ditch, and the papers and documents were at the same time unfortunately destroyed.

A low range of dungeons was discovered under-ground, close to the moat; and so contrived, that if those within had forced a passage through, they would have let in the water of the ditch and been suffocated. In one of these a skeleton was found hanging to an iron cramp in the wall. In reading the accounts of the demolition of this building, one feels that indignation should have melted the stone-walls like flax, and that the dungeons should have given up their dead to assist the living! Surely it must be allowed that John Bull's former horror of these doings was more in character than his late patronage and admiration of them as indispensable to the existence of social order. The Bastille was begun in 1370, in Charles V.'s time, by one Hugh Abriot, provost of the city, who was afterwards shut up in it in 1381. It at first consisted only of two towers: two more were added by Charles VI. and four more in 1383. Two days after it was taken, it was ordered by the National Assembly to be razed to the ground, and in May 1790, not a trace of it was left.

and ardor were borne on the shoulders of the rest, crowned with laurel. They were escorted up the hall by near two thousand of the populace, their eyes flaming, their hair in wild disorder, variously accoutred, pressing tumultuously on each other, and making the heavy floors almost crack .beneath their footsteps. One bore the keys and flag of the Bastille, another the regulations of the prison brandished on the point of a bayonet; a third (a thing horrible to relate!) held in his bloody fingers the buckle of the Governor's stock. In this order it was that they entered the Hôtel-de-Ville to announce their victory to the Committee, and to decide on the fate of their remaining prisoners, who, in spite of the impatient cries to give no quarter, were rescued by the exertions of the commandant La Salle, Moreau de St. Mery, and the intrepid Elie. Then came the turn of the despicable Flesselles, that caricature of vapid, frothy impertinence, who thought he could baffle the roaring tiger with grimace and shallow excuses. " To the Palais-Royal with him!" was the word; and he answered with callous indifference, " Well, to the Palais-Royal if you will." He was hemmed in by the crowd and borne along without any violence being offered him to the place of destination; but at the corner of the Quai Le Pelletier, an unknown hand approached him, and stretched him lifeless on the spot with a pistol-shot. During the night succeeding this eventful day, Paris was in the greatest agitation, hourly expecting (in consequence of the statements of intercepted letters) an attack from the troops. Every preparation was made to defend the city. Barricadoes were formed, the streets unpaved, pikes forged, the women piled stones on the tops of houses to hurl them down on the heads of the soldiers, and the National Guard occupied the outposts.

While all this was passing, and before it became known at Versailles, the Court was preparing to carry into effect its designs against the assembly and the capital. The night between the 14th and 15th was fixed upon for their execution. The new minister, Breteuil, had promised to re-establish the royal authority within three days. Marshal Broglie, who commanded the army round Paris, was invested with unlimited powers. The Assembly, it was agreed upon, were to be dissolved, and forty thousand copies of a proclamation to this effect were ready to be circulated throughout the kingdom. The rising of the populace was supposed to be a temporary evil, and it was thought to the last moment an impossibility that a mob of citizens should resist an army. The Assembly was duly apprized of all these projects. It sat for two days in a state of constant inquietude and alarm. The news from Paris was doubtful. A firing of cannon was supposed to be heard, and persons anxiously placed their ears to the ground to listen. The escape of the King was also expected, as a carriage had been kept in readiness, and the Body-Guard had not pulled off their boots for several days.

In the Orangery belonging to the Palace, meat and wine had been distributed among the foreign troops to encourage and spirit them up. The Viscount de Noailles and another deputy, Wimpfen, brought word of the latest events in the capital, and of the increasing violence of the people. Couriers were dispatched every half-hour to gather intelligence. Deputations waited on the King to lay before him the progress of the insurrection, but he still gave evasive and unsatisfactory answers. In the night of the 14th, the Duke de Liancourt had informed Louis XVI. of the taking of the Bastille and the massacre of the garrison on the preceding day. "It is a revolt!" exclaimed the monarch taken by surprise. "No, Sire, it is a Revolution," was the answer. This turn of affairs, of which his ministers had kept him ignorant, determined the King to present himself to the Assembly, and assure them of his friendly intentions; for there is no meanness or duplicity of which persons in his station are not capable, because they think they cannot be degraded by the one, and are not responsible for the other. He entered the Assembly just as Mirabeau had finished his invective against the presents, the encouragements and caresses lavished by the Queen, the Princes, and courtiers on the troops the day before. He was received at first in a mournful silence; but no sooner had he declared that "*he was only one of the people*," than they loaded him with acclamations, rose with one accord. and conducted him back to the palace. The credulity of subjects is in proportion to the insincerity of sovereigns; for, as professions are all they ever get from them, they are obliged to be doubly grateful for the mere demonstrations of good-will or casual overtures to an amicable

understanding.    Louis, two days after, entered Paris, preceded
by a deputation of the Assembly, with Bailly and La Fayette at
its head.    He was welcomed with shouts by the people, who had
changed in a moment from fear and suspicion to the most unbounded confidence.    The taste of princes for popularity must
be small indeed, since they can so easily command it by a word
or look, and since they in general prefer reigning over the fears
instead of courting the affections of their subjects.    Perhaps they
despise what is so cheaply and unworthily earned, or shrink with
a natural disgust from offers of service and attachment where
there can be no real sympathy, where the most abject homage is
due to Majesty on the one side, and where all emanating from it,
even insult and oppression, is to be regarded as grace and favor
on the other.    The voluntary love of the people is insipid!
There was manifestly no disposition on the part of the nation or its
representatives, to come to an open rupture with the monarch.
On the contrary, they hailed with the most lively gratitude and a
kind of doating fondness, every mark of condescension on the part
of the Court, or appearance of making common cause with them;
as the child is pleased with the gay colors and forked crest of
the serpent that is going to strike its fangs into it.

The commotions in the metropolis were followed by disturbances in the provincial towns and in the country places, where
many of the ancient *chateaus* were set on fire, and other unjustifiable excesses committed.    This, however, was almost inevitable.
The ill-usage of the peasantry had been of so long standing, so
barefaced and galling, that it could not but engender a burning
and deep-seated resentment, which with the first opportunity would
break out into acts of violence and revenge.    The Grand Seigneurs had so long treated them with every aggravation of contempt, cruelty, and hardship, presuming on their rank and power,
that the instant their hands were untied, they fell upon them with
all the maddening sense of accumulated shame and wrong.    The
restraint of fear being removed, they had no jot of love to hold
them back.    They looked upon their superiors as their natural
and declared enemies (whom they had got in their power), not as
their natural protectors and benefactors.    They submitted to their
old trammels from compulsion and necessity alone, and were

ready to shake them off with every sign of impatience and abhor
rence. These first excesses were the consequence (wherever
they occurred) of a spontaneous local feeling; and were neither
authorized by the Assembly nor the result of any concert between
the different places; for such was the want of communication,
and the stagnation of activity and intelligence in France previous
to the Revolution, that the most important events were often not
known for some days at the distance of only a few leagues from
Paris.* Necker was at the same time recalled, and traversed
France in a kind of triumph. He was now at the height of his
popularity, from which he soon after declined, from the half-
measures he pursued, and from his taking part with some of those
against whom the indignation of the people was excited, as having
encouraged the firing of the troops on the patriots on the 14th.
Necker was one of those timid spirits who adhere to the nicest forms
of justice in the midst of the most violent commotions—(a sort of
*petits-maitres*, who are as afraid of spoiling a certain ideal standard
of perfection in their own minds, as a courtier is of soiling a birth-
day suit)—and soon after retired from the scene of the Revolution
(for which he was unfit) in effeminate disgust, but without ever
going over to the other side. Buonaparte met him at Geneva in
1800, when he was as full of himself and his financial schemes as
ever. He was a man of principle, and of a certain literal understanding, but wanted strength of character to conform to circumstances or to govern them; and from an over-chariness of reputation, was afraid to approve what under any supposition, or by
any party, could be condemned as wrong. While the world was
tumbling about his ears, he was weighing the grains and scruples
of morality. Such self-satisfied casuists neutralize every cause,
and are the outcasts of every party.

The DECLARATION OF RIGHTS was shortly after promulgated by
the Assembly (on the model of that of America), and in the night

---

* See Arthur Young's Travels. The circumstance of the setting fire to
the old castles, and expelling their proprietors, is slurred over by some late
French writers, but it is clearly made out by this ingenuous and authentic
observer. In fact, the country was too hot to hold these persons, who had
been from time immemorial the terror and scourge of their immediate
neighborhood.

of the 4th of August the important and decisive decrees were passed, abolishing the remains of feudal jurisdiction, seignorial rights, tythes, the game laws, the *gabelle*, the inequality of imposts, and the total exemption from them claimed by certain classes. These Acts and this Declaration produced an entire and beneficial change in France, if liberty and justice are benefits, and made all the divisions of the kingdom and all classes of society politically equal; subject to the same laws, capable of arriving at the highest honors in the state, entitled to choose their own representatives, and masters of their own labor. The vastness of this change, from a servile, arbitrary, and abject state to one of freedom and manly independence, was an enormity not to be paralleled in the eyes of those who " prefer custom before all excellence;" and the King, with the advice of those most nearly allied to him in blood and situation, prepared to evade giving his assent to it by flight. He professed himself ready to correct certain positive and temporary abuses in the government and finances; on any change in the others, which were of a permanent and, therefore, infinitely more pernicious nature, he put an absolute *veto*, by treating them as coming under the head of property and the essential privileges of the higher classes. In reality, the people had so far been the property, the sport, and the victims of the higher classes, that the relation in which they had hitherto stood to each other in all their dealings by the laws and usages of society, could hardly be abrogated without a violent revulsion, or an entire remoulding of all the elements of the state. In the debates on the new constitution also, the King's own title and place in it had been canvassed and commented upon. This was adding gall to bitterness. From this time a rupture became inevitable, a cordial reconciliation impossible: for from this time two claims were brought to issue, the *right of prescription* and the *right of the public good*, both clear and consistent in themselves, but absolutely incompatible with each other, between which no common judge or measure could be found, and in the collision of which one or other of the parties must be crushed to atoms; because every approximation between such hostile elements only increased the violence of their antipathy, and every concession, by making them more tenacious of what was left, only widened the breach between

them. The Revolution was hurried on to its accomplishment by
principles or prejudices, over which the will of individuals had a
very slight control ; for each person's private character or pretensions became merged in great masses of feeling and opinion.
Those who think that a little more candor, a little more firmness,
a little less rashness might have hit upon a middle course and
reconciled all differences, seem not to read human nature or history right. Grant that Louis XVI. was a man of upright and excellent intentions, still he was a king. Was he weak ? He was
descended from a long line of powerful ancestors. Had he the
good of his people sincerely at heart? He had also to leave an
inheritance, an untarnished crown, to his posterity ! Had he
possessed strength of mind to look down on all these prejudices,
that would hardly have rendered him less formidable to his opponents. It must have sounded a little strange to him, at his time
of day, to have his place and power made a subject of debate, a
question to settle, as if he were a king of yesterday, or a constable
newly appointed to office. It was not unaccountable that an arbitrary monarch, claiming by right of twenty descents, should feel
some qualms, some tremors, some backwardness and hesitation to
have his prerogative called in question, its abuses restrained, its objects defined, its origin sifted and cavilled at, any more than it is
strange that a whole people, having the opportunity, should wish to
curtail the right to seize upon their persons, to dictate laws to their
assemblies, to confiscate their property. Both were natural and
in order ; and it might easily be foreseen that the repugnance of
either party to come to terms would increase till it could only be
satisfied by the absolute and final submission of the other. It is
in vain to regret the catastrophe; the struggle was from the commencement and in its nature a fatal one.

The changes in the principles and forms of the government
which had been adopted by the National Assembly, and to which
the King at length gave an ungracious and imperfect assent, must
have completely alienated the mind of the monarch, since they
implied that he was only the steward, not the proprietor of the
common-weal. The Princes of the Blood had already fled with
their retainers to the frontier, where they were busy in exciting
the hostility of foreign powers against a Revolution which admit-

ted all Frenchmen to the rank of men and citizens, subject to the
law, but no longer subject to the caprice and tyranny of the privileged classes ; and the King was secretly contriving how to join
them, after making one more trial of the dispositions of the
military.

As this is a new crisis in the Revolution, it will be as well, before we proceed farther, to take a glance at that state of things
which called forth such tender regrets in the partisans of the old
system, and sooner than abandon which they were resolved to
plunge their country and Europe in seas of blood.   Justice was
openly bought and sold like any other commodity in the market.
The law was only a convenient instrument in the hands of the
rich against the poor.   He who went into a court of justice without friends or without money to seek for redress, however gross
his provocation, was sure to come out of it with insult added to
the original injury, and with a sickening and humiliating sense of
his own helpless and degraded situation.   If he had a handsome
wife or daughter, or was entrusted with any great man's secrets,
he had less need to despair.   The peasants were over-worked,
half-starved, treated with hard words and hard blows, subjected
to unceasing exactions and every species of petty tyranny, both
from their haughty lords and their underlings ; while in the cities
a number of unwholesome and useless professions and a crowd of
lazy menials pampered the vices, or administered to the pride and
luxury of the great.   The roads and villages were infested with
beggars and various objects of disease, neglect, and wretchedness.
The modes of education, and the notions respecting the treatment
of the children of the poor and of the sick were full of superstition
and barbarism, which no pains were taken to eradicate, and led to
the most distressing consequences.   The hopes and labors of the
husbandman were constantly ruined by the inroads of wild boars
and other animals of chase ; and if any of these were destroyed
in a fit of impatience or from the pressure of want, the offence was
never forgiven, as directed less against the property than the exclusive pleasures of the proprietors of the soil.   The tythes were
an additional and heavy burden ; in the imposition of taxes no
favor was shown to the comforts or necessaries of the poor, while
the privileged classes were wholly exempted from them.   If a

rich man struck a poor one, the latter must submit in silence; if
he was robbed of a house or orchard, and he complained, he was
sent to prison. Instances have even been known of the common
people passing along the streets, or workmen on the tops of houses,
being shot at as marks and killed in sport, and no notice taken.
There was no such thing as liberty of the press or trial by jury,
nor any public trial or confronting of witnesses. The great mass
of the people were regarded by their superiors as of a lower species, as merely tolerated in existence for their use and convenience; the object was to reduce them to the lowest possible state
of dependence and wretchedness, and to make them sensible of it
at every step. The human form only (and scarcely that) was
left them: in other respects the dogs and horses of the rich were
better off, and used with less cruelty and contempt. The arbitrary arrests of the court were not so frequent as formerly, but
there was no security against them; so that the people felt thankful for the forbearance of power, instead of being indignant at its
exercise, like the poor bird that cowers and trembles after having
just escaped the talons of the hawk. To speak truth, to plead the
cause of humanity, was sure to draw down the vengeance of government, and was to sign the warrant of your own condemnation.
Loyalty was a sordid calculation of interest or a panic-fear. No
erectness of spirit, no confidence, no manly boldness of character;
but in their stead, trick, cunning, smiling deceit, tame servility, a
total want of public principle; and hence, in a great measure,
arose the excesses of the Revolution, when power got into the
hands of a people wholly unused to it, and impatient of every obstacle to their wishes, from want of respect for themselves or reliance on one another. Hence the treachery and vacillation of
leaders, the fury of parties. Marat, before the Revolution, ad-
dicted himself wholly to the study of abstruse science, and avoided
meddling with politics from the avowed dread of the Bastille: it is
not surprising that in a mind like his this painful and pusillanimous feeling should seek to revenge itself, when its turn came,
by inspiring the same terror in others. The manners of the court
were also carried to the extremes of frivolity and depravity, so as
to take alike from virtue its dignity, from vice its blush. The
clergy, shut out from the charities of domestic life, strove to tar-

nish what they could not enjoy, and to turn the general profligacy to the profit of their own peculiar calling. Their sanguinary bigotry was changed to a covert scepticism not less odious, and into a sleek and dangerous complaisance to the vices of individuals and the abuses of power. In the court, corruption; in the church, hypocrisy; levity and licentiousness in the people. The influence of the *haut ton* (as it was called) had spread far and wide—had tainted literature, and given a false and mischievous bias to philosophy, by transforming court-vices into incontrovertible principles of human nature. Society was in a false position. All that was really left of loyalty was the admiration of the last new court-dress; of religious zeal, a desire to witness some imposing church-ceremony, or to slide into a vacant preferment: what little there was of household faith or homely honesty in common life was trampled under the feet or dissipated by the example of the higher classes. The ancient government and institutions had lost their hold on the prejudices and feelings of the community, and remained chiefly as a stumbling-block in the way of improvement, or as a Gothic ruin, ready to fall upon and crush those who attempted it; and it was high time that they should be swept away to make room for a more rational, and in the present circumstances of the world, a more natural order of things. A system, originating in the feudal times and in the dark ages, and bent on maintaining its ground in an age of reason and inquiry, is as great a solecism in the moral world, as an apparition at noon-day would be in the physical one. Ridicule and disgust in that case inevitably succeed to awe and wonder. Every thing is forced and spurious in such an incongruous and disjointed state of the public mind. Old prejudices and institutions remain only to prevent the growth or warp the direction of the new ones, which, while this is the case, cannot take effect to any good or consistent purpose. One of two things must, therefore, occur; it is necessary either that society should retrograde, which is hardly possible, or that it should "take progression forward," which it will do in spite of every obstacle opposed to it.

It has been pretended that the National Assembly proceeded upon merely abstract and gratuitous principles to level what has lately been termed "the beautiful fabric of the French Monarchy" with the ground, and to get rid of the solid benefits of their ancient laws and constitution, from being suddenly enamored of a vague, fanciful, and impracticable theory. Alas! if they were reduced to recur to extreme and speculative principles, it was because " from the sole of the foot to the crown of the head" there was no soundness to be met with in the old system. So far is this charge from being true, that there is hardly one of those reforms which they effected that was not called for over and over again in the *cahiérs* or instructions to the deputies, and that was not a subject of notorious and bitter complaint throughout the country. This is matter of fact and record. I shall go a little into the details, with the assistance of an author whose information and candor are acknowledged on all hands.

" The enrolments for the militia, which the *cahiérs* call *an injustice without example*, were another dreadful scourge on the peasantry; and as married men were exempted from it, occasioned in some degree that mischievous population, which brought beings into the world, in order for little else than to be starved. The *corvées*, or police of the roads, were annually the ruin of many hundreds of farmers; more than three hundred were reduced to beggary in filling up one vale in Lorraine: all these oppressions fell on the *tiers état* only; the nobility and clergy having been equally exempted from *tailles*, militia, and *corvées*. The penal code of finance makes one shudder at the horrors of punishment inadequate to the crimes. It is calculated that, upon an average, there were annually taken and sent to prison or the galleys, 2340 men, 896 women, 201 children (total, 3437) for smuggling salt. All families and persons liable to the *taille* in the provinces of the *grandes gabelles*, were enrolled, and their consumption of salt for the *pot* and *salière* (that is, the daily consumption, exclusive of salting meat, &c.) estimated at seven pounds a head *per annum*, which quantity they were forced to buy whether they wanted it or not, under the pain of various fines, according to the case.

" The *capitaineries* were a dreadful scourge on all the occupiers of land. By this term was to be understood the paramountship of certain districts, granted by the King to princes of the blood, by which they were put in possession of the property of all

game, even on lands not belonging to them; and what is very singular, on manors granted long before to individuals; so that the erect-
ing of a district into a *capitainerie* was an annihilation of all manorial rights to game within it. This was a trifling business in comparison of other circumstances: for in speaking of the preservation of
the game in these *capitaineries*, it must be observed that by game
must be understood whole droves of wild boars and herds of deer not
confined by any wall or pale, but wandering at pleasure over the
whole country to the destruction of the crops; and to the peop-
ling of the galleys by the wretched peasants who presumed to kill
them in order to save that food, which was to support their helpless children.   The game in the *capitainerie* of Montceau in four
parishes only did mischief to the amount of 184,263 livres per
annum; no wonder then that we should find the people asking,
' *Nous demandons à grands cris la destruction des capitaineries et
celle de toute sorte de gibier.*'*   And what are we to think of
demanding as a favor the permission—'*De nettoyer ses grains, de
faucher les prés artificiels et d'enlever ses chaumes sans égard pour
la perdrix ou toute autre gibier.*'†   Now an English reader will
scarcely understand it without being told, that there were numerous edicts for preserving the game which prohibited weeding and
hoeing, lest the young partridges should be disturbed; steeping
seed, lest it should injure the game; manuring with night-soil,
lest the flavor of the partridges should be injured by feeding on
the corn so produced; mowing hay, &c., before a certain time,
so late as to spoil many crops; and taking away the stubble which
would deprive the birds of shelter.   The tyranny exercised in
these *capitaineries*, which extended over four hundred leagues of
country, was so great, that many *cahiérs* demanded the utter suppression of them.   Such were the exertions of arbitrary power,
which the lower orders felt directly from the royal authority: but,
heavy as they were, it is a question whether the others, suffered
circuitously through the nobility and clergy, were not yet more
oppressive.   Nothing can exceed the complaints made in the
*cahiérs* under this head.   They speak of the dispensation of justice in the manorial courts, as comprising every species of despot'sm: the districts intermediate—appeals endless—irreconci-

---

* Cahiérs de Tiers Etat de Mantes et Meulan.                † Ibid.

iable to liberty and prosperity ; and irrevocably proscribed in the
opinion of the public ;* augmenting litigations, favoring every species of chicane ; ruining the parties, not only by enormous expenses
on the most petty objects, but by a dreadful loss of time.   The
judges commonly ignorant pretenders, who hold their courts in
*cabarets* (public houses), and are absolutely dependent on the
*Seigneurs*, in consequence of their feudal powers.   They are described as vexations '*qui font le plus grand fleau des peuples*†—
*Esclavage affligeant*‡—*Ce régime désastreux.*'§   That the *féo-
dalité* be for ever abolished.   The countryman is tyrannically enslaved by it.   Fixed and heavy rents ; vexatious processes to secure them ; appreciated unjustly to augment them ; rents *soli-
daires* and *revanchables ;* rents *chéantes* and *levantes, fumages.*
Fines at every change of the property, in the direct as well as
collateral line ; feudal redemption (*retraite*) ; fines on sale to the
eighth, and even the sixth penny ;   redemptions (*rachats*) injurious
in their origin, and still more so in their extension ; *bannalité* of the
mill, of the oven, and of the wine and cider-press ;‖ *corvées* by
custom ; *corvées* by usage of the fief; *corvées* established by unjust decrees : *corvées* arbitrary, and even fantastical ; servitudes,
*prestations*, extravagant and burthensome ; collections by assess-
ments incollectible ; *aveux, minus, impunissemens* ; litigations
ruinous and without end ; the rod of seignorial finance for ever
shaken over their heads ; vexation, ruin, outrage, violence and
destructive servitude, under which the peasants, almost on a level
with Polish slaves, can never but be miserable, vile, and oppressed.
They demand, also, that the use of hand-mills be free ; and hope
that posterity may be ignorant, if possible, that feudal tyranny in
Bretagne, armed with the judicial power, has not blushed, even
in these times, at breaking hand-mills, and at selling annually
to the indigent the faculty of bruising between two stones a

---

* Rennes.                † Nevernois.                ‡ Tiers Etat de Vannes.
§ Clermont Ferrand.
‖ By this horrible law the people were bound to grind their corn at the
mill of the *Seigneur* only ; to press their grapes at his press only ; and to
bake their bread in his oven ; by which means the bread was often spoiled,
and more especially wine, since in Champagne those grapes which pressed
immediately made white wine, would, by waiting for the press, which often
happened, make red wine only.

measure of buckwheat or barley. The very terms of these complaints are unknown in England, and consequently untranslata-
ble. What are those tortures of the peasantry in Bretagne,
which they call *chevanchés, quintaines, soule, saut de poison, bai-
ser de mariées ; chansons ; transporte d'œuf sur un charette ; silence de grenouilles ;* corveé a misericorde ; milods ; leide ; coup-
onage ; cartelage ; barage ; fouage ; marechaussé ; ban vin ; ban
d'août ; trousses ; gelinage ; civerage ; taillabilité ; vingtain ;
sterlage ; bordelage ; minage ; ban de vendanges ; droit d'ac-
capte.*

"In passing through many of the French provinces, I was struck
with the various and heavy complaints of the farmers and little
proprietors of the feudal grievances, with the weight of which
their industry was burthened ; but I could not then conceive the
multiplicity of the shackles which kept them poor and depressed.
I understood it better afterwards from the conversation and ac-
knowledgments of some *Grand Seigneurs*, as the Revolution
advanced ; and I learnt that the principal rental of many estates
consisted in services and feudal tenures, by the baneful influence
of which the industry of the people was almost exterminated. In
regard to the oppressions of the clergy as to tythes, though the
ecclesiastical tenth was levied in France more severely than usual
in Italy, yet was it never extracted with such horrid greediness
as is at present the disgrace of England. Notwithstanding
the mildness in the levy of this odious tax, the burthen to people
groaning under so many other oppressions united to render their
situation so bad that no change could be for the worse. But these
were not all the evils with which the people struggled. The ad-

---

* This is a curious article: when the lady of the *Seigneur* lay in, the
people were obliged to *beat the waters* in marshy districts, to keep the frogs
silent, that she might not be disturbed: this duty, a very oppressive one,
was commuted into a pecuniary fine.—Resumé des Cahiérs, tom. iii. pp.
316, 317.

The *colombiers* were another instrument of oppression and injustice.
These were groves of wild pigeons, kept up for the amusement of the great ;
and if the peasants entered or approached within a given distance of them,
the punishment was the galleys, or even death. On every feature of the
old government, on every object it touched, on every measure or contrivance it adopted, might be written—*Sacred to Injustice!*

ministration of justice was partial, venal, infamous.  I have, in
conversation with many very sensible men, met with something
of content with their government in all other respects than this;
but upon the question of expecting justice to be really and fairly
administered, every one confessed there was no such thing to be
looked for.  The conduct of the parliaments was profligate and
atrocious.  Upon almost every cause that came before them, interest was openly made with the judges; and woe betide the man
who with a cause to support had no means of conciliating favor,
either by the beauty of a handsome wife or other methods.  There
was also a circumstance in the constitution of these parliaments but
little known in England, and which under such a government as
that of France, must be considered as very singular.  They had
the power and were in the constant practice of issuing decrees
without the consent of the crown, and which had the force of laws
through the whole of their jurisdiction; and of all other laws
these were sure to be the best obeyed; for as all infringements
of them were brought before sovereign courts, composed of the
same persons who had enacted these laws, (a horrible system of
tyranny!) they were certain of being punished with the last severity.  Their constitution, in respect to the administration of justice, was so truly rotten, that the members sat as judges even in
causes of private property, in which they were themselves the
parties, and have in this capacity been guilty of oppressions and
cruelties, which the crown has rarely dared to attempt."—Young's
Travels, vol. ii. p. 515.

So far, then, is it from the historic fact, that the French Revolution was a monstrous chimera, the offspring of Utopian dreams
and romantic imaginations, pampered by too much ease and liberty
in the former state of things, that the ancient *régime* was an absolute nuisance, and it was felt to be so in all its branches, and by
all classes except those who were directly interested in its abuses.
It was hardly a system of governing men, but of torturing and
insulting them; proceeding on an avowed contempt of the rights
and welfare of the people, setting at naught their comforts and
happiness as not to be taken into the account, sacrificing every
principle of law or equity to the least of its caprices; taking a
pride and pleasure, and considering it as its peculiar privilege and

most dignified employment to interfere in all their concerns, to harass them at every turn, and to keep them in a state of constant alarm and annoyance and helpless dependence, and to make them feel at every moment, and by every possible means, that they were made not to set up any fantastical, preposterous, and presumptuous claims to freedom or happiness, but solely for the great to exercise their spleen, caprice, vanity, greediness, insolence, and cruelty upon. How to get rid of this complicated mass of folly, absurdity, impertinence, violence, and injustice, pointing only to the advantages and aggrandizement of the few, and to substitute in its stead a system of real government, law and liberty, founded on the good of the many, was the question. It could hardly be done without violence, for the higher orders set their faces against it ; but the voice of reason and humanity prevailed, and this great benefit was effected for mankind.* "The people," concludes the writer whom I have here quoted, "suffer much and long before they are effectually roused; nothing, therefore, can kindle the flame, but such oppressions of some classes or orders in the society, as give able men the opportunity of seconding the general mass ; discontent will soon diffuse itself around ; and if the government take not warning in time, it is alone answerable for all the burnings, and plunderings, and devastation, and blood that follow. The true judgment to be formed of the French Revolution must surely be

* The *cahiers* of the deputies of the *tiers etat* almost uniformly denounced and called for the abolition of the abuses above renumerated : the *cahiers* of the nobility, on the contrary, demanded as steadily, that all their feudal rights should be confirmed ; that the carrying of arms should be strictly prohibited to every body but noblemen ; that the infamous arrangements of the militia should remain on the old footing ; that breaking up wastes and enclosing commons should be prohibited ; that the nobility should alone be eligible to enter into the army, church, &c. that *lettres de cachet* should continue ; that the press should not be free ; and in fine, that there should be no free corn-trade. There was the same ill spirit manifested in the instructions given to the clergy by their own body. They maintain, for example, that the liberty of the press ought rather to be restrained than extended ; that the laws against it should be renewed and executed ; that admission into religious orders should be, as formerly, at sixteen years of age, that *lettres de cachet* are useful, and even necessary. They solicit to prohibit all division of commons, to revoke the edict allowing inclosures ; that the export of corn be not allowed ; and that public granaries be established

gair.ed from an attentive consideration of the evils of the old government; when these are well understood, with the extent and
universality of the oppression under which the people groaned,
(oppression which bore upon them from every quarter,) it will
scarcely be attempted to be urged, that a Revolution was not absolutely necessary to the welfare of the kingdom." But in proportion as this change was great and desirable, so was the opposition
to it violent, determined, and lasting. The Princes of the Blood
were among the first to sound the alarm, and to fly from an object
abhorrent to their pretensions and prejudices, the sight of their
country's freedom; and they lived to reap the benefit of their
early opposition and antipathy to it!

The scarcity which prevailed in Paris occasioned a tendency
to riot and disorder. Under a pretence of repressing it, the court
summoned a number of troops to Versailles; doubled the Body
Guard on duty; and sent for the dragoons and the Flanders regiment. All this, in the irritable and agitated state of the public
mind, excited hourly apprehensions of a counter-revolutionary
movement, of the flight of the King, and the dissolution of the
Assembly. In the different places of public resort, it was observed that black or yellow cockades and unusual badges were
worn; the enemies of the Revolution manifested an approaching
triumph; and the Court by its imprudence confirmed these
alarming symptoms. The officers of the Flanders regiment were
entertained by those of the King's Guard, in a sumptuous manner. The dragoons, the Swiss Guards, and several others were
also present at this banquet, which was given in the great hall
of the palace, never appropriated but to solemn occasions. All
of a sudden the King entered in a hunting-dress, followed by the
Queen, holding the Dauphin in her arms; thus (as they always
do) by a meretricious and theatrical artifice, appealing to the
common affections of our nature, to overturn the common interest and rights. The acclamations were loud and incessant: the
health of the Royal Family was drank by the troops, with drawn
swords in their hands; and when after some time Louis XVI.
withdrew, the band struck up the air—" O Richard! O my King!
the universe abandons thee!" The scene then took a more disorderly and extravagant character, the wine and music having

banished all reserve from the guests. They sounded the charge, scaled the lodges, as if they were mounting to an assault; and spreading themselves through the galleries of the palace, were received by the ladies of the court with a profusion of congratulation, and decked out with ribbons and white cockades.

The same ceremony was repeated on the 3d of October, which had taken place on the 1st, and the Queen declared herself enchanted with the day. All was now gloom and suspicion. The refusal of the King unconditionally to sanction the *Declaration of Rights*, (after having agreed to the decrees of the 4th of August,) his deliberate temporizing and increasing distrust combined with the dread of famine to produce this effect. While things were in this state, a girl entered a guard-house, seized a drum, and paraded the streets of Paris, calling out " Bread, bread !" and in a short time she was surrounded with an immense concourse of women, who repeated the same cry, and, with Maillard at their head (one of those who had distinguished themselves at the taking of the Bastille) set off for Versailles. The French and National Guards resolved upon following in their train. Fayette, who for a long time strove all he could, but in vain, to dissuade them from their purpose, at length accompanied them. The appearance of this female troop at Versailles caused considerable dismay, as it ought; for as the interference of the multitude implies an extraordinary agitation of men's minds, and some grief which has penetrated to the bottom of society and turned it *upside down*, so the interference of a female mob shows a more extreme case still. They must be pressing dangers, acute diseases indeed, which provoke such rude and unwarranted practitioners to volunteer their services. If their remoteness from power and grossness of apprehension make them bad judges of the remedy, at least it is not a trifling cause that takes them out of their ordinary routine of action, and urges them into the presence of their betters to demand one. There are no sort of people who have less impertinence, or who are less disposed to meddle with what does not concern them than the mob.——Maillard and his women appeared before the King and the Assembly in the character of suppliants, and went away satisfied with the assurances they received. But it was next to impossible that some cause of dissension should

not arise between this disorderly troop and the Body Guard, who
were the object of so much dislike and apprehension.   A quarrel
presently ensued, and an officer of the Guard struck a Parisian
soldier with his sword, and received in return a musquet-shot in
his arm.   The engagement became general, and must have ended
fatally, but for the darkness of the night coming on, and the order
which was issued for the Guard to retire.   But as they were accused of being the aggressors, the multitude were not to be pacified, broke into their quarters, and wounded two of them.   The
rain, which fell in torrents, fatigue, and the forbearance of the
soldiers put a stop to the affray ; and the arrival of Fayette,
with the National Guard, promised to restore tranquillity.

At the palace all was still ; and after a harassing night, at
two o'clock the Royal Family retired to sleep.   But towards six in
the morning, some of the rioters of the preceding day, more unsettled than the rest or waked up sooner by accident, strolling round
the palace, spied a grating open, apprised their companions of it,
and got in.   These persons saw a *Garde-du-corps* at a window,
and accosted him with a volley of abuse ; he fired and hit one of
them.   They then rushed furiously on the soldiers, who defended
the passages foot by foot, and with the greatest obstinacy.   One
of the latter had just time to inform the Queen of her danger, who
fled, half naked, to the apartment of her husband.   Fayette no
sooner heard of this unexpected attack on the royal residence,
than he mounted on horseback, and repaired without loss of
time to the spot.   He found the French Guards already there,
who had, with much difficulty protected the King's Body Guard
from the fury of the mob.   But the palace was still a scene of
the most excessive disorder.   The people assembled in the court-
yard with loud cries demanded the appearance of the King.   He
came forward and showed himself.   They then insisted on his
setting out for Paris, which he agreed to do.   The Queen was
to accompany him thither ; but so strong were the prejudices
against her, that it was first necessary to make her peace with
the people.   Fayette led her forward to the front of the balcony,
and bowing, kissed her hand with the greatest respect.   The people assented with shouts of applause.   He then advanced with
  e of the Body Guard, placed his own tri-colored cockade in his

hat, and embracing him, the people cried, " Long live the *Gardes-du-corps !*" ·The people bear no malice, and hence, from a consciousness of their infirmity, their impatience and rashness in revenging injuries at the moment and on the first object that presents itself, before the fit is overblown. The *Odia in longum jaciens quæ conderet auctaque promeret* is reserved for other breasts. Fayette by his address and well timed gallantry on this occasion probably prevented much mischief, and succeeded in escorting the Royal Family in safety to Paris. He was eminently fitted to shine in scenes like this, which required a certain calm benignity of manner and a thorough consciousness of the most perfect uprightness of intention.

The division of the kingdom into departments, with the abolition of the provincial jurisdictions, occasioned some opposition in Languedoc and Bretagne, and in the parliaments of Metz, Rouen, Bordeaux, and Thoulouse, who appear to have been more tenacious of their local privileges than zealous for the rights and equal happiness of the people at large. A more serious difficulty arose out of the abolition of the tythes and the sale of the church-lands as national property. The Revolution had commenced with financial difficulties ; and Necker, with unlimited powers and credit, and his great opinion of himself, had not been able to relieve the general embarrassment. The court had run the nation into debt ; and the nation, to clear itself at a crisis not merely of present exigency, but of inconceivable future importance, reclaimed the property in the hands of the church, guaranteeing the objects of a pious or charitable nature, for which it had been originally bequeathed. The clergy cried out *Sacrilege,* and from this time became inveterate enemies of the Revolution. They began everywhere to stir up the people against it, and denounced those who purchased any part of the ecclesiastical domains as excommunicated. The abolition of monastic vows soon after (in the beginning of 1790) was another blow to their privileges, and an affront to their supposed sanctity of pretensions. Their subsequent appointment by the state, instead of by divine ordination, was an additional aggravation of their quarrel with the Assembly. The sale of the church-lands and the various difficulties thrown in the way of its execution led to the famous system of *assignats,* which was at one time the occasion of so much distress and ridicule, and was appealed to, on the one hand, as the sure forerunner of the ruin, on the other, as the only means of the salvation of France, by those who look no deeper for the ruin or salvation of states than the symbols and nominal signs of wealth. The sale of church property and of forfeited noblemen's estates, in which this paper-currency originated, whatever might be the immediate embarrassments or absurdities attending its issue, has had the ultimate effect of giving and securing to hundreds of thousands of peasants a field, a cottage, and leisure to read. Benefit unspeakable of the Revolution, its sheet-anchor, its pride and strength!

As the anniversary of the 14th of July was set apart for a grand civic display, it was thought proper to signalize its approach by a new patriotic sacrifice. The Assembly abolished titles of nobility, armorial bearings, liveries, and orders of chivalry. This step, though of less vital importance than the rest, was perhaps called for in the heat of the moment, and as a counteraction to the disproportioned and mischievous value which had been set on these distinctions. It may be thought, possibly, that the great ends of liberty and justice having been recognised and secured, names and things of ornament might be left to take their chance with time and common sense; and that the triumph of equality, which had cancelled the legal claims and shattered the castle-walls of the old *noblesse*, might have spared their silver crests and motley coats as something to amuse their leisure and exercise their heraldic ingenuity upon. But passion converts things that are trifling and frivolous into importance; and names are more closely allied to things than we at first imagine. A *Grand Seigneur* will perhaps stand up for a title of courtesy or a device in his escutcheon as sturdily as his ancestor would for the power of life and death over his vassals; but he would not do so but that the empty sign is connected by tradition and memory with the real power, and fosters the same spirit. It is therefore necessary, in making clear work, to get rid of both, the sign with the thing signified, as long as it is made a point of; since it is always sound policy to dispossess an adversary of any vantage ground which he is obstinate in defending. With this reservation, the rule for establishing revolutions, no doubt, is to make sure of essential and universally acknowledged benefits, or to consolidate the triumph we have gained over grievous wrongs, instead of extending our conquests to matters of vague or fanciful import. Otherwise, we run a risk of bringing the whole once more into question. But reformers in general are not satisfied unless they can proceed from the solid and practical to the doubtful and insignificant; and it is well if they stop here, and do not press on with redoubled ardor, and in the spirit of wanton defiance and contradiction to the violent, the extravagant, and the obnoxious parts of their system.

The grand confederation of the Champ-de-Mars took place on the 14th of July, 1790, the anniversary of the taking of the Bastille. All Paris had been busy for several weeks in making preparations for this magnificent festival. At seven in the morning, the corporations of the city, the members of the National Assembly, the Parisian Guards, the deputies from the departments and from the army, set out from the former site of the Bastille, traversed the length of the Rue St. Honoré, and crossed the Seine on a bridge of boats, amidst discharges of artillery, the sounds of music, and the joy of the people. The procession entered the Champ-de-Mars, under a triumphal arch decorated with patriotic inscriptions, when each division of the assembled multitude repaired to the place assigned it with banners floating, and amidst loud shouts of applause. Four hundred thousand spectators were seated on benches of turf, ranged round this wide space: in the middle was placed an altar after the antique fashion; near it, raised upon an eminence conspicuous from afar, were the King, the Royal Family, the National Assembly, and the members of the municipality; the other bodies, civil or military, were placed not far off, each under its particular banner. The Bishop of Autun, assisted by four hundred priests, with white surplices and tri-colored scarfs, celebrated mass to the sound of martial music, and afterwards consecrated the royal standard and the banners of the eighty-three Departments. A profound silence ensued throughout the vast assembly, and Fayette advanced the first to take the civic oath. Borne in the arms of the soldiers to the altar of the country, amidst the acclamations of all present, he repeated in an elevated voice, in his own name, and in that of the army and the people, " We swear to be faithful to the nation, to the law, and to the King, and to maintain the Constitution decreed by the National Assembly and accepted by him." In an instant the discharges of artillery, the eager cries of the multitude, the clash of arms, the sounds of music again were blended together, and rent the air with deafening thunder. The Assembly took the same oath, and then Louis XVI. standing up, swore "to employ all the power delegated to him to maintain the Constitution decreed by the Assembly, and which he had accepted." The Queen, too, played her part in the ceremony, perhaps hurried away by the contagion of the moment and the imposing effect of the surrounding scene, and held up the Dauphin in her arms as a pledge of universal confidence and satisfaction. For the time, distrust, jealousy, reserve, dissimulation seemed to be forgotten ; and the majesty of an anointed King did not disdain to stoop and mingle with the assembled pomp and plenitude of power in a free people. The wish on the one side that the monarch should long continue the King of a free people, was answered by a ready assent on the other, that the people should be free. Vain and short-lived illusion! The rain fell in torrents nearly the whole day, (the sun only once breaking out to cast a transient gleam upon the pageant,) but this circumstance took little from the effect of the ceremony or the heartfelt enthusiasm of the spectators. The rejoicings of the day were prolonged into the night; games, illuminations, dancing succeeded. A ball was given on the spot where, a year before, the Bastille stood. A medal was afterwards struck in commemoration of this, which has been well called " a mighty people's coronation-day."

# CHAPTER V.

## COALITION AGAINST FRANCE.

THUS far the Revolution had gone on well, with the ordinary success of revolutions, where the force of reason and public opinion triumphs over arbitrary power and notorious abuses—with little violence, with little bloodshed, (and that casual and unauthorized,) and with an apparent disposition to abate its eager, whirling motion, and settle down into a constitutional monarchy, more popular than that of England, but less so than the government of the United States of America. The vessel of the state, having made its desired haven, slackened its course, and was inclined to repose in quiet under the shadow of the laws, and on the seeming union between prince and people. From the summer of 1790 to August, 1792, no restlessness of temper was manifested, no exorbitant, uneasy craving after innovation : few additional changes had been made or even suggested, little was done in the way of pulling down, much to build up and perfect what had already been chalked out. The starts, the flaws, and angry impatience of the existing order of things were during this period on the side of the Court, not of the people. The latter had thrown off their yoke, and were pleased with the terms of freedom they had obtained. Their subsequent convulsive movements and wild extravagance, both in theory and practice, took their rise not in the necessary, irregular impetus implied (as is pretended) in the very nature of all political reform, but in the insidious or barefaced attempt to arrest its progress by secret machinations or by open force, and to crush it altogether. The favorable and lofty aspect which it at first assumed and maintained, while left to itself, was soon changed to one of gloom and distraction, when beset with enemies without and within—a change which its friends had to regret, at which its antagonists rejoiced, and endea vored by every means within their reach to make worse. It has been usual (as men remember their prejudices better than the truth) to hold up the Coalition of the Allied Powers as having for its end and justification the repressing the horrors of the French Revolution; whereas, on the contrary, those horrors arose out of the Coalition, which had for its object to root out not the evil, but the good of the Revolution in France. History will confirm this sentence, and will set its mark of reprobation on those who did all in their power to impede the march of truth and freedom (with impudence and hypocrisy at their side), and sooner than relinquish a tittle of their own pride and monstrous pretensions, to convert the fairest prospects into a scene of devastation and blood, bringing about the very calamities they predicted, by driving a whole people to despair and madness, no less by the threats and vengeance denounced, than from the hopes and possession of liberty snatched from them. To understand what followed, we may pause here for a moment to take a view of the state of feeling of both parties.

We have in the last chapter seen what was the condition of the mass of the French people previous to the Revolution. The change from such a state of things, at once exciting odium and contempt, to that which had been established on its ruins, was so new, so great and beneficial, it carried such relief and conviction to every breast, to the meanest peasant or lowest mechanic, (for every human being feels that he has a heart with a capacity for enjoyment or suffering, which ought not to be wilfully and wantonly sported with by his fellow-man, a truth which all the sophistry in the world cannot overturn, and which was now erected into a principle, and promulgated as the foundation of all law and government,) this change was so satisfactory and so welcome, as at first to occasion some surprise that it did not meet with universal approbation; and this surprise soon turned into hatred of those who doubted or opposed the common good. The difference, not between the new and old philosophy, but between the natural dictates of the heart and the artificial and oppressive distinctions of society, was so vast and obvious, that the people in general could not conceive it possible for any one to be sincere or merely mistaken in withholding their claims. From Nature's bastards, they had become her sons, children of one common parent; in all their towns and villages you were met with songs of triumph, with the festive dance and garlands of flowers, as in a time of jubilee and rejoicing; and those who did not join in hailing their emancipation from thraldrom, as the dawn of a new and golden era after the long night of slavery, could only be actuated by perversity or malice. They were juggling fiends or mischievous apes, making mocks and mows at humanity, and who wished to blot out the light of reason, and to stifle once more the breath of liberty. Hence originated an impatience, a disgust, an intolerant spirit and a mutual antipathy, like that between different sects in religion; the one party seeing only the common rights they had regained, the other only the exclusive advantages they had lost. The nobles were accordingly looked upon as an abstraction of pride and selfishness, the priests of hypocrisy. An aristocrat was a being of another species, cut off from common sympathy or pity; he was like a bloated snake or spotted leper, whose touch was infection, whose sight was painful. The pretension of the few to lord it over the many was regarded as a monstrous assumption of superiority, which, the longer it had been usurped, and the more recently the disguise had been stripped from it, was entitled to less mercy. They were therefore hunted down like wild beasts shortly after; and having themselves denied the privileges of humanity to others, on system and in cold blood, were in their turn denied its benefits on the spur of the occasion and in the frenzy of the moment. They had hard measure dealt them; but they had not much right to complain, having themselves determined to give no quarter.

There was at the same time, it must be allowed, an extreme *bonhommie* and an unpardonable want of thought in the people in not expecting this result and being shocked at it. They seemed to suppose, that because a new light had struck them, the rest of the world were to be convinced as easily as they were; and that because they had been willing converts to the public good, others, who existed only on abuses and privileges, would be as forward to make the same disinterested and heroic sacrifice. That they did not, was accounted by the patriotic side a contradiction in terms, a flying in the face of nature. But this is neither a wise nor a

politic view of the subject, and should be corrected to prevent
mistakes in future.   It is impossible ever to effect any good for
mankind till we are aware of the obstacles offered to it, and of the
resistance we have to encounter from prejudice, pride, and interest.   It seems an easy thing in theory for priests and nobles to
make a virtue of necessity, and act the part of good citizens and
pious Christians, or for an arbitrary monarch to subside with
grace and dignity into the patriot-king; but the more nearly we
examine the subject, the more difficulties we shall find at every
step.   Looking at the oppression and injustice practised in
France under the old government, it might be thought strange, in
one point of view, for any human being to be found to advocate
so gross and mischievous a system.   But to those personally concerned, and with the aid of flattery and self-love, the very oppressions, vexations, and cruelties exercised seemed to carry their
own justification with them, by representing those who were the
objects of them in the most degrading and contemptible light, and
as incapable of any better treatment than they received.   Extreme inequality sharpens the edge of pride and disdain; and
these, when at their height, deaden all sense of natural right and
wrong.   While the vassal submitted without repining to his fate,
he deserved to suffer : if he resisted, it was flying in the face of
all authority and duty.   The lower classes had been so often
made use of as beasts of burden, that they had in the estimation
of their superiors forfeited all claims to humanity; and when
they at length resumed their native shape, it was resented as an
unheard-of and daring piece of presumption by their former masters, who could by no means stomach the change or tell what to
make of it.   They concluded that what had always been, must
always be ; that the distinctions of rank and their great superiority in personal accomplishments were the obvious consequences
of an original difference in blood, just as the butterfly is superior
to the caterpillar; and that clowns and artificers were the natural
drudges of lords and fine gentlemen.   Modern effeminacy and
fastidious refinement dazzled the vanity of some, and blinded them
to the plain and manly principles of independence ; while others
bent their gaze on the dim twilight of antiquity—and not finding
the ancestors of the great mass of mankind in books of heraldry,

regarded them as of no account whatever. Even the tardy sense
of justice would make them reject every other supposition with
a kind of abhorrence, for they could no otherwise defend their
having so long abused the human form ; and they must either
acknowledge the odiousness and absurdity of their own pretensions, or look down upon the bulk of the species with scorn and
loathing. We see indeed in persons of this class,* who were
exceptions to the general rule, and superior to selfish and sordid
motives, the unconquerable force of habit—how difficult they
found it to reconcile themselves in reality to what they had ardently desired in theory, and how soon they withdrew, one by
one, from the race of popularity on which they had entered,
not able to breathe out of the thick and unwholesome atmosphere of tradition and prejudice to which they had been accustomed ! If this was the case even with men of reflection and of
enlarged and liberal views, what must have been the scorn, the
fear, and hatred of those who were eaten up by their own pride
and passions only, and who had never so much as dreamt that
the universe was not a plaything made for their amusement ?

As for the clergy, the Revolution, if it did not make them
humble, made them zealous. There were many *Tartuffes* among
them who thought Heaven was concerned in the defence of their
wealth, and who were ready to call down its vengeance on the
enemies of the church. Numbers of them, who before were
hypocrites or lukewarm, became bigots. Their self-interest
alarmed and strengthened their piety ; their piety lent a seeming, and often a real sanctity, to their worldly passions. In the
best of them, the cause and defence of religion was the prevailing
motive : it was not without its effect, from sympathy and opposition, in the worst. They could not fail to perceive that their *all*
was at stake ; and when this is the case, the understanding is apt
to put itself to school to the will. By their *all*, we are not to
imply merely their external possessions, but their spiritual rank
and character, the whole ground-work of their opinions, studies,
acquirements, the influence they had exercised in the world, and
the authority they still claimed over the bodies and souls of men.
From reverend men they became, by the new light, cheats and

* Such as the Duke of Liancourt and others.

impostors : from giving laws to the world, and leading it blindfold, their pretensions were turned into a laughing-stock ; they
were alike scoffed at by the philosophers, and " baited with the
rabble's curse." If they were men, they could never tamely
brook this change ; nor be cordially, or under any circumstances,
reconciled to a Revolution that had produced it. At best, their
spiritual domination was gone from them ; they were become
mere cyphers in the state. The more rudely the mask had been
torn from their failings, the closer would they try to keep it on ;
the more absurd and fantastical their articles of faith or forms of
worship, the more sophistry would they employ both to themselves and others in palliating their grossness ; the more base and
unremitting had been their subservience to power, the more would
they strain every nerve and undergo every privation to restore
that power, that it might be a shield to them, and a triumphant
answer to their enemies. It was not that they themselves were
attacked, but it was a question whether all that they ever held, or
professed to hold sacred and venerable, should be made into a jest
and bye-word. The *esprit de corps* was too deeply wounded for
them to remain neuter ; their part was decidedly and finally allot-
ted them by the circumstances in which they stood, and by the
necessity to prop up the throne on which the altar leant for mutual support. To have acted otherwise than they did, would have
been a professional and mental *felo-de-se.* It was an error to suppose that any arguments or concessions could soften them, or
divert them from the settled purpose of recovering this self-consequence. Such characters are not unnatural, but incorrigible.

To proceed to the last point, the temper and patience with which
the King was likely to submit to the various experiments for
paring down his crown to a philosophic and constitutional standard. A lioness robbed of her young is not more furious than
an absolute monarch deprived of the smallest tittle of his power.
The convulsive start, the quivering of the flesh, the scalding tear,
the querulous tone, the swelling rage, and the faint smile would
be a subject for a great actor or poet to express. To question his
right is a deadly offence which calls for instant and signal punishment. From the moment that he knows or suspects that you do
not look upon his person as sacred, that you think him a mere

mortal, or that a single hair of his head is not of more worth than
the lives of millions of men, he conceives a surprise, fear, and
loathing in his breast which nothing can alter or appease. For
him to be taken to task, to have his designs thwarted, his power
circumscribed by the people, is an usurpation of the brute over
the God against all reason and nature. He stands up for his superiority with the instinct of self-preservation, and will sooner
part with life than forfeit his just right ; for the notion of Majesty
is so bound up with his being that he cannot breathe, it is torture
to him to exist without it. To trench upon this is to tread upon
the forked adder. He may be the mildest and best-natured of
men ; this makes no difference whatever—the slightest mark of
disrespect curdles his blood the same like poison, fevers his brain
the same like madness. And what wonder ? Do we not see the
pride and self-will of human nature going to all lengths in the
most ordinary cases, and maintaining its ground with every
thing to mortify and humble it ? Is not a man's idea of his own
merit and importance proof against every disadvantage of birth,
fortune, opinion, conscience, folly, and shame ? And what will
not this idea be in the mind of a king, pampered as it has been
from his cradle by flattery, confirmed by prejudice, consecrated
by religion, seated on a throne, blazing from the altar, woven into
the language and history of the country, and handed down from
age to age without the formal consent or intervention of his subjects, from whom he claims obedience as God's vicegerent upon
earth ? And is it to be supposed that he will give up this rank
tamely, or not rather die in the attempt to recover the last iota of
that right, the doubting of which he considers as sacrilege, treason, rebellion or worse against every law, divine or human ? To
tell him of the right of the people to be free is a cruel irony, as if
he hindered them. To have it hinted, however gently, that he
reigns by and for the people, millions of whom he has been
taught to regard as cyphers who were nothing without him at
their head, or as worms that he might crush at his pleasure or
spare at his mercy, is a thing as odious as it is incredible to his
imagination, and the stain of which is to be washed out with
rivers of blood. To suppose that a man so qualified and brought
up will voluntarily relinquish his exclusive pretensions, will fore

go or divide his sovereignty with the people in the way of friendship and good-will, is to expect milk from tigers, honey from the
scorpion. It cannot be. It is not that I blame him for being
what he is, a king; but I blame those who think he can ever forget that he was one. He is what they have made him, for the
tyrant is the work of slaves; but let them beware how they proceed, gravely and by piece-meal, to undo their own handy-work.
It is no child's-play, the *uncrowning* of a monarch! Thenceforth
there can be no compromise, no cordiality, no reliance on his
good-nature or promises or imbecility; for the weakest monarch
knows that he is a king, and his fancied wrongs give him the right
and spirit to resort to every means of violence or artifice to remain
so. There was nothing to prevent Louis XVI. from becoming a
popular and constitutional monarch but his having been born an
absolute one; and this circumstance alone made it quite as impossible for the old monarchy ever to be firmly and quietly settled in
his person on the new basis, as for his head to be restored to his
body after it was severed from it. In these reflections we may
trace the real principles of the rise, fate, and progress of the
French Revolution.

Mirabeau (on whom the court had just then fixed their eyes as
a person likely to stop what he had so great a share in accelera-
ting) died in April, 1791; and his death, which was sudden, and
by some attributed to poison, was lamented by all France. He
was the alarm-bell of the Revolution, the mouth-piece of the Assembly, the very model of a French orator: if he had been less
of a mountebank or actor, he could not have produced the effect
he did. He caught with singular felicity and animation the feeling of the moment, and giving it a tenfold impulse by his ges-
ture, voice, and eye, sent it back with electrical force into the
breasts of his audience. He seized the salient point of every
question, saw the giddy fluctuation of opinion, and rushed in and
turned it to his own advantage. By his boldness and promptitude he exercised a dictatorial power over the Assembly, and
held them in subjection by a brilliant and startling succession of
pointed appeals, as Robespierre afterwards did by the reiterated
and gloomy monotony of his denunciations. Mirabeau bore a resemblance to the late Lord Chatham in his commanding tone and

personal apostrophes, but with more of theatrical display and rhetorical common-place.  He died just in time to save his popularity, or to prevent his becoming, in all probability, an abject and formidable deserter from the cause of the people; for after his death a clandestine correspondence with the Queen's party was discovered by the minister Roland; and on this occasion his bust, which stood in the hall of the Legislature, was veiled with a graceful mixture of reproach and regret.

The Princes, and particularly the Count d'Artois, had for some time been busily employed, in concert with the emigrant nobles and clergy, or what, in the language of the period, was called *exterior France*, in organizing the insurrection of the provinces and the invasion of the kingdom by the foreign powers.  The declaration of Mantua, signed by that prince, in conjunction with the Emperor of Austria and the King of Sardinia, and settling the amount of the contingent of troops to be furnished by each of the contracting parties, bears date the 20th of May, 1791.  Austria was to send 35,000 men into Flanders; the Circles of the Empire, 15,000 into Alsace; the Swiss Cantons, 15,000 upon Lyons; Sardinia, the same number into Dauphiny; Spain was to augment the army of Catalonia to 20,000 men; Prussia was favorably disposed to the Coalition, and the King of England was to take an active part in it as Elector of Hanover.  But as it was indispensable to act in unison and prevent any partial insurrection, the treaty was to be kept secret till the latter end of July.  Calonne was employed as minister at this juncture by the Count d'Artois; Count Alexander Durfort was the confidential messenger between Leopold and Louis XVI.

But the latter, either from an apprehension of trusting himself in the hands of the Emigrants and foreigners, or from a natural vacillation of purpose, determined, in the interim, to confide his cause and person to General Bouillé, a devoted and skilful partisan, who had taken the oath of fidelity to the Constitution solely that he might be able to place the army at the disposal of the King.  For some time a close correspondence had been kept up between them; everything was prepared for the reception of the royal fugitive.  Under pretence of some hostile movement on the frontier, a camp was established at Montmedy, and detachments of soldiers lined the road to Paris, in order, it was said, to protect a convoy of gold and silver to pay the troops. The Royal Family, on their side, had made every necessary arrangement, and taken every precaution to lull suspicion. On the night of the 20th of June, at the moment fixed for their departure, they quitted the Thuilleries separately and in disguise, passed the sentinels, repaired to the Place de Carrousel, where a carriage awaited them, and set off in the direction of Chalons and Montmedy.*

The next day, when the news was known, Paris was seized with a stupor, which soon gave place to indignation. Groups of the most violent description were collected, and suspicion did not spare even Bailly or Fayette as accomplices in the event. People foresaw in the King's flight the invasion of France, the triumph

* Several accidents threatened to defeat this project in the very commencement. The King was challenged as he was going out of the gate of the Thuilleries, and only escaped detection by answering to the name of Sullivan Craufurd, to whom he bore a strong resemblance. A deputation of some of the ministers passed him as he was stooping down to buckle his shoe in one of the galleries. He, however, reached the place of rendezvous; and with Madame Elizabeth, the young Princess, the Dauphin disguised as a little girl, and Madame de Tourzel, the governess of the children, got into a hackney-coach, which was driven by Count Ferzen, a Swedish nobleman and a favored lover of the Queen; who, the more completely to avoid suspicion, whistled as he sat on the coach-box, which is considered as a mark of the lowest vulgarity in France. They had to wait in this situation, and in a state of the greatest anxiety, for the Queen, who having left the palace in company of one of the Guards, and neither she nor her guide knowing any thing of the streets of Paris, she had lost her way, and did not arrive for above an hour after her time. At the barrier the lights of a wedding had nearly discovered them. Having passed the Porte St. Martin, the hackney-coach was overturned into a ditch, and the party got into a berline with six horses which was waiting for them. Madame de Tourzel, under the name of the Baroness Korff, passed for a mother travelling with her children; the King was supposed to be her valet-de-chambre. To favor the deception, the Baroness had twice made the same journey to Montmedy. Count Ferzen took leave of them on the outside of the barriers, returned to Paris to see whether the King's flight was discovered, and set out himself the next day for Brussels. It was the same nobleman who was afterwards sent to the congress of Rastadt, as plenipotentiary from the Swedish monarch, and who was assassinated at Stockholm, in 1810, in a popular tumult.—Monsieur, with his wife, fled at the same time to Flanders by a separate route.

of the Emigrants, the return of the ancient *régime* with aggravated evils, or a long civil war. The conduct of the National Assembly, however, soon restored tranquillity and confidence. They summoned the ministers and authorities to their bar, took the executive power upon themselves for the time, charged the minister Montmorin to inform the cabinets of Europe of their pacific intentions, dispatched commissioners to the army to receive the oath of fidelity, not in the name of the King, but in their own, and transmitted orders into all the Departments to prevent every person from leaving the kingdom. Meanwhile, the King and his family proceeded undiscovered for some stages; as he retired farther from Paris he grew more confident, and suffered himself to be seen; and at St. Menehould he was recognized by Drouet, the postmaster's son, (from the likeness to the head on an assignat,) who followed him to Varennes to give the information, where he was questioned and stopped on the evening of the 21st. The next morning Romeuf, aide-de-camp to Fayette, arrived with the decree of the Assembly, commanding his detention, which the Queen snatched and tore in pieces. Bouillé, on learning the arrest of the King, hastened to his rescue with a regiment of cavalry, but came too late; when he reached Varennes, the King had been gone some hours. After the failure of his plan, the General had no other alternative but to quit the army and the kingdom. The Assembly no sooner heard of the return of the Royal Family, than it sent three of its members, Petion, Latour-Maubourg, and Barnave, to reconduct them to Paris. It was during this journey (which took up eight days, under a burning sun, and amidst clouds of dust, raised by incessant gaping crowds) that Barnave, touched by the unaffected conversation of the King, and the fascinating address of Maria-Antoinette, became a convert to the Royal cause. So much more influence has the smile of princes than the welfare of nations! Petion gave offence by his rough manners; so that no attempts were made to gain him over to the court. On arriving at Paris (by the Champs-Elysées) they passed through an immense multitude, who expressed neither disapprobation nor applause, but observed a long and deep silence—the King smiling and saying, " Here I am, good people!" and the Queen bridling, and ready to burst with rage and shame.

From this period the republican party began to show itself, who wished the downfal of the King and of the monarchy; and subsequent events did not tend to weaken this party or feeling. Louis XVI. was now pretty generally thought to harbor sentiments and designs, of which neither his countenance nor his words were a sufficient index, and against which it was necessary to have some better security than his own protestations. He was for a while suspended from his functions, and had a guard placed over him; his footsteps were narrowly watched, and he was only suffered to walk out at certain hours in the garden of the Thuilleries: but in consequence of an eloquent and artful appeal by Barnave to the moderation and magnanimity of the representatives of a great nation, the Assembly agreed to overlook what was past; at the same time making a decree, that if in future the monarch should violate the oath of fidelity to the Constitution, or league with foreign enemies, or put himself at the head of an army to wage civil war, he would thereby have forfeited the throne, and would from that time be liable to be proceeded against like any other citizen. A vast concourse of persons of all classes assembled in the Champ-de-Mars to petition against this sentence of amnesty and oblivion, and to propose an appeal to the people as to the continuance of Louis XVI. in office. The petition was drawn up by Brissot, who afterwards fell a victim to the fury of the Robespierre party, for not voting the death of the King; and it required the interference of an armed force, headed by La Fayette, to disperse the mob. Some lives were lost. Fayette, by his forwardness on this occasion, forfeited some of his popularity, which he never entirely regained.

While Paris and the Assembly remained in this state of agitation and suspense, the Allies, thrown into consternation by the arrest of the King, proceeded to take a decisive part in affairs, which allowed no alternative to the French people, as long as they aspired to the rank of men or freemen. Monsieur, the King's brother, who had fled at the same time with him, arrived at Brussels with the assumed title and powers of regent. The Emigrants, having no other hope left, called loudly for the intervention of Europe; more than two hundred members of the Assembly, who had at different times withdrawn from it, protested against the validity of its decrees; Bouillé published a threatening bombastic letter, in the hope of intimidating it. Finally, the Emperor, the King of Prussia, and the Count d'Artois met together at Pilnitz, where they signed the famous treaty of the 27th of July, 1791, which gave its sanction to the invasion of France, and commenced the war of the Revolution; which was not a war of government against government, or of one country against another, but of power against liberty, of kings against the people; and which neither did nor could end till one or the other was completely overthrown. When the Bourbons were restored in 1814 and 1815, the contest came to a natural termination. England did not openly join the Coalition (though it gave it every secret encouragement) till after the death of Louis XVI., which event it might easily have prevented; not by making his acquittal the price of its neutrality, but by putting a stop, by a firm and manly declaration, to the invasion of France by the Allies, and to the French monarch's consequent tampering with them for assistance, which led to his destruction, and to the disasters that followed. From the moment that war was found to be inevitable, the Revolution, which had hitherto been suspended on the edge of a precipice, was like a loose fragment of rock thrown down a declivity, that bounds from projection to projection, makes strange havoc, and overturns all obstacles in its progress, and increases every instant in fury and impetuosity. Let us try, in a hasty sketch, to follow its headlong and irregular course, as far as is necessary to our present purpose.

In the declaration signed at Pilnitz the Sovereigns avowedly considered the cause of Louis XVI. as their own. They insisted that he should be allowed full liberty to go where he pleased, that is, to join their standard; that he should be restored to his throne, with all his former pr vileges; that the Assembly should forthwith be dissolved; and the Princes of the Empire having possessions in Alsace and Lorraine re-instated in their feudal right. In case of refusal to comply with these terms, France was threatened with a war and with the utmost displeasure of the High Allied Powers. This lordly menace incensed instead of discouraging the nation and the Assembly. It was asked, by what right the Sovereigns of Europe exercised a despotic sway in the internal government of France? But since a band of haughty

Princes, with their hordes of satellites, were determined to degrade and wage war on a great and free people, the challenge
was accepted ;—the frontiers were ordered to be put in an immediate state of defence ; a hundred thousand national troops were
levied, and France awaited the momentous struggle to which it
was called with alacrity and confidence.

Shortly afterwards, the National Assembly having achieved
its noble task, and appointed meetings for the election of its successors, drew to a close, and was dissolved by the King in a
speech of excessive cordiality and friendly condescen ion, occasioned, perhaps, by satisfaction at the event, and the prosp·ct
of undoing all that it had done in the interval before it met again.
Part of it is worth citing, as an instructive specimen of regal
adulation. "I trust you will be the interpreters of my sentiments," he said to the deputies, "when you return among your
fellow-citizens. Tell them all that the King will always be their
first and their most faithful friend ; that he has need of their love,
and that he can only be happy with and through them." This
was declared to be a discourse after the manner of Henry IV. ;
and the monarch withdrew, in the midst of the most unbounded
expressions of attachment and esteem, to contrive new plots
against the Constitution, and to form new leagues with its enemies.
Then Thouret, the president, declared with a loud voice, and
turning towards the people, that "the Constituent Assembly had
accomplished its object, and that its sittings ended there." The
Assembly, in dissolving itself, had precluded its members from
being re-elected to the following one, with a refinement in disin-
terestedness, after the example (as it was said) of the legislators
of antiquity. This tendency to imitate antiquity has often led
the French astray. In the present case, it endangered the
stability of the work, to throw an air of purity and magnanimity
over the character of those who had been instrumental in effecting it. But even virtue and honor may have too high a standard.
In the race of patriotism, the first thing to be attended to is to see
that the Common-wealth suffers no detriment ; the second is to
place our own motives above suspicion. We may, however, pardon the impolicy of the measure for the rareness of the example,
and as a weakness incident only to the best and loftiest minds.

The humane and benevolent are refined, and refinement leads to fastidiousness. The selfish and brutal, on the contrary, never stand on ceremony, or "mince the matter;" and for this reason, so often triumph over their more scrupulous and well-meaning adversaries. Robespierre was the author of the proposal in question; and it has been attributed to his envy of the talents and eloquence displayed by some of his coadjutors in the preceding Assembly, and his wish to exclude them from the following one. But as he would also exclude himself by the same resolution, this seems hardly possible. His conduct was, more probably, owing to a sort of political pedantry, a barrenness of resources, and a literal tenaciousness of purpose, which was the original sin of his understanding, and of which he was apparently no less the dupe, than others were the victims.*

The King opened the sittings of the Legislative Assembly (which met on the 1st of October 1791) with an ill grace, thus compromising the character of candor and good-nature, which he affected, through a puerile inconsistency. Averse to the bad, repenting of what was good in his intentions, he provoked enemies without commanding respect. He sent a cold answer to the deputation that waited on him, and then appeared in person, with a countenance by no means calculated to do away the first unfavorable impression. The cause of this distance and haughty reserve was the composition of the new Assembly, which was much more popular than had been expected by the Court. Power still trusts to Fortune, as its natural ally, till undeceived by the event, and even then still trusts on. Another ground of distaste was, that some over-zealous members had proposed to withhold from the King the title of *Sire*, or *Majesty*, but this idle project was soon over-ruled. The Legislative Assembly consisted then chiefly of a few undecided stragglers, who trimmed between the

---

* Robespierre, instead of being a *sansculotte* or sloven, was a *dandy* in his dress, and when he came to cut off heads, still continued to wear powder. His refinements in theory, his cruelties in practice might come under the denomination of political *dandyism*, or were the height of the fashion, the opinion of the day carried to excess and outrage, because he had no feelings of his own to oppose to a cant-phrase or party-Shiboleth, or to qualify a verbal dogma.

Court and the Revolution; the *Gironde*, who inherited the mild wisdom and eloquent enthusiasm of the first National Assembly, but with a stronger infusion of the spirit of the period, such as Brissot, Vergniaud, Condorcet, Siéyes, and others; and the *Mountain*, or men of nerve and action, of whom Danton was at the head. Most of the latter were men who had grown out of the Revolution, and partook of its impulse, some more, others less violently, according to their previous dispositions. The studious or philosophical character of the first Assembly appeared much less in this, which had to contend with pressing emergencies, instead of laying down general principles: the one was occupied in forming a Constitution out of scattered and unknown elements, which the other was called upon to defend to the utmost against the shock of hostile states and parties. The clubs of the Corde-liers and Jacobins, in which Robespierre and Camille-Desmoulins figured, and the *Commune*, or municipality of Paris, led by such men as Santerre and Legendre, also began to have considerable influence and even authority. These bodies were a kind of roll-ers to the Revolution, when its motion was otherwise impeded; suggested, nay, dictated measures of violence or safety to the Assembly on any sudden exigency or burst of popular feeling; could act with more promptitude and effect from being shackled by no forms or dignified responsibility; and by means of this formidable adaptation to the unforeseen and rapid changes of the time, from being the auxiliaries, in the end became the masters. They were, in fact, a self-appointed executive power, with the energy and determination of a single chief and the wild irregu-larity of a lawless multitude, borne along indeed by the tumultu-ous agitation of public events, but often precipitating them to remediless destruction.

The Assembly, from its commencement, was placed in trying circumstances. Its first object was to demand an explanation of their hostile demonstrations from the foreign powers, and in case of not receiving a satisfactory answer, to declare war imme-diately. Nothing could be obtained but ambiguous excuses, a repetition of the same unwarrantable claim to interfere with the internal regulations and political independence of France on the part of the Emperor, and the continued preparations and

insolent threats of the Emigrants. The answer to all this was
an indignant and unavoidable one, namely, that the French people were not the subjects of the Emperor of Germany, and war
was accordingly declared without one dissentient voice. By
thus striking the first manly blow, France did not assuredly become the aggressor, though it has been hypocritically pretended
so. Three armies were appointed under the command of Luckner, La Fayette, and Rochambeau; and a decree was at the same
time passed, containing an act of attainder against the King's brothers, as in conspiracy and correspondence with the enemies of the
country, provided they did not return within three months to
France; confiscating the property of the emigrant nobles, and
banishing a number of refractory priests, who refused to take the
oath required by the Constitution, and did all they could to stir up
the people against the Government.

The King's ministers, however, did nothing : there was an in-
ertness and an evident want of sincerity. Not to take active and
vigorous measures of defence was to deliver the country, bound
hand-and-foot, into the power of the Allies. There was an indecision
and double-dealing in the conduct of the King himself, an overt
disapprobation, a covert encouragement of the proceedings of the
Princes and the Sovereigns. The effect of this benumbing influence was soon felt by the people and produced, as its natural
consequence, impatience and disgust. It was necessary to strike
a terror into the enemy, to inspire the nation with enthusiasm. A
change of ministers was loudly called for and agreed to by the
King, who yielded with apparent indifference to every suggestion
and every demand. Dumouriez and Roland were the two principal members of the new cabinet, the one being appointed minister of the interior, the other of foreign relations. Roland was a
plain honest man, without much pretension, but thoroughly attached to the cause of the people, and more fit to have been born
in a republic than to bring about a revolution, or to contend with
the violence and intrigues of party, to which, urged on by his
wife's enthusiasm and masculine intellect, they both fell victims.
He was remarkably simple and unaffected in his manners; and
on one occasion going to court with strings instead of buckles in
his shoes, the master of the ceremonies at first refused him ad-

mittance, but not daring to persist, he turned round in despair to Dumouriez, who humored him by exclaiming—*"Ah! Monsieur all is lost!"* Dumouriez was a man of an entirely opposite character, brilliant, enterprising, full of expedients, without principle, and so ambitious of effect, that sooner than not produce it every instant, he was willing to sink (the martyr of egotism) into insignificance and infamy all the rest of his life. This infirmity was not peculiar to the individual, but is characteristic of a community. To note it, therefore, belongs to history; it should be pointed out, defined as distinctly as possible, they should be warned against it, that in future it may not produce the same sinister effects, not only on the fate of a country, but of the world. The national vanity of the French unfortunately has no relief, no selection in it; it is voracious of every kind of food and impatient of the least delay. Place a Frenchman in any situation, no matter what, provided he is an object of attention, he is satisfied; his self-complacency supplies the rest. Have we not seen, not one, but a succession of generals betraying their standards, and marching at the head of the enemy in triumph? Have we not seen crowds of patriots making first the ruins of the throne and then the carcass of their country a pedestal for their pride to stand upon, and so that they were gazed at with wonder and incredulity, fancying themselves objects of admiration to the universe? Their inverted ambition does not climb the steep and rugged path of duty and of honor, but runs, like water, wherever it can find a declivity. The rest of mankind, if defeated, submit to their fate with what grace they may; the French alone make a boast of being beaten, and even of having contributed to it by their treachery and want of principle. They are never on the losing side. Their buoyancy of spirit soon rises from defeat unhurt—

> "And in its liquid texture mortal wound
> Receives no more than does the ambient air."

But they should remember, that though vanity may have a hundred lives, honor has but one!

The French, on the first signal for hostilities, showed great enthusiasm and ardor for the combat; yet all the good-will in the world, could not, in the commencement, supply the deficiency of

numbers, means, and skill.    While the new levies were raising,
the actual force of the country was disposed of in the following manner.    The whole of the vast frontier from Dunkirk to
Huninguen was entrusted to the command of the three generals
above-mentioned.    On the left, from Dunkirk to Philippeville, the
army of the north, about 50,000 strong, was under the orders of
Marshal Rochambeau.    Fayette had the command of the army in
the centre, composed of 45,000 men and 7000 horse, and stationed between Philippeville and the lines of Weissembourg.
Lastly, the army of the Rhine, consisting of 35,000 men and 8000
horse, was under the direction of Marshal Luckner, from Weissembourg to Basle.    The frontier of the Alps and of the Pyrenees was entrusted to General Montesquiou, whose army was
very inconsiderable ; but that side of France was not at this time
in danger.

   Marshal Rochambeau's advice was to remain on the defensive,
and merely guard the frontier.    Dumouriez, on the contrary, proposed to begin the attack, and thus have the advantage of the first
blow.    His plan, which was approved of, consisted in a sudden
incursion into the Netherlands, which, as they had lately attempted
to throw off the Austrian yoke, it was thought, would be favorable to the French arms.    This invasion was to have been conducted by a combined movement from three different points of
attack, viz. by the troops under Theobald Dillon, who was to
march with 4000 men from Lille on Tournay ; by those under
Biron, amounting to 10,000 men, who were to proceed from Valenciennes to Mons ; and by a part of La Fayette's Army, who
were to set out from Metz, and fall on Namur by forced marches,
through Stenai, Sedan, Mezieres, and Givet.    The plan, which
was too difficult of execution for raw troops, however able in the
conception, totally failed.    No sooner had Theobald Dillon's corps
passed the frontier, and got within sight of the enemy, than they
were panic struck, took to flight, and hurrying their general along
with them, assassinated him on the spot.    Almost the same thing
took place with those under Biron.    Fayette, hearing of these disasters, immediately retreated ; and Rochambeau, unwilling to be
the mere instrument of schemes undertaken without his approbation, threw up his command.    This disgraceful check added fresh

7*

fuel to the discontent that prevailed at Paris.   The Court was
more than ever suspected of keeping up an understanding with
the enemy, and the cry of *sauve qui peut* which had thrown the
French ranks into confusion, was attributed to its emissaries.  The
Assembly ordered a camp of 20,000 men to be formed round
Paris, and the enrolment of several companies of pikemen in the
National Guards.   Both these measures, the one as providing the
Assembly with a military force, the other as introducing the populace into the army, were sharply criticised by the Constitutional
party—a set of men existing at all times, who never can arrive
at a conception beyond the *still-life* of politics, and in the most
critical circumstances and in the convulsion and agony of states,
see only the violation of forms and etiquette.   This class of persons began from its outset to cripple the Revolution by petty trammels and trifling objections, as the Lilliputians attempted to bind
Gulliver with pins fastened in the ground; nor is it surprising,
that with the instinct of self-preservation and the rage of power,
men of greater energy of character, but with less principle, found
it necessary to get rid of their importunity by acts of violence and
proscription.   The King grew daily more reserved with his ministers.   It was then that Roland addressed to him that famous
letter (said to have been written by Madame Roland) which occasioned their dismissal and the resentment and tumultuary rising
of the people of Paris in consequence.   Mallet du Pan was sent
with secret instructions to the Allied Powers; while Dumouriez,
having helped by his officiousness to dissolve a ministry of which
he composed a part, repaired to the army; and La Fayette, from
his camp at Maubeuge, wrote to the Assembly, demanding the
suppression of the Jacobins, and the putting a stop to the farther
tendency of the Revolution to vulgarity and democracy.   In the
mean time, the Revolution kept on its course; the hostile pressure
from without produced a correspondent reaction from within; and
all intermediate parties and subordinate distinctions were crushed
or set aside in the mortal struggle between those who were resolved to destroy the Revolution altogether, and those who were
prepared to defend it to the last extremity, and to sacrifice every
other object to that paramount consideration.

On the anniversary of the 20th of June 1792, under pretence

of celebrating that memorable day, and planting a tree in honor
of liberty, a collection of about 8000 men set out from the Fauxbourg St. Antoine, and directed their steps towards the place where
the Legislature sat.   Their leaders asked for leave to present a
petition and to defile before the Assembly.   After a violent debate,
the deputation was admitted.   Their orator expressed himself in
threatening language, talking of a resort to the original right of
the people—"resistance to oppression"—as explained in the *Declaration of Rights ;* demanded the expulsion of the discontented
members, who (he said) would do well to join their friends at
Coblentz, (where the Princes were ;) and insisted that the King
should either second the exertions of the armies in defence of the
country, or resign a situation of which he made so ill a use.   The
Assembly agreed to take their petition into consideration, recommended respect for the laws, and permitted them to defile in its
presence.   The procession, which by this time amounted to 30,000
persons, men, women, and children, National Guards, recruits
armed with pikes, and bearing flags and trophies with the most
inflammatory inscriptions, traversed the hall, singing the well-
known tune of *Ca ira!* and crying out " *The nation for ever!
The sansculottes for ever!   Down with the veto!"*   The mob was
headed by Santerre and the Marquis St. Hurugues.   On quitting
the Assembly, they proceeded towards the Thuilleries with the
petitioners in front.

 The outer gates of the palace were opened to them by order of
the King ; the multitude then rushed into the interior.   They ascended the stairs to the royal apartments ; and while they were
breaking down the doors with the blows of an axe, Louis XVI.
desired them to be thrown open, and presented himself to the assailants, attended only by a few persons.   The popular tide was
arrested for a moment by this unlooked-for circumstance ; but the
crowd without, not being restrained by the presence of the King,
continued to press forward.   Those about him had the precaution
to place Louis XVI. in the recess of one of the windows.   On no
occasion did he display greater firmness or presence of mind than
on this highly distressing one.   Hemmed in by the National
Guard, who helped to keep off the crowd, seated in a chair which
had been raised on a table, in order that he might be able to

breathe more freely and be seen by the people, he preserved a
countenance calm and unruffled.   To those who rudely demanded
the sanction of the decrees against the Emigrants and the refractory priests (which the King had hitherto declined signing) he replied steadily, "This is neither the mode nor the time to obtain it
from me."   Having had the courage to refuse what was the
essential object of this sudden commotion, he did not think it worth
while to quarrel with an outward symbol which to him signified
nothing, and which in the eyes of the spectators was the badge of
liberty.   He put a red cap on his head, which was held up to him
on the point of a pike.   The crowd were exceedingly delighted
with this mark of condescension ; and presently after they overwhelmed him with applause, when nearly choking with heat and
thirst, he drank without any hesitation out of a wine-glass offered
him by a workman, who was half-drunk.   Meanwhile, Vergniaud, Isnard, and some other deputies of the Gironde hastened to
protect the king, to speak to the people, and put an end to this extraordinary scene.   The Assembly, which had just before broken
up its sittings, met on the instant, alarmed at this outrage, and
sent several successive deputations to Louis XVI. to serve him as
a safeguard.   At length the Mayor Petion arrived: he mounted
on a chair, harangued the crowd, intreated them to retire without
committing any disorders, and they obeyed.   These singular disturbances, which had for their object to enforce the sanction of
the late decrees and the recal of the popular ministers, ended without having broken out into any actual violence, but without having
attained their original purpose.

The proceedings of the 20th of June were followed by a strong
remonstrance on the side of the Constitutionals.   Both La Fayette
and the Duke de la Rochefoucauld Liancourt proposed to take
the King and place him at the head of their troops at Rouen and
Compiegne ; but the monarch declined their offers, choosing rather
to owe his deliverance to the Allied Powers, who were at hand.
Fayette, considerably disappointed, made a last effort in favor of
the royal cause.   He repaired to Paris, presented himself unex-
pectedly at the bar of the Assembly, and demanded the punishment of the outrages of the 20th of June, the closing of the clubs,
and the suppression of the revolutionary meetings.   He was coldly

received by the Assembly, who, however, were inclined to overlook the well-meant eccentricity of his conduct, and invited him
to the honors of the sitting. He still had hopes from the assistance of the National Guards; but the Court itself contrived to
defeat his projects in that quarter. So little sympathy do such
romantic mediators find with either party, who would do even
more mischief to their own side of the question, but `that their
enemies, who perfectly know their own minds, will have nothing
to say to their offers of conditional service and qualified approbation, but are determined to push matters to extremities and assert
their real designs, stripped of all equivocation or disguise. This
was the last attempt of the Constitutional party towards an adjust-
ment between the King and the people. Fayette returned to the
army, which both he and Dumouriez (who had taken the command under Luckner at the camp of Maulde) endeavored to bring
into some state of discipline and order, previously to the approach
of the Allied troops.

At this crisis the Gironde no longer doubted of the overthrow
of the Constitutional party, and foresaw plainly that Louis would
not rest contented, till he had either re-established the ancient
monarchy with all its privileges and safeguards, or hurled himself from the throne by his obstinacy, feebleness, and insincerity.
Vergniaud, one of their most powerful orators, did not scruple to
affirm that " it was *in the name of the King* that the Emigrants
were assembled, that the Sovereigns were leagued together, that
the foreign armies hovered on the frontier, that the troubles in the
interior took place." He broadly accused the monarch of paralyzing the energy of the nation by his repeated refusals to comply
with its wishes, and of thus delivering up France to the Coalition.
Then founding himself on an article in the Constitution, which
declared that *if the King put himself at the head of an army and
directed its force against the nation, or if he did not by a formal
and timely disavowal oppose any such enterprise which might be
executed in his name, he should be judged to have abdicated the
throne ;* and putting the supposition that Louis XVI. had de-
signedly crippled the means of defence and resources of the country, he asked if it would not be right to address him in these
terms :—" O King, who without doubt have believed with the

tyrant Lysander, that the truth was of no more avail than falsehood, and that it was necessary to amuse men with oaths as they amuse children with cockle-shells, who have feigned the appearance of attachment to the laws only to retain the power which might enable you to brave them, of attachment to the Constitution only to remain on a throne whore you might the better destroy it, think you to abuse our confidence with hypocritical pretences? Think you to mock our misfortunes with the cunning of your excuses? Was it then to defend us to oppose the foreign troops with a force that did not leave a doubt of its defeat? Was it to defend us to reject every plan tending to fortify the frontier? Was it to defend us to encourage a general who spurned the Constitution, and to damp the courage of those who enforced it? Did that Constitution leave you the choice of the ministers for our welfare or for our ruin? Did it make you the chief of our army for our glory or our shame? Did it, in fine, allow you the right of the *veto*, a civil list and so many privileges, only that you might be at liberty constitutionally to destroy the Constitution and the Empire? No, no! Man whom the generosity of Frenchmen has not been able to render grateful, whom the sole love of power has touched, you are henceforth nothing for that Constitution which you have so unworthily broken through, for that people whom you have so unworthily betrayed!"

Soon after followed the famous Manifesto of the Duke of Brunswick; and on the heels of that (as might be expected) the well-known 10th of August, which was fatal to the Monarchy. The Duke of Brunswick was advancing at the head of 70,000 Prussians, and as many Austrians, Hessians, and Emigrants. He himself, with the Prussians, was to pass the Rhine at Coblentz, and march on Paris by Longwy, Verdun, and Chalons. The Prince of Hohenloe was to operate on the left in the direction of Metz and Thionville, with a body of Hessians and Emigrants, while General Clairfayt was to lead the main body of the Austrians against Fayette, who was stationed before Sedan and Mezieres, and to reach the capital by way of Rheims and Soissons. Thus the royal fowlers spread their nets round France, but this time caught only chaff. Sweden had been detached from the Coalition by the death of Gustavus; Spain by a change of ministry, the

Count d'Aranda having succeeded the Marquis Blanca-Florida; neither England nor Russia had yet openly acceded to it. On the 25th of July, just as the army quitted Coblentz, the Duke of Brunswick published his ever-memorable proclamation in the name of the Emperor and of the King of Prussia. In this proclamation he reproached those who had usurped the reins of administration in France with having troubled social order and overturned the legitimate government; with having directed both against the King and his family attacks and violences renewed daily; with having arbitrarily quashed the rights and possessions of the German Princes in Alsace and Lorraine; finally, with having completed the measure of their guilt by declaring an unjust war on his Majesty the Emperor, and invading his provinces in the Low Countries. He declared that the Allied Sovereigns marched into France to put an end to the frightful anarchy that reigned there; to repel the attacks made on the altar and the throne; to restore the King to the security and liberty of which he was deprived, and to place him in a situation to exercise his lawful authority. In consequence, he made the National Guards and civil authorities answerable for all disorders till the arrival of the troops of the Coalition. He summoned them to return to their ancient allegiance. He added, that the inhabitants of cities who should dare to defend themselves would be punished on the spot as rebels, with all the rigor of martial law, and their houses demolished or burnt: that if the city of Paris did not set the King at entire liberty, and pay him the respect which was his due, the Coalesced Princes would render all the members of the Legislative Assembly, of the Department and Municipality, and of the National Guard, personally responsible and liable to military execution without hope of pardon; and farther, that if the Palace of the Thuilleries was forced or insulted, the Princes would take a terrible and exemplary revenge by giving up Paris to military execution, and by not leaving one stone of it upon another. On the other hand, he promised the inhabitants of Paris the interposition of the good offices of the Allied Princes with Louis XVI. with a view to obtain forgiveness of their manifold offences and errors, provided they showed a prompt obedience to the orders of the Coalition.

This impolitic and vaunting proclamation, which laid open the designs and pretensions of the Allies, the Emigrants, and the Court in all their arrogance and cruelty, which menaced a whole people with the return of their ancient slavery, and with immediate vengeance and summary punishment for having dared to shake it off, excited but one cry of indignation, but one vow of resistance from one end of France to the other; and whoever had not joined heart and hand in it, would have been justly regarded as guilty of impiety towards his country, and the still more sacred cause of mankind. From hence we may fairly date the excesses and horrors of the French Revolution. This proclamation, the deliberate and haughty tone in which it pronounced its dictatorial mandates, the assumption of an undisputed right over the French people and the human species at large as a herd of slaves who were taunted with their pretensions to be any thing else as rebellion and insolence, the lordly claim set up over them, which showed in burning daylight the degradation from which they had escaped, the crying injustice with which they were threatened, and which was not even attempted to be glossed over, exasperated their passions and exhausted their patience, as well it might; and the contrast between what they had hoped and what they were apprehensive of, almost turning their brain, they struck at the spectre of power which haunted them like a filthy night-mare, wherever they could encounter it in a tangible shape, with fear and hatred, without mercy and without remorse. I must stop here to express my admiration, which has often amounted to stupor, at two things; first, that these very Prussians, who put forth this Manifesto of their designs, sentiments, and principles, should for twenty years afterwards have yelled out dolorous complaints of the ill-usage and unprovoked aggressions of France, and that there should have been found hypocrisy enough in the world to believe and pity them; secondly, that at the end of that twenty years and a little more, these very Prussians should have twice carried their threats, so gallantly resisted at first, into execution to the very letter (turning a bravado into a prophecy) without a blow struck, with scarce a word of remonstrance or a blush of shame from a people that had once dared to call itself free, great, and the mistress of the world. Neither does it lessen my regret or indignation on this

occasion, that England had a principal share in so ignomini>us a
triumph, which "called every drop of blood in her veins bastard,"
and which was proclaimed by the words, "Your King is at hand"
—the same who had been for more than twenty years digesting
the principles of the Duke of Brunswick's Manifesto into a Charter !

The Gironde wished for the dethronement of Louis XVI. by a
decree of the Assembly ; the popular leaders, Danton, Robespierre, Camille Desmoulins, Marat, &c. by means of an insurrection.   The latter party were the most determined, and they
carried their purpose into effect first.   On the 26th of July an
explosion was to have taken place, but was prevented by the interference of the Mayor Petion.   On the 8th of August the accusation of Fayette was proposed in the Assembly ; it was negatived after a long and stormy discussion, but those members who
voted against it were hissed and maltreated by the mob on coming
out.   On the following day, the effervescence was extreme.   The
section of *Quinze Vingts* declared that if the sentence of abdication
were not pronounced the same day, at midnight the tocsin would
sound, and there would be a general rising of the people.   This
resolution was transmitted to the forty-eight sections, who all approved of it, except one.*   The Mayor, who was applied to by
the Assembly, replied that he could do nothing if the people were
determined to take the power into their own hands.   The attack
on the Thuilleries was fixed for the 10th of August.

The Court had been for some time apprised of its danger, and
had put itself in a posture of defence.   The inside of the palace
was lined with Swiss troops to the number of eight or nine hundred, with officers of the Guard, and a body of gentlemen and
loyalists, who had come armed with pistols and sabres.   Mandat, the commander of the National Guard, had also repaired to
the Thuilleries with his staff ; and Petion was summoned to give
an account of the state of Paris, and to authorize the repelling
force by force.   At midnight, the report of a cannon was heard,
the tocsin rang, and the insurgents assembled and established a
provisional council of the Commune at the Hôtel-de-Ville.   Meantime, the National Guard took the direction towards the Thuilleries ; the cannoneers were planted with their guns at the entrance

* The Filles-St. Thomas, or Lepelletier

of the avenues; and the Swiss and volunteers defended the apart. ments within. The **Assembly**, alarmed by the ringing of the tocsin, met under the presidency of Vergniaud. They sent for Petion, who was detained at the Palace, and ordered him to repair to his post; but no sooner did he arrive at the Hôtel-de-Ville, than he was put under arrest by the provisional council, who wished no other authority that day than their own. The Council also summoned Mandat, who came after some hesitation, charged him with having instructed the troops to fire on the people, ordered him to the Abbaye, and on going out he was killed on the steps of the Hôtel-de-Ville. Santerre was immediately appointed to the command of the National Guard in his stead.

The Court thus found itself deprived of its firmest supporter. The National Guard would not strike a blow without him. The sight of the nobles and royalists had also given them a disgust, and Mandat had in vain urged the Queen to send away this troop: she replied angrily, "These gentlemen have come to defend us, and we reckon upon them!" Dissension was already sown among the defenders of the palace, when Louis XVI. passed them in review about five in the morning. He visited the different parts of the palace, accompanied by Madame Elizabeth, the Dauphin, and the Queen, whose Austrian lip and aquiline nose more curled than usual gave her an air at once dignified and forbidding. The King was exceedingly dejected, and his reception by the troops was doubtful and discouraging. Some cried "*Long live the King!*" while others answered by the counter-cry of "*Long live the nation! Long live Petion!*" He was greeted with the loudest acclamations by the battalions of the Filles-St. Thomas and the Petits-Pères, who were ranged along the terrace close to the palace. But as the King traversed the garden to visit the Pont-Tournant, the new-raised companies of pike-men pursued him with cries of "*Down with the veto! down with the traitor!*" and quitting their station, turned the guns against the Thuilleries. Two other battalions, placed in the inner courts, followed their example, and took up an offensive position. The King on returning to the palace was pale, and evidently disturbed; and the Queen said, "All is lost! this unlucky review has done more harm than good!"

While this scene was passing at the Thuilleries, the insurgents advanced from different quarters, having taken advantage of the night to force the arsenal, and to distribute arms. The column of the Fauxbourg St. Antoine, about 15,000 strong, and that of the Fauxbourg St. Marceau, consisting of 5000 men, had commenced their march about six in the morning. The crowd increased every moment. The Marseillois and Breton troops proceeded as their advanced guard along the Rue St. Honoré, and drew up in order of battle on the Carrousel, with their guns pointed against the palace. The Syndic Rœderer addressed them and urged them to disperse, but was answered by a discharge of cannon. He then, finding that the populace were everywhere masters, returned hastily and in great trepidation to the palace. The King was holding a council with the Queen and the ministers. A municipal officer had a few minutes before given the alarm of the approach of the insurgents. "What is it they want?" asked the Keeper of the Seals, Joly. "The abdication," replied the officer. "Let the Assembly then pronounce it," rejoined the minister. "But after the abdication, what is to follow then?" said the Queen. The messenger bowed his head and was silent. At the same moment Rœderer entered, and completed the consternation of the Court by stating that the danger was extreme—that the multitude had become totally unmanageable, and that the King and Royal Family had no other chance of safety than by taking refuge in the bosom of the Legislative Assembly. The Queen at first rejected this advice with the most lively indignation: "I will sooner," she exclaimed, "see myself nailed to the walls of the palace than leave it:" and turning to the King with a pistol in her hand, added, "Now is the time to show youself, sir." The King made no reply to this extravagant appeal; and Rœderer interposing, persuaded him to repair to the hall of the Assembly. He dismissed his ministers and attendants, saying, "Gentlemen, there is nothing more to do here;" and followed by his family and a few individuals of his household, crossed the garden*

* The Assembly at this time, and from the period of its leaving Versailles, held its sittings at a large riding-house which then stood between the Place Vendôme and the gate of the garden of the Thuilleries, facing (what is now) the Rue Castiglione. The garden was not surrounded by railing, but by a wall.

through a line of Swiss, and the battalion of the Petits-Pères and the Filles-St. Thomas. But at the gate of the Feuillants, the mob, which was immense, obstructed his passage; and it was with difficulty he reached the Assembly, exposed to the insults, the threats, and the revilings of the people. This was a result very different from that held out in the manifesto of the Duke of Brunswick; and the glaring contrast between the pretensions there set up and the indignities now offered him by the meanest of the rabble must have drained the cup of bitterness to the very dregs. Having entered the hall of the Assembly, he said, "Gentlemen, I am come here to prevent a great crime : I must always think I am in safety with my family in the midst of you."—"Sire," replied Vergniaud, who occupied the chair, "you may depend on the Assembly, who have sworn to die in defence of the laws." The King then took his place by the side of the President; but Chabot having observed that it was impossible for them to deliberate in presence of the King, he withdrew into a small recess behind the President, from whence he could see and hear all that passed. After the departure of the monarch, there was no longer any motive for assaulting the Thuilleries; but the combatants were drawn up face to face, and a furious conflict ensued. The Bretons and Marseillois had forced their way into the courts of the palace, under the guidance of an officer of the name of Westermann, a friend of Danton's, where they were joined by the cannoneers who had been placed there to repulse them. The Swiss soldiers at first threw their cartridges out of the windows in token of amity; but as the insurgents pressed into the interior of the palace, a quarrel arose, when the Swiss directed a fatal fire amongst their ranks and dispersed them for a minute. But the Marseillois soon returning in force, attacked the Swiss with their cannon, repulsed, surrounded, and cut them in pieces. It was no longer a combat but a massacre; and the assailants gave themselves up to every kind of disorder. The Assembly were kept for some time in a state of anxiety and apprehension. The cannon continued firing, and the event seemed doubtful. At length the cry of "*Victory!*" was heard from the people, and the fate of the monarchy was then decided. A deputation from the new Municipality soon after entered, followed by innumerable others, to demand the abdication. The Assembly did not dare to take this step upon itself, but Vergniaud mounted the tribune in the name of the Commission of Twelve, and proposed the calling a new National Convention, the dismission of the ministers, and the suspension of the King from the exercise of his authority. These propositions were unanimously agreed to. The popular ministers were recalled, the long-pending decrees were passed, commissioners were dispatched to tranquillize the armies, and Louis XVI. was ordered first to the Luxembourg, from whence he was transferred as a prisoner to the Temple, by the formidable and implacable Commune. The 23d of September was fixed for the opening of the new extraordinary Assembly, and the deciding the fate of the monarchy.

The Departments and in general the army gave in their assent to the change of government. Fayette alone made an attempt at a counter-movement. Enamored of that first step in the Revolution, of which he had been a principal instigator, and to which he had pledged himself as a friend at once to liberty and the laws, he was determined, with a strange mixture of prejudice and romance, that it should advance no farther under pain of his displeasure, and was always for bringing it back to this technical point of perfection with Quixotic perseverance and in spite of circumstances. He seemed to consider a Revolution as too much an affair of taste and decorum. He worshipped the Constitution of 1789 in the shrine of his imagination, to which no one else paid the smallest regard, and was in danger of sacrificing to this chronological chimera the future prospects of freedom. He had been a knight-errant in the American Revolution, and thought himself bound to maintain the character of that of his own country equally pure and immaculate, though as affairs stood the thing was impossible. Its course was too irregular and Pindaric for his taste, and yet he persisted in fond attempts (the offspring, doubtless, of the goodness of his heart and the rectitude of his own intentions), to " lure this gentle tassel back" by smiles and threats, and tie it by a silken thread to the foot of the throne. No man is wiser from experience or suffering, or can cast his thoughts and actions in any other mould than that which nature has assigned them ; or so true a patriot (than whom a better or honester

man breathes not) would not, after his own and his country's
" hair-breadth 'scapes" and bleeding wrongs, have tried to *hamper* the Revolution in its last struggles with the same cobweb,
flimsy refinements that he did in its first outset.  To politicians
of this visionary stamp, the slightest motives have always the
greatest weight ; for they only see how much their own side falls
short of imaginary perfection, and have no conception of the
*damning* alternative opposed to it, or of the abyss that yawns to
receive them.

On the present occasion, La Fayette wished to employ the
services of the 30,000 men who were under his command in
restoring the King to the throne.  For this purpose he concerted
measures with the municipality of Sedan, where he had his head-
quarters, as well as with the Directory of the department of Ardennes.  He seized the three commissioners sent to his army,
Kersaint, Antonelle, and Peraldy, and shut them up in the tower
of Sedan.  While he was pursuing these ill-judged projects, as
if it were in a time of perfect peace and leisure, the invading
army which had set out from Coblentz ascended the Moselle and
advanced towards the frontiers.  The French troops, in consideration of the extreme danger, were disposed to repel an actual
enemy rather than to patch up an imaginary Constitution.
Luckner, who had at first sided with Fayette, deserted him, and
the latter perceived it was necessary to yield to circumstances.
He quitted the army, accompanied by Bureau de Pusy, Latour-
Maubourg, and Alexander Lameth, and directed his steps along
the advanced posts of the enemy to Holland, intending to proceed
to America, his adopted country.  But he was discovered by the
Austrians, and taken prisoner, together with his companions.
Contrary to all the laws of nations, he was treated as a prisoner of war, and confined first in the dungeons of Magdebourg
and afterwards of Olmutz.  For four years of the most severe
captivity, suffering under all sorts of privations, ignorant of the
fate of liberty and his country, he displayed the most unshaken
courage, and refused to purchase his release from the frightful lot
that awaited him at the expense of a few submissions compromising the sacred cause he had espoused.  Tempers like his, mild,
amiable, upright, sincere, are better qualified to endure the inflic-

tions of arbitrary power than to enter into that arduous and deadly strife with it which can alone ensure a triumph over it. It is theirs to do and to feel what is manly and becoming in their own persons ; but, thinking to shame their opponents out of their unjust pretensions by the example of what is right, they fall victims to their own candor and moderation ; and bad men are left to finish the work which good ones have begun!

The popular party who had brought about the 10th of August, did not relax in their daring designs. After having procured the removal of Louis XVI. to the Temple, they next proceeded to demolish all the statues of the kings, and to efface the emblems of royalty ; they annulled the law which required certain conditions of property as essential to the enjoyment of civil rights, and insisted on the appointment of an extraordinary tribunal *to try the conspirators of the 10th of August,* that is, those who had resisted the popular conspiracy of the day. Thus does power always use names as it pleases! This tribunal sat, and condemned a few persons to death ; but it proceeded too leisurely and formally to give satisfaction to the Commune, who were impatient of justice in the most wholesale way, and contented with no half-measures. The leading members of the Commune were Marat, Panis, Sergent, Duplain, Lenfant, Lefort, Jourdeuil, Collot d'Herbois, Billaud Varennes, Tallien, and others ; but Danton was undoubtedly its head, who has been called the Mirabeau of the mob ; a man of gigantic courage, stature, and voice, whose words rolled in thunder above the noise of the most tumultuous assemblies, and whose energy rising with the occasion, and unchecked by fear or remorse, launched the thunderbolt of popular vengeance at the enemies of the Revolution, and so far saved his country by dire measures in a dire necessity ; but who being equally without malice* or principle, relapsed into indolence and thoughtlessness again, when the blow had been struck ; and him-

---

* He spared all those who personally applied to him ; and of his own accord saved the lives of Dupont, Barnave, and Charles Lameth, who were in some sort his personal antagonists, by letting them out of prison in time It would have been an additional reason with Robespierre to proceed to ex tremities, and would have given additional zest to his cruelty, to show that he was proof against every such plea of weakness or magnanimity.

self fell a martyr to those who from a more untired cruelty or a bigotted faith in crime, aimed at converting the resort to terror and violence which he had recommended as a measure of expediency into a system of government. He had been the great mover of the insurrection of the 10th of August; had been present everywhere to superintend its execution ; had gone from the Sections to the barracks of the Bretons and Marseillois to spirit them up, and from these had hastened to the Fauxbourgs ; and by a zeal and foresight that steadily contemplates its end and is prodigal of its means, set aside a throne which had become a stumbling-block in the way of the Revolution, and the rallying-point of its enemies.

The Prussians advanced to their avowed and nefarious object, and passed the frontier, after a march of twenty days. The army of Sedan was without a leader, and incapable of resisting such superior and well-disciplined forces. Longwy was invested on the 20th of August; bombarded and taken on the 24th. On the 30th the Allies were before Verdun, commenced the bombardment; and this place once taken, the road to Paris lay open. The inhabitants were in the utmost consternation. The Executive Council, composed of the ministers, came to the Committee of Public Safety to know what was to be done. It was on this trying occasion that Danton, rejecting every common-place means of defence which had been proposed, cut the knot of the question and sundered the bands of slavery which were prepared to be thrown over them, by saying, " *Il faut faire peur aux royalistes !*" And, as the Committee seemed to shrink and stand aghast at the terrible suggestion, the import of which they too well understood, he repeated, "Yes, I say we must put the royalists in fear!" Out the words came, and they never went back till they had effected and more than effected their purpose. He concerted along with the Commune the means of carrying them into execution. Domiciliary visits were paid in the most mournful silence ; a great number of refractory priests, nobles, and other disaffected persons were inclosed in the prisons of the Abbaye, Conciergerie, and La Force. In the night between the 1st and 2d of September, the news came of the capture of Verdun ; and the Commune, taking advantage of the breathless pause of fear and expectation, executed their plan; the tocsin sounded, the drums beat, the barriers were closed, and for three days the prisons ran with blood. Few indeed of those devoted to destruction escaped: three hundred of the most depraved and desperate characters that the metropolis afforded did the work of death, while the members of the Commune looked on, and judged with calm, unrelenting severity. The threat of vengeance and summary punishment, which had been so loudly promulgated, "like a devilish engine back recoiled" upon its advisers and accomplices; and the intended victims of an exterminating proscription were transformed into its frantic executioners. Fear, pride, revenge had changed sides. The people were goaded from tame into wild beasts. Not they, but their boastful oppressors turned pale, and crouched to the earth. Liberty, like the bruised adder, turned and struck its mortal fangs, inflamed with rage and hate, into those who wished to crush it. The vilest and meanest of mankind were brought into contact with the pampered and high-born—rag-sellers, dog-clippers, thieves, mendicants, with the haughty noble, the dignified prelate, the elegant courtier; and for one short hour misery showed to grandeur no more mercy than it had always received from it! The Assembly attempted in vain to stop the effusion of blood; the ministers also tried to interfere, but their hands were tied; a nod from the terrible Commune decided every thing; the mob either took a share in the scene, or stood gazing on; the soldiers who had to guard the prisons, durst not hinder the murderers; while others were afraid to express any opinion, lest they too should be singled out as objects. One universal feeling of terror, distrust, and vengeance had taken possession of the public mind, and the Commune had found out the only vent for it in violence and blood. Every thing else seemed idle and out of tune.

This was properly the commencement of the *reign of terror*, and we have seen pretty plainly what was the occasion of it. However great an evil in every point of view, it was, perhaps, necessary to France to enable her to weather the storm. This is not meant as a compliment either to France or to the reign of terror. The truth must be spoken here. To no other country in the world would it have been necessary; but such as her old

government had made her, such she must show herself, in order
to shake off that government. What France needed was courage
to face external danger, steadiness to adhere to certain fixed principles. She had neither the one nor the other in a noble, manly
way; they must, therefore, be forced and purchased at any rate.
To a great people the danger is sufficient to awake the courage;
to a free people the love of liberty is sufficient title to be free. In
England (dull as we are) a thousand enemies would only call up
a thousand champions to answer them. But in France the extremity of the danger only produces a correspondent degree of
fear, unless they can inspire others with a greater fear; and to
meet their adversaries, they must already have triumphed over
them by proxy. Having cut the throats of the royalists in prison,
they looked upon them as poor wretches and themselves as
heroes, and thus recovered spirit to face them in the field. A
massacre was therefore a necessary prelude to a victory, and
they could only "screw their courage to the sticking-place"
against a host of enemies, by glutting their resentment and cruelty with an easier prey. Neither is this justly to be attributed to
a natural ferocity, but rather effeminacy of character. The
sterner virtues are not natural to them, and they can only be produced in them in extreme cases, and by the most violent means.
Again, an abstract principle with them goes for nothing. *Liberty, equality, patriotism*, are fine words to talk about; but so are
many others—*loyalty, religion, honor*. To rouse or keep alive
any strong enthusiasm, there must be a dramatic effect added to
the conviction of truth and justice. Liberty must have its festivals, its garlands, its altars; and when these fail or are soiled, its
tragic stage, its scaffolds, its daggers, and the slider of the guillotine. Otherwise the interest soon flags—they would be sick of
it in a month. But give them excitement, and there is nothing
they will stop at under its impulse; nothing is too lofty, nothing
too vile for them; and a prison-floor turned into a shambles, a
bleeding head stuck upon a pole in honor of liberty, would do
more to attach them to it than all the good it could do to millions
of men for ages to come. One of their own orators (Louvet)
said on this occasion, "A great people know how to defend their
capital without massacring prisoners." If so, the French are not

a great people ; for they massacre prisoners, and they do not defend their capital—without it !

The Revolutionists had now thrown away the scabbard, and
had no hope of pardon but in victory ; despair, if nothing else did,
must now give them energy and firmness.   All the citizens capable of bearing arms had been enlisted in the Champ-de-Mars, and
sent forward on the 1st of September to join the armies.   The great
difficulty was in the choice of a general.   Kellermann, who had
succeeded Luckner, Custine, Biron, Labourdonnaie, though well
qualified to fill the rank of second in command, had not the requi-
sites to direct an extensive line of operations, on which the fate of
France hung.   Dumouriez alone had sufficient talent, but he
wanted the confidence of the patriotic party ; yet as there was no
one else adequate to the crisis, he was appointed by the Executive
Council to the command of the Army of the Moselle.

Dumouriez instantly repaired from the camp of Maulde to that
of Sedan.   He called a council of war on the spot ; and in opposition to the general advice, which was to retire on Chalons or
Rheims behind the Marne, carried the project of posting himself
on the forest of Argone, through which the enemy must pass to
reach Paris.   By a bold and rapid march he succeeded in occupying the four outlets of the forest with upwards of 20,000 men
under his command and that of General Dillon.   It was here he
wrote to the minister of war, Servan:   " *Verdun is taken : I am
waiting for the Prussians.   The camp of Grandpré and that of Is-
lettes are the Thermopylæ of France ; but I shall be more fortunate
than Leonidas.*"   This is concise and spirited ; and at the same
time an example of that love of running parallels between themselves and the ancients which is the weak side of French imagination.   The Greeks and Romans were great naturally, or because they made the most of the circumstances in which they
were placed, and not from an idle affectation of resembling any
other people.   French heroism is always expressed by an historical metaphor.

In this position Dumouriez was at liberty to await the enemy and the arrival of his own succors.   Beurnonville had
orders to march to his assistance with 9000 men, Duval with
7000, and Kellermann was to come from Metz with 22,000.

These were to join him by the middle of September; it was only
necessary therefore to gain time.   He had, however, left the
passes of Chêne-Populeux and Croix-au-Bois not sufficiently
guarded.   The Prussians accordingly seized upon these two
posts, and had well-nigh turned him in his camp at Grandpré and
forced him to lay down his arms.   He decamped in the night of
the 14th, passed the Aisne, and took up a position at St. Menehould.   He had already delayed the march of the Prussians
through the forest of Argone; the season, as it advanced, grew
worse; his own troops were every day more inured to the hardships of war; and on the junction of Beurnonville and Kellermann, which took place on the 17th of September, the French
army amounted to nearly 70,000 men.   The Prussian army had
regularly followed the movements of Dumouriez.   On the 20th
they attacked Kellermann at Valmy, in the hope of cutting off
the retreat of the French on Chalons.   A brisk cannonade commenced on both sides.   The Prussians then pushed forward in
columns to the heights of Valmy, intending to carry them.   But
Kellermann also formed his infantry in columns, enjoined them
not to fire, but to wait for the approach of the enemy to charge
with the bayonet.   At the same time the cry of " *The Nation for
ever!*" repeated from one end of the line to the other, astonished
the Prussians no less than their firm and undaunted posture.
The Duke of Brunswick, disappointed, made his battalions fall
back, and though the Austrians afterwards rallied, the fortune of
the day remained with the Revolutionary army; and this trifling
success produced, both on the troops and on public opinion in
France, all the effects of the most decisive victory.*   From this
period may be dated the discouragement and subsequent retreat
of the enemy.   The Emigrants had represented the march to
Paris as a military promenade.   The Prussians were without
magazines, without food, and instead of an open country, found
every day a more determined resistance: the roads were cut up
by the rains, the soldiers had to wade up to their knees in mud;
and the bad water and raw grain which they were obliged to eat,

* Five-and-twenty years after, when liberty, independence, glory, all
but the memory of the past was fled, Kellermann bequeathed his heart to
be buried in the field of Valmy

brought on the most destructive diseases. The Duke of Brunswick, in apprehension of losing his whole army, counselled a retreat, in opposition to the opinion of the King of Prussia and the
Emigrants. Negociations were opened, in which he merely insisted on the restoration of the King to a constitutional throne;
but the Convention had in the meantime met, and had proclaimed
the Republic; and the Executive Council replied, that the French
Republic could listen to no terms till the enemy had evacuated
the French territory. The Prussians, sometimes annoyed in their
retreat by Kellermann, repassed the Rhine at Coblentz, towards
the latter end of October, 1792. The French again took possession of Verdun and Longwy; and Dumouriez set out for Paris,
to enjoy his victory and concert measures for the invasion of the
Netherlands. The campaign had been everywhere successful.
In Flanders, the Duke of Saxe-Teschen had been compelled to
raise the siege of Lille, after a fruitless and cruel bombardment
of seven days; Costine had taken Treves, Spire and Mayence;
on the side of the Alps, General Montesquiou had penetrated into
Savoy, and General Anselm into the county of Nice. The
French armies, everywhere fortunate, had taken the offensive,
and the Revolution was for this time saved.

# CHAPTER VI.

### THE NATIONAL CONVENTION.

THE Convention met the 20th of September, 1792, and opened its deliberations on the 21st.   In its first sitting it abolished royalty and proclaimed the Republic, dating the Revolution from this period.   Not having enemies enough to contend with abroad, it was divided from the first into two parties, the Gironde and the Mountain, that attacked one another with unceasing virulence. Robespierre was the principal object of the denunciations of the more moderate party, who saw from afar his tyrannical sway, and attributed to him in a great measure the massacres of the 2d and 3d of September.   Robespierre having pretended that no one durst accuse him to his face, a tall, thin, pale figure of a man advanced slowly from the other end of the hall, and mounting the tribune, said in a deep, sonorous voice, *C'est moi qui l'accuse, Robespierre !''*   (It is I who accuse you, Robespierre.)   He then proceeded to inveigh bitterly against the secret designs of Robespierre, his base flatteries of the people, his supposed share in the massacres of the prisons, and to vindicate the friends of the Revolution from having any hand in this odious transaction, as well as the people of Paris in general, who, he said, knew how to repel their foes, but not to assassinate those whom they had in their power.   " All Paris was before the Thuilleries on the 10th of August, and participated in the events and sentiments of that day.   Not 400 persons, led by a stupid horror, were to be seen before the prisons on the 2d and 3d of September, while half that number executed their bloody task within."   And then returning to Robespierre, he charged him with being accessory to the blood that had been shed, and with an insatiable thirst and craving after more, at each pause repeating the emphatic words, " *C'est moi qui t'accuse, Robespierre !''*   This was the famous Louvet, after-

wards one of the proscribed members, and who has given so interesting an account of his own, and the sufferings of his party,
in his Memoirs of that period.

Robespierre was screened by the Convention, and by his own
followers; but the weight of the accusation fell on Marat, who
appeared at the bar of the Convention to exculpate himself. He
had in his journal, entitled *The Friend of the People*, recommended a dictatorship, and preached up assassination as a civic
virtue; and now, amidst loud cries of reprobation and the stupe-
faction of his hearers at his audacity, he frankly declared what
he thought on each of these topics. He was less a hypocrite
than Robespierre, had no ulterior designs, and used no artifice in
concealing his principles, but rather made a merit of exposing
them in their worst light. There was no atrocity which, from a
gloomy temper and a spirit of dogmatism, he could not persuade
himself was right, and which he would no· proceed unblushingly
to obtrude upon others, being equally devoid of modesty or discretion. Others had more delight in the actual spilling of blood:
no one else had the same disinterested and dauntless confidence
in the theory. Marat might be placed almost at the head of a
class that exist at all times, but only break out in times of
violence and revolution; who, without natural sensibility or even
strong animal passions, are the dupes of every perverse paradox that
gratifies their desire of intellectual power; who form crime into a
code, and who proclaim conclusions that make the hair of others
stand on end, not only with the most perfect calmness and compo-
sure, but with the redundant zeal and spirit of proselytism belonging to saints and martyrs. There can be little doubt that Marat
regarded himself as an apostle of liberty; and the more undenia-
bly wrong he was, the more infallible he thought himself, the
very violence and harshness of his opinions rivetting them the
more on his conviction, and the circumstance of every one else
being against him, only proving his infinite superiority to the rest
of mankind and irritating his habitual petulance into the frenzy
of fanaticism. Disappointed vanity would step in to confirm this
original morbid bias. Outrageous paradoxes are the resource
of mediocrity of understanding, as bombastic metaphors are a
sign of a frigid imagination. Perhaps this sort of theoretical and

gratuitous barbarity, by which Marat sought to be distinguished, makes more enemies, and shocks the general feeling more than any excesses of passion or cruelty; for these last, however we may lament or shudder at them, are confined to the individual act, do not stagger our faith in virtue, or make us, by reflection abhor ourselves. In the other case, the mind conceives a disgust and impatience at what appears to cast a blot and an imputation on the order of the moral world. Urged by the enthusiasm of insulted virtue, and her hatred of the doctrines of Marat, the handsome and high-spirited Charlotte Corday wore a dagger in her bosom as a charm against the contagion of such revolting sophistry, and at length seized an opportunity to rid the world of an intellectual monster. The same attempt was made twice on Robespierre, and failed, probably from its being the result of a less determined plan and less rooted antipathy.*

The bickerings and animosity between the Mountain and the Gironde, that broke out with the first opening of the Convention and continually increased in acrimony and personality, did not come to a decisive issue till after the death of the King; and the moderation and scruples of the Brissotins on this occasion proved fatal to them. The Mountain went along with the popular tide, and indeed did all they could to excite the rage and fermentation of the passions; and this impulse, as it was the most violent, so it was the most powerful at the moment, and naturally prevailed.

For some time men's minds were prepared for the King's trial. The Jacobin Club resounded with invectives against him; reports the most injurious were circulated against his character; his condemnation was loudly called for as necessary to the establishment of liberty on a sure basis. The popular societies in the departments poured in addresses to the Convention to the same effect; the Sections also presented themselves at its bar, and even went so far as to parade before them on litters those who had been wounded on the 10th of August, and who came to demand vengeance on this account against Louis Capet, for so they affected to call Louis XVI. This is in the worst style of revolutionary mock-heroics. I do not object to striking an enemy hard, if he is an enemy, and if you strike him at all; but surely

* See Brissot's character of Marat, Appendix, No. 4.

to expect that he is not to defend himself, or to show the wounds received in civil strife, where all is supposed to be voluntarily risked as well as braved for one's country or for conscience' sake, as beggarly claims to pity or incentives to revenge, is dastardly and pusillanimous to the last degree. It is a wretched assumption of a question which has only been decided by the event, and a cowardly advantage taken of a fallen foe. But here again we have the everlasting craving after effect, produced by any means whatever, and under the most paltry pretence. The Parisians insulted Louis, and strove to degrade him by bald and opprobious epithets in his low estate, which entitled him doubly to every consolation of courtesy and humanity (the great political question being reserved entire)—but there was a contrast, there was a change of scene, a melo-dramatic opportunity not to be missed; though had he been restored to that full regal power which alone could make him an object of fear or enmity, they would have crouched in abject submission at his feet. Those who insult over misfortune are the first to fawn on power. The king was assailable, the man was sacred.

Public resentment joined with party-motives to urge the unfortunate monarch to his fall. Unluckily, about this period the discovery of the cabinet of steel redoubled the rancor of the people, and the despondency of the King's defenders. After the 10th of August several papers had been found in the bureaus of the Civil list, which had but too clearly proved the secret understanding kept up by Louis XVI. with the disaffected priests, the Emigrants, and Europe. In a report drawn up under the Legislative Assembly, he had been accused of a design to betray the state and overturn the revolution. He was there reproached with having written on the 16th of April, 1791, to the Bishop of Clermont, saying, that "if he ever recovered his power, he would reestablish the ancient government and the clergy in all their former privileges;" with having more recently declared war only with a view to hasten the approach of his deliverers; with having been in habits of correspondence with men who wrote to him in this manner:—"The war will compel all the powers to unite against the factious wretches who at present tyrannize over France, in order that their chastisement may serve hereafter as a

8*

warning to all those who may be tempted to trouble the repose of empires ; you may reckon on the assistance of 150,000 Prussians and Austrians, and on an army of 20,000 Emigrants :"—with having been in accord with his brothers, whose interference he disclaimed in his public declarations ; in fine, with never having ceased to use every means for the overthrow of the Constitution.    Additional proofs were now brought forward in support of these allegations.    There was at the Thuilleries, concealed behind a wainscote pannel, a hole cut in the wall, and closed with a sliding-door of iron.    This secret recess was pointed out to Roland, when minister ; and here were found the documents of all the plots and intrigues of the Court against the Revolution, the cabals with the popular leaders to increase the constitutional power of the King, with the aristocracy to bring back the ancient *régime*, the manœuvres of Talon, the arrangements with Mirabeau, the propositions of Beaulieu, which had been accepted, to march the army to Paris, and dissolve the Assembly by main force.    These proofs of treachery and double-dealing enraged the people more than ever against the King : the bust of Mirabeau was broken in pieces at the Jacobins, and the Convention (as was before observed) had that which was placed in the hall of their sittings veiled.

The discussion relative to the attainder of the King was opened on the 13th of November, and opinions appeared strongly divided on the question.    The Brissotins were (generally speaking) satisfied with the abdication of Louis XVI. which they had in a great measure effected, and objected to all further proceedings against him as illegal and impolitic ; they were absolutely averse to his death.    There was another party, who contended by some wretched sophistry for a judicial proceeding, and wished to have him tried by form of law, though there was neither law to condemn him, nor judges to try him, nor form of sentence to be passed upon him.    The violent Revolutionary party, which began to domineer in the Convention, were equally disinclined to admit the inviolability of the King or the propriety of a legal proceeding against him, but persisted in considering the condemnation of Louis as a question of state, and an act of national justice. They had not only strong prejudice, but also common sense on their side, as far as related to the mode of viewing the subject. "Citizens," exclaimed St. Just, one of the most determined and powerful of their speakers, " I undertake to prove that the opinion of Morrison, which sanctions the inviolability of the person of the King, and that of the Committee, who propose to try him as a simple citizen, are equally false. For myself, I say that the King ought to be judged as an enemy ; that we have not to judge, but to put it out of his power to destroy us ; that being no longer any thing in the compact which binds Frenchmen together, the forms of proceeding must be sought not in the civil law, but in the laws of nature and nations ; and that all the delays and scruples on this occasion are so many offences against the safety and inviolability of the state. The same men, let us not forget, who are about to pronounce sentence on the King, have also to found a Republic. But those who attach so much undue import-ance to the just chastisement of a King, will never found a Re-public. Citizens, if the people of Rome, after six hundred years of virtue and hatred against tyrants, if Great Britain, after the death of Cromwell, witnessed the return of the regal power in spite of all its energy ; what ought not those among us who are good patriots and friends of liberty to fear at seeing the axe tremble in your hands, and a people, from the first hour of its liberation, respect the memory of its chains ?"

The exact contrary conclusion ought to have been drawn. Those who instantly lose sight of the past can have no security for the future. Were the French people all of a sudden to for-get that they had ever had a monarchy, or to make light, by a mere flourish of rhetorical fortitude, of the dreadful alternative to which either the King or people were exposed ? But to have done with reflections, as useless as they are painful.—Robespierre followed on the same side of the question. He had manifested extreme hardihood and extreme pertinacity during the whole of this trying discussion. His cadaverous appetite was not to be diverted from its course, and he saw that he could not do better, in order to impress on the Revolution that stern, relentless, homi-cidal character which he wished, than to begin the banquet of blood by the body of an anointed King. Addressing himself to the Convention, he said, " You are not, and you cannot be in this case other than statesmen. You have not a sentence to pronounce for or against an individual, but a measure of public safety to enact. A dethroned king in a republic is only good for two things; either to trouble the tranquillity of the state and undermine liberty, or to cement both one and the other. Louis was King, the Republic exists; the *famous* question which occupies you is decided by these single words. Louis cannot be tried; he is already tried, condemned, or the Republic is not justified. I demand that the Convention declare Louis XVI. a traitor to the French people, guilty in the eyes of humanity, and condemn him to death on the instant in virtue of the insurrection of the 10th of August."

This reasoning is not very convincing or captivating; but it is, like all Robespierre's declamation, a disjointed tissue of rhapsodical common-places, forced into an abortive union by dogmatical assertion, and where, in the midst of an utter barrenness of thought or illustration, there is an appearance of coming to the point with great directness and simplicity. He was a mere party orator, and in common times and on general subjects, would have produced no effect whatever; but in a period of violent agitation when men's passions were set afloat and driven along in the same furious current, the very destitution of natural powers was an advantage, as it gave exclusive and tyrannic scope to his intensity of purpose, fell in with the overstrained humor of his hearers, who wanted practical results, not logical conclusions, or ingenious digressions, and whose inflamed zeal lent to his unmeaning antithetical dilemmas all the force of self-evident propositions. For instance, what can be more absurd, and at the same time more artful or effectual, than the proposing in the speech just cited to condemn the King "in virtue of the insurrection of the 10th of August," as if the rebellion against a monarch inferred a right to bring him to the block, and as if this insurrection must not only be just and right in itself, but a foundation to build all future violence upon? Yet it was certainly that which gave the Convention the courage, the will, and the power to accomplish the King's death; and it was therefore the strongest argument to which a thorough-paced demagogue could appeal. In like manner (for it is important to know in all circumstances what it is that gives power over the human mind) his celebrated speech in his own defence is dry and prosing, unconnected and unreadable ; but the blind zeal of his partisans, and his own inveteracy of manner, his look, and particularly his hard, unaltered eye, which betraying no misgiving or compunction, overcame and lured others into his toils, converted its very defects into beauties, as if his bosom labored with a weight of conviction which no words could be found adequately to express, and the charges against him were too weak and absurd to admit even of a refutation.

With respect to the part he took against the King, he was right in arguing the point as a question of state, and not of law. If the law did not reach it, some other principle must, if the public safety was concerned ; for neither the law nor the king, which are but instruments, are above the general good, which is the end of all law and sovereignty. He who is placed above the law (should he forfeit the privilege of his station) is necessarily reduced to a state of nature, and placed out of the protection of the law. He is not, indeed, amenable to the law, but he becomes, by that very circumstance, a hostage to the commonwealth, or he might waste and destroy it at his pleasure. As there is no law in that case made and provided, an appeal must be made to common sense and equity, which do not answer in a voice less loud or intelligible, because they speak their oldest and most natural language. That any one should be placed entirely out of the reach of responsibility is a fiction in law, a courtesy of speech not to be understood as applicable to extreme cases. If the person of the King were strictly inviolable, according to the letter of the law and Constitution, then the Convention could have no right to imprison or banish him, as a measure of security ; and yet this was the mildest treatment proposed for him by the Constitutional party. If he were strictly inviolable, he might enter the Convention, and dispatch its members individually without the possibility of resistance. This, it may be said, is an absurd case ; but was it not the same thing if by a sign, a breath, he could encourage an army of 100,000 men to come and do so ? And was no precaution to be taken against this treason which had already been practised, and would still be persisted in as long as he lived ? Would his banishment prevent

his return at the head of his hordes of foreigners and bands of emigrants ?    The effect of this doctrine is to tie the hands of liberty
and to make men and nations passive under the stroke of despotism, like sheep under the knife.    The condemnation of Louis
XVI. stands on the same broad and firm foundation as that of
Charles 1. of England ; and the object of both was, as I imagine,
to remove the most dangerous enemy of the state, and also to set
an example and establish a principle, that if kings presume on being placed above the law to violate their first duties to the people,
there is a *justice above the law*, and that rears itself to an equal
height with thrones.    This view of the subject makes the rulers
cautious, makes the people bold ; or even if it be said that such
an example is of no use, for that kings are incorrigible, yet at any
rate it takes away that servile awe and dread with which the people were wont to shrink from the contest with power and authority, like the warriors in Homer, who were afraid to encounter the
immortal gods in battle, because they were invulnerable and im-
passive to blows and death !    If a common man is detected as a
spy, or in the act of conveying important information or encouragement to the enemy's camp, he is hanged up without judge
or jury ; no man intercedes for him ; no man writes his epitaph ;
it is a thing of course.    But the case is different with a king.    In
the eye of prejudice it may be so, but in the eye of reason it is
aggravated ; for it is the very circumstance of his being a king
that adds to his power and demonstrates the necessity of removing
him.    It was not Louis XVI. that was properly the subject of debate, but the last remains of arbitrary power, of which he was the
representative, that phantom of the past, that rose in irreconcilable
antipathy to the prospect of future freedom, that no voice could
charm, no art could tame ; that, affecting magnanimity and moderation in public, clung in secret to every vestige of power and
prerogative, that shrunk in fear and loathing from an acknowledgment of the people's rights, and scrupled no treachery, no violence, no shameless league that promised a chance of finally an-
nulling and disowning them—it was this phantom of kingly power
that was struck at, that tottered and fell headless with Louis XVI.,
and with it the opinion, the paralyzing prejudice that that power
was sacred, inviolable, and *that* one life of more consequence than

the lives of all other men. In fine, the end and object of this act, "which was not done in a corner," was to let the world see that there was a majesty of the people as well as of kings, which might be too long insulted and trifled with, and that when the one came into collision with the other, the latter must kick the beam. Or be it that *le malheur et la pitié* should never be parted; but is pity only due to the misfortunes of kings, or the sword of justice only to be blunted in favor of those who wield it? For scenic effect, the individual case bears most dressing up; but the death of a king, his power and office apart, is no more than that of a common man; and we should remember, that

> " The poor beetle that we tread upon,
> In corporal sufferance feels a pang as great
> As when a giant dies."

If a son or brother had dethroned Louis, had imprisoned, had beheaded him (a thing that happens every day, except where reason and philosophy temper absolute power,) no one would have heard of it, or after a buzz of idle wonder, it would have been hushed up by the sycophants and jobbers of courts as a family-affair; the actual proprietor might have been ejected, the reversion of despotism would have remained untouched. A regicide is a parricide, but a parricide is not a regicide in the pages of heralds and court-scribes. But when a mighty people, when mankind strike the blow, and abate the nuisance altogether, and take the power into their own hands, so that the change is for the benefit of millions, then an appeal is made to outraged humanity, and tears and groans must never have an end, because at the same expense of life and anguish, a great principle is established, and a nation declared free. This, then, is not the language of humanity, but of hypocrisy and servility; or is fit only for the writers of melo-dramas and elegies.*

---

* Buonaparte has left his opinion as to what ought to have been the conduct of the Constituent Assembly with regard to Louis XVI. after the flight to Varennes.—"Great as this error was" (the Constitution they established) "it was less flagrant, and had less deplorable consequences than that of persisting in re-establishing Louis XVI. on the throne, after the affair of Varennes. What then ought the Assembly to have done? It ought to have sent commissioners extraordinary to Varennes, not to bring the

The behavior of Louis XVI. on his trial was simple, manly, and affecting. He rested his defence chiefly on a positive denial of any knowledge of the letters and documents that were brought as proofs against him. His advocates on this occasion, Malesherbes (who nobly volunteered his services on the refusal of Target), Tronchet, and Désèze, did themselves great and lasting honor by their eloquence, intrepidity, and disinterested zeal. The Convention pronounced his condemnation by a majority of only 26 voices, out of about 700. The smallness of this majority was made a plea to set aside the sentence. "Decrees are passed by a simple majority," said a member of the Mountain. "True," it was replied, "but decrees may be recalled, whereas the life of a man cannot be recalled." Some were for relieving themselves from the responsibility by an appeal to the nation, but this, it was thought, would betray a distrust of the cause, and might also breed a civil war. The sitting of the Convention which concluded the trial lasted seventy-two hours. It might naturally be

King back to Paris, but to clear the way for him, and to conduct him safely beyond the frontiers; to have decreed, by virtue of the Constitution, that he had abdicated; proclaimed Louis XVII. King; created a regency, confided the care of the Dauphin during his minority to a Princess of the house of Condé, and composed the Council of Regency and the ministry of the principal members of the Constituent Assembly. A government so conformable to principle, and so national, would have found means to remedy the disadvantages of the Constitution; the force of events would soon have led to the adoption of the necessary modifications. It is probable that France would have triumphed over all her enemies, foreign and domestic, and would have experienced neither anarchy nor revolutionary government. By the time of the King's majority the Revolution would have been so well rooted, that it might have defied every attack. To act otherwise, was intrusting the steering of the vessel, during the most violent storm, to a pilot no longer capable of conducting her; it was calling the crew to insurrection and revolt, in the name of the public safety; it was invoking anarchy."—*Memoirs*, vol. iii. p. 3.

"'Tis better as it is."—We shall have occasion to see hereafter what was his opinion on the subject of the King's death. In all these questions Buonaparte was influenced by political calculations and available circumstances, of which he, perhaps, would have made something, but which, ordinarily speaking, would have come to nothing. Men in general require to be governed by abstract principles or strong passions; and both lead to very downright conclusions.

supposed that silence, restraint, a sort of religious awe would have pervaded the scene ; on the contrary, every thing bore the marks of gaiety, dissipation, and the most grotesque confusion. The farther end of the hall was converted into boxes, where ladies, in a studied dishabille, swallowed ices, oranges, liqueurs, and received the salutations of the members, who went and came as on ordinary occasions.    Here the door-keepers on the Mountain side opened and shut the boxes reserved for the mistresses of the Duke of *Orleans-Egalité ;* and here, though every sign of approbation or disapprobation was strictly forbidden, you heard the long and indignant " *Ha, ha's !*" of the Mother-Duchess, the patroness of the bands of female Jacobins, whenever her ears were not loudly greeted with the welcome sounds of death.

The upper gallery, reserved for the people, was during the whole trial constantly full of strangers and spectators of every description, drinking wine and brandy as in a tavern.  Bets were made as to the issue of the trial in all the neighboring coffee-houses.  *Ennui,* impatience, disgust sat on almost every countenance.  Each member seemed to ask, whether his turn came next ?  A sick deputy, who was called, came forward wrapped up in his night-cap and night-gown, and the Assembly, when they beheld this sort of phantom, laughed.  The figures passing and repassing, and rendered more ghastly by the pallid lights, and that in a slow and sepulchral voice only pronounced the word *Death ;* the Duke of Orleans hooted, almost spit upon, when he voted for the condemnation of his relative ; others calculating if they should have time to go to dinner before they gave their verdict, while the women were pricking cards with pins in order to count the votes ; some of the deputies fallen asleep, and only waked up to give their sentence ; Manuel, the secretary, trying to falsify a few votes in favor of the unfortunate King, and in danger of being murdered for his pains in the passages ; all this had the appearance rather of a hideous dream than of the reality.  When Malesherbes went to carry the tidings to the King, he found him with his head reclined on the table, in a musing posture ; and he observed to him at his entering, " I have been for these two hours trying to recollect what I have ever done to incur the ill-will of my subjects."  The very en

deavor showed goodness of heart and a certain simplicity of character ; but it would be long before one taught from his childhood
to believe that he could do no wrong, would find just ground of
offence in his behavior to his people.   The execution of the sentence was fixed for the 21st of January, 1793.   Louis mounted the
fatal scaffold with firmness ; after administering the last sacrament,
his confessor addressed him, " Son of St. Louis ! ascend into heaven !"   He however manifested some repugnance to submit to
his fate, and would have addressed the spectators, staggering to
one side of the platform for that purpose, when the drums beat,
and he was suddenly seized by the executioners and underwent
the sentence of his judges.   It is said that the indecent haste and
eagerness of these men to complete their task arose from orders
having been issued to the soldiers, in case of any attempt at a rescue, to fire at the scaffold, and that they were afraid of being
themselves dispatched if any alarm were given, or there were
any symptoms of commotion among the crowd.   One person
tasted the blood, with a brutal exclamation, that it was " shock-
ingly bitter ;" the hair and pieces of the dress were sold by the
attendants.   No strong emotion was evinced at the moment ; the
place was like a fair ; but a few days after, Paris, and those who
had voted for the death of the monarch, began to feel serious and
uneasy at what they had done.   Louis XVI. had occupied his time
while in prison, where his confinement was strict, chiefly in con-
soling his wife and sister, and in instructing his son.   He discovered neither impatience, regret, nor resentment.   The truth is,
that great and trying situations raise the mind above itself, and
take out the sting of personal suffering, by the importance of the
reflections and consequences they suggest.   He read much, and
often reverted to the English history, where he found many examples of fallen monarchs, and one among them, condemned like
himself by the people.   He was attended during the whole time,
and in his last moments, by his old servant, Clery, who never left
him.   The names of those who are faithful in misfortune are sacred in the page of history !   The Queen followed her husband
to the block, after an interval of almost a year.   There were circumstances of a dastardly and cold-blooded barbarity attending
the accusation against her.   But the Revolutionary spirit had

then attained its highest virulence and fury. She expressed her apprehensions of being torn in pieces by the mob on her way to the scaffold, and was gravely assured by one of the *gendarmes* who accompanied her, that "she would reach it without meeting any harm!" It is an affecting incident, that just before she expired she turned round her head to look back at the Thuilleries, and then laid her neck on the block.*

One might have concluded that the death of Louis XVI., which removed one great cause of dissension, and united all Europe in an extended and formidable league against them, would have healed or abated the animosity of the different parties towards each other, instead of which it increased and inflamed it to a pitch of inconceivable fury and madness.

The common object of their distrust and suspicion being gone, they immediately fell upon one another, for their passions were so excited that they required some object to vent themselves upon ; and the greatness of the danger that threatened them, so far from producing candor or forbearance, rendered them more irritable, jealous, and vindictive, drove them upon desperate measures, and when they could not wreak their disappointed malice on the common foe, they turned round on their rivals, as the most obvious

---

* When Santerre took back the King from his trial the first day he kept on his hat the whole way; on which the latter jocularly remarked, "The last time you took me to the Temple, in your hurry you forgot your hat, and now you are determined to make up for the omission." The treatment of the Dauphin is another of those abominations which show the extent of the revolutionary re-action at this period, when, to express their contempt for the old system, men fancied that nothing but *slang* was decent, and that every thing but outrage was affectation. This is the true *low-life* of democracy, which feeling no respect for any thing, can only exalt one side by degrading the other, and can allow no merit in an adversary, lest it should outweigh its own meanness and want of it. On the contrary, we ought to allow the utmost to the opposite claims and pretensions, and then say that ours are still higher. Let a king be all but sacred—yet no individual is of as much consequence as a whole people. That is enough to insist upon if we only stick to that—but if we fight only with nonentities, we shall fall prostrate before the least show of resistance or argument. Servility does not consist in paying respect to the persons of others, but in supposing that this personal respect includes a compromise of every principle of freedom and justice.

resource that presented itself, and accused them of being accomplices in the reverses of the Republic, or at any rate, of causing them by their lukewarmness and indifference. The whirl of the political machine was so violent and irregular, that it was dangerous, nay, fatal to all that came within its reach. The popular party not only enforced the most severe and sanguinary laws against those who were known or suspected to be adverse to the Revolution, but they pursued with the same spirit of intolerance all those who did not approve of their extreme rigor, or who differed with them but a hair's breadth as to any measures or principles to be adopted. They took summary justice of those who laid themselves open to the charge of *Moderantism*, which was a watchword for imprisonment and death; made the most trifling distinctions capital offences; and as their passions became more inflamed and their action more questionable, grew naturally more impatient of the shadow of opposition to them. The ordinary proneness of the French character to be led away by circumstances or the impulse of the moment was heightened into tragic caricature and deformity at the present crisis. Like people out at sea on a raft and reduced to the last extremity, they seemed to lose all discretion, common sense, and humanity. No set of actors on a stage could mouth or rant or stare more furiously—no den of bravos could stab more causelessly for a word or look, than these demure philosophers and enlightened patriots of the eighteenth century. Too much blinded by passion to have any doubt of the success of their cause, they instantly threw the blame of any unexpected failure in the progress of the armies on treachery in the General, which soon involved in its ramifications all those to whom they had any distaste at home. The futility did not lessen the confidence of the charge, for the same strength of prejudice that suggested it without reason, supplied the proofs; and the more incredible and extravagant any proposition, the more readily was it admitted in this morbid state of mind. There is a tendency in the mind to all strong excitement, whether of good or evil; and in truth, evil has this advantage over good, that it is the strongest excitement of the two. It was, therefore, *con amore*, that these persons conjured up phantoms of conspiracy and danger to keep their imaginations in play; they dipped their hands

in blood to persuade themselves that they were in earnest, and to
wipe out effeminate and slothful scruples.  The habit became a
want, and called for the application of a continually increasing
stimulus to produce the customary sense of energy and self-complacency.  This impetuous, headlong impulse not only became
the ruling passion in the breasts of the leaders, but communicated
itself by sympathy to all around.  He who was maddest was
wisest; and he who startled the multitude by the most groundless
alarms or the most offensive proposals, was sure to gain the
greatest number of hearers and converts.  This craving after
excitement.was pampered into a disease, a *mania ;* and no matter
who or what the subject, it was necessary to bring out new plots,
new accusations, new horrors for the public entertainment, like a
succession of new pieces at a theatre.  The Revolution ran wild,
and was contained in its orbit only by the pressure of external
force, which had indeed given it its extraordinary and eccentric
impulse.  There was a suspension of all the common charities,
a concentration of all the ill-humors of the state ; suspicion alone
was virtue; he who mounted the tribune to denounce his neigh-
bor was alone a friend to his country ; he who grasped the assassin's knife was alone safe from it.  Even talents and eloquence,
though on the popular side, incurred an imputation as not sufficiently civic.  Literature was an invidious distinction, a frivolous
digression from the great question ; and those only, who with
Stentorian lungs could bawl out a few vulgar, ferocious watch-
words and signals of party-proscription, that the many could
repeat after them, that implied hatred without a cause, and led
to mischief without an object, were considered as the models of
pure patriotism and republican simplicity.  The superior accomplishments of the Brissotins were as fatal to them as their moderation and humanity.  Pedantry and formality were carried to as
great a height in matters of speculation, as rage and bigotry in
practice.  The plans and theories of constitutions and governments were infinitely varied and uncalled-for ; the *Decade* superseded the week ; Sunday was abolished, and the names of the
days were altered ; a new table of weights and measures was
adopted ; proposals were made for an universal language ; projects of general pillage, of agrarian laws, and for the destruc-

tion of commerce, were promulgated; the Thuilleries were, in the same spirit, ploughed up into a potatoe-garden; the worship of Reason was substituted for that of the Supreme Being; and every thing, as may be supposed in this state of things, under-went a change. It was intended to reverse all the old ideas and establishments, to make every thing an experiment, and to begin society *de novo.* The rage of paradox succeeded to the torpor of prejudice, and philosophy consisted in setting common sense at defiance, and in giving a loose to the idlest suggestions of fancy. Each of these changes, as it occurred, was looked upon as an im-portant revolution; and woe be to him who had hazarded the smallest objection to the most insignificant or absurd among them!

Mr. Burke has made fine havoc of the "Abbé Siéyes's pigeon-holes, crammed full of Constitutions," and laughs at the stress laid upon the figure of the Departments, whether round or square. The obstinacy and insanity of the leaders, and the frivolous pre-texts on which they proceeded to the utmost extremities against each other, have been often appealed to to throw a ridicule and odium on the Revolution itself. And at first sight and to the petu-lance of party-spirit it may seem so. But if we consider farther, the reverse conclusion will hold good; for the very circumstance of the disproportioned importance of these pretexts and the narrow shades of difference to which they were reduced as the grounds of their deadly quarrels, though it exhibits a revolting picture of the heated state of party-feeling and of the evils attendant on a contest for power, shows also that the great principles of the Revolution remained untouched. The different candidates for popularity and heads of factions quarrelled about minor points, because they durst not quarrel about greater ones. Whoever had brought any of these into question, would soon have found the difference to his cost. They might dispute for instance about the form of the Departments, their size or number, but no one pro-posed to re-establish the privileges of the ancient corporations, the revocation of the sale of national domains, the restoration of tithes, of the *corvées* or game-laws, or the exemption of the most opulent part of the community from the payment of taxes. The chief handle which the Jacobins made use of against the Gironde was, that they did not strain some of these great and original principles (such as the hatred of royalty) to the very utmost point of possible tension. They did not however owe their fall (one of the greatest blots and scandals of the time) merely to the wanton insolence of their rivals, but to the defection of Dumouriez and the treachery (as it was called) of General Mack, in which they were absurdly and most unjustly implicated by the fury of the multitude.

And what is this popular fury that is so much talked about, and that commits such strange havoc? Is it a phantom, a thing without a cause? No, it has always a motive equal to the rage it feels and the mischief it does. Nothing but the immediate, irresistible sense of extreme danger or extreme wrong either can or does excite it, or take from it in its paroxysms of impatience and despair all sense of right and wrong, all distinction of friend or foe, so that we may judge even from its extravagance of the depth of its provocation. It is this flame, kindled not of straw or stubble or the breath of a demagogue, but of a thousand burning wrongs, that spreads on all objects a lurid glare, blood-stained, gorgeous, confounding all forms, dazzling the strongest sight. When Marat mounted the tribune with the list of proscribed patriots in his hand, and dictated to the astonished Convention what names to put in, what names to strike out, it was not that poor, distorted scare-crow figure and maniac countenance that inspired awe and silenced opposition; but he was hemmed in, driven on, sustained in the height of all his malevolence, folly, and presumption by 80,000 foreign bayonets, that sharpened his worthless sentences and pointed his frantic gestures. Paris, threatened with destruction, thrilled in his accents; Paris, dressed in her robe of flames, seconded his incendiary zeal: a thousand hearts were beating in his bosom, which writhed like the Sybil's; a thousand daggers were whetted on his stony words. Had he not been backed by strong necessity and strong opinion, he would have been treated as a madman; but when his madness arose out of the sacred cause and impending fate of a whole people, he who denounced the danger was a "seer blest;" he who pointed out a victim was the high-priest of freedom. It was this popular fury, the feeling of the last bewildering extremity with the resolution to meet it, that was the soul of Jacobinism; it was this that having to do

with " that dragon old, that was and is and is to be," spared no
pains, scrupled no means, dealt blow for blow, and answered
threat with threat, that signed an order for an execution or planned the array of a battle ; it was this that inspired the Furies of
the Guillotine, and sat and smiled in the galleries of the Convention with the *tricoteuses* of Robespierre !* It was this that mouthed out blasphemies and rant, and by its very froth and trashiness
proved the sacredness and solidity of its cause, for nothing else
could redeem such baseness. It was this that led to the ruthless
destruction of all old customs, establishments, names, and forms,
the total razure of the old edifice of society that there might be
nothing left of it but a bye-word. It was this that threw a slur
on arts and elegance, and made the *salus populi* the sole law ; for
of what use are arts and elegance in a famine or a shipwreck ?
This gave an air of hardness, crudeness, and barbarity to the Revolution, but armed it in panoply all-proof. The Brissotins were
humane and accomplished, but what would their humanity or accomplishments avail in the camp of the Allies or in a *clique* of
royalists ? There is no adequate measure between the public
good and private regards; and when the former is urged to the
edge of the precipice, and ready to be dashed in pieces, every
thing else must be sacrificed to save it. The Allies might easily
have put an end to the horrors at which their delicacy was so
much shocked, by making peace at any period of the Revolution.
Why then did they not ? It would have been compromising the
royal cause. Why then were the people to be the first to give in ?
If the principles of despotism authorized the prolonging all these
horrors, the principles of freedom might justify the enduring
them to the utmost. Let us hear no more of the cant on this
subject.—

Dumouriez after the death of the King conceived designs of
putting an end to the Revolution and playing a distinguished part
himself on the stage of the world. He had (as we have seen)
gone to Paris, after the retreat of the Prussians, to concert measures for the invasion of the Austrian Netherlands. He returned

* Female knitters, who passed their mornings in the galleries of the
Convention, and applauded with soft murmurs the most sanguinary measures and speeches.

to the army on the 20th of October, 1792, and commenced an at
tack on the enemy on the 28th. At the head of the army of Belgium, 40,000 strong, he marched from Valenciennes on Mons,
supported on his right by the army of the Ardennes, amounting
to 16,000 men under General Valence, who directed his route
from Givet to Namur, and on his left by the army of the North,
18,000 strong, under general Labourdonnaie, who advanced from
Lille on Tournay. The plan which a year before had failed for
want of sufficient experience now succeeded. The Austrian
army, posted in front of Mons, waited to give battle in its entrenchments. Dumouriez completely defeated them ; and the
victory of Jemappes opened the Netherlands to the Republic, and
recommenced once more the ascendancy of the French arms in
Europe. Having beaten the enemy on the 6th of November,
Dumouriez entered Mons on the 7th, Brussels on the 14th, and
Liege on the 28th. Valence took Namur, Labourdonnaie made
himself master of Antwerp ; and by the middle of December the
occupation of the Low Countries was entirely achieved. The
French army, masters of the Meuse and of the Scheldt, went into
winter-quarters, after having driven the Austrians behind the
Roër.—From this moment hostilities commenced between Dumouriez and the Jacobins. The latter, by a decree of the 15th of
December, organized the conquered country into a republic, established clubs on the model of the parent society, made requisitions, rendered their yoke more insupportable than that of the
Austrians, and defeated all Dumouriez's projects of independence
for the Netherlands, or of ambition for himself. He went to Paris
to complain, and to try to save Louis XVI., but returned to the
army without having obtained either of his objects, dissatisfied and
determined to make any new victories serve to effect a change of
politics.

The frontiers of France were this time about to be attacked by
nearly all the powers of Europe. England joined the coalition
against France, the last and most formidable of its enemies. On
learning the news of the death of Louis XVI. our cabinet sent back
the French ambassador Chauvelin, and drew Holland into the
quarrel with it, under pretence of the opening of the Scheldt by
order of the French government. This pretence could deceive

no one, and was like the stratagem of those foolish birds that
bury their heads in the sand, and think nobody can see them.
Our statesmen of this period, Mr. Pitt and others, were so wrapped
up in words and rhetorical common-places, that they fancied
them an impenetrable covering.   Continental politicians, who are
jealous of the maritime preponderance of England, and suppose
us to be a mere money-getting nation, have assigned commercial
aggrandizement as the motive of the war.   This is an utter mistake.   Our conduct at the peace showed it ; we gave up all that
we might have claimed as a trading country.   Our object from
first to last was the disinterested defence of the legitimate government, which is so much the more remarkable as our own was not
legitimate ; or, as Mr. Wyndham exclaimed emphatically at the
time, our motto was, " Perish commerce, live the Constitution !"
We somehow chose to fancy the fate of our own free government
intimately interwoven with that of the old despotic government of
France.   If the consequence had been the entire ruin of our commerce and the loss of our possessions in both the Indies, we
should have gone to war nevertheless.   It was not our merchants,
but the court and clergy who gave the tone at this period.   The
people were strongly divided, or upon the whole against it.
Spain had lately undergone a change of ministry ; the famous
Godoy, duke of Alcudia, and since Prince of Peace, having been
placed at the head of affairs, through the influence of Great Britain
and the Emigrants.   This power broke with France, after inter-
ceding in vain for Louis XVI. and offering its neutrality as the
price of the life of the King.   Naples followed the example of
the Pope, who had entered into the same league.   Switzerland,
Sweden, Denmark, and Turkey remained neuter.   Russia was
at this time occupied with the second partition of Poland, in preventing which the champions of social order and legitimate government did not feel themselves concerned.   All their thoughts
were directed against France.

The Republic had its frontiers threatened by the most warlike
troops in Europe.   It would shortly have to contend with 45,000
Austro-Sardinians on the Alps ; 50,000 Spaniards in the passes
of the Pyrenees ; 70,000 Austrians and Imperialists, reinforced
by 38,000 English and Dutch, on the Lower Rhine and in the

Netherlands; 33,400 Austrians between the Meuse and the Moselle, and 112,600 Prussians, Austrians, and Imperialists on the Middle and Upper Rhine. To make head against so many enemies, the Convention decreed a levy of 300,000 men. This measure of external defence was accompanied by one of extreme rigor for the internal security. At the moment that the new-raised battalions quitted Paris, and presented themselves to the Convention for that purpose, the Mountain called for the establishment of a tribunal-extraordinary to support the Revolution within, while the troops were going to defend it on the frontier. The tribunal, composed of nine members, was to have the power of life and death without jury and without appeal. The Gironde, by opposing this arbitrary measure, only lessened their popularity and brought their patriotism into question ; for they seemed to favor the secret enemies of the Republic by objecting to a tribunal destined to punish them, as if such a tribunal must necessarily be impartial and infallible in its decisions. All they could obtain was the introduction of juries and the exclusion of the most violent of the proposed members, while they themselves had any influence, though this did not last long.

The principal efforts of the Coalition were directed against the eastern frontier of France from the North Sea to Huninguen. The Prince of Cobourg, at the head of the Austrians, was to attack the French on the Roër and the Maese, and penetrate into the Netherlands ; while the Prussians marched against Custine, took Mayence, and followed up the plan of invasion of the preceding year. Dumouriez, more occupied with his own vain projects than with the perils of the country, threw himself on the left of these operations, and entered Holland at the head of 20,000 men. He was to be joined at Nimeguen by 25,000 men under Miranda. He took Breda and Gertruydenberg ; but as he was preparing to attack the other fortresses, and dreaming of making himself master of Holland and marching to Paris at the head of his victorious troops to put an end to the Revolutionary Government, the army of the right suffered the most alarming reverses, the Austrians having forced Miranda to raise the siege of Mæstricht, crossed the Meuse, and put the French army near Liege completely to the rout. Dumouriez received an order from the

Executive Council, which he found himself obliged reluctantly to obey, to quit Holland instantly and put himself at the head of the Belgic troops.

At the news of these disasters, the Jacobins became outrageous. With their headstrong perversity, which would listen to no remonstrance, they incontinently attributed them to an understanding between the generals and the Brissotins. They agreed to fall upon the latter in a body in the Convention on the night of the 10th of March, 1793. The tocsin was sounded, the barriers closed, but several circumstances prevented the execution of the plot: the Brissotins, apprised of the schemes, kept out of the way, the rain fell in torrents, and the minister of war, Beurnonville, had a skirmish with a band of the insurgents, and dispersed them at the head of a battalion of Breton volunteers. Vergniaud the next day denounced the conspiracy and demanded an investigation. In his strong and glowing language, he said, " We march from crimes to amnesties, and from amnesties to crimes. A large number of citizens have persuaded themselves to consider the invitations of robbers as the ebullitions of generous souls, and robbery itself as a means of public safety. We have witnessed the developement of that strange system of liberty, according to which they say to you, ' You are free, but think as we do, or we denounce you to the vengeance of the people ; you are free, but bow the neck before the idol to which we offer incense, or we denounce you to the vengeance of the people ; you are free, but join with us in persecuting the men whose probity and talents we dread, or we denounce you to the vengeance of the people !' Citizens, it is to be feared that the Revolution, like Saturn, will successively devour its children, and in the end engender despotism with the evils that attend it !" These striking words produced a transient impression on the Convention, but the measures of inquiry proposed by Vergniaud came to nothing.

The Jacobins were disappointed at the ill-success of their first attempt upon their adversaries ; however, the insurrection which soon after broke out in La Vendée gave them new courage. The war of La Vendée was one of those events which were nearly inevitable in the Revolution. This country, thrown as it were on one side of France, having scarcely any intercourse with the capital, not being a thoroughfare to other places, without roads, without large towns, consisting of villages and hamlets, remote, poor, and ignorant, remained almost in its ancient feudal state. There was no middle or independent class, neither books nor commerce; and the peasantry, receiving all their notions from the priests, were attached like vassals to the soil and to its lordly proprietors, as in the early times. The Revolution was to them an event alike unexpected and unaccountable. The priests and nobles, finding themselves strong in these provinces, had not emigrated. This was, therefore, the true centre or rallying-point of the counter-revolution, for here the doctrines and principles of the ancient *régime* were to be found in their original integrity. It is true, the exactions and vexations of the old system were here kept up with greater severity than almost anywhere; but their being ground down by them did not make the inhabitants less prone to the earth, nor less desirous to drag others, if they could, into the same situation. Probably, too, the extreme servitude of the peasants was compensated for by some of the correspondent advantages, the patronage and hospitality of the chivalrous times and manners; at least, all the sentiments and prejudices of that age remained in full force.* There was to have been a general rising in 1792 under the Count de la Rouairie, which failed in consequence of his having been arrested at the time; but on the occasion of raising the levy of 300,000 men, to recruit the Republican armies, the insurrection broke out afresh. The insurgents beat the Gendarmerie at St. Florens, and at first chose for their chiefs the waggoner Cathelineau, Charette, an officer of marines, and the game-keeper Stofflet. Shortly, 900 communes had risen at the sound of the tocsin; and then the noble chieftains Bonchamps, Lescure, La Rochejacquelin, D'Elbée, and Talmont joined the others. The troops of the line and the battalions of the National Guard, who marched against the insurgents, were everywhere defeated and driven back. The Vendeans had become masters of Chatillon, Bressuire, and Vihiers, and formed themselves into three armies of 10,000 or 12,000 men each; the first under Bonchamps on the banks of the Loire, the second placed in the centre under D'Elbée, the third was stationed in the Lower Vendée under

* See Memoirs of the Countess La Rochejacquelin.

Charette.  A council of war was appointed to direct their operations, and Cathelineau was chosen generalissimo.  This was from the beginning one of the chief scourges of the Revolution—a wound that was never thoroughly healed, and from which gall and bitterness issued in the greatest profusion.

On the first intelligence of this formidable insurrection, the Convention took measures of greater severity than ever against the priests and emigrants.  All those belonging to the privileged classes were disarmed; and if they took part in any military movement, they were outlawed.  The old emigrants were banished forever, on pain of death if they returned; and their goods confiscated.  On the door of each house the name of every inhabitant was to be inscribed; and the Revolutionary Tribunal, which had been adjourned, commenced its dreadful functions.  Just at the same time, and blow upon blow, came the account of fresh military disasters.

Dumouriez, on rejoining the army of the Netherlands, tried to make head against the Austrian general, the Prince of Cobourg.  He found his men disheartened and in want of every thing; and wrote a threatening letter to the Convention, accusing the Jacobins, who denounced him in return.  After this, having brought his army into some order and engaged in a few skirmishes, he risked a general battle at Nerwinde and lost it.  The Netherlands were evacuated; and Dumouriez, placed between two fires, beaten by the Austrians and assailed by the Jacobins, had recourse to an expedient too common at this time,—to save the wreck of his fortune and not be entirely baffled in his schemes of personal ambition, he sold his country.  He had conferences with Colonel Mack, and agreed with the Austrians to deliver them up several strong places on the frontier as pledges, while he marched to Paris to restore the monarchy.  It is supposed that he wished to place the young Duke of Chartres on the throne.  It is not likely that the Allies would have cared one rush what he intended, when he had once put the liberties of France into their power.  The Jacobins, ever on the alert, and acquainted with his intrigues, sent three of their members, Proly, Percira, and Dubuisson, to sound him; to whom he made no secret of his motives or his designs.  It appeared upon coming to an explanation that he had a strong dislike to the Jacobins and as strong a predilection for a king, which the French people must have at any rate—of their own choice if they would ; if not, he would force one upon them. In talking thus big, however, he was reckoning without his host. To effect his blustering pretensions, he must first bring over the army to his views, and deliver Lille, Condé, and Valenciennes into the enemy's hands. In both these preliminary steps he failed. No sooner was the Convention informed of his designs than they ordered him to their bar ; he refused to obey. They then sent four representatives, Camus, Quinette, Lamarque, Bancal, and the minister of war Beurnonville, to arrest him in the midst of his army. On their reading him the decree of the Convention, and threatening to suspend him from his functions if he longer delayed to accompany them, he cried out, " This is too much ;" and delivered up the Commissioners as hostages to an Austrian guard in attendance. By this act of revolt he had committed himself beyond retreat. He made one more attempt upon Condé, but it failed like the first ; and the army, who would not be instrumental to his treachery, abandoned him with reluctance to his fate. Dumouriez had but one choice left, he went over to the Austrian camp with the Duke of Chartres, Colonel Thouvenot, and two squadrons of Berchiny : the rest of his army returned to the camp of Famars, to join the troops commanded by Dampierre. Not to speak of higher motives, the improvidence and presumption of Dumouriez were extraordinary, and are difficult to be accounted for but on the principle that from the rapid and unforeseen succession of events, no one looked to consequences ; the present object was as much as they could attend to, and in the excessive excitement and agitation of the moment, men were disposed to attribute the strong impulse they received from without to their own energy and self-importance, and to imagine they could direct the course of the torrent as they pleased, instead of being merely the sport and victims of external circumstances.— The Convention, on hearing of the arrest of the Commissioners, lost no time in declaring Dumouriez a traitor to his country, authorized every citizen to dispatch him, set a price upon his head, decreed the famous Committee of Public Safety, and banished the Duke of Orleans and all the Bourbons from the Republic.

Though the Brissotins condemned Dumouriez as much as the Mountain, yet they were accused of being secretly his accomplices, and from his defection may be dated their fall. In fact, the public mind, both by multiplied dangers and repeated treachery, was worked up to a pitch little short of frenzy: the Jacobins and the majority of the Convention wished and found it necessary to give to this feeling the extremest impulse of which it was capable both by words and actions: the Gironde not only did not go the same lengths, but blamed and strove to throw a damp on those who did; they therefore became odious to their antagonists as courting a fair and spotless popularity while they did all the disagreeable but (as they conceived) indispensable work of the Revolution, and they were determined to get rid of them, cost what it would. Nor did they rest till they had effected this object, partly urged on by jealousy of their rivals, partly by a strong sense of the urgency of the moment, and partly by an indifference to or rather a complacency in the dreadful means, by which their triumph (and that of the Republic) was to be secured.

Several furious and indecent altercations took place time after time. Threats and recriminations passed. Marat and Hebert, the most profligate and inflammatory writers on the side of the Mountain, were denounced by the other party; imprisoned, and released in triumph by the mob. Isnard, one of the principal Brissotins, was displaced, and Herault Sechelles appointed President of the Convention in his stead. Insurrection followed insurrection; the armed force was called out not to quell them, but to join them. A sacrifice was wanted for the altars of fear and vengeance, nor was the public impatience to be appeased without it; and after a violent conflict and tumultuary sitting, during which the members of the Gironde evinced the greatest intrepidity and firmness, while Henriot, the commander of the National Guard, pointed his cannon against the Convention, Marat mounted the tribune, and dictated to the Assembly a list of the obnoxious members, striking out and inserting what names he pleased at his own option. He struck out the names of Dussaulx, Lanthenas, and Ducos, and inserted that of Valazé. The list of illustrious patriots who were thus proscribed, and whose names will be forever an honor and a disgrace to their country, stands thus: Gensonné, Guadet, Brissot, Gorsas, Petion, Vergniaud, Salles, Barba-roux, Chambon, Buzot, Birotheau, Lidon, Rabaud, La Source, Lanjuinais, Grangeneuve, Lehardy, Lesage, Louvet, Valaze, the minister for foreign affairs Le Brun, the minister of finance Claviere, and the members of the Committee of Twelve, Kervelegan, Gardien, Rabaud-St. Etienne, Boileau, Bertrand, Vigée, Molliveau, Henri La Riviere, Gomaire, and Bergoing. This happened on the 2d of June; and from this time the Convention was dictated to by the Committees, the Clubs, or by sudden and frequent insurrections of the people. Thus fell the Gironde, the true representatives of liberty; men of enlightened minds, of patriotic sentiments, and mild and moderate principles, but who necessarily gave place to those men of violence and blood, who, rising out of the perilous and unnatural situation in which the Republic was placed, were perhaps alone fitted, by their furious fanaticism and disregard of all ordinary feelings, to carry the Revolution triumphant through its difficulties, by opposing remorseless hatred to the cold-blooded and persevering efforts of tyranny without, and cruelty and the thirst of vengeance to treachery and malice within. Virtue was not strong enough for this fiery ordeal, and it was necessary to oppose the vices of anarchy to the vices of despotism.

Some of the Girondins, with their usual indecision and want of concert, remained after the 2d of June to take their trial and answer the charges against them, such as Vergniaud, Gensonné, Ducos, Fonfredé, &c.; the others fled, as Petion, Barbaroux, Gaudet, Louvet, Buzot, Lanjuinais, and so on. The last were the most obnoxious, and concluded themselves in the most imminent danger. They retired to Evreux, in the Department of Eure, where Buzot had great influence, and from thence to Caen in Calvados. This town became the centre of an insurrection against the Convention under General Wimpfen, which Brittany soon after joined. It was from hence that Charlotte Corday set out for Paris, for the purpose of taking away the life of Marat, which she carried into effect. On her trial she answered her judges with great calmness and frankness that her object (which she had long meditated) was to rid her country of a tyrant; and she suffered with unmoved constancy and a beautiful modesty of

9*

character, being less afraid of death than insult. Her appearance and behavior so captivated a young man of the name of Adam Lux, of Mayence, that he loudly demanded to share her fate, and was executed with her. The blow she had aimed, though mortal, did not, however, produce the immediate result she intended. Marat after his assassination became an object of greater enthusiasm than ever to the multitude; his name was invoked in all public meetings, his bust was placed in all the popular societies, and the Convention was constrained to award him the honors of the Pantheon.

Nearly at the same time, Lyons, Marseilles, and Bordeaux took up arms against the Convention, and a great many of the southern Departments favored the revolt. The Royalists seized the opportunity to turn the spirit of disaffection to their own advantage. Lyons had always had a bias towards the ancient *régime* from its extensive and lucrative manufactures of silk and embroidery, which rendered it dependent on the higher classes. As long ago as the year 1790, and while the emigrant princes were at the court of Turin, it had attempted a rising, but without effect. After the 10th of August, 1792, Chalier, an Italian mountebank and a pretended imitator of Marat, was sent there. From his cruelty and insolence, he soon came to blows with the inhabitants; his party was vanquished, and he himself taken prisoner and executed. While the Convention was calling the people to an account for this outrage, the insurrection of Calvados broke out; Lyons on this openly raised the standard of revolt, levied an army of 20,000 men, and gave the command of its forces to the royalist general Precy, and to the Marquis de Virieux, at the same time concerting hostile measures with the King of Sardinia.

At Marseilles the news of the 31st of May and 2d of June had stirred up the partisans of the Gironde. Rebecqui, their deputy, who was one of them, had proceeded thither in all haste; but on finding the turn which things were likely to take in the hands of the Royalists, he threw himself in despair into the harbor of Marseilles. Toulon, Nismes, Montanban, and the principal cities of the south followed the same example. Bourdeaux, Nantes, Brest, and L'Orient, were all favorably inclined to the cause of the proscribed members, but were held in check by the Jacobin party, and by the necessity of resisting the Royalists of the West. The latter, after their first successes, had taken possession of Bressuire, Argenton, and Thouars. On the 6th of June the Vendean army, composed of 40,000 men under Cathelineau, Lescure, Stofflet, and La Rochejacquelin, marched against Saumer and took it by storm. Cathelineau, having left a garrison in this place, proceeded to and took Angers, passed the Loire, and under pretence of marching upon Tours and Mans, turned suddenly towards Nantes, which he attacked on the right bank, while Charette was to attack it on the left. Every thing seemed conspiring to overwhelm the Convention with destruction. Menaced with civil war in the South and in the West, its armies were beaten in the North and in the Pyrenees. The wreck of the army of Dumouriez, which had united at the camp of Famars under the command of Dampierre, had been obliged to retire, after sustaining a defeat, before the cannon of Bouchain : Dampierre himself was killed. Custine had been called from the army of the Moselle to that of the North, without doing any good. Valenciennes, Condé were taken ; the army, chased from position to position, retired behind the Scarpe in front of Arras. Mayence, pressed by famine and the enemy, was forced to capitulate. The affairs of the Republic could not be in a worse situation.

The first thing the Convention did in these circumstances was to adopt the new Constitution, and offer it to the acceptance of the primary assemblies. This Constitution, which had been drawn up chiefly by Herault de Sechelles, corresponded with the notions of the time ; it was one of pure democracy. It annulled the qualifications which had been required by the first Constitution (of 1789) to enable individuals to vote ; it allowed of no intermediate body of electors, and made every citizen eligible to the highest offices in the state. It had so far the advantage, that it acted up to the theory upon which its authors set out: what evils might have resulted from it in practice does not appear, for it was suspended as soon as approved of, and the Revolutionary government established in greater rigor than ever. In the meanwhile, the Convention were every day more and more aware of the dangers of their situation. The deputies of the forty-four thousand municipalities came to accept the Constitution. Being admitted to the bar of the Convention, after giving in their approbation, they demanded a law authorizing the arrest of all suspected persons and the levy in mass of the people. Danton seconded this recommendation in his abrupt, emphatic manner, and proposed to enforce the requisition of 400,000 men. " It is," he said, " by discharges of artillery that we must announce the Constitution to our enemies. The time is come to take a last and solemn oath, that we will all devote ourselves to death or annihilate the tyrants!" This oath was instantly taken by all the deputies and citizens in the hall at the time. A few days after, Barrière, in the name of the Committee of Public Safety, which was become the chief organ of the Convention and of the Revolution, came to propose measures of a still more comprehensive nature. " Liberty," said he, " is become the creditor of all the citizens ; some owe it their industry, others their wealth ; these their counsels, those their arms ; all owe it their blood. Thus then all the French people, both sexes, all ages are called upon by their country to defend freedom. All the faculties moral or physical, all resources political or commercial belong to her ; all the metals, all the elements are tributary to her. Let every one occupy his post in the national and warlike movement which is about to take place. The young will fight, the married men will forge arms, transport the baggage and artillery, and bring in supplies of provisions ; the women will employ themselves in making clothes for the soldiers, will construct tents, and will act as sick nurses in the asylums for the wounded ; the children will make old linen into lint ; and the aged, resuming the office which they held among the ancients, will cause themselves to be borne into the public places, will there inflame the ardor of the young warriors, will teach the hatred of kings and the unity of the Republic. The national buildings will be converted into barracks, the public places into workshops, the floors of cellars will serve to prepare saltpetre ; all saddle-horses will be required for the cavalry, all carriage-horses for the artillery ; the guns used for shooting, and pikes will suffice for the service of the interior. The Republic is for the present a vast city besieged, France must become one immense camp." The last sentence pretty clearly explains the whole question of the situation of the country, both at the time and during the entire period of the Revolution. This speech of Barrière is not an unfavorable specimen of the eloquence of the period. What it wants in force, it probably made up by volubility of utterance; or in richness of illustration by vehemence of gesticulation. Like all eloquence that trusts much to physical animation or the excitement of the moment, it suffers, and its spirit evaporates by being transferred to paper and with the lapse of time. The French speakers are rather actors than orators, and in both points of view are extravagant and mannered. The most lasting and universal eloquence is that which is the least an ebullition of animal spirits or of popular common-places, which abounds the least in action and clap-traps, and consequently has not its full effect at the time. There is no style that unites all advantages.

The measures proposed by Barrière were decreed on the spot. All Frenchmen from the age of eighteen to twenty-five were to take arms; the troops were recruited with requisitions of men, were maintained by requisitions for food. The Republic in a short time possessed fourteen armies, and 1,200,000 soldiers. France, which had been transformed into a camp and a workshop for good citizens, had become a prison for the disaffected. Before they marched against declared enemies, they wished to make sure of secret ones, and the famous law *Of the Suspected* was passed. Strangers and the partisans of the ancient order of things, of all degrees and classes, moderate republicans and constitutional royalists, were put under arrest to be kept in custody till a peace. An army of 6000 soldiers and 1000 cannoneers was ordered to watch the interior. Each indigent citizen received an allowance of forty sous a day to attend to the duties of his post, and certificates of *civism* were given to those who were fixed upon to co-operate in the great work of deliverance. Thus precautions were taken to meet the difficulties which rose up on all sides, and the results answered to the energy and zeal called into action.

The insurrection of Calvados was suppressed the first. The favorers of the Girondins, who were at the head of it, were not hearty in the cause, and gave in their submission at Caen, where the Commissioners of the Convention did not soil their victory

with blood.   On the other side of France, General Cartaux advanced against the insurgents of the South, beat them twice,
entered Marseilles, and Provence submitted as Calvados had done.
Toulon still held out, the royalists there having called in the aid
of the English fleet under Admiral Hood, who with 8000 Spaniards took possession of the harbor and forts, and proclaimed the
Dauphin as Louis XVII.   The Revolutionary Commissioners
made their triumphal entry into the revolted capitals ; Robert
Lindet was sent to Caen, Tallien to Bourdeaux, Barras and
Freron to Marseilles.   Lyons was besieged by Kellermann, who
commanded the Army of the Alps.   It was surrounded on all sides,
and made a vigorous and obstinate defence ; but pressed by hunger, and without hope of succor from the Piedmontese troops
which had been repulsed by the French general, it surrendered.
Some months after, Toulon, the only formidable point of resistance left in the South, was obliged to yield without a blow to the
skilful combinations of Buonaparte as commandant of artillery
there, whose distinguished military talents were first shown on
this occasion, of which a more particular account will be given
in the sequel.

The Convention was on all sides victorious.   The Vendeans,
having failed in their attempt upon Nantes, after losing a great
number of men and their General Cathelineau, retreated within
their own territory.   Here they withstood for a time a feeble
and desultory mode of warfare, till the Convention sent General
Lechelle against them ; who, seconded by the garrison of Mayence, 17,000 strong, who had marched out with the honors of
war, but who could not serve against the Coalition by the terms
of their capitulation for a year, defeated the insurgent troops in
four several engagements, and killed three of their generals,
Lescure, Bonchamps, and D'Elbée.   Eighty thousand of them
attempted to emigrate and cross Brittany, but were intercepted,
put to the rout, and slaughtered at Grandville, Mans, and Save-
nay, and scarcely a handful of them escaped to return to their
own country.   These disasters, with the taking of the Isle of
Noirmoutiers and the death of La Rochejacquelin, left the
Republicans masters of the field.   The Committee of Public
Safety, thinking the insurrection suppressed but not extinguished,

resorted to a terrible system of extermination to prevent its breaking out afresh. General Thurreau occupied La Vendée with
sixteen entrenched camps; twelve moveable columns, with the
appropriate title of *Infernal Columns*, scoured the country in all
directions, carrying fire and sword along with them, burnt down
the woods, carried off the cattle, and spread terror and havoc
through the adjoining districts. The spirit of the unfortunate
people was, however, only subdued for a while by these extreme
measures, which served to exasperate rather than heal the original cause of discontent; it rose again and again in spite of defeat, and proved in the end, and long after, triumphant. Perhaps
in all cases, after repelling force by force, clemency is the
soundest policy, and the surest means of disarming prejudice.
It is impossible to provide against future contingencies, except by
absolute destruction, since mere intimidation cannot answer this
purpose beyond the present moment; or when appalling and
excessive, leaves an odium on any cause which by no means
adds to its strength or security. Had the system of conciliation
practiced by Buonaparte been tried in the first instance and after
the first decisive reverses, probably the wounds inflicted on local
attachments and rooted bigotry might not have been so deep as to
be incurable.

The foreign armies had been repulsed in like manner on the
frontier of France. After the taking of Valenciennes and Condé,
and laying siege to Maubeuge and Quesnoy, the Allies directed
their march on Cassel, Hondscoote, and Furnes under the command of the Duke of York. Custine had been replaced by
Houchard, who beat the English at Hondscoote and forced them
to retreat. Houchard was himself succeeded by Jourdan, who
took the command of the army of the North, gained the great
battle of Watignies over the Prince of Cobourg, raised the siege
of Maubeuge, and assumed the offensive along his whole line of
operations. The same success attended the Republicans in other
quarters. What Jourdan had performed with the Army of the
North, Hoche and Pichegru did with the Army of the Moselle,
and Kellermann with the Army of the Alps. The Allies were
everywhere repulsed and kept in check. The new generals
were chosen by the faction of the Mountain; and the new suc-

cesses were attributable to the enterprising and patriotic genius
of Carnot, who directed the triumphant campaigns of 1793 and
1794.

During the continuance of this period, the Committee of Public Safety exercised the most terrible severity within the Republic. It crushed its enemies without, it exterminated them within.
Lyons was made a terrible example of; its name was changed
to that of Ville-Affranchie, its buildings razed to the ground, its
inhabitants dispatched in groups by discharges of grape-shot.
Collot d'Herbois, Fouché, and Couthon were sent to superintend
these revolting executions. Nearly the same scenes were repeated at Marseilles, at Toulon, and Bourdeaux, and even with
aggravated cruelty and an abominable levity at Nantes, Cambray,
and Arras, under Carrier and Joseph Lebon, who seemed to have
worked up their natural ferocity or patriotic rage to the frenzy
of demons. At Nantes ship-loads of victims were sunk in the
river,* and young men and women tied naked together and
drowned in this manner, which was called a *republican marriage.* The inhabitants and municipalities of towns which had
thrown off their allegiance to the Convention were shot promis-
cuously and as it were in sport, as they came out to meet the
Commissioners and to give in their submission. The whole
country seemed one vast conflagration of revolt and vengeance.
The shrieks of death were blended with the yell of the assassin
and the laughter of buffoons. The excesses daily and hourly
committed might be supposed to sharpen the invention and harden
the feelings; or natural ferocity combining with the most brutal
levity, took advantage of the license of the time and of the strong
measures of retribution and precaution which were no doubt
necessary, to carry their sanguinary impulses or wanton caprices
into effect, unquestioned and applauded. It was thus that one of
the Parisian rabble plucked Bailly by the beard when waiting
for the executioner, and said, "You tremble, Bailly!" to which
he answered, "It is with cold, then!" Lavoisier, Chamfort, Barthelemy, Malesherbes, all that was most enlightened, disinterested,
patriotic, fell a sacrifice, as if in scorn and wanton defiance.
Humanity, that had been mocked, outraged, "struck most serpent-

* To the number of several hundreds.

like," seemed to hurl back the taunt and foul injury, and steel itself against remorse, respect, and pity. Never were the finest affections more warmly excited, or pierced with crueller wounds.[*] Whole families were led to the scaffold for no other crime than their relationship ; sisters for shedding tears over the death of their brothers in the Emigrant armies, wives who lamented the fate of their husbands, innocent peasant-girls for dancing with the Prussian soldiers, a woman giving suck, and whose milk spouted in the face of her executioner at the fatal stroke, merely for saying as a group were conducted to slaughter, "Here is much blood shed for a trifling cause !" It would be endless to repeat the instances, some of which were as affecting as others were shocking. Such were the effects ; we have seen the cause, the provocation offered by those who hoped that the blows that Liberty gave herself, and dealt with indiscriminate fury on all round her, would sooner or later ensure their hated triumph.

Among the rest Maria Antoinette was beheaded on the 16th of October, 1793 ; and the Girondins, to the number of twenty-one, on the 31st of the same month ; viz. Brissot, Vergniaud, Gensonné, Fonfredé, Ducos, Valazé, Lasource, Sillery, Gardien, Carra, Duprat, Beauvais, Duchâtel, Mainvielle, Lacaze, Boileau, Lehardy, Antiboul, and Vigée. Sixty-three of their colleagues, who had protested against their arrest, had been imprisoned with them, but did not undergo the same fate. During the trial these illustrious victims showed the greatest courage and calmness. Vergniaud for the last time, but in vain, took the audience captive with his eloquent accents. Valazé, on hearing the sentence, stabbed himself with a poniard, and Lasource said to the judges : "*I die at a time when the people have lost their reason ; you will die on the day that they recover it.*" The condemned patriots walked to the place of execution with all the stoicism characteristic of the period, chaunting the Marseillois Hymn, and applying it to their own situation :

> "Allons, enfans de la patrie,
> Le jour de gloire est arrivé :
> Contre nous de la tyrannie
> Le couteau sanglant est levé," &c.

---

[*] See Appendix, No. 5.

The other chiefs of this party almost all came to a miserable
end.    Salles, Gaudet, Barbaroux were discovered in the caverns
of St. Emilou, near Bourdeaux, and perished on the public
scaffold there.    Pétion and Buzot, after wandering about for some
time, put an end to themselves, and were found dead in a field,
half-devoured by the wolves.    Rabaud-St. Etienne was betrayed
by an intimate friend.    Madame Roland was also condemned,
and suffered with the constancy of a Roman matron.    Her husband, on hearing of her death, quitted his place of concealment,
and killed himself in the middle of the high-road.    Condorcet,
who had been outlawed some time after the 2d of June, was
seized, but escaped punishment by taking poison.    Louvet, Kervelegan, Lanjuinais, Henri La Riviere, Le Sage, La Reveillere-
Lepaux were the only ones who in secure retreats waited for the
end of this furious tempest.

From this time to the death of Robespierre the *reign of terror*
was established without intermission or obstacle.    Not only those
who disapproved of the existing system were persecuted with the
utmost rigor and acrimony, but all those who did not approve of
the utmost severity exercised against the first, on the slightest
suspicion and on the most ridiculous grounds, fell equally a sacrifice (in a continually widening circle) to their ill-timed scruples
and moderation ; party succeeded party, and the most daring and
unprincipled was sure to prevail.    There was one answer to
every objection, *the enemies of the country were to be destroyed at
all events,* and all those who differed with you a hair's breadth as
to the means of saving the Republic, or drew back from the necessity of the wildest and most unwarrantable step that had this
pretext, were of course the enemies of their country, and came
under the proposed penalty.    The original opponents of the Revolution, seeing the pass to which things had come even beyond
their expectations, redoubled their efforts to increase the dismay
and confusion, by affecting the utmost horror at their own handi-
work.—The sun of Liberty was in eclipse, while the crested
hydra of the Coalition glared round the horizon.    The atmosphere
was dark and sultry.    There was a dead pause, a stillness in the
air, except as the silence was broken by a shout like distant thunder or the wild chaunt of patriotic songs.    There was a fear, as

in the time of a plague; a fierceness as before and after a deadly strife. It was a civil war raging in the heart of a great city as in a field of battle, and turning it into a charnel-house. The eye was sleepless, the brain heated. Sights of horror grew familiar to the mind, which had no other choice than that of being either the victim or the executioner. What at first was stern necessity or public duty, became a habit and a sport; and the arm, inured to slaughter, struck at random and spared neither friend nor foe. The soul, harrowed up by the most appalling spectacles, could not do without them, and "nursed the dreadful appetite of death." The habit of going to the place of execution resembled that of visiting the theatre. Legal murder was the order of the day, a holiday sight, till France became one scene of wild disorder, and the Revolution a stage of blood.

The chief actor in this tragic scene, the presiding demon of the storm was Robespierre. He ruled the Committee of Public Safety, who ruled the Convention by an instinct of terror, by the scent of blood. He was urged on in his pitiless career by fear, which he had by natural constitution, and by vanity, which arose from education and circumstances. Austere, simple in manners, incorruptible,* inflexible, he attained to distinction by the strictness of his principles, by the unity of his purposes, and by a certain want of versatility and resources, which confined him to that place in the political machine into which opportunity had forced him, and for which alone he was fitted. Brought up with hopes of making a figure at the bar, and prevented by want of capacity for public speaking, disappointed vanity is said to have become the ruling passion of his life, and the love of power the sole unremitting motive of all his actions. As he could not inspire admiration, he would at least excite fear; and as he could not distinguish himself by a superior display of talents, he would be foremost in the field of action by the unbending and remorseless nature of his will. He had no other passions or pursuits to divert him from this single one; the dryness and rigidity of his understanding made him a dupe and instrument of certain abstract

* "At the time," says Napoleon, "that he was deluging France with blood, if Pitt had offered him two millions of money to betray the Republic, he would have rejected it with disdain."

dogmas; and the regularity of his life and the absence of common vices, lent a color, both in his own eyes and those of others, to his pretensions to political virtue. It is remarkable that he lived in the same house from the time he came from Arras till he was taken to the scaffold—a house in the Rue St. Honoré, belonging to a carpenter of the name of Duplessis, whose daughter he was to have married. Tallien, who knew him well, said of him, that he had more virtue than those who beheaded him; that he meant well, but was a coward. The truth is in one word, he was a natural bigot, that is, a person extremely tenacious of certain feelings and opinions, from an utter inability to conceive of any thing beyond them, or to suppose that others do; and he was ready, like all such persons (monks, inquisitors, sectaries) to sacrifice every thing to the establishing those opinions, and strengthening the influence that enabled him to do so. Instances have been cited of personal pique and malice, but this could not have been the case generally; and the mass of his victims who did not come up to his standard of political orthodoxy must have been consigned to the guillotine, as heretics were handed over to the secular power, without any hatred except to their opinions and want of faith.

From a little before the death of the King to the condemnation of the Girondins, he had been advancing gradually in popularity and power, and had been uniform, indefatigable, inexorable in the pursuit of his objects till after the fall of the principal Brissotins; and then he so far relaxed that he interposed to save the sixty-three remaining deputies, and did so with effect, in this showing more management than fanaticism or cruelty, as if he was bound to remove the leaders who stood in his way as rivals, but was willing to make friends of the rest. After this, he strove to make a clear stage, and to narrow the question of patriotism and public spirit to very circumscribed limits. By extravagant assumptions and the unbounded and unfeeling exercise of power, he had worked himself up to an incredible pitch of arrogance and self-sufficiency. He considered his doctrines as infallible, his will as law; whoever opposed the one or doubted the other was, in his mind, worthy of condign punishment, and forthwith consigned to it as a defaulter to the public good, without reprieve or delay. The least offence against the Republic, the smallest disrespect to its guardians or to the "true patriots," was a crime of the highest magnitude; and not to denounce or pursue this offence with unrelenting severity, or to feel pity for the sufferers, or hesitation as to the justice of their sentence, was equally to betray the interests of their country, and to deserve death. The majesty of the Republic was inviolable, and every slight offered to it was unpardonable. It was a sort of *demonism* in political orthodoxy, by which, under pretence of providing for the extreme safety of the country, all the inhabitants would be swept out of it, and made over to a speedy death, so that they could no longer harbor designs against the state or breathe a murmur against its head. It in fact gave him *carte-blanche* to hunt down and proscribe whom he pleased, on the true and infallible principles of the greatest possible good to the community. In this manner he first got rid of Hebert, Anacharsis Cloots, Chaumette, and the leaders of the Commune, as enemies to the Republic by spreading atheism and indecency. He next got rid of Danton and Camille-Desmoulins, as enemies to the Republic by setting an example of immorality in their lives and moderation in their writings. Danton fell a sacrifice to this deliberate and technical system of proscription, by being too proud to defend himself, too indolent to crush his adversary. Legendre attempted a friendly defence of him, and in the language of the day, "answered for his purity as for his own." But the favorable disposition which this bold declaration drew forth was instantly stifled by a few words from Robespierre. Danton was advised to escape, but showed a reluctance to do so; and even at the last moment, when assured that the Committee were deliberating on his arrest, said, "They dare not!" There are certain terms on which all men desire to live; and he who has prided himself on daring every thing against others is not willing to sink so low in his own estimation as to believe it possible that they should venture to retaliate upon him. A little before this, Danton had an interview with Robespierre, whose manner was cold and dry. He remonstrated against indiscriminate severity, and observed, "It was time to distinguish between the innocent and the guilty!" "And who has told you," replied Robespierre, "that a single innocent person has suffered?" Danton, turning to a friend who accompanied him, made answer, " What say you ? Not a single innocent person has perished !" This speech of Robespierre shows either consummate hypocrisy, or rather that he had arrived at the highest possible pitch of voluntary self-deception, which was determined to allow of no imputation on his past conduct that no check might be put upon it in future. It was only by shutting his eyes, obstinately and on system, that he could hope not to be staggered by the havoc he made around him. Hebert and his crew of atheists* had died miserably. Danton and his friends, Lacroix, Philippeau, Westermann, and Camille-Desmoulins, displayed the greatest intrepidity and spirit both at their trial and death. Camille-Desmoulins, a young and high-spirited enthusiast, could not to the last comprehend his fate, or even believe it : " Behold," he said, as he was led to execution, " the reward of the first apostle of liberty !" Danton amused himself, during his trial, with throwing little paper-pellets at his judges. When the sentence was pronounced, he cried, " I draw Robespierre after me ; Robespierre will follow me ;" and died with the name of his wife on his lips.

Robespierre associated himself most intimately with St. Just and Couthon. The latter was his creature, a man with a mild expression of countenance, and who had lost the use of one side of his body, but in whom feebleness and pain were joined with a remorseless cruelty of disposition. St. Just was not more than five-and-twenty ; with regular and striking features, long dark hair, austere in manners like Robespierre, but more enthusiastic, and the image of a thousand religious or political fanatics, who being of a gloomy temperament and full of visionary aspirations, think that good is always to be worked out of evil, and are ready to sacrifice themselves and the whole world to any scheme they have set their minds upon. He was nicknamed the *Apocalyptic* When the object was to intimidate the Convention, it is said St. Just was charged with the report of the Committee of Public Safety : when it was intended to take them by surprise, Couthon

---

* I should be sorry if there were a single word approaching to *cant* in this work. I do not mean that an atheist as such must perish miserably, but he who, like the persons in question, makes use of an obnoxious opinion to gain notoriety and insult others, is a bully and naturally a coward.

was employed : if there arose any murmur of disapprobation or any hesitation, Robespierre came forward ; and with a word or look, all returned into silence and terror. The union of these men was formidable to others, and in the end proved fatal to their own safety. They separated themselves more and more from the other members of the Committee, who in return became jealous of their exclusive and domineering influence. Besides, the tone of the Triumvirate was too saturnine and morbid for the licentious spirit of the times. Except the delight in blood, there was nothing in common between them and the multitude. They wished to repress impiety and immorality. Robespierre himself aimed not merely at being a dictator in politics, but a stern and inflexible censor of faith and morals. He had done himself considerable harm by procuring toleration for the Catholic religion, and by bringing forward a decree, acknowledging the existence of the Supreme Being. Indeed to read his speeches, one would suppose that he was a perfect pattern of piety and goodness ; a man of purer eyes than to behold iniquity ; and who, in order that it might not exist, required to have the lives of all men laid at his feet to be extinguished at the least alarm to patriotism or virtue. About this time a young girl, named Cecilia Renault, made an attempt on his life ; and being questioned what her business was with him, said she wanted to see what a tyrant was like.* The Clubs, the Convention rang with the most fulsome congratulations on his escape. which was openly attributed to the Good Genius of the Republic and to the interposition of the Supreme Being, in gratitude for having proclaimed his existence ! Such was the madness of the times. No small share of ridicule was thrown on him for his supposed connection with an old woman of the name of Catherine Theot, who had set up for a prophetess, and who had foretold a new Messiah. Several sarcasms were pretty broadly directed against Robespierre in a report made by Vadier on the subject, and the seeds of dissension thus sown soon grew to a head. In the mean time, he delivered a fine discourse on patriotism, humanity, and all the virtues. Barrère also made an eloquent and striking report on the best means of

* A man of the name of Admiral also watched for him with the same purpose, but not finding him, struck Collot d'Herbois.

putting a stop to mendicity; and regular reports were read on
the state of literature and the fine arts, which breathed nothing but refined taste and feeling.  The French are a mercurial
people, and pass with wonderful ease " from grave to gay, from
lively to severe."  Nothing can engross them long or wholly.
The Committee of Public Safety devoted, at the time we speak
of, twenty hours out of the four-and-twenty to business.  They
had to attend the Committee in the morning, the Convention in the
evening, and sat up nearly all night in examining papers and
writing out reports.  How they got through it they knew not—
except that their country's welfare required their services!
They thought themselves heroes, martyrs, and that they were
not only playing a conspicuous part on the stage of the world,
but entitling themselves to the gratitude and admiration of posterity.  They resembled men in a dream.  Shortly after all this,
the Parisians danced in the Gardens of the Thuilleries as if
nothing had happened; the guillotine was laid by as a child's
plaything; and the surviving actors in the scene lurked in
obscure corners, like old family-portraits, out of date and never
thought of!

The day fixed for the celebration of the new religious worship
decreed by the Convention through the whole extent of the Republic now approached.  Robespierre was unanimously chosen
president of the Convention, that he might act as high-priest of
the ceremony.  He appeared on this occasion at the head of the
Assembly, his countenance beaming with confidence and joy,
which was a thing unusual with him.  He walked a certain
number of paces before his colleagues, attired in a splendid dress,
holding flowers and ears of corn in his hand, and the object of
universal attention.  He addressed the people from a platform in
front of the Thuilleries, hung with appropriate designs by the
celebrated David.  All looked forward to something extraordinary
as the result of this imposing attitude and ostentatious display, his
enemies expected an attempt at usurpation, the people in general
a relaxation of the system of severity.  How little this was to
understand the nature of the passions!  The glossy sleekness of
the panther's skin does not imply his tameness, and his fawning
eye dooms its prey while it glitters.  He went on as before.  No

ray of hope appeared even in his harangue to the people, which was as dull as it was dispiriting. "To-day," he cried, "let us give ourselves up to the transports of a pure enjoyment! To-morrow we will combat vice and tyranny anew!" These ideas had taken such strong possession of his mind that he was haunted by them; nor could he relieve them by any others. He was no longer a voluntary agent, but the mere slave of habitual and violent excitement, which he could not do a moment without. Only two days after, Couthon came to the Convention to propose a fresh law which gave the Revolutionary tribunal new and unlimited powers, and subjected to their decision the lives of the members of the Convention itself. This was thought too much. Ruamps said, "If this law passes, we have only to blow out our brains with a pistol;" and moved an adjournment. Robespierre opposed the adjournment, and said that since faction had ceased, the Convention had learned to decide on the spot. The law passed after a few minutes discussion. But the next day, some members seriously alarmed returned to the charge, particularly Merlin and Bourdon de l'Oise, who wished to insert a saving clause for the protection of their own body from the power of the tribunal. At this unexpected opposition Robespierre grew insolent and furious, and Merlin's clause was withdrawn *as injurious to the Committee.* This hideous law, which condemned without a jury, without defence, without evidence, and without a trial all classes and orders of men, lasted about two months, during which time *fournées*, that is, batches of victims came into fashion, and fifty persons on an average were every day sent to the guillotine; but it was the last triumph of Robespierre and his party.

While they had other enemies to contend with, all went on well; but left to themselves, dissensions arose among them, old grievances were ripped up, they were at odds on the subject of religion, Billaud Varennes and others preferring the worship of Reason to the worship of the Supreme Being; and Robespierre, who was insatiable in his demands and drew the lines of proscription closer and closer round him, beginning to indicate victims out of his own party and snuff the blood of his coadjutors, they grew suspicious and alarmed and turned against him. Mortified at finding that they were not ready to put their lives in his hand, he became shy and retired, absented himself from the Committee and the Convention, and only repaired occasionally to the Club of the Jacobins, where ne mourned over the fate of the proscribed patriots, the danger of the Republic, and talked of dying. He had the whine as well as the spring of the tiger; and disappointed of his prey, turned round to lament over himself as an injured and persecuted man. St. Just was with the Army of the North. He wrote to him to return immediately. From the reception of the latter by the Committees, who were cold and suspended their debates when he entered, he perceived there was no time to lose. They concerted measures together, and the next day, July 26th (1794), Robespierre came to the Convention at an early hour, mounted the tribune, and pronounced a long and elaborate discourse in his own defence, and concluding (for he was not to be diverted from his object) with a proposal to purify the Committees and rid the Convention of corruption, that is, to sacrifice all those in either who were not the creatures of his will and did not agree with all his notions of liberty and justice. Not a murmur of disapprobation or applause was heard, but a long silence prevailed after he had ended; and the members looked at each other in fear and uncertainty. At length, Lecointre moved the printing of the discourse. This proposal was the signal for a general commotion. Bourdon de l'Oise opposed the printing of the discourse, which however was carried; but the members of the Committees threatened by Robespierre, seeing the tameness of the Convention, rallied and attacked him one by one; Vadier began, and Cambon, Billaud Varennes, Panis, and others followed, each taking courage from the other. Freron proposed to rescind the law which placed the lives of the Convention at the disposal of the Committees; but it was the members of these Committees that were the greatest enemies of Robespierre, and it was only in concert with them that he could be overthrown. Freron had observed that while this law remained in force, the deputies durst not express their opinions. "He who dares not express his opinion freely for fear of the Committee," said Billaud Varennes, "is not worthy to be a representative of the people." So the motion of Freron was withdrawn, but the vote to print the discourse of Robespierre was also recalled, and it was ordered to be submitted to the examination of the Committees. He went from the Convention to the Jacobins, where he was received with enthusiasm, and where he complained of the conduct of the Convention in sending his discourse to be judged of by his enemies, and talked of being ready, if it were necessary, to drink the cup of Socrates. "I will drink it with you," exclaimed a member of the Club; "the enemies of Robespierre are the enemies of their country.' It was agreed that the Club and the Commune should be ready next day for an attack on the Convention, to which Robespierre was to repair early with his friends.

The Committees, united by their common danger, deliberated the whole night. St. Just appeared among them, and they endeavored to detach him from the Triumvirate, but in vain. "You have grieved my heart," he said a parting from them, "but I go to open it to the Convention." The members of the Convention had come to an understanding during the night, though with difficulty, the Mountain with the Right and with the Plain—all were resolved against Robespierre. The members met early on the 27th of July. Towards eleven o'clock, they collected in the passages of the hall, encouraging one another. Bourdon de l'Oise, a member of the Mountain, approached the moderate Durand Maillane, and pressing his hand, cried "Oh! the brave men, the members of the Right!" Rovere and Tallien did the same, and joined their felicitations to those of Bourdon. At noon, through the door of the hall, they saw St. Just mount the tribune. "Now is the time," said Tallien. Robespierre had placed himself on a seat in front of the tribune, no doubt to intimidate his antagonists by his looks. St. Just began to complain of the behavior of the Convention. He was suddenly interrupted by Tallien who said, "No good citizen can refrain from shedding tears over the unfortunate state of the country; we hear of nothing but misconduct and dangers to be apprehended from the members of the government: I demand that the curtain which conceals these secret enemies be entirely torn asunder!"—"It must, it must," was repeated from all parts of the assembly. Billaud Varennes then took up the question. "Yesterday," said he, "the Jacobin Club was filled with men who vomited out calumnies against the true patriots, and who threatened to cut the throats of the Natiónal Convention: I see one of them on the Mountain."—"Let him be instantly seized," was the general cry, and the guards took him into custody. Billaud continued. He said that the Convention was placed in the most imminent peril, and that it would perish, if it was irresolute. "No, no," replied all the members, "we swear to save the Republic;" and the galleries applauded and cried, "*Long live the National Convention!*" Lebas attempted to justify the Triumvirs, but could not be heard; and Billaud Varennes renewed his attacks on Robespierre, denounced his plans of dictatorship, and named his accomplices. All eyes were turned on the latter; he remained for a long time unmoved, but at last he could contain himself no longer, and rushed to the tribune. Instantly the words, "*Down with the tyrant! down with the tyrant!*" were heard on all sides, and hindered him from speaking. Tallien then said, "I just now demanded that the veil should be torn off; it is so completely. I yesterday saw the sitting of the Jacobins; I trembled for the country; I saw the army of the new Cromwell formed, and I armed myself with a poniard to pierce his bosom, if the National Convention had not the courage to decree his accusation!" He then drew out his poniard, brandished it in the eyes of the Convention,* and demanded the arrest of Henriot, the Commandant of the armed force, which was immediately carried amidst the cries of "*Long live the Republic!*" Billaud also obtained a decree for the arrest of three of Robespierre's most daring accomplices, Dumas, Boulanger, and Dufresne. Vadier reverted to the subject of Catherine Theot, whom he considered as an agent of the Triumvir. "Let us not turn the question from its true object," interrupted Tallien. "I will take care to bring it back to it," said Robespierre.—"Let us attend to the tyrant," replied Tallien; and attacked him anew with greater vigor. Robespierre, who had several times endeavored to speak, who by turns ascended and descended the steps of the tribune, whose voice was always drowned by the cries of "*Down with the tyrant!*" and by the noise of the bell which the president Thuriot shook incessantly, made one last effort to obtain a hearing. "For the last time, I

---

* Was this before or after Mr. Burke drew out his in the English House of Commons?

ask, will you suffer me to speak, president of assassins?" But Thuriot continued to ring the bell as before. Robespierre, then, having in vain turned round to the galleries which remained immoveable, addressed himself to the Right side of the Convention. "Men of pure minds, men of virtue," he exclaimed, "it is to you I appeal; grant me a hearing, which assassins refuse me!" Not a word of encouragement or reply, but a dead silence. Then for the first time disconcerted, he went back to his place, and sunk down on his seat, overcome with fatigue and rage. His mouth foamed, his voice failed. "Wretch," said a member of the Mountain, "the blood of Danton chokes thee!" His arrest was then decreed. His brother desired to incur the same sentence, and Lebas also at his own request was included in it. The members against whom this decree passed were the two Robespierres, Couthon, Lebas, and St. Just. The last, after remaining a long time in the tribune with unchanged countenance, returned to his seat: during this long and agitated scene, he had shown no signs of dismay. The accused were delivered over to the Gendarmes, who led them away amidst general acclamations. Robespierre as he left the hall said, "The Republic is lost, and robbers triumph!" It was half-past five in the afternoon; the sitting was suspended till seven o'clock.

Henriot with Payan and Fleuriot had been waiting at the Hôtel-de-Ville, and sent word to Robespierre to stand firm and not fear any thing. Henriot in the mean time, as he paraded the streets with a pistol in his hand, inciting the citizens to take arms against the Convention, was seized and sent to the Committee of General Surety. The Commune or Municipality of Paris on hearing of the arrest of Robespierre, hastened to the spot and liberated both him and his accomplices from prison, conducting them to the Hôtel-de-Ville amidst cries of "*Robespierre for ever! Perish the traitors!*" The Convention, as soon as it met again, was informed of the change in the state of affairs, the rising of the Commune, the release of the prisoners, and the fury of the Jacobins. Some of the members of the Committee of General Surety now came running to the Convention with the alarming intelligence that Coffinhal at the head of 2000 cannoneers had rescued Henriot out of their hands, and that their commandant had prevailed on these men to turn their pieces against the Convention.   The President on this put on his hat in sign of distress and declared, "It was time to die at their posts."   All the members were resolved, and they immediately outlawed Henriot.   Fortunately he could not prevail on his cannoneers to fire, and this decided the events of the day.   The Convention also placed the conspirators as well as the insurgents of the Commune out of the protection of the law, and assembled a force to march against them.   The Sections who had hitherto hesitated, doubtful of the issue, now declared in favor of the Convention, and their battalions defiled in succession before them.   It was now midnight.   The conspirators had not stirred from the Hôtel-de-Ville.   Robespierre, after being welcomed with shouts of applause and promises of victory, was admitted to the general council and seated between Payan and Fleuriot.   The Place de Grève was full of men, of bayonets, pikes and cannon.   They waited only for the arrival of the Sections, for whose favorable disposition Henriot answered, as well as several of their own deputies who were present.   Every thing seemed to augur success.   An executive commission was appointed, addresses were prepared for the armies, and lists of proscription made out.   But at a little after midnight none of the Sections had appeared, no order had been issued, the Triumvirs still sat, and the multitude assembled in the Place de Grève began to waver in their resolution, when some emissaries of the new raised troops glided in among them, crying " Long live the Convention !"   The proclamation was then read putting the Commune hors la loi ; and after hearing it, the mob quietly dispersed.   Henriot, coming out soon after to encourage them, to his utter amazement found the Place de Grève empty.   At this instant the troops of the Convention came up, surrounded the Hôtel-de-Ville, occupied the avenues, and then, before any warning of their approach had been given, raised the cry of " Long live the National Convention !"

The conspirators finding all lost attempted to escape from the hands of their enemies by destroying themselves.   Robespierre shattered his jaw-bone with a pistol-ball.   Lebas followed his example, but succeeded better.   The younger Robespierre threw himself headlong from the window of the third story, but survived

his fall. Couthon gave himself several stabs with an irresolute
hand. St. Just awaited his fate. Coffinhal blamed the hesitation
of Henriot as the cause of their failure, and leaped into a com-
mon-sewer, through which he escaped. The others were taken
to the Convention. Bourdon entered, crying "Victory, victory!
the traitors are no more!"—"The wretched Robespierre is without," said the President, "borne on a litter; you would not have
him brought in?"—"No, no!" said a number of voices, "let him
be conveyed to the Place de la Revolution!" He was left some
time at the Committee of General Surety, previously to his being
transferred to the Conciergerie. Here, stretched on a table, his
visage disfigured and bathed in blood, exposed to the gaze, the
taunts, and maledictions of the crowd, he heard the different parties exult in his fall, and charge him with all the crimes that had
been committed; whereas it was much more their own versatility,
joining in with whatever power was uppermost and trampling on
whatever side was weakest, that was the cause of all the mischief.
He manifested a great deal of insensibility during the scene.
He was removed to the Conciergerie, and then brought before the
Revolutionary Tribunal, who after identifying his person and that
of his accomplices ordered them for execution. The 10th of
Thermidor (July 28th) towards five o'clock in the afternoon, he
ascended the fatal car, where he was placed between Henriot and
Couthon, mutilated like himself. His head was enveloped in a
bloody cloth, his color was livid and his eyes sunk. An immense
multitude pressed round the car, exhibiting the most marked and
extravagant joy. They congratulated, they embraced one another; they loaded him with execrations, and came as near as
possible to have a better view of him. The Gendarmes singled
him out with the point of their sabres; and when the procession
came opposite his house in the Rue St. Honoré, they stopped, and
a group of women was formed, and they danced round the dying
bier of him, whose chariot-wheels they would have dragged the
day before (aye, and the day after, had he been successful) over
a thousand victims. As for him, he seemed to look upon the
crowd with pity. St. Just regarded them with a steadfast eye,
the others, to the number of twenty-two, were more dejected.
Robespierre mounted the scaffold last, and the moment that his

head fell, the people applauded, and continued to do so for some minutes. The shout was echoed till it reached the gloom of prisons, where it was a reprieve from death to many who hourly expected their fate.*

This was the end of the *reign of terror,* a reign that has been the wonder of our times, and the chief actors in which will not be absolved by posterity, however it may qualify the decision or prejudices of the moment. Perhaps, under all the circumstances, the system adopted (however dreadful) was necessary to repel the unprincipled aggressions or secret treachery of the enemies of the Republic; the transient evil, though great, was less than the evil aimed at by the opposite side, which was no other than the final and utter extinction of the hopes, rights, and dignity of human nature. But a good cause may require the aid of bad men and bad passions to contend on equal terms with the extent of means and inveterate malignity arrayed against it by the worst; nay, it must do so, since good men have not the strength of nerve or stock of virtue to make the sacrifices or incur the responsibility unavoidable in that deadly strife which evil wages with good, power with liberty, kings with their subjects. Pure patriotism and philanthropy may be wound up to strike a terrible blow on some particular occasions; but a succession of such acts hardens the heart and revolts the feelings: the good and humane either shrink from the trial or become corrupted by their "great office," and the bad come forward to relieve them from the painful alternative. A man may at first imbrue his hands in blood from a strong sense of necessity or from a sincere love of his country; but in process of time, the love of justice or his country will become the professed and ostensible motive, the original repugnance will wear off, and the love of shedding blood will be an appetite and a disease in his mind, so that he will shed blood for the sake of shedding it. The execution will outrun the warrant; and for one deed of dire necessity, there will be a score of acts of volun-

---

* In some cases, the event was announced to the prisoners by the waving of handkerchiefs from the tops of houses; and in one instance a family whose friend was allowed to stick a slip of paper to their linen when returned to them with the words "*Je me porte bien,*" knew that some important change had happened from the simple addition, "*Ah! que je me porte bien!*"

tary and systematic barbarity. The leaders in the Revolution were placed in a situation above humanity. They must either be or become demons. If they yielded to the amiable infirmities of human nature, they must give up the cause of liberty and independence; in order to ensure the triumph of the last, they must first triumph over their own most cherished feelings. It is possible that the feelings of justice and mercy should survive a series of barbarous and cruel acts, sustained by the sacred sense of duty; but it is barely possible—or if in one case, not in many. The act will oftener soil the motive than the motive will purify the act. There may be one Brutus, but not an assembly of Brutuses.

The excesses of the French Revolution have indeed been considered as an anomaly in history, as a case taken out of every rule or principle of morality by comparison with any thing else. But there are three tests by which we may form a tolerably fair estimate of the characters and motives of those concerned in it. First, do we not see the hold which the love of power and all strong excitement takes of the mind; how it engrosses the faculties, stifles compunction, and deadens the sense of shame, even when it is purely selfish or mischievous, when it does not even pretend to have any good in view, and when we have all the world against us? What then must be the force and confidence in itself which any such passion, ambition, cruelty, revenge, must acquire when it is founded on some lofty and high-sounding principle, patriotism, liberty, resistance to tyrants; when it aims at the public good as its consequence, and is strengthened by the applause of the multitude? Evil is strong enough in itself; when it has good for its end, it is conscience-proof. If the common bravo or cut-throat who stabs another merely to fill his purse or revenge a private grudge, can hardly be persuaded that he does wrong, and postpones his remorse till long after—he who sheds blood like water, but can contrive to do it with some fine-sounding name on his lips, will be in his own eyes little less than a saint or martyr. Robespierre was a professed admirer of Rousseau's *Social Contract* and the *Profession of Faith of a Savoyard Vicar;* and I do not conceive it impossible that he thought of these when the mob were dancing round him at his own door. He would certainly have sent any one to the guillotine who should have con-

10*

futed him in a dispute on the one or have ridiculed the other ; but this would not prove that he had altered his opinion of either. He was a political pedant, a violent dogmatist, weak in argument, and who wished to be strong in fact. Every head he cut off, he felt his power the greater ; with the increase of power, he felt his opinions confirmed, and with the certainty of his opinions, the security for the welfare and liberty of mankind. These were the rollers on which his actions moved, spreading ruin and dismay in large and sweeping circles; these were the theoretical moulds in which cruelty, suspicion, and proscription were cast, which, according to the abstractedness, or what, in the cant of the day, was called the *purity* of his principles, embraced a wider sphere, and called for unlimited sacrifices. The habitual and increasing lust of power and gratification in counting his victims did not enable him to disentangle the sophistry which bewildered him or prove to him that he was in the wrong, but the contrary, however the actual-results might occasionally **stagger him**: to save was in his mind to destroy, to destroy **was to save** ; and he remained in all probability as great a contradiction to himself as he has **been** an anomaly and riddle incapable of solution to others. The fault of such characters is not the absence of strictness of principle or a sense of duty, but an excess of these over their natural sensibility or instinctive prejudices, which makes them both dangerous to the community and hateful in themselves by their obstinate determination to carry into effect any dogma or theory to which they have made up their minds, be the objections or consequences what they will. Such instruments may indeed be wanted for great and trying occasions ; but their being thrown into such a situation does not alter the odiousness of their characters nor the opinion of mankind concerning them. **The action alone is** certain ; the motive is hid; the future benefit doubtful. Fame and even virtue are to a certain degree commonplace things! This "differences" Robespierre from characters of mere natural ferocity, or from the tyrants of antiquity, who indulged in the same insatiable barbarity only to pamper their personal pride and sense of self-importance. Robespierre was nothing in himself but as the guider of a machine, the mouth-piece of an abstract proposition ; he would hurt no one but for differing from him in an opinion which he had worked himself up to believe was the link that held the world together, the peg on which the safety of the state hung, the very " keystone that made up the arch" of the social fabric, and that if it was removed, the whole fell together to cureless ruin.

Secondly, let those who deny this view of the subject explain if they can the conduct of religious persecutors and tyrants for conscience' sake. The religious and the political fanatic are one and the same character, and run into the same errors on the same grounds. Nothing can surely surpass the excesses, the horrors, the refinements in cruelty, and the cold-blooded malignity which have been exercised in the name and under the garb of religion. Yet who will say that this strikes at the root of religion itself or that the instigators and perpetrators of these horrors were men without one particle of the goodness and sanctity to which they made such lofty and exclusive pretensions ; that they were not many of them patterns of sincerity, piety, and the most disinterested zeal, (who were ready to undergo the same fate they inflicted on others;) and that in consigning their opponents to the stake, the dagger, or the dungeon, they did not believe they were doing God and man good service ? The kindling pile, the paper-caps of the victims at an *auto-de-fé*, the instruments of torture, the solemn hymn, the shout of triumph, the callousness of the executioner, the gravity of the judges are circumstances sufficiently revolting to human nature ; but to argue from hence that those who sanctioned or who periodically assisted at such scenes were mere monsters of cruelty and hypocrisy, would be betraying a total ignorance of the contradictions of the human mind. All sects, all religions have retaliated upon one another where they had the power, and some of the best and most enlightened men have been zealots in the cause. We see by this how far an opinion, the conviction of an abstract and contingent good will carry men to violate all their natural feelings and all common ties conscientiously and in the face of day ; nor should we imagine that this is confined to religion. I grant that religion being of the highest and least questionable authority has caused more fanaticism and bigotry, more massacres and persecutions than any thing else ; but whatever cause, religion, patriotism, freedom, can strongly excite the affections and agitate large masses of men, will produce the same blind-fold and headlong zeal, and plead the same excuse for the excesses of its adherents. At the same time I think that those who have been most forward to distinguish themselves as bigots and persecutors have been generally men of austere, vindictive, and narrow minds; and their names are branded in history accordingly.

Thirdly, there is some affinity between foreign and civil war. We pour molten lead on the heads of those who are scaling the walls of a city; but this would be of no use if those within could be found delivering up the keys with impunity. Why then are all our pity and complaints reserved for the evils of civil war, since the passions are as much excited and the danger as great in the one case as in the other? No one will compare Shaw the Lifeguards'-man with the celebrated Coup-Tête; the one was a gallant soldier, the other a sneaking villain; yet the one cut off as many heads in a day as the other: it is not the blood shed then, but the manner and motive; the one braved a formidable enemy in the field, the other gloated over a hapless victim. We distinguish the soldier and the assassin; to be just, we must distinguish between public and private malice. But here comes in the hypocrisy or cowardice of mankind. In war, the enemy is open and challenges your utmost malice; so that there is nothing more to be said. In conspiracy and civil strife, the enemy s either secret and doubtful or lies at your mercy; and after the catastrophe is over, it is pretended that he was both helpless and innocent. entitled to pity in himself and fixing an indelible stain on his dastardly and cruel oppressor. Here then is again required in times of revolution, that *moral courage*, which uses a discretionary power and takes an awful responsibility upon itself, going right forward to its object, and setting fastidious scruples, character, and consequences (all but principle and self-preservation) at defiance.

What were the leaders of the Revolution to do? Were they to suffer a renewal of the massacres of Ismael and Warsaw, by those tender preachers of morality and the puling sentimentalists that follow in their train, who think to crush men like worms and complain that they have trod on asps? They not only had these scenes fresh before their eyes, but they were in part the same identical persons who threatened to treat them with a second course of them? "Rather than so, come Fate into the lists and champion us to the outrance!"—seems to have been the motto of the Revolutionists and their reply. Were they not to anticipate the ignominious blow prepared for them by their insolent invaders? Or should they spare those who stood gaping by and beckoning others on to their banquet

of blood? But the number of these last increased, and made it difficult to know where to strike. It was this very uncertainty that
distracted and irritated the Government; and in the multitude and
concealment of their adversaries, hurried them forward to indiscriminate fury. What the Revolution wanted, and what Robespierre did for it in these circumstances, was to give to the political
machine the utmost possible *momentum* and energy of which it was
capable; to stagger the presumption and pride of the Coalition by
showing on the opposite side an equally inveterate and intense degree of determined hostility and ruthless vengeance; to out-face;
to out-dare; to stand the brunt not only of all the violence but of all
the cant, hypocrisy, obloquy and prejudice with which they were
assailed; to stamp on the revolution a *practical* character; to wipe
out the imputation of visionary and Utopian refinément and consequent imbecility from all plans of reform; to prove that " brave
Sansculottes were no triflers;" and to enlist all passions, all interests, all classes, and all the resources of the country in the one great
object, the defence of the Republic. The decks were cleared as for
a battle, all other considerations, scruples, objections were thrown
on one side; and the only question being to save the vessel of the
state, it was saved. Under this impulse the Revolution went on
through all chances and changes, "like tumbler-pigeons making all
sorts of summersaults and evolutions of figure," but never losing
sight of its goal, and arriving safe at its place of destination. All
feelings, all pretensions, all characters, levity, brutality, rage, envy,
ambition, self-interest, generosity, refinement were melted down in
the furnace of the Revolution, but all heightened the flame and
swelled the torrent of patriotism. The blaze thus kindled threw its
glare on all objects, so that the whole passed in a strange, preternat-
ural light, that precluded the discrimination of motives or characters.
Nor was it necessary to distinguish to a nicety. The great point was
to distinguish friends from foes, and for this purpose they were put
to a speedy probation. Otherwise, it was not asked whether a man
wore a long beard or a short one, whether he carried an axe or a
pike, no attention was paid to the *dramatis personæ* or to costume—
but all to the conduct of the fable and to bring about the catastrophe!
Every state contains within itself the means of salvation, if it will
look its danger in the face and not shrink from the course actually

necessary to save it. But to do this, it must rise to the magnitude of the occasion, above rules and appearances. France, baited, hunted down as she was, had but one resource left to retaliate on her aggressors, to throw aside all self-regards and all regards for others, and in order to escape from the toils spread around, to discard all obligations, and cut asunder the very nerves of humanity. Few persons could be found to help her at this exigency so well as Robespierre. The Brissotins, who were fine gentlemen, would have been entangled in " the drapery of a moral imagination :" Robespierre, to give no hold to his adversary, fought the battle naked and threw away both shame and fear. When it comes to the abstract choice between slavery or freedom, principles are of more importance than individuals ; it is to be apprehended that an energy and pertinacity of character that would not have exceeded the occasion, would not have come up to it ; and we see that when the dread of hostile invasion or domestic treachery no longer existed and tyrannized over the minds of men, the reign of terror ceased with the extreme causes that had provoked and alone rendered its continuance endurable.*

The army under all these circumstances remained firm and unshaken. They seemed to regard the errors and calamities of the country with an indulgent eye as the errors of a parent—knew their own place and duty which was to protect her, and to present a stern and erect aspect to the enemy. A republican severity and simplicity of manners was daily gaining ground among them. Even the generals appeared for a while to partake of the steadiness and energy of the government ; whether they beat or were beaten, entered into no cabals with the Allies ; and the rapid and violent whirl of the political machine might be said for a wonder to have suspended the versatility of the national character.

* I have not tantalized the reader by making it a question whether the dramatic interest which Robespierre's system excited in Paris, or the newspaper interest it excited through Europe was not a set-off to the actual sufferings of the individuals who came within its grasp, as some writers have alleged in extenuation of the hardships of the subjects of despotic governments who have not a house over their heads or a rag to cover them, that they have at least the pleasure of seeing the fine palaces and fine liveries of the great. I would only observe that Legitimacy is come to a fine pass, when instead of the *Jus Divinum* and the absolute will of the sovereign, all that its ablest defenders can say in its behalf is reduced to the pleasure which the people have in looking at it as a raree-show.

# CHAPTER VII.

### THE SIEGE OF TOULON.

It was during the height of the reign of terror and of civil strife, that Buonaparte was appointed by the Committee of Public Safety to take the command of the artillery at the siege of Toulon. If the French government at this period carried their measures of internal security to an excess of suspicion and cruelty, they spared no pains in repelling external aggression with the utmost vigilance and vigor. In fact, the excesses of the French Revolution were to be considered in the circumstances of the time and from the character of the people, as the natural but deplorable result of the general and almost frantic spirit of resistance to the threat of subjugation and oppression without.

In consequence of the events which took place at Paris on the 31st of May and 2d of June (the arrest and expulsion of members of the Gironde party from the Convention) Mars as we have seen, revolted and sent a number of troops to the assistance of Lyons, which was at this time in possession of the royalists, and besieged by Kellermann. General Cartaux, who had been detached from the army of the Alps with 2000 men, beat the Marseillois at Orange, drove them out of Avignon,* and entered Marseilles on the 25th of August, 1793. Toulon received the principal inhabitants of Marseilles concerned in this insurrection within her walls, and in concert with them gave up the place to the English squadron that blockaded the harbor.

---

\* Buonaparte is said to have had the principal share in this event, by placing a battery on the heights of Villeneuve facing Avignon, and dismounting one of the cannon of the insurgents on the opposite side of the river, and by a second fire killing one of their cannoneers. On this the latter refused to fight any longer against republican artillery, and the insurgents evacuated the city and retired towards St. Remy.

This was a dreadful blow to the Republican party, inasmuch as besides twenty or twenty-five ships of the line which were stationed there, Toulon contained several noble establishments and immense naval stores.   On the first announcement of the intelligence, the French General La Poype set out from Nice with 4000 men, accompanied by the representatives of the people, Freron and Barras : he advanced in the direction of Saulnier, following the line between Cape Brun and Fort Pharaon, on the eastern side of Toulon.   On the other side, General Cartaux, with the representatives of the people, Albitte, Gasparin, and Salicetti, advanced on Beausset and observed the passes of Ollioules, which were in possession of the enemy.   The combined troops, English, Spanish, Neapolitans, Sardinians, and others, collected from all quarters, were masters of the place itself and of all the defiles and avenues for six miles round it.   On the 8th of September General Cartaux made an attack on the passes of Ollioules, and carried them.   His advanced posts were within sight of Toulon and the sea : he took Six-Fours to the west of the harbor, and repaired the fortifications of the little post of Nazer.   The division of General Cartaux, consisting of 7000 or 8000 men, was separated by Mount Pharaon behind Toulon, from that part army commanded by General La Poype, which caused inconvenience and the want of co-operation between them. A difference of opinion prevailed as to the mode of conducting the siege ; that is to say, whether the principal attack should be made on the left or on the right of the town.   On the left were the forts of Pharaon and La Malgue, which last is a strong and carefully constructed fortification ; on the right there was only the fort of Malbosquet, which is little else than a field-fort, though difficult of access from its situation.   This fort being once taken, the besiegers would be close to the ramparts of the town ; so that in reality there could be no question that this was the true point of attack, and hither therefore all the reinforcements from the interior were sent.   It was a few days after the taking of the passes of Ollioules that Napoleon arrived from Paris (whither he had been sent on some special mission) to take the command of the besieging train.   He, with other non-commissioned officers and ensigns, had been promoted, according to the principles of the

Revolution, to the higher ranks of the artillery, for which many of them were well qualified, whilst others had neither the capacity nor information necessary for the important situations to which chance, with the spirit of the time, had raised them. The principle, however, was on the whole a good one ; for in this lottery of promotions, though there must needs be many failures, yet those who possessed real talents and bravery had an opportunity to distinguish themselves, and were almost sure of being brought forward (in proportion to their merits) in the service of the Republic.

Napoleon on his arrival found the head-quarters still at Beausset. The troops were busy in making preparations to burn the Allied squadrons in the road of Toulon ; and the next day the new Commandant of the Artillery went with the General-in-Chief to visit the batteries. What was his surprise to find a battery of six twenty-pounders placed close to Ollioules at two gun-shots from the shore, and quite out of reach of the English vessels ; and the volunteers of the Côte d'Or and the soldiers of the regiment of Burgundy employed in heating the balls at the different country-houses in the neighborhood, as if red-hot cannon balls were easily transported from place to place ! Napoleon instantly set about reforming this state of things. His first care w
about him several officers of artillery who had been employed before the Revolution, and whom the troubles of the time had displaced. He appointed his old comrade, Colonel Gassendi, to the superintendence of the arsenal at Marseilles. At the end of six weeks he had succeeded in collecting and completing a park of two hundred pieces of artillery. The batteries were advanced forward and fixed on the most advantageous points of the shore, the consequence of which was that some large vessels were dismasted by them, several smaller ones sunk, and the English were forced to abandon that part of the harbor.

While the preparations for the siege were going on, the army received considerable reinforcements. The Committee of Public Safety sent plans and instructions relative to the conduct of the siege, drawn up by General D'Arçon of the engineers. These were read in a council of war called on the occasion, at which Gasparin, a popular representative and a sensible and well-in

formed man, presided.   Napoleon, who for the last month had
been examining the ground, and was become thoroughly acquainted with its peculiarities, recommended the plan of attack
which afterwards succeeded.   He regarded the suggestions of the
Committee as totally useless under the circumstances of the case,
as in his opinion a regular siege was not at all necessary.   In
fact, allowing that a position could be gained, from which, with a
certain number of mortars and cannon and furnaces for red-hot
balls, a fire could be kept up on every point of the greater and
lesser roads, it was evident that the combined squadron would be
compelled to abandon them, and the garrison would then be reduced to a state of strict blockade, the communication with the
squadron, which would be forced to stand out at sea, being cut
off.   Such a position was to be found at the extreme point of the
promontory of Balagnier and L'Eguillette, between the two harbors and nearly opposite to the town.   This he had remarked
some weeks before to the General-in-Chief, but the English had
in the mean time become so sensible of its importance, that they
had landed 4000 men there, had cut down the wood covering the
promontory of Cair, which commanded the whole position, and
had employed all the aid they could get from Toulon, having re-
c        'en to the galley-slaves, to entrench themselves there,
making it into what they called "the Little Gibraltar."   This
point, which a month before might have been seized upon without
any difficulty, now required a serious attack ; for which purpose
it would be most advisable to form batteries mounted with twenty-
four pounders and mortars, in order to destroy the epaulments
which were constructed of wood, to break down the palisades,
and throw a shower of shells into the fort ; and that then, after a
vigorous fire of eight-and-forty hours, the works should be storm-
ed by picked troops.   Two days after the capture of the fort, Napoleon gave it as his opinion that Toulon would belong to the Republic.   This plan of attack was warmly discussed, and at length
unanimously agreed to.

According to the proposed plan, the French raised five or six
batteries over against Little Gibraltar, and also platforms for fifteen mortars.   A battery of eight twenty-four pounders and four
mortars had at the same time been thrown up against Fort Mal-

bosquet nearer the town, the construction of which was a profound
secret to the English, the workmen being entirely hid from view
by a plantation of olives. It was intended that this battery should
not be unmasked till the moment of marching against Little Gibraltar; but on the 20th of November the Representatives of the
People went to inspect it, when they were informed by the cannoneers that it had been completed eight days, and that no use had
yet been made of it. Without further inquiry, the Representatives ordered them to open a fire, and accordingly the cannoneers with great readiness opened an alternate fire from the battery. General O'Hara, who commanded the Allied Army at
Toulon, was much surprised at the erection of so considerable a
battery close to Fort Malbosquet, and gave orders that a sortie
should be made at day-break. An hour before day, he in consequence sallied out of the garrison with 6000 men, and meeting
with no material obstacle, his skirmishers only being engaged,
spiked the guns of the battery.

In the mean time the drums beat to arms at the French head-
quarters; and Dugommier, who had just then taken the command, in haste rallied his troops, which occupied the line from
Fort Rouge to Malbosquet, and were too much scattered to make
an effectual resistance at any single point. The Commandant of
Artillery posted himself on a rising ground behind the battery,
where he had previously established a _dépôt_ of arms. There was
a communication from this spot to the battery, by means of a sup-
plementary branch or continuation of the trench. Perceiving
from hence that the English troops had drawn up to the right and
left of the battery, he conceived the project of leading a battalion that was stationed near him along this concealed passage.
By this manœuvre he succeeded in coming out unperceived
among the brambles close to the battery, and immediately commenced a brisk fire upon the English, whose surprise was such
that they imagined it was their own troops to the right, who by
some mistake were firing on those to the left. General O'Hara
hastened towards the spot, thinking to rectify the supposed mistake, when he was wounded in the hand by a musket-ball, and a
French serjeant seized and dragged him prisoner into the trench.
The disappearance of the English General was so sudden that

his own troops did not even know what was become of him. By
this time Dugommier, with the troops that he had rallied, had got
between the town and the battery : this movement disconcerted
the opposite party, who forthwith commenced their retreat. They
were hotly pursued to the gates of the fortress, which they entered precipitately, and without having been able to ascertain the
fate of their General. Dugommier himself was slightly wounded. A battalion of volunteers from the Isere distinguished itself
in this action.

General Cartaux, as we have seen, had conducted the siege at
its commencement; but the Committee of Public Safety had
found it necessary to supersede him. He was a vain man,
usually covered from head to foot with gold-lace ; and when Napoleon first presented him with his credentials, he said he could
do very well without him, but that he was welcome to share the
honors of the victory without having had any of the trouble. He
was originally a painter by profession; and for his success
against the Marseillois had been promoted to the rank of Brigadier-General and General of Division. He was ignorant of the
art of war as well as of most other things ; but was not an ill-
disposed man, and had been guilty of no excesses on the taking
of Marseilles. Doppet, who succeeded him, was a Savoyard by
birth, and had been bred a physician. He thought of nothing
but denunciations, and had no idea of the nature of war. Nevertheless, by a singular chance, he was very near taking Toulon
within forty-eight hours after his arrival. A battalion of the
Côte d'Or and another of the regiment of Burgundy, being on
duty in the trenches before Little Gibraltar, had one of their men
taken by a Spanish company on guard at the redoubt ; they saw
their comrade ill-treated and beaten, while the Spaniards offered
them every insult by shouts and indecent gestures. The French
being provoked beyond patience, ran to their arms, commenced a
brisk fire, and advanced against the redoubt. On this the Commandant of Artillery immediately hastened to the General-in-
Chief (Doppet,) who was not aware of what was going on. They
galloped to the scene of action together, and there perceived how
the matter stood. Napoleon persuaded the General to support
the attack, assuring him that it would not be productive of greater

loss to advance than to retire.  The General accordingly gave orders for the different corps of reserve to be put in motion; all were quickly on the alert, and Napoleon marched at their head. Unluckily an aid-de-camp was killed by the side of the General-in Chief.  Doppet was panic-struck; and ordering the drums to beat a retreat, recalled the soldiers at the very moment when the grenadiers, having driven back the skirmishers, had reached the gorge of the redoubt, and were about to enter it.  The troops were highly incensed, and complained that painters and physicians were set over them.  The Committee of Public Safety recalled Doppet; and at length feeling the necessity of employing real military men, sent Dugommier, who had seen fifty years' service, was covered with scars, and was dauntless as the sword by his side.

The garrison was all this while obtaining reinforcements, and the public watched the progress of the siege with anxiety.  They could not understand why every effort should be bent against Little Gibraltar, a place so insignificant and in a contrary direction to the town.  All the popular societies rang with denunciations on the subject.  Provence complained of the long duration of the siege.  A scarcity began to prevail, and increased to such a degree, that Freron and Barras, having given up all hopes of the prompt reduction of Toulon, wrote in great alarm from Marseilles to the Convention to take into consideration whether it would not be better to raise the siege, repass the Durance, and resume offensive operations again after the harvest.  A few days after the Convention received this letter, Toulon was taken, and the letter was then disowned by the Representatives as a forgery. Dugommier having resolved that a decisive attack should be made upon Little Gibraltar, the Commandant of the Artillery threw 7000 or 8000 shells into the fort, while thirty twenty-four pounders battered the works.  On the 18th of December, at four in the afternoon, the troops left their camps, and marched towards the village of Seine, a little on one side of the English.  The plan was to attack at midnight, in order to avoid the fire of the fort and of the intermediate redoubts which had been constructed at the foot of two hillocks close to it.  At the instant when every thing was ready, the Representatives of the People called a council to deliberate whether the attack should proceed or not : either they wished thus to throw the blame of a failure on the General, or with many others despaired of success on account of the dreadful weather, the rain falling in torrents. Dugommier and the Commandant of Artillery ridiculed these fears; two columns were formed, and set out to attack the fort. The Allied troops, to shelter themselves from the balls and shells which showered upon the fort, usually occupied a station at a small distance in the rear of it. The French were in hopes of reaching the works before them ; but the English had a line of skirmishers in front of the fort, and as the musquetry commenced firing at the very foot of the hill, the Allied troops came up in time to its defence, when a very smart fire was immediately opened. Case-shot showered all around. At length, after a most furious attack, Dugommier, who, according to his usual **custom**, headed the leading column, was obliged to fall back ; and in the utmost despair cried **out, "I am a lost man!"** Success was indeed in every way important at a crisis when the want of it ordinarly conducted the unfortunate General to the scaffold.

The fire of the cannonading and musketry continued. Captain Muiron of the artillery, a young man full of bravery and presence of mind, and who was aid-de-camp to the Commandant of Artillery, was detached with a battalion of light infantry and supported by the second column, which followed at the distance of a musket-shot. He was thoroughly acquainted with the position, and availed himself so well of the windings of the ascent, that he conducted his troops up the hill without sustaining any loss. He debouched at the foot of the fort, rushed through an embrasure ; his soldiers followed him, and the place was taken. The English and Spanish cannoneers were all killed at their guns, and Muiron himself was dangerously wounded by a thrust from the pike of an English soldier. When Dugommier had been three hours in the redoubt, the Representatives of the People came with their drawn swords in their hands (the Baillie Jarvies of the scene) to load the troops with eulogiums on their conduct. If, however, not brave in themselves, they were " the cause of bravery in other men ;" made those who lay at the mercy of their caprice and importunate demands look about them, and let it be

understood in a manner that was neither to be mistaken nor gain-
sayed, that "the Republic expected every man to do his duty!"

At break of day, the French marched on Balagnier and
L'Eguillette, which were already evacuated. The twenty-four
pounders and the mortars were brought to line these batteries,
whence they hoped to cannonade the combined fleets before noon ;
but Napoleon deemed it not advisable to fix them there. They
were of stone, and the engineers who had constructed them had
been guilty of an oversight in placing a large tower of masonry
just at their entrance so near the platforms, that whatever balls
might have struck them would have rebounded on the gunners,
besides the splinters and rubbish. They therefore planted cannon on the heights behind the batteries, which could not open
their fire till the next day ; but no sooner did the English Admiral, Lord Hood, see that the French had possessed themselves of
these positions than he made signal to weigh anchor and get out
of the roads immediately. He then went to Toulon to make it
known that there was not a moment to be lost in putting out to
sea.* A council of war met, and agreed that the place was no
longer tenable. They accordingly proceeded to issue orders, as
well for the embarkation of the troops, as for the burning and
sinking such French vessels as they could not carry away with
them, and setting fire to the marine establishments. Notice was
also given to the inhabitants that those who wished to leave the place
might embark on board the English and Spanish fleets. When
these disastrous tidings were spread abroad, a scene of confusion
arose, which it would not be easy to describe, any more than the
disappointment and astonishment of the garrison and of the unfortunate inhabitants, who but a few hours before, calculating on the
great distance of the besiegers from the place, the slow progress of
the siege during four months, and the daily arrival of reinforcements, not only hoped to effect the raising of the siege, but to become
masters of Provence. The surprise and consternation manifested
at so unforeseen a reverse bore testimony to the skill and genius
of this which was Napoleon's first military enterprise. The plan
was what no one suspected ; and yet when it had succeeded,

* It has been said he wished first to make a desperate attempt to retake
Little Gibraltar.

nothing could appear simpler.  It was only going a little out of
his way to take the town by attacking the fleet, which was its
chief defence.  The secret of this, as of all enterprises of origi-
nality and boldness, consisted in looking at the real circumstances
and possibilities of the case instead of trusting to routine or the
opinion of others, and in seizing (out of a great number of doubtful means that offer) on those that led most effectually and certainly to the end.  It was also highly creditable to the discernment and promptitude of the English Admiral that he saw the important use that might be made of the possession of Little Gibraltar beforehand, and lost not a moment in preventing the disastrous
consequences after it was taken.

In the night Fort Poné was blown up by the English, and an
hour afterwards a part of the French squadron was set on fire.
Nine seventy-four gun ships and four frigates fell a prey to the
flames.  The fire and smoke from the arsenal resembled the
eruption of a volcano, and the thirteen vessels which were burning in the road were like so many magnificent displays of fire-
works.  The masts and forms of the vessels were distinctly visible in the blaze, which lasted for many hours and had a striking
effect.  Sir Sidney Smith took a very active share in this transaction.  The Spaniards were entrusted with the destruction of two
powder-vessels ; but instead of sinking, blew them up, which occasioned a tremendous shock.  It was of course sufficiently mortifying to the French to see such valuable resources and so much
wealth consumed within so short a space of time.  The English
had not time to blow up Fort La Malgue, as was expected.  Napoleon then went to Malbosquet.  It was already evacuated.  He
ordered the field-pieces to sweep the ramparts of the town and
heighten the confusion by throwing shells from the howitzers into
the harbor, until the mortars which were upon the road with their
carriages could be planted on the batteries, and shells thrown from
them in the same direction.  General La Poype took possession
of Fort Pharaon, which the Allies no longer attempted to keep.
During this time, the batteries of L'Eguillette and Balagnier kept
up a constant fire on the vessels in the roads.  Many of the English ships were much damaged.  The batteries continued to play
all the night, and at break of day the English fleet was seen out

at sea. By nine o'clock a high Libeccio wind got up, and the English ships were forced to put into the Hyeres.

Many thousand families at Toulon had followed the English, so that the Revolutionary tribunals found but few victims in the place; all the persons most deeply implicated in the late transactions had left it  Nevertheless, between one and two hundred unfortunate wretches were shot within the first fortnight.* Orders afterwards arrived from the Convention for demolishing the

* The manner of doing this was sufficiently infamous. Only eight or ten persons of any consequence, who had wished to fly, remained behind; a great sacrifice to the offended Genius of the Republic was wanted and these were too few. A stratagem was therefore resorted to. Proclamation was made that all those who had been employed in the arsenal while the English were in possession of the town, were to repair to the Champ de Mars and give in their names; and they were led to believe that it was for the purpose of employing them again. Nearly two hundred persons, head-workmen, inferior clerks, and others in subaltern situations, went accordingly in full confidence, and had their names registered. It was thus proved by their own confession that they had retained their places under the English government, and the Revolutionary Tribunal immediately sentenced them to be shot.—It was during his stay at Toulon at this period that Buonaparte saved the Chabrillant family, who were brought into the harbor on board a Spanish prize, from the fury of the mob. It was just after the fall of Robespierre, and the inhabitants were by no means reconciled to the change. No sooner was it known that about twenty Emigrants had been landed (though by no fault or wish of their own) than a crowd collected at the arsenal and in the streets, and were proceeding to the prisons to slaughter these unfortunate persons. It was in vain that the Representatives Mariette and Cambon, who were of the moderate party and themselves suspected, attempted to dissuade them from their purpose; they were in danger of being themselves hud up to the lamp-post. It was late in the day, and the crowd were growing outrageous; the Guard came up and were repulsed. At this crisis Napoleon recollected among the principal rioters several gunners who had served under him during the siege: he mounted a platform; the gunners enforced respect to their General, and obtained silence; he had the good fortune to produce an effect: they were restrained from further violence by his assurance that the Emigrants should be delivered up and sentenced the following morning. It would have been no easy matter to persuade them of what was perfectly evident, namely, that these Emigrants had not infringed the law, as they had not returned voluntarily During the night he had them put into some artillery-waggons and carried out of the town as a convoy of ammunition; a boat was waiting for them in Hyeres roads, where they embarked and were thus saved.

buildings of Toulon : the absurdity of the measure did not prevent its partial execution, and many houses were pulled down
which it was, of course, subsequently found necessary to rebuild.
During the siege of Toulon, the Army of Italy had been attacked
on the Var.   The Piedmontese had attempted to invade Provence,
and had got nearly as far as Entrevaux ; but being defeated at
Gillette, they retreated within their lines.    The news of the
taking of Toulon caused a lively sensation in Provence and
throughout France, particularly as success was unexpected and
almost hopeless.   From this event may be dated the rise of Napoleon's reputation ; he was made Brigadier-General of Artillery
in consequence, and appointed to the command of that department
in the Army of Italy.   General Dugommier was appointed Commander-in-Chief of the Army of the Eastern Pyrenees.   He always spoke in the highest terms of Buonaparte, and sent him
word from time to time of his successes.

It was at the siege of Toulon that, standing by one of the batteries where a cannoneer was shot dead at his side, Buonaparte
took the ramrod which had fallen out of his hands, and charged
the gun several times.   He by this means caught an infectious
cutaneous disease, which was not completely cured till many
years after, and which often did great injury to his health.   It
was here also he became acquainted with several officers, who
were afterwards the most strongly attached to him ; among others
with Duroc.   On one occasion, while constructing a battery, he
wanted some one to write a letter for him.   A young man stepped forward to offer his services.   The letter was hardly finished,
when a cannon-ball striking near him, covered him all over with
earth.   " Good," said the writer, " we shall not want sand this
time."   This sally, together with the coolness he displayed, was
the making of the young soldier's fortune.   It was Junot.   Doppet, to whom Buonaparte is not very favorable, has, however,
made a very honorable mention of him in his *Memoirs* of the campaign.   He says, " Whenever he visited the outposts of the army,
he was always sure to find the Commandant of Artillery at his ;
he slept little, and that little he took on the ground, wrapped in
his mantle : he hardly ever quitted his batteries."   So watchful
was he for the enemy and for fame.

Before joining the Army of Italy, Napoleon superintended the fortifying the coasts of Provence and the Isle of Hyeres, shortly after the English quitted it. He divided the coast-batteries into three classes: those intended to protect harbors for fleets and men-of-war, those for the protection of merchant-vessels, and those erected on projecting headlands to guard the coasting-trade and prevent cruisers from landing on shore; but in this judicious and economical arrangement he had everywhere to encounter the warm opposition and remonstrances of the public authorities and popular societies, who in their officious self-importance or idle apprehensions were anxious to have expensive batteries erected at every little village or hamlet that happened to be situated near the sea-side.

Napoleon joined the head-quarters of the Army of Italy at Nice in March, 1794. It was at that time commanded by General Dumerbion, an old and brave officer, who had been for ten years a captain of grenadiers in the troops of the line. His military knowledge was considerable; he had carried on the war between the Var and the Roya, and knew the positions of the mountains that cover Nice perfectly well; but he was confined to his bed by the gout half his time. The new General of Artillery visited all the advanced posts, and reconnoitred the line occupied by the army. On returning from this inspection, he laid a Memorial before General Dumerbion, relating to the unsuccessful attempt of General Brunet to force the enemy beyond the High Alps the year before, and to the right method of effecting this object by taking possession of the Col di Tende. If the French could thus fix themselves in the upper chain of the Alps, they would secure almost impregnable positions, which requiring but a few men to maintain them would leave a greater number of troops disposable for other service. These suggestions were laid before a council, at which the Representatives Ricors and Robespierre the younger were sitting: they were unanimously approved of. Since the taking of Toulon, the opinion entertained of the General of Artillery was such as of itself to inspire considerable confidence in his plans.

On the 8th of April, 1794, a part of the army under the command of General Massena (General Dumerbion being confined to his bed by a fit of the gout) filing along the edge of the Roya by Menton, crossed the river. It then separated into four columns, three of which proceeded severally towards the sources of the Roya, the Mervia, and the Taggio, and the fourth advanced upon Oneglia. The last column fell in with a corps of Austrians and Piedmontese upon the heights of St. Agatha, repulsed, and defeated them. The General of Brigade, Brulé, was killed in the action. The head-quarters were removed to Oneglia, which is situated on the sea-coast, and troops were immediately sent forward to occupy Loano, still farther east. From Oneglia the French troops ascended to the sources of the Tanaro, beat the enemy on the heights of Ponte-Dinairo, seized on the fortress of Ormea, where they took four hundred prisoners, entered Garessio, and made themselves masters of the road from that place to Turin. The communication with Loano was kept up by way of Bardinetto and the Little St. Bernard.

The fault of General Brunet had been that he had come in front of the enemy, and endeavored, by mere dint of obstinacy, to dislodge them from an almost unassailable position and push them across a rugged barrier into their own country. Napoleon, by directing the movement of the troops obliquely along the valleys of the Roya, the Nervia. and the Taggio, and by means of those which had debouched in Piedmont by the sources of the Tanaro, had taken them in rear. The Piedmontese troops occupying the camp at Saorgio might be cut off and taken prisoners ; but the loss of an army of 20,000 men was too serious to be risked by the court of Sardinia, which was alarmed, and justly so. The Piedmontese troops, therefore, lost no time in abandoning those famous bulwarks which had been drenched with so much blood, and where they had acquired no inconsiderable renown. Saorgio was immediately invested, and soon after capitulated. The Piedmontese remained on the Col di Tende till the 7th of May, when, after a severe action, they were driven from it ; and thus all the upper regions of the Alps fell into the hands of the French. By this skilful and well-concerted plan, boldly carried into effect, the Army of Italy had also gained more than sixty pieces of cannon. Saorgio was well stocked with provisions and ammunition of every kind, being the principal *dépôt* of the Piedmontese army. The Com-

mandant of Saorgio was afterwards tried and shot by order of the
King of Sardinia, on the ground that he might have held out
twelve or fourteen days longer. It is true the event would have
been the same, as the Piedmontese army could not have come to
his assistance; but in war, the Commandant of a place is not to
judge of events, but to defend it to the very last hour. The
French kept possession of the ground they had occupied from
May till September, when they learned from Nice that a considerable Austrian force was advancing on the Bormida, and General Dumerbion in consequence set forward to reconnoitre the
enemy and to seize their stores, which he was informed had been
pushed on as far as Caire. The Representatives Albitte and
Salicetti accompanied the French army; the General-Comman-
dant of the Artillery was called upon to direct the operations;
and it was on this occasion that he narrowly escaped being summoned to the bar of the Convention on the following extraordinary
charge.

Napoleon, it appears, while employed in inspecting the fortifications at Marseilles, was applied to by one of the Representatives
there, who informed him that certain popular societies intended
to attack and plunder the powder-magazines. The General of
Artillery, in order to prevent this, furnished him with a plan for
constructing a little wall with battlements upon the ruins of Fort
St. James and Fort St. Nicholas, which had been destroyed by
the Marseillois at the beginning of the Revolution. The expence
was trifling; but some months after, a decree was passed for
summoning the Commandant of Artillery at Marseilles to the bar
of the Convention, as having projected a plan for restoring the
Forts of St. James and St. Nicholas in order to withstand the
patriots. The decree specified the Commandant of Artillery at
Marseilles; but Napoleon was at this time General of Artillery
in the Army of Italy. Colonel Seigny, who was the person designated by the words of the decree, had to go to Paris according
to its literal tenor. When this officer presented himself at the
bar, he proved that the plan was not in his hand-writing, and that
he knew nothing about the matter. The circumstance was explained, and Napoleon was discovered to be the person in question; but the Representatives of the Army of Italy, who were in

great need of his services to direct the campaign at this crisis,
wrote to Paris, after putting him under a temporary arrest, and
have such explanations to the Convention as it was satisfied with.

The French in pursuance of the plan laid down crossed the
straits of the Bormida ; and on the 26th of September came to Bal-
astreno, whence they proceeded to Caire or Cairo. Here they fell
in with from 12,000 to 13,000 Austrians manœuvring on the plain,
who no sooner saw the French army approaching than they retreated upon Dego; and being attacked here, after a slight action
in which they lost some prisoners, retired to Acqui. Having
taken Dego, the French halted. They had secured possession of
several magazines, and ascertained that there was nothing to fear
from the Austrian detachment. The march of the French spread
considerable alarm through this part of Italy. The army returned to Savona, traversing Upper and Lower Montenotte. General Dumerbion wrote to the Convention to say that "it was to
the skilful dispositions of the General of Artillery that he in a
great measure owed the success of the expedition."

The remainder of the year 1794 was spent in putting the positions occupied by the French army into a state of defence, particularly Vado, where a part of the troops had been stationed to
protect this port from the English cruisers. The knowledge that
Napoleon acquired by this means of all the positions of the
neighborhood was highly useful to him when he became Commander-in-Chief of the same army, and enabled him to venture
on the bold manœuvre to which he owed the victory of
Montenotte at the opening of the campaign of Italy in 1796.
This may show how intimately application and industry are
connected with genius and capacity. Others who were placed
in the same circumstances with himself derived no advantage
from them, or probably made no minute inquiries or accurate observations from not seeing the use of them or having any object
in view. Napoleon with all his talent would not have performed
what he did, if he had neglected his opportunities of acquiring
local and technical information. But it was the very strength
and comprehensiveness of his mind that made him indefatigable
in his observations and researches from foreseeing the results and
having certain principles in view by which the individual details

were combined with grandeur of effect. Success in any pursuit
implies incredible labor and pains; but it is at the same time a
genius for any pursuit that alone gives a passion for it, or that
can supply the patience necessary to master the preliminary steps
from distinctly perceiving the consequences to which they led or
that can in the end turn them to any account. Buonaparte applied himself to the study of his art with a secret consciousness
of his future destiny, and never looked at an old tower or a moun-
tain-pass but he saw Victory perched upon it! In January, 1795,
he passed a whole night in company with General St. Hilaire on
the Col di Tende, from whence at sun-rise he surveyed those fine
plains which were already the subject of his meditations. *Italiam! Italiam!* This circumstance probably suggested to his
brother Lucien the fine passage in which he describes Charlemagne passing a night among the Alps. In May of this year he
quitted the Army of Italy, and returned to Paris. Aubry, at
that time at the head of the Military Committee and secretly attached to the cause of the Bourbons, had purposely deprived him
of his situation as General of Artillery, and put him on the list of
generals who were intended to serve in La Vendée. The command of a brigade of infantry had been assigned to him; but he
declined this offer, and flung up his commission.

When Kellermann, who had taken the command of the Army
of Italy, was driven from the positions of Vado, St. Jaques, and
Bardinetto, and even talked of evacuating the Genoese territory,
the Committee of Public Safety grew alarmed and called together the different Representatives who had been deputed to the
Army of Italy, in order to consult them. Pontecoulant, who succeeded Aubry in the war-department, was one among others who
pointed out Napoleon as eminently qualified to give an opinion on
the subject—a piece of service for which Buonaparte showed his
gratitude by promoting the minister to a seat in the Senate
when he afterwards became Consul. Napoleon was summoned
to the topographical Committee, and laid down the line of the
Borghetto for the troops—a suggestion that saved the French
army and preserved the coast of Genoa, notwithstanding the repeated attacks of the enemy. At the end of the year (1795)
General Scherer superseded Kellermann in the command; and

on the 20th of November, having received reinforcements from
the army of the Pyrenees, attacked the Piedmontese general De-
vins at Loano, drove him from all his positions, and had he been
sufficiently enterprising, might have conquered all Italy ; but instead of pursuing his advantages, he returned to Nice, and went
into winter-quarters. The enemy did the same.

Napoleon passed most of his time at Paris in meditation and
retirement. He went out but seldom, and had few acquaintances.
He endeavored to forget the sense of mortification and neglect by
a more intense application to his professional studies. This was
the time to prepare himself for the career that lay before him,
and it required all his attention and efforts. He had done something, he had still more to do. Genius is at first shy and taken
up with itself. The new world of thought or enterprise that is
forming in the imagination jostles against and repels the actual
one. This begets an appearance of distance and reserve, because
there is a series of reflections going on in the mind that mark out
a path for themselves and unfit it for the ordinary intercourse of
familiar life. We do not wonder at people in common life who
are absent and thoughtful, if we know that any particular object
engrosses their attention or clouds their brow : but the life of a
man of genius from its commencement is a preparation for the
arduous task he has imposed upon himself. His soul is "like a
star and dwells apart," till it is time for it to disclose itself, and
burst through the obscurity that environs it. Or as an old poet
has expressed this finely, though quaintly—

> "The noble heart that harbors virtuous thought,
> And is with child of glorious, great intent,
> Can never rest until it forth have brought
> The eternal brood of glory excellent."

At a later period of his life, when he had discharged his debt
to Fame, and when men of narrow minds would have become
stiff and haughty with their elevation, he grew proportionably
easy and familiar, and no one was more unreserved, gay, and
communicative, even to exuberance, in conversation. It has been
pretended that about this time Buonaparte had thoughts of offering
his services both to England and the Porte ; for the latter of which

assertions there is so far a foundation, that he proposed to the
Government to send him with other French engineers to assist
the Turks (who were in alliance with France), against the Rus-
sians; but this was perhaps a feint, and answered its end, for
Jean de Bry, one of the Council, observed that if he could be of
such use to the Turks, they had the more need of his services at
home. He sometimes went to the Théâtre Feydeau,·where he
happened to be when he first heard of the rising of the Sections;
and frequented the Corazza coffee-house in the Palais-Royal,
where he used to meet some of his old companions in arms, as
well as several actors of the day, and where the celebrated Talma
is said to have once paid his reckoning for him, for which he had
left his sword in pledge. He himself however contradicts the
truth of this anecdote, and says that he was personally known to
Talma only after he became First Consul.

11*

# CHAPTER VIII.

## THE QUELLING OF THE SECTIONS.

IF a nation of a species lower than men had undertaken a Revolution, they could not have conducted it worse than this of France, with more chattering, more malice, more unmeaning gesticulation, and less dignity and unity of purpose. Scarcely had the *reign of terror* ceased, and the Government been restored to something like stability and order, when within a few months the volatile genius of this people, impatient of liberty or repose, and eager for some new theatrical display, since the daily procession of the *guillotine* no longer kept them in a state of excitement and dismay, seemed anxious to get rid of the Revolution altogether: by way of interlude decked out the youth of the city (*La Jeunesse Dorée*) in the Chouan uniform, and instigated the Sections to revolt against the Convention with a view to restore royalty. When one follows the succession of parties and events which resemble the shifting of the scenes in a pantomime, the oscillation from one dangerous extreme to another, without any motive but the love of change or contrast; when one sees the uniform readiness to spill blood (as the sovereign panacea), the impulse which this appeared to give to the public mind, and the equal readiness and even infatuated determination to relinquish the object which such tremendous sacrifices had been made, the instant t. object was attained, out of sheer fickleness and perversity, or cannot help feeling a sudden burst of spleen, and a disposition t excuse Robespierre and others for thinking that liberty an patriotism alone had not sufficient charms for the Parisians with out the aid of terror, and that it was necessary to resort to extreme violence to compress their extreme versatility. Again, Buonaparte, who was at Paris during the time of this reaction, must have been struck with the folly and extravagance he witnessed, and might then probably have come to the conclusion (on which he acted afterwards) that a people so prone to vanity and mischief might be led by the love of glory and conquest to maintain their external independence, but were as unfit as possible for the enjoyment of a system of regulated and constitutional liberty. The best intentions and the best principles in the world are thrown away upon a nation whose chief delight is in novelty and in a sort of treachery to itself.

The first inclination of the popular party after the death of Robespierre was to keep up the Revolutionary tribunal, and continue nearly the same system under different auspices; but the scheme failing, things took a totally opposite turn. The sixty-three Deputies who had been proscribed for protesting against the expulsion of the Brissotins on the 31st of May, were first recalled to the Convention; and afterwards, all that remained of the victims of that day. The violent party had lost the assistance of the Commune, the principal leaders of which had fallen with Robespierre; but they still had the support of the Jacobins and the Fauxbourgs. The Convention closed the sittings of the one and disarmed the other. The Revolutionary tribunal was still permitted under certain restrictions; those who had been imprisoned by it as suspected persons were let out slowly, one by one, and Barrère attempted in vain to save the president, Fouquier-Thinville, one of those who had dipped his hands with most insolence and fury in the blood of his fellow-citizens, and whose name excited general horror. A month after the fall of Robespierre, Lecointre of Versailles denounced Billaud-Varennes, Collot d'Herbois, Barrère, Vadier, Amar, and Vouland, bringing twenty-three distinct charges against them. Tallien had just before inveighed bitterly against the system of terror; and Lecointre was emboldened in his attack by the effect which Tallien's words had produced. Alas! every thing here seems referable to the study of effect, to a mixture of cowardice and vanity. No fixed principles, no steady convictions, and determination to abide by them in spite of consequences; but an habitual readiness to abandon or outrage the plainest truths, according to the immediate chances of personal disgrace or triumph. The accusation of Lecointre against the accomplices of Robespierre failed the first time, and was declared calumnious by the Convention: soon after, they contented themselves with passing to the order of the day upon it; the third time, it was carried tumultuously, and the objects of it were condemned to banishment. Thus the first time a charge is brought, it only excites surprise at the boldness of the experiment: the second time, the ice being broke, there is an apprehension that it will be carried; and this anticipation of defeat makes all eager to concur in it, lest they should be considered as parties implicated, though the grounds of the accusation remain in all respects the same as before. It is not the truth or justice of the case that determines the question, but the confidence of success that encourages the attack and silences opposition.

What contributed to increase the unpopularity of the members of the Committee, was the publicity given to the cruelties of Carrier and Joseph Lebon, its two Commissioners at Arras and Nantes. Lebon, young, of a sickly temperament, and naturally compassionate, had discovered considerable humanity in his first mission to Cambray; but he was reproached with his moderation by the Committee, and was sent to Arras (his own and Robespierre's birth-place) with the express injunction to show himself a little more *revolutionary*. In order not to be behind-hand with the inexorable policy of the Committee, he lent himself to the most unheard-of excesses; mixed up debauchery with extermination; had the guillotine always standing by him, which he called *St. Guillotine*, and kept company with the executioner, whom he admitted to his table. Carrier, having more victims at his disposal, had even surpassed him: he was bilious, fanatical, naturally blood-thirsty. He only waited for an opportunity put in practice all that the imagination of a Marat had not ev dared to think of. Being sent to the neighborhood of a rebel d triet, he condemned to death the whole hostile population, priest women, children, the old, the young. As the scaffolds did n suffice, he had superseded the Revolutionary tribunal by a ban of assassins, who took the appellation of the *Company of Marat*— and the guillotine by boats with false bottoms, by means of which he drowned crowds of victims in the Loire. As many (it is said) as eight hundred persons at a time, of different ranks, ages an' sexes, were precipitated into the river in this inhuman manne

and when any of these unfortunate wretches clung in despair to
the sides of the barges, if in the struggle their hands got loose,
their executioners amused themselves with cutting them across
the wrists with their sabres, or knocking them on the head with
their poles. Innocent young women were stripped naked in the
presence of their butchers and tied to young men, and both were
cut down or thrown into the river together—and this kind of murder was called by an opprobrious nickname.

Cries of vengeance and horror were raised against these acts of
atrocity, say the French historians, after the 9th of Thermidor;
yet when, a short time before, Carrier himself sent them a de-
tailed account of his proceedings, and added with a sort of triumphant sneer, " *Quel torrent revolutionnaire que la Loire !*" the
Convention received this piece of barbarous levity with applause.
Surely the dictates of humanity or decency do not depend on the
dates of the almanac. An act of lawless cruelty and revenge
may be endured, while it is deeply lamented, in a dreadful crisis;
but that it should be made a subject of sport and merriment, is
not to be endured or palliated under any circumstances. In other
countries they attempt to resist or remonstrate against oppression
at the time; in France the successful perpetrators are applauded
like favorite actors on a stage, and they are only punished when
all the mischief and danger is over, by what is termed a *reaction*.
The style of this period corresponds very much with the tone of
its sentiments, and equally shows the inflamed and exasperated
state of the public mind that could dictate or tolerate such bombast. " At the name of Carrier," says the reporter of his correspondence at the time, " the smoking chart of La Vendée unrols
self before your eyes. *Thousands of salamanders from amidst
e furnace of that wide waste feed the fire which consumes the
epublic.* You hear the crackling of the flame which devours
th manufactures and hamlets, cities and men; the ruins of
stles mingled with the wreck of cottages—melancholy and de-
rable equality, which exists only in devastation! I see by
glare of the blaze, those who have kindled it, darting across
burning beams of falling houses, like birds of prey, on the
sures they contain. Even the asylum of patriotism is not
ected; the enemies taken with arms in their hands, and those

who lay them down, are precipitated into the same gulph; the
common foe, and the friend who leads our soldiers to victory,
who procures them by sure indications the means of necessary
subsistence, perish alike; and the same regard is paid to the patriot and the rebel." We may see by this flagrant style that the
popular brain had been over-wrought; images of death, of havoc
and destruction floated familiarly and mechanically before it;
and the degree of excitement was the only thing considered, the
kind (whether good or evil) was a matter of absolute indifference.

Carrier, when called upon for his defence, threw the blame of
what he had done on the cruelties of the Vendeans themselves and
on the undistinguishing fury of civil war. "When I was giving
my orders," said he, "the air seemed still to resound with the
civic chaunts of twenty thousand martyrs to liberty, who had
shouted *Long live the Republic!* in the midst of tortures. How
is it possible for humanity, dead in these terrible crises, to make
its voice heard? Those who accuse me, what would they have
done in my place? I saved the Republic at Nantes. I have lived
only for my country, and I am prepared to die for it." Out of five
hundred members, four hundred and ninety-eight voted in favor of
the sentence against Carrier. What added to his unpopularity and
hastened his condemnation, was the evidence of ninety-four of the
most respectable inhabitants of Nantes, persons sincerely attached
to the cause of the Revolution, and who had resolutely defended
their city against the Vendeans, but who were implicated in the
same fate with them and sent to Paris in chains as Federalists.
If they had happened to have been brought before the Revolutionary tribunal during the zenith of its power, they would have fallen
like so many others under the fangs of its merciless system. This
instance alone is enough to show that the system of terror resorted
to at this period exceeded its professed objects, however stern and
implacable; and that the rage of patriotism, like every other,
soon "made the food it lived upon," that it constructed crimes and
fabricated excuses, in order to exercise its sense of power and
glut its love of vengeance on all who came by any accident within its unhallowed grasp, without distinction and without remorse.
Two reflections arise here. The first is, that it is unjust to attribute the corrupt state of moral feeling, the want of moderation

and magnanimity, the ferocity or apathy displayed on these occasions, to the French Revolution.   Instead of throwing an indelible reproach upon it, they seem rather to vindicate its necessity.
They were committed by men who had received a Bourbon education, and had for the most part imbibed their ideas of what was
fair and honorable from the precepts of priests and the example
of nobles.   *Coup-Tête* with his axe and his beard, his hand and
his heart, was ready-made for his part, and sprung all-armed out
of the filth and rottenness of the ancient *régime*, like Pallis out of
the head of Jupiter.   The license of the time indeed gave a
greater scope to such characters, when in the fury of civil contest the hateful passions were most in request ; but the former
state of things had left no dearth of such materials and such
characters to work with.   It would be more a matter of wonder,
and would lessen the value of the change, if a people suddenly
emancipated from a long, ignoble, and dastardly servitude, all
at once displayed the wisdom and manliness of character of a
people regularly trained to the possession and to the use of freedom.   Secondly, we shall do well to consider whether this stain
of cruelty and intolerance, instead of being confined either to the
French Revolution or French character, is not too applicable to
all ages and nations, whether free or enslaved, refined or barbarous ; and how far this original and rancorous bias in our own
breasts is merely hindered from breaking out by circumstances,
or "skinned and filmed over" by custom and appearances.  Very
common characters would work up into Revolutionary monsters!

The *reaction*, to which Carrier had appealed in his own justification, soon began to spread in a contrary direction.   The South
of France became a scene of counter-revolutionary excesses, of
the same character and almost as terrible as those of the Revolutionary Committees themselves.   Massacres in mass, private assassination, were the order of the day.   *Companies of Jesus* and
*Companies of the Sun* took place of *Companies of Marat*, and
exacted as severe a retribution.   At Lyons, at Aix, at Tarascon,
at Marseilles, they slew all those confined in the prisons who had
participated in the late transactions, pursued those who had escaped in the streets, and without any other form or notice than
the reproach, "Behold a *Matavin!*" (the nickname they gave to

their opponents) slew them, and threw them into the river.    At
Tarascon they precipitated them from a high tower on a rock
which bordered on the Rhone.    Thus the infliction of cruelty and
terror went its round, and was not confined to any particular class
or side, but was the consequence of the maddening spirit and
delirium of the time and the mutual hatred of the different factions
towards each other.

The Jacobins and the Fauxbourgs were dissatisfied with the
arrest and trial of the *terrorist* Deputies.    The latter more than
once raised an insurrection, and marched to the Convention, crying out, " Bread, the Constitution of the year 93, and the release
of the imprisoned Deputies !"    On one of these occasions they
rushed in considerable numbers into the Hall of the Convention,
and a scene of the most frightful disorder ensued.    Boissy-d'-An-
glas took the chair which Vernier had quitted.    He was not popular, being at the head of a Committee of Subsistence for supplying the people with bread ; and from the slow and inefficient
manner in which they proceeded, he was called *Boissy-Famine*.
He was even suspected of keeping back the supplies of provisions,
in order to make the people desperate and favor the designs of the
royalist faction, with which he was secretly connected.    The
rioters took aim with their pieces at Boissy-d'-Anglas, when a
deputy of the name of Ferand, rushing forward to protect him,
was dragged out into the lobbies, his head lopped off, and held up
on a pike before the President of the Convention to induce him to
pass the resolutions required by the insurgents.    Boissy-d'-An-
glas remained firm, inflexible in the midst of threats and insults ;
and when the bleeding head of Ferand was presented to him,
bowed respectfully to it.    There is a strange mixture of the horrible and ludicrous with the sublime in this scene, which is not
lessened when we are told that the calmness of countenance assumed by the chief actor in it was but a mask for clandestine designs, and the courage he displayed inspired by a lurking hatred
and contempt for the people.    In this period of political scene
shifting and violent tergiversation, there is not only no trusting to
appearances, but even the most heroical actions become equivocal
by their pretended connection with problematical circumstances.
Boissy-d'-Anglas was the intimate friend of Aubry, who is also

supposed to have superseded Buonaparte with a view to rob the
Republic of his talents and future victories.   In France every
thing is attributed to stratagem and intrigue on the slightest
grounds: one thing is certain, that where people are always on
the watch for such motives, they are more likely to act from them,
and that a downright simplicity and straight-forwardness cf character is the last thing to be looked for.   The assassin of Ferand
was discovered, but rescued by the mob.   This ill-timed and sanguinary insurrection hastened the fate of the members of the
Committees under arrest, who, with several *Cretais* (the wreck
of the Mountain faction, who had countenanced the rioters), were
condemned and sent to the fortress of Ham.   These disorderly
risings of the common people might be mischievous, but were no
longer formidable.   They wanted the clubs, they wanted the terrible municipality with Henriot at its head, knocking at the gates
of the Convention, and crying with a voice of thunder and a front
of brass, " The Sovereign People is at hand !" they wanted public
opinion on their side ; and above all, they wanted Prussian manifestos and the dread of the Allied powers, hanging imminent over
Paris, and threatening them with military execution and lasting
debasement and servitude.   The brain pressed on that nerve
started into sudden frenzy : otherwise, it was tame and light
enough.

The arms of the Republic were, about this time, everywhere
victorious; and the public mind, reassured in that respect, had
leisure to come to its senses in other things.   In the beginning of
1795 peace was concluded with Spain and Prussia ; and, at the
same time, Pichegru overran and conquered Holland, drove away
the Stadt-Holder, and thus deprived Great Britain of its footing on
the Continent.   Seeing no prospect of crushing France by means
of foreign powers, the British Cabinet united itself more closely with
the Emigrants, and in concert with them projected the disastrous
expedition to Quiberon.   Hoche had nearly stifled the war in La
Vendée by a mixture of vigor and prudence hitherto unattempted.
He had beaten the scattered remains of the enemy's troops, driven
away their cattle, which he restored to them in exchange for their
arms, and gained over many of their priests by separating the cause
of religion from that of politics.   The spirit of disaffection still in

deed existed, but had scarcely the means of showing itself; and
the differences between their only surviving chiefs, Charette and
Stofflet, gave the finishing blow to the hopes of the royalists in
that quarter.   Charette had even consented to make peace with
the Republic, and a sort of treaty had been entered into at Jusnay
between him and the Convention.   The Marquis de Puisaye, a
man of intrigue and adventure rather than the enthusiast of any
party, had conceived the project of transferring the nearly extinguished insurrection of La Vendée into Brittany.   There already
existed in Morbihan bands of Chouans, composed of the refuse of
all parties, of men thrown out of employment and desperate, of
hardy smugglers, who made predatory incursions into the enemy's
territory, but could not keep the field like the Vendeans.   Puisaye
had recourse to Great Britain to extend the Chouan system, and
led the English ministers to expect a general rising in Brittany,
and from thence throughout the rest of France, if they would only
furnish the skeleton of an army, ammunition, and musquets.

The Quiberon expedition (the favorite and memorable scheme
of the late Mr. Windham, then Secretary at War) included the
most active and spirited of the Emigrants, almost all the officers
of the ancient French marine, and in short all those of that party
who, tired of exile and the miseries of a wandering life, were desirous to try fortune once more.   The English fleet accordingly
landed on the small peninsula of Quiberon 15,000 Emigrants,
6000 republican prisoners who had enlisted in hopes to return
to France, 60,000 musquets, and a complete equipment for an
army of 40,000 men.   Fifteen hundred Chouans joined this little
army on its disembarkment, when it was immediately attacked
by General Hoche.   He succeeded in turning it; the republican prisoners who were found in its ranks deserted from it, and
it was defeated after the most obstinate resistance.   In the deadly
war between the Emigrants and the Republic, the vanquished
were treated as outlaws, and no quarter was given to them.
Their loss was a severe and irrecoverable blow to the Emigrant
party.

The expectations founded on the armies of Europe, on the
progress of internal discord, and on the attempt of the Emigrants
having failed, recourse was next had to the discontented Sec-

tions. It was hoped to bring about the counter-revolution by means of the new Directorial Constitution. This Constitution was nevertheless the work of the moderate republican party ; but inasmuch as it gave the ascendant to the middle classes, the royalist intriguers indulged confident expectations of entering by their means into the Legislature and the Government. The Convention having suppressed the Jacobins and the Fauxbourgs in order to put an end to anarchy and violence, the *Jeunesse Dorée* thought this a proper time to insult their fellow-citizens as Republicans, and the Sections rose against the Convention to annul its authority now that it was mildly and beneficially exercised, and to restore despotism and the ancient *régime :* upon what principle it is impossible to guess, except that mentioned by Luther, that " human reason is like a drunken man on horse-back—set it up on one side, and it is sure to fall over on the other." Or rather, passion is only satisfied with mischievous extremes—moderation and wisdom appear to be its bane—and reason is the dupe of sophistry and passion.

The Convention notwithstanding held an even course, and was determined to keep it. To avoid the error of the first Constituent Assembly, which had involved France in endless troubles by the prudery of excluding its members from the subsequent Assembly, the Convention decreed the re-election of two-thirds of its members. This prompt and seasonable step, which had for its object to save the country from the return of anarchy or a counter-revolution, excited the greatest possible ferment : the Royalist Committee came to an understanding with the journalists and shop-keepers of Paris ; the Fauxbourg St. Germain, hitherto deserted, was filled from day to day with Emigrants in the Chouan uniform, who made no secret of their design of restoring absolute power, while the Section Lepelletier (or Filles-St. Thomas) under the guidance of La Harpe,* Lacretelle, and other literary drivellers, at once the accomplices and dupes of the reviving party, declared loudly (in order to arrive by a diversion at the same end) that all power resided in the assembled people. The struggle be-

* This writer appears to have been much such a politician as he was a critic, neglecting the essence for the form, and more taken up with the means than the end.

came more and more furious: the majority of the Sections of
Paris sided with the Section Lepelletier in rejecting the decree
of the Convention, who however, on the 1st of Vendemaire pronounced both that and the Constitution to have been acceded to
by the majority of the primary assemblies throughout France.
The Sections had now nothing to do but to submit ; but as they
had farther objects in view or were led on by those who had, they
were by no means disposed to do so.   They proceeded to nominate
the electors, who were to choose the new members after their
own fashion ; and to organize an armed force to defend their
meetings.   The Convention, apprised of the coming storm and
not inclined tamely to yield to it, collected the troops from the
camp of Sablons, delegated its powers to a Committee of five persons, Colombel, Barras, Daunou, Letourneur, and Merlin of
Douai, who were charged with the care of the public safety ;
enrolled a *Battalion of the Patriots of Eighty-nine* (amounting to
fifteen or eighteen hundred old revolutionists, who had been objects of persecution to the *réactionnaires* in the southern departments), and on the 11th at night sent to dissolve the assembly of
electors by force, but they had already adjourned.   During the
night of the 11th, the decree which dissolved the college of electors and armed the Battalion of Patriots of Eighty-nine, produced
the greatest consternation and was represented as a return to the
system of terror.   The Section Lepelletier did every thing in its
power to incite the other Sections to revolt.   The Convention, no
less alarmed, resolved to give the first blow and bring the affair
to a conclusion by disarming the refractory Sections.

On the 12th of Vendemaire (October 3d) at seven or eight
o'clock in the evening, General Menou, accompanied by the
Representatives of the People, who always attended on such occasions as Commissioners of the army of the Interior, proceeded
with a numerous escort to the place of rendezvous of the Section Lepelletier to put the decree of the Convention in execution.
The infantry, cavalry, and artillery were all crowded together in
the Rue Vivienne, at the extremity of which stood the Convent
of the *Filles-St. Thomas*.   The Sectionaries occupied the windows of the houses in this street.   Several of their battalions drew
up in line in the court-yard of the Convent, and the military force

which General Menou led found itself placed in **an** embarrassing predicament. The Committee of the Section having designated themselves as a deputation of the Sovereign People in the exercise of their original functions, which the Convention had usurped, they refused to obey its orders; and after an hour spent in useless conferences, General Menou and the Commissioners withdrew by a sort of capitulation, without having dissolved or disarmed the meeting. The Section thus victorious declared themselves in permanence; sent deputations to the other Sections, boasting of **its** success and urgently recommending the measures best calculated to insure the common triumph. In this manner it prepared for the contest of the 13th of Vendemaire (October 4).

Napoleon, who had been for some months attending the Committee which directed the movements of the Armies of the Republic, was at the Théâtre Feydeau, close to the top of the Rue Vivienne, when he heard of the extraordinary **scene that was** passing so near him. He went to the spot, curious to observe all the circumstances. Seeing the troops baffled, he hastened to the gallery of the Convention to witness the effect of the news and mark the character and coloring that would be given to it. The Convention was entirely at a loss what to do. The Representatives, wishing to exculpate themselves, eagerly accused Menou, attributing to treachery (according to the fashion of the time) **what arose from unskilfulness alone. Menou was** put under arrest. Several deputies then appeared at the Tribune, stating the extent of the danger, which was but too clearly proved by the intelligence that **arrived every moment from** different quarters. Each member proposed the General in whom he reposed the greatest confidence to succeed Menou. The Thermidoriens wished for Barras, but this choice was by no means agreeable to the other parties. Those who had been on duty with the Army **of** Italy at Toulon and the members of the Committee of Public Safety who were in daily communication with Napoleon, recommended him as the person most likely to extricate them from their present danger, on account of the promptitude **of his resources** and the firmness and moderation of his character. Mariette, who belonged to the party of the Moderates, and was one of the lead-

ing members of the Committee of Forty, approved of this selection. Napoleon, who was in the crowd and heard all that passed,
considered for above half an hour of the course he should adopt.
At length he made up his mind and repaired to the Committee,
where he pointed out in the most forcible manner he was able the
impossibility of directing so important an affair while clogged by
three Representatives, who would in fact take the whole management into their own hands, and impede all the operations of the
General :—he added that he had witnessed the occurrence in the
Rue Vivienne, and that the Commissioners had been most to
blame, though they had come forward as angry accusers. Struck
with the truth of this reasoning, but unable to remove the Commissioners without a long discussion in the Convention, the Committee to reconcile all parties (for they had no time to lose) determined to nominate Barras General-in-Chief, appointing Buonaparte second in command under him. Thus they got rid of the
services of the three Commissioners without giving them any
cause of umbrage. As soon as Napoleon found himself invested
with the actual command of the forces that were to protect the
Convention, he went to one of the apartments in the Thuilleries,
where Menou remained in custody, in order to procure from him
the necessary information as to the strength and disposition of the
troops and the state of the artillery. The regular army consisted of only 5000 soldiers of all arms, whereas the ... tional
Guard at the disposal of the insurgents amounted to 40,000 men.
The park of artillery was composed of forty pieces of cannon,
then collected at Sablons (about five miles from Paris) and
guarded by twenty-five men. It was one o'clock in the morning.
Buonaparte immediately dispatched a major of the 21st Chasseurs (this major was Murat) with 300 horse to the camp at Sablons to bring off all the artillery to the Garden of the Thuilleries.
Had another moment been lost, he would have been too late. He
reached Sablons at three in the morning, where he fell in with the
head of a column from the Section Lepelletier, which was coming to seize the park ; but Murat's troops being cavalry and the
ground a plain, the Sectionaries did not think proper to risk an
engagement. They accordingly retreated, and at five o'clock in
the morning the forty pieces of cannon entered the Thuilleries.

Between six o'clock and nine Napoleon planted his artillery at the head of the Pont Louis XVI. the Pont-Royal, and the Rue de Rohan, at the Col-de-sac Dauphin, in the Rue St. Honoré, at the Pont-Tournant, &c. entrusting the guarding of it to officers of known fidelity. The matches were lighted, and the little army was distributed at the different posts or kept in reserve in the Gardens and at the Carrousel. The drums beat to arms in every quarter. During this interval the National Guards were posting themselves at the outlets of the different streets contiguous to the Palace and the Garden of the Thuilleries : their drums even came and beat the charge on the Carrousel and the Place Louis XV. The danger was imminent ; 40,000 National Guards, well armed and long since trained to discipline, were in the field and highly incensed against the Convention. The troops of the line entrusted with its defence were comparatively few in number, and might easily be led astray by catching the enthusiasm of the populace. To increase its disproportioned force, the Convention had distributed arms to about 1500 individuals called the Patriots of 89, who were divided into three battalions and placed under the command of General Berruyer. These men fought with the most determined valor ; their example influenced the other troops, and they were mainly instrumental to the success of the day. A committee of forty members, which had been chosen from the Committees of Public Safety and General Security, managed all the proceedings, discussed much, but resolved on nothing ; while the urgency of the danger increased every moment. Some proposed that the convention should lay down their arms and receive the Sections as the Roman Senators received the Gauls. Others wished the members to withdraw to Cæsar's camp on the heights of St. Cloud, there to be joined by the Army of the Coasts of the Ocean ; and others recommended that deputations should be sent to the forty-eight Sections to make them various offers.

During these vain discussions, a man named Lafond (an old Garde-du-Corps) debouched on the Pont-Neuf, about two o'clock in the afternoon, at the head of three columns from the Section Lepelletier, while another detachment of the same body advanced from the Odeon to meet them. They joined in the Place Dauphin.

General Cartaux, who was stationed on the Pont-Neuf with 400
men and four pieces of cannon, with orders to defend both sides
of the bridge, quitted his post, and fell back on the wickets of the
Louvre.    At the same time, a battalion of National Guards occupied the Infant's Garden.   They pretended to be faithful to the
Convention, but nevertheless seized this post without orders.   On
the other side, the church of St. Roche, the Théâtre Français,
the Hôtel de Noailles were occupied in force by the National
Guards.   The posts of the Conventional troops were not above
twelve or fifteen paces from them.   The Sectionaries sent women
to corrupt the soldiers; even the leaders came forward several
times unarmed and waving their hats, as they said to *fraternize!*
The danger rapidly spread.   Danican, the general of the Sections,
sent a flag of truce to summon the Convention to remove the troops
that threatened the people, and to disarm the *Terrorists*, meaning
the patriots of 89.   The bearer traversed the posts with his eyes
bandaged and with all the formalities of war, about three o'clock.
He was then introduced into the midst of the Committee of Forty,
amongst whom his menaces caused much alarm, but he obtained
nothing.   Night was coming on; the populace might have
availed themselves of the darkness to climb from house to house
to the Thuilleries itself, which was closely blockaded.   Napoleon
had 800 muskets, belts, and cartridge-boxes brought into the hall
of the Convention, to arm the members and the clerks as a corps
of reserve.   This measure alarmed several of them, who then began to comprehend the seriousness of the circumstance.   At
length at four o'clock some muskets were discharged from the
Hôtel de Noailles, and some of the balls struck on the steps of the
Thuilleries, and wounded a woman who was going into the Gardens.   At the same moment Lafond's column debouched by the
Quai Voltaire, marching on the Pont-Royal, and beating the
charge.   The batteries then got ready: an eight-pounder at the
Cul-de-Sac Dauphin opened the fire on the church of St. Roche opposite occupied by the insurgents, which served as a signal.   After
several discharges the church was carried.   Lafond's column,
taken in front and flank by the artillery placed on the quay even
with the wicket of the Louvre and at the head of the Pont-Royal,
was routed; the Rue St. Honoré, the Rue St. Florentin, and the

places adjacent were swept by the guns. About a hundred men attempted to make a stand at the Théâtre de la Republique, but were dislodged by a few shells. At six o'clock in the evening, all was over. A few cannon-shots were heard from time to time during the night; but they were fired to prevent the barricades which some of the inhabitants attempted to form with casks. There were nearly two hundred of the Sectionaries killed or wounded, and almost an equal number on the side of the Convention; the greater part of the latter fell at the gates of St. Roche. The Representatives, Freron, Louvet, and Siéyes, evinced great spirit. The Section of the Quinze-Vingts in the Fauxbourg St. Antoine was the only one that assisted the Convention, sending 250 men to its aid. The Fauxbourgs, however, containing the poorest of the people, though they did not rise in favor of the Government, did not act against it. The strength of the armed force of the Convention employed on this occasion, reckoning the Representatives themselves, was about 8500 men.

Assemblages still continued to form in the Section Lepelletier. On the morning of the 14th some columns marched against them by the Boulevards, the Rue Richelieu, and the Palais-Royal. Cannon had been planted in the principal streets, so that the Sectionaries were speedily dispersed, and the rest of the day was passed in traversing the city, visiting the rendezvous of the insurgents, seizing arms, and reading proclamations; in the evening order was universally restored, and Paris was completely quiet. After this important service, when the officers were presented to the Convention in a body, Napoleon was chosen by acclamation Commander-in-Chief of the Army of the Interior, Barras being no longer allowed to combine his military functions with the character of Representative. General Menou was delivered up to be tried by a Council of War; but Buonaparte saved him by insisting that the Representatives were more in fault than he, and should be condemned first. Lafond was the only person executed. This young man was an emigrant,* and had displayed great courage in the action: the head of his column on the Pont-

---

* This circumstance alone points out the complexion of the affair. The Royalists made use of the Constitutionalists as tools, and the latter seem to have been at all times proud of the occupation.

Royal had formed again thrice under the fire of grape-shot, be
fore it entirely gave way.   The officers were very desirous to
save him ; but the imprudence of his answers made it quite impossible.   It is not true that the troops were ordered to fire only
with powder at the commencement of the action, (which would
have served to embolden the insurgents and endanger the
troops ;) but towards the latter part of the affair, when success was no longer doubtful, they were told to fire with blank
cartridges.

After the 13th of Vendemaire, Napoleon had to re-organize the
National Guards as well as those of the Directory and Legislative
Body—a circumstance that conduced very much to his success
on the famous 18th of Brumaire.   He left so favorable an impression on these different corps, that on his return from Egypt,
although the Directory had prohibited its Guards from paying
him any military honors, their order was without effect, and the
soldiers could not be prevented from beating *To the Field !* the
moment he appeared.   The foundation of fame and greatness is
laid regularly step by step, so that the brilliant renown which at
last astonishes the world is but the echo of the common consent
of all those with whom a really powerful mind has come in contact ; instead of being the result of caprice or accident, according
to the opinion of some, who would persuade us that the adventurer can at any time start up and play the hero !   Great and
first-rate talents, it is true, are often concealed from observation,
and are not suspected, till a proper occasion offers for them to
display themselves ; but from the first moment that such an
opportunity occurs, they do not fail to stamp their impression on
outward circumstances and opinion, as surely as the seal leaves
its impression on the wax !   The few months during which
Napoleon was at the head of the Army of the Interior were replete
with difficulties and disturbance, arising from the installation of
a new government (that of the Directory,) the members of which
were divided among themselves as well as often opposed to the
Councils ; the silent ferment which existed among the old Sectionaries, who were still powerful in Paris ; the active turbulence
of the Jacobins, who used to meet at the Society of the Pantheon
the foreign agents who fomented discord in all quarters ; and

above all, from the horrible famine which at that time raged in the capital. Ten or twelve times the scanty allowance of bread, which the Government usually distributed day by day, entirely failed. The Society of the Pantheon caused the Directory increased uneasiness ; in consequence of which the General-in-Chief had the doors of their assembly-room sealed up. The members stirred no more for the present ; but some time after Babœuf, Antonelle, and others connected with it set on foot the conspiracy of the camp of Grenelle. Napoleon at this period frequently had occasion to harangue the people in the streets and market-places, at the Sections and in the Fauxbourgs ; and it is worthy of notice, that of all parts of the capital the Fauxbourg St. Antoine (which had been regarded as the most violent, and was the first that rose and demolished the Bastille at the commencement of the Revolution) was the one which he always found most ready to listen to reason and the most susceptible of gener ous motives.*

It was while he commanded at Paris that Napoleon became acquainted with Madame de Beauharnais. After the disarming of the Sections, a youth ten or twelve years of age presented himself to the staff to solicit the return of a sword which had belonged to his father, formerly a General in the service of the Republic. This youth was Eugene Beauharnais, afterwards Viceroy of Italy. Napoleon, touched by the nature of his petition and by his boyish eagerness, granted his request. Eugene burst into tears, when he beheld his father's sword. The General, pleased with his sensibility, behaved so kindly to him, that his mother thought herself obliged to wait on him the next day to thank him for his attention. Every one has heard of the extreme grace of the Empress Josephine, and of her sweet and captivating manners. Napoleon was struck at this first interview. Their acquaintance soon became more tender and intimate ; and it was

---

* One day as he was addressing the crowd, a fat woman interrupting him said, "Never mind these smart officers, who, so that they themselves get fat, do not care who else is starved." Buonaparte, who was then very thin, turned round and said, "Look at me, good woman, and then tell me which of us two is the fattest ?" This repartee turned the laugh against her, and the mob dispersed

not long before they were married.* This connection proved
fortunate and happy for both parties; and well perhaps would it
have been, had it also proved lasting!

Scherer who commanded the Army of Italy had not profited as
he might have done by the victory of Loano. He was constantly
writing to the Directory for money and horses; and as they
could supply him with neither, he threatened to evacuate the
coast of Genoa and repass the Var. The Directory, at a loss
what to do, turned their thoughts to the General of the Interior.
His reputation for boldness and skill, and the confidence reposed
in him by the Army of Italy, naturally pointed him out as the
fittest person to retrieve the present embarrassing situation of
affairs. These considerations determined the Government to ap-
point him Commander-in-Chief of the Army of Italy. He left
Paris to join them on the 14th of March, 1796. General Hatry,
a veteran of sixty, succeeded him in the command of the Army
of Paris, which had become of less importance, now that the crisis
of the scarcity was over, and the Government was more settled.
Buonaparte was between six and seven and twenty when he took
upon him this new command. Some one taunting him with his
youth on this occasion, he is said to have given the memorable
answer, " In a year's time I shall be dead or old!" Or as it was
variously reported afterwards, " In a year's time I shall have Milan,"—*J'uarai Milan*,†—(meaning the name of the city or a
thousand years.)

* In March, 1796.—Madame Beauharnais was by birth a Creole of St.
Domingo. Her name originally was Marie-Joseph Rose Tascher de la
Pagerie. When a child, a black sorceress had foretold that she should be
one day more than a queen. Her husband had been a general in the Republican armies, and had fought valiantly in the battles on the Rhine; but
merely on suspicion as being noble, had been arrested and suffered death
four days before the fall of Robespierre. His wife had been thrown into
prison also, where she became acquainted with Madame Fontenai, afterwards Madame Tallien, through whom she was introduced to Barras and
into the political circles of the day. Buonaparte left Paris a few days after
they were married; and during the first campaign in Italy, when all Europe rang with his exploits, constantly wrote letters to her, bemoaning their
separation, and full of the most passionate and even *home-sick* feelings. On
his way to join the army, he turned aside to Marseilles to visit his mother
and family who were residing there.                    † Mille ans.

# CHAPTER IX.

## CAMPAIGN IN ITALY.

BUONAPARTE reached Nice, the head-quarters of the army, the 27th of March, 1796.* The picture of the army which General Scherer laid before him was even worse than any thing he had been able to conceive. The supply of bread was precarious; no distributions of meat had been made for a long time. The cavalry was in the worst condition possible, though it had been on the Rhone to recruit its strength; but it had suffered for want of provisions. The arsenals of Nice and Antibes, it is true, were well furnished with artillery, but destitute of the means of transporting it from place to place, all the draught horses having perished for want. There were no means of conveyance left but five hundred mules. The low ebb of the finances was such that Government with all its efforts could only furnish the chest of the army with two thousand louis in specie to open the campaign with, and 40,000*l.* in drafts, part of which were protested. Marshal Berthier preserved among his papers an order of the day, dated shortly after from Albenga, granting an extraordinary gratification of three louis-d'ors to each General of Division. The army thus destitute had nothing to expect from France; all its dependence was on victory and its new General: it was only in the plains of Italy that it could find carriage-horses for the artillery, clothe the soldiers, and mount the cavalry. This, however, was a bold and almost hopeless undertaking; for the troops consisted

---

* He was well received by the other Generals, some of them of high standing. Massena and Augereau bore testimony to his military talents, and expressed their readiness to serve under him. Decrès, afterward Minister of Marine, who had been intimate with him, hearing he was to pass through Toulon, ran to congratulate him as an old acquaintance. But his manner, without having any thing injurious in it, put a stop to his eager zeal, and he never after attempted any familiarity with him.

of only 30,000 men actually under arms, with thirty pieces of cannon at their command; while they stood opposed to 80,000 men and two hundred pieces of cannon. The army of the Allies, commanded by General Beaulieu, an officer who had acquired considerable reputation in the campaigns of the North, was divided into two grand corps; the Austrian, 45,000 strong, under Lieutenant-General D'Argenteau, Melas, Wukassowich, Liptay, and Sebottendorf; and the Sardinian, amounting to 25,000 men, under the Austrian General Colli and Generals Latour and Provera. The rest of the forces of the King of Sardinia were employed to garrison the fortresses, or defend the frontier of the higher Alps, under the command of the Duke of Aoste. The French army was composed of four effective divisions of infantry and two of cavalry, under Generals Massena, Augereau, Laharpe, Serrurier, Stengel, and Kilmaine; it amounted to 25,000 infantry, 2500 cavalry, 2500 artillery, sappers, &c.; total, 30,000 men. The nominal strength of the army, according to the Government returns, was indeed 100,000 men; but out of these 30,000 were killed or taken prisoners, 20,000 were at Toulon, Marseilles, and Avignon, and the rest dispersed in the hospitals, *dépôts*, and fortresses on the coast of Genoa or in the passes of the mountains. Had the French army been under the necessity of engaging in a general action, its inferiority in numbers, in artillery, and cavalry must have prevented it from making an effectual stand: it had therefore to make up for its inferiority in numbers by rapid marches, for the want of artillery by the nature of its manœuvres, and for its inferiority in cavalry by the choice of positions. On the other hand, the character of the French soldiers was excellent, without which nothing could have been done. They had distinguished themselves and were grown inured to war on the summits of the Alps and of the Pyrenees. Poverty, danger, and hardships are the school in which good soldiers are bred.

The state of affairs daily grew worse; there was no farther time to be lost. The army could no longer procure subsistence where it was, and must either advance or fall back. Napoleon gave orders to advance and thus surprise the enemy in the very opening of the campaign by striking a decisive blow. The headquarters had never been removed farther than Nice since the commencement of the war; he at once put them on their march for Albenga half-way between Nice and Genoa. All the persons on the civil list had long considered themselves as permanently stationary where they were, and were much more intent on providing the comforts of life for themselves than on supplying the wants of the army. Napoleon, on reviewing the troops, addressed them thus:—"Soldiers, you are naked and ill-fed! Government owes you much and can give you nothing. The patience and courage you have shown in the midst of these rocks are admirable; but they gain you no renown; no glory results to you from your endurance. It is my design to lead you into the most fertile plains in the world. Rich provinces and great cities will be in your power: there you will find honor, glory, and wealth. Soldiers of Italy! will you be wanting in courage or perseverance?" This speech from a young General of six-and-twenty, already distinguished by well-earned success, was received with eager acclamations.

In the beginning of 1796, the King of Sardinia, whose military and geographical situation had procured him the title of *Porter of the Alps*, had fortresses at the outlets of all the passes leading into Piedmont. For the purpose of penetrating into Italy by forcing the Alps, it would have been necessary to gain possession of one or more of these fortresses; a work of considerable risk and difficulty, as the roads did not allow of bringing up a battering-train, and the mountains are covered with snow during three quarters of the year, which leaves little time for besieging fortresses. Napoleon conceived the idea of turning the whole chain of the Alps, and entering Italy at the very point where these lofty mountains terminate, and where the Apennines begin. Mont Blanc (a little to the south of the Lake of Geneva) is the most elevated point of the Alps, whence the range of these mountains decreases slowly in height towards the Adriatic as well as towards the Mediterranean as far as Mount St. Jaques, where they end, and where the Apennines begin to rise gradually as far as Mount Velino near Rome. Mount St. Jaques is therefore the lowest point both of the Alps and Apennines. Savona, a sea-port and fortified town near this place, was well situated as a *dépôt* and point of support. From this town to La Madonna it is three miles, whence it was reckoned six miles to Carcari by a road which might in a few days be rendered practicable for artillery. From Carcari there are carriage-roads leading into Piedmont and Montferrat. This is the only point by which Italy can be entered without passing over high mountains; and here the elevations of the ground are so trifling, that at a later period (during the Empire) a canal was projected for joining the Adriatic to the Mediterranean by the Po, the Tanaro, the Bormida, and by locks from that river to Savona. The plan of invading Italy on this side gave hopes of separating the Austrian and Sardinian armies; as Turin and Milan might be marched upon with equal facility in this direction, and the Piedmontese would be interested in covering the one, the Austrians the other.

In pursuance of the design of turning the Alps and invading Italy by the Col di Cadibona, it was necessary to collect the whole army on its extreme right; a dangerous operation, had not the snow then covered all the passes of the Alps, so as to prevent the enemy from attacking them while making this change of position from the defensive to the offensive order. Serrurier posted himself at Garessio, on the other side of Mount St. Jaques to observe Colli's camp near Ceva: Massena and Augereau took possession of Loano, Finale, and Savona along the coast; Laharpe menaced Genoa, and his vanguard, led by Cervoni, occupied Voltri. The French minister demanded of the Senate of Genoa a passage by the Bocchetta and the keys of Gavi; a demand which spread alarm through this city, and even as far as Milan.

Beaulieu hastened with all speed to the aid of Genoa. He advanced to Novi, and divided his army into three corps; the right at Ceva, under Colli, was ordered to defend the Stura and the Tanaro; the centre, under D'Argenteau, marched on Montenotte to intercept the French army in its way to Genoa, by falling on its left flank and cutting it off from the road of La Corniche; Beaulieu in person marched with his left on Voltri by the Bocchetta to protect Genoa. By this manœuvre, which at first seemed skilful enough, he had in fact disconnected his force, as no communication was practicable between his left and his centre, except round the back of the mountains; while the French could unite in a few hours, and fall in a mass on either of the enemy's corps, on the defeat of either of which the other would be compelled to retreat. Iu consequence of this plan, General D'Argenteau, with the Austrian centre, encamped on Lower Montenotte on the 10th of April, and on the 11th marched on Montelegino, to debouch by La Madonna on Savona. Colonel Rampon, who was ordered to guard the three redoubts of Montelegino, hearing of the enemy's march, pushed forward a strong reconnoitring party to meet him, which was driven back from noon till two in the afternoon, when it regained the redoubts, which D'Argenteau in vain attempted to carry in three successive assaults; and his troops being fatigued, he was forced to take up a position, intending to turn the redoubts in the morning. General Cervoni, who had been attacked by Beaulieu before Voltri on the 10th, defended himself through the day, fell back during the evening and the night of the 11th, and joined Laharpe's division, which on the 12th before day-break was drawn up in the rear of Rampon on Montelegino. During the night Napoleon marched with Augereau's and Massena's divisions, the latter of which debouched by the Col di Cadibona and by Castellazzo behind Montenctte. At day-break on the 12th, D'Argenteau, surrounded on all sides, was attacked in front by Rampon and Laharpe, and in flank and rear by Massena's division. The rout of the Austrians was complete; those that were not killed were either taken or dispersed: four stand of colors, five pieces of cannon, and 2000 prisoners were the trophies of this day. Beaulieu, in the meantime, presented himself before Voltri, but found nobody there; had a long conference with Nelson, the English Admiral, and did not hear till the 13th of the loss of the battle of Montenotte and the entrance of the French into Piedmont. He was then obliged to retreat suddenly, and by such bad and circuitous roads, that it took him two days to reach Millesimo, and twelve to evacuate his magazines at Voltri and in the Bocchetta.

On the 12th the head-quarters of the French army were removed to Carcari. The Allies occupied Dego and Millesimo, which cover the two great roads into Piedmont and Lombardy. But on the next day but one (the 14th) the battle of Millesimo opened both these roads to the French. The enemy had strengthened his right by occupying the hill of Cossaria, which commands

12*

both branches of the Bormida. On the 13th, Augereau, whose troops had not been engaged at the battle of Montenotte, attacked the right of the line opposed to him with such impetuosity, that he carried the defiles of Millesimo and surrounded the hill of Cossaria. The Austrian General Provera, with his rear-guard 2000 strong, was cut off; in this desperate situation he took refuge in an old ruined castle, where he barricadoed himself. From its top he saw the Sardinian army preparing for the battle of the following day, and conceived hopes of being released. Napoleon tried (but without being able to succeed) to gain possession of the castle of Cossaria. The next day the two armies engaged; Massena and Laharpe carried Dego after an obstinate conflict, Menard and Joubert took the heights of Biestro. All Colli's attacks, for the purpose of delivering Provera, were fruitless; so that the latter in despair laid down his arms. Great advantages resulted from this victory in the quantity of artillery and ammunition, as well as the number of prisoners taken. It also separated the Austrian and Sardinian armies. Beaulieu removed his headquarters to Acqui on the Milan road; and Colli proceeded to Ceva, to oppose the junction of Serrurier and to cover Turin.

Meantime, Wukassowich's division of Austrian Grenadiers, which had been sent on from Voltri by Sassello, reached Dego at three o'clock in the morning of the 15th of April, and easily carried the village, in which there were only a few French battalions. Their arrival occasioned some panic, as it was difficult to imagine how the enemy could have got to Dego, while the advanced posts on the Acqui road remained undisturbed. Napoleon marched to Dego, which was retaken after a very smart action of two hours. Adjutant-General Lanusse, who was afterwards a General of division, and fell at the battle of Alexandria in Egypt in 1801, was chiefly instrumental to its success, which at one time appeared doubtful. At the head of two battalions of light troops he climbed the left side of the hill of Dego, whither some Hungarian Grenadiers hastened to oppose his progress: twice the two columns advanced and were obliged to fall back; but the third time Lanusse, placing his hat on the point of his sword, rushed forward, and by his example decided the victory. This exploit, which took place in the sight of the General-in-Chief, procured him the rank of brigadier-general. Generals Causse and Bonnel were killed ; they came from the Eastern Pyrenees, and the officers who had served in that army always displayed remarkable courage and impetuosity. It was at the village of Dego that Napoleon for the first time took notice of a lieutenant-colonel, whom he made a colonel. This was Lannes, who afterwards became a Marshal of the Empire and Duke of Montebello, and evinced the greatest prowess in a hundred battles. Buonaparte always showed no less superiority in the quickness with which he discovered bravery than in the generosity with which he rewarded it.

After the action of Dego, operations were principally directed against the Piedmontese, and it was thought sufficient to keep the Austrians in check. Laharpe was placed in observation at the camp of San Benedetto on the Belbo, where, from the scarcity of provisions, the soldiers were guilty of several excesses. Serrurier, having heard at Garessio of the battles of Montenotte and Millesimo, occupied the heights of San Giovanni di Murialto, and entered Ceva on the same day that Augereau arrived on the heights of Montezemoto. Colli had already evacuated the town on the 17th, and retreated beyond the Corsaglia, leaving the artillery of his camp behind him, which he had not time to carry off, and placing a garrison in the fort. The arrival of the victorious army on the summit of Montezemoto was a sublime spectacle. From that position the troops beheld the immense and fertile plains of Piedmont ; the Po, the Tanaro, and a multitude of other rivers meandered in the distance ; in the horizon a glittering circle of snow and ice bounded the rich valley at its feet. Those gigantic barriers, which rose like the limits of another world, which nature had rendered almost impassable, and on which art had lavished all its strength, had yielded as by enchantment. "Hannibal forced the Alps," said Napoleon, eyeing those stupendous mountains, "and we have turned them !"

The army passed the Tanaro, and for the first time found itself in the plains, where the cavalry became necessary. General Stengel, who commanded it, crossed the Corsaglia at Lezegno on the right bank of that river, near its junction with the Tanaro. On the 20th, Serrurier, while passing the bridge of St. Michel to attack the right of Colli's army, as Massena was passing the Tanaro to

turn his left, met Colli's troops, who had become sensible of the
danger of his situation, and had abandoned it in the night to retire
to Mondovi. The French General was repulsed and forced to
turn back, partly from the want of discipline in the troops, some
of them having taken to pillage. On the 22d, however, he debouched by the bridge of Torre, Massena by that of St. Michel,
the General-in-Chief by Lezegno, advancing in three columns on
Mondovi, where Colli had intrenched himself. Serrurier carried
the redoubt of La Bicoque, and thus decided the battle of Mondovi. The town with all its magazines fell into the power of the
victor. General Stengel, who had advanced too far into the plain
with a thousand horse in pursuit of the enemy, was attacked in
his turn by the Piedmontese cavalry, which were excellent, and
while making his retreat in good order, received a mortal thrust
in a charge, and fell dead on the spot. Murat came up at the
head of three regiments and put the Piedmontese to flight.
General Stengel was a native of Alsace, and an excellent officer,
combining the fire and activity of youth with the judgment of age.
Two or three days before his death, having been the first to enter
Lezegno, the General-in-Chief arrived a few hours later, and
found that the defiles and fords had been reconnoitred, guides procured, the curate and post-master questioned, provisions bespoke,
and every thing he could wish for in readiness. Stengel was
short-sighted, and this circumstance proved fatal to him. We can
hardly lament those who fell in this early struggle for independence—happier than those who lived to see its end! Death closed
their eyes on victory; nor did they think they should fall in vain.

The loss of the Piedmontese in this battle amounted to 3000
slain, eight pieces of cannon, ten stand of colors, and 1500 prisoners, among whom were three Generals. After the battle of
Mondovi, Napoleon marched on Cherasco, Serrurier advanced on
Fossano, and Augereau on Alba. Beaulieu had proceeded from
Acqui towards Nezza-della-Paglia with half his army, to make a
diversion in behalf of the Piedmontese, but too late; he fell back
on the Po as soon as he heard of the treaty concluded at Cherasco. This last is a fortified place, and supplied the French
troops with artillery-magazines. The army then passed the
Stura and encamped before the little town of Bra. Serrurier's

junction had thrown open the communication with Nice by Ponte-di-Navi; and reinforcements of artillery, with all the stores that could be got ready, also arrived from thence. In the late actions the army had made acquisition of a great quantity of cannon and horses; and a few days after entering Cherasco, the artillery could furnish sixty guns well supplied and horsed. The soldiers, who had been without rations for the last ten days, now received them regularly; pillage and disorder, the usual accompaniments of want and hurried marches, ceased; the appearance of the army was improved and its losses repaired; soldiers pouring in by every road from all the *dépôts* and hospitals of the coast of Genoa on the mere report of the victories gained by the army and of the abundance it enjoyed. The Court of Sardinia in these circumstances saw no other alternative but to propose an armistice. Count Latour, a cavalier of the old school, and Colonel Lacoste, an intelligent and liberal-minded man, were charged with the King's powers; and the terms proposed were, that the King of Sardinia should secede from the Coalition, and send a plenipotentiary to Paris to treat for a definitive peace; that Ceva, Coni, and either Tortona or Alexandria should be immediately surrendered to the French army, with all their artillery and stores; that the French should continue to occupy their present positions, and a free communication be allowed them by the military roads to and from France; and that Valenza should be evacuated by the Neapolitans and placed in the hands of the French General till he should have effected the passage of the Po. Colonel Murat, principal aid-de-camp, was dispatched to Paris, by way of Mount Cenis, with this capitulation and twenty-one stand of colors. His errand caused great joy in the capital. Junot, who had been sent forward after the battle of Millesimo by the Nice road, arrived later. In the course of a month from the opening of the campaign, the Legislature had five times decreed that the army of Italy had deserved well of its country.

From this time the Austrians, left to fight their own battles, might be pursued into the interior of Lombardy. But would it be prudent to do so? Many thought it madness to attempt the conquest of Italy with so small an army and with a hostile kingdom in their rear. These persons were for revolutionizing Pied-

mont before they ventured farther; but Buonaparte saw little
danger on this side, now that the fortresses were given up, and
was of opinion that the French army ought not to halt till they
had reached the Adige, the best line of defence against the Austrian succors, which would soon, no doubt, pour down from the
Tyrol and the Frioul. This counsel prevailed. To dare is, in
critical circumstances, often the means of success; as to carry into
effect what to others appears madness is the surest sign of genius.
Ordinary minds are appalled no less by the magnitude than by
the danger of an enterprise. Buonaparte's clearness of percep-
tion and promptness of resolution were alike conspicuous through
the whole of the campaign, and it is the union of these two qualities that distinguishes the hero from the mere speculative dreamer
or fool-hardy adventurer. From Cherasco he addressed a proclamation to the army, in which traces may be found of the con-
trariety of sentiment and the apprehensions that were entertained.
" Soldiers, you have in fifteen days gained six victories, taken
twenty-one stand of colors, fifty-five pieces of cannon, and several fortresses, and overrun the richest part of Piedmont: you
have made 15,000 prisoners, and killed or wounded upwards of
10,000 men. Hitherto you have been fighting for barren rocks,
made memorable by your valor, though useless to your country,
but your exploits now equal those of the Armies of Holland and
the Rhine. You were utterly destitute, and you have supplied
all your wants. You have gained battles without cannon, passed
rivers without bridges, performed forced marches without shoes,
and bivouacked without strong liquors, and often without bread.
None but republican phalanxes, the Soldiers of liberty, could
have endured what you have done; thanks to you, Soldiers, for
your perseverance! Your grateful country owes its safety to
you; and if the taking of Toulon was an earnest of the immortal campaign of 1794, your present victories foretell one more
glorious. The two armies which lately attacked you in full confidence, now fly before you with consternation: the perverse men
who laughed at your distress and inwardly rejoiced at the triumph
of your enemies, are now confounded and trembling. But, Soldiers, you have yet done nothing, for there still remains much to
do. Neither Turin or Milan are yours: the ashes of the con-

querors of Tarquin are still trodden under foot by the assassins of Basseville. It is said that there are some among you whose courage is shaken, and who would prefer returning to the summits of the Alps and Apennines. No, I cannot believe it. The victors of Montenotte, Millesimo, Dego, and Mondovi are eager to extend the glory of the French name!"

On the 15th of May the definitive treaty of peace with the Court of Sardinia was signed by Count Revel at Paris, by which the fortresses of Alexandria and Coni were surrendered to the Army of Italy; Susa, Brunetta, and Exilles were to be demolished, and the Alps opened; the King of Sardinia being left with no other fortified places than Turin and Fort Bard, and the Coalition thus deprived of the assistance of a power which could send from fifty to sixty thousand men into the field, and was still more formidable from its situation. This treaty must have been extorted by main force, and shows the brilliant success of Napoleon's arms, as the King of Sardinia was father-in-law both to Monsieur and the Count D'Artois, and it was at his court that the first plan of the Coalition was concerted.

The gates of the fortresses of Coni, Tortona, and Alexandria were opened to the French in the beginning of May. The headquarters were fixed at Tortona. Beaulieu had retreated beyond the Po, and prepared to defend the passage of that river opposite Valenza. An article in the concluding part of the armistice stipulated for the surrender of that town to the French to enable them to pass the Po there. This was a *ruse de guerre*. With the same view to mislead, scarce had Massena reached Alexandria when he pushed forward parties in the direction of Valenza. Augereau left Alba to encamp at the mouth of the Scrivia. Serrurier and Laharpe repaired to Tortona, where the grenadiers of the army were assembled to the number of 3500 men. With these choice troops, with the cavalry and twenty-four pieces of cannon, Napoleon, suddenly turning to the right, advanced by forced marches on Placenza to surprise the passage of the Po. The moment the intended object was unmasked, all the other divisions abandoned their posts and followed him with the utmost expedition. On the 7th of May, at nine o'clock in the morning, he arrived before Placenza, having marched sixteen leagues in thirty-six hours. He proceeded to the bank of the river, where he remained till the passage was effected, and the van was on the opposite side. The ferry-boat of Placenza carried 500 men or 50 horses, and crossed in half an hour. The river is very rapid and about a quarter of a mile in breadth. Lanusse passed first with 500 grenadiers. Two squadrons of the enemy's hussars in vain opposed their landing. In the night of the 7th the whole army had come up, and on the 9th the bridge was finished.

Liptay's division of the Austrian army, consisting of eight battalions and eight squadrons, arrived during the night from Pavia at Fombio, one league from the bridge of Placenza. On the 8th in the afternoon it was discovered that the steeples and houses of the village were embattled and filled with troops, and that cannon were planted on the roads which crossed some rice-fields. It became of the utmost importance to dislodge the Austrian general from Fombio, where he might receive great reinforcements, and it would be unsafe to be compelled to give battle with so large a river in the rear. Napoleon gave orders for such dispositions as the nature of the ground required, and in an hour the village was carried and the Austrians routed with the loss of their cannon, three standards, and above 2000 prisoners. The wreck of this corps threw themselves into Pizzighettone, which only a few days before was thought too far from the seat of war to be put in a state of defence. It had been ascertained from the prisoners that Beaulieu was on his march to encamp behind Fombio. It was therefore possible that some of his troops, not knowing what had happened in the afternoon, might advance to Codogno, to take up their quarters there, and the troops were instructed accordingly. Laharpe drew up in front of this place; and Massena took post at the head of the bridge across the Po, to support him in case of need. The General-in-Chief after giving orders for the most vigilant look-out returned to his head-quarters at Placenza. What had been foreseen took place. Beaulieu on hearing of Napoleon's advance on Placenza put all his troops in motion, in hopes of coming up in time to prevent the passage of the river. A regiment of cavalry that preceded the column in which he was, stumbled on Laharpe's advance posts, and turned back to give the alarm. The French bivouacs were speedily under arms: after discharging a few shots, they heard no more of the enemy. Laharpe went forward with a piquet and some officers to ascertain what was the matter; but returning by a different path from that by which he set out, the troops who were on the watch took him for the enemy; they received their General with a brisk fire, and he fell dead, pierced by the bullets of his own soldiers. Laharpe was a Swiss of the canton of Vaud. His hatred of the government of Berne had exposed him to persecution, from which he had sought an asylum in France. He was an officer of distinguished bravery and much beloved by his troops, though of an unquiet temper. It was remarked that during the action of Fombio, on the evening preceding his death, he had appeared absent and dejected, giving no orders, seemingly deprived of his usual faculties, and overwhelmed by some fatal presentiment. The news of this melancholy accident reached head quarters at four in the morning. Berthier was instantly dispatched to this division of the vanguard, and found the troops in the greatest distress.

On entering the States of Parma, Napoleon at the passage of the Thebbia received envoys from the Prince, suing for peace and for protection. This was granted on condition that the Duke paid two millions in French money, furnished the stores of the army with a quantity of hay and wheat, and supplied 1600 horses for the artillery and cavalry. It was on this occasion also that Napoleon exacted a contribution of works of art to be sent to the Museum at Paris, being the first instance of the kind that occurs in modern history. Parma furnished twenty pictures chosen by the French Commissioners, among others the famous St. Jerome of Correggio. The Duke offered £80,000 to be allowed to keep this picture; the opinion of the army-agents was decidedly in favor of accepting the money. The General-in-Chief said, there would very soon be an end of the two millions of francs; while the possession of such a masterpiece by the city of Paris would remain a proud distinction to that capital, and would produce other *chefs-d'œuvre* of the same kind. Vain hope! Not a ray of the sentiment or beauty contained in this picture dawned upon a French canvas during the twenty years it remained there, nor ever would to the end of time. A collection of works of art is a noble ornament to a city, and attracts strangers; but works of genius do

not beget other works of genius, however they may inspire a taste
for them and furnish objects for curiosity and admiration.    Correggio, it is said, the author of this inimitable performance,
scarcely ever saw a picture.    Parma, where his works had been
treasured up and regarded with idolatry for nearly three hundred
years, had produced no other painter like him.    A false inference
has been drawn from works of science to works of art, as if there
could be a perpetual addition and progression both in one and the
other: but science advances because it never loses any of its
former results, which are definable and mechanical; whereas art
is wholly conversant with indefinable and evanescent beauties and
can never get beyond the point to which individual nature and
genius have carried it.    The accumulation of models and the
multiplication of schools, after the first rudiments are conquered
and the language is as it were learnt, only create indolence, distraction, pedantry, and mediocrity.    No age or nation can ever
ape another.    The Greek sculptors copied Greek forms; the
Italian painters embodied the sentiments of the Roman Catholic
religion.    How is it possible to arrive at the same excellence
without seeing the one or feeling the other?    From the time that
men begin to borrow from others instead of themselves, and to
study rules instead of nature, the progress of art ceases.    In Italy
there has not been a painter worthy of the name for the last hundred and fifty years!    It was not amiss, in one point of view, that
the triumphs of human genius should be collected together in
the Louvre as trophies of human liberty; or to deck out the
stern, gaunt form of the Republic which was declared incapable
of maintaining the relations of peace and amity with the richest
spoils of war: otherwise these works would make most impression
and are most likely to give a noble and enthusiastic impulse to the
mind in the places which gave them birth and in connection with
the history and circumstances of those who produced them:—
torn from these, they lose half their interest and vital principle.
Besides, the French see nothing but what is French.    Barbarism
and rusticity may perhaps be instructed, but false refinement is
incorrigible.    They have no turn for the fine arts, music, poetry,
painting.    They have indeed caricatured and ill-colored the Greek
statues, as they have paraphrased the Greek drama; but that is

all. This people are " born to converse, to write, and live with ease," but they are qualified for nothing that requires the mind to make an arduous effort or to soar beyond its ordinary flight. Buonaparte could do and did a great deal for France; but he could not *unmake* the character of the people. Give them David's pictures, and they are satisfied; and no other country will ever quarrel with them for the possession of the prize!*—Still, justice should be done to the taste and judgment with which the selection was made, which was no less striking than the universality of the sources from whence it was drawn. As a gallery, the Louvre was unrivalled: even the Vatican shrinks before it. Not a first-rate picture is to be met with on the Continent, but it found its way to the Louvre. Among other claims to our gratitude and wonder, it shortened the road to Italy; and it was "a journey like the path to heaven," to visit it for the first time. You walked for a quarter of a mile through works of fine art; the very floors echoed the sounds of immortality. The effect was not broken and frittered by being divided and taken piecemeal, but the whole was collected, heaped, massed together to a gorgeous height, so that the blow stunned you, and could never be forgotten. This was what the art could do, and all other pretensions seemed to sink before it.

School called unto school; one great name answered to another, swelling the chorus of universal praise. Instead of robbery and sacrilege, it was the crowning and consecration of art; there was a dream and a glory, like the coming of the Millennium. These works, instead of being taken from their respective countries, were given to the world, and to the mind and heart of man, from whence they sprung. The shades of those who wrought these

---

* This celebrated artist, looking at some fine Caraccis no longer in the Louvre, said to a friend who was with him, "Don't you remember the time when we were sufficiently absurd to admire those daubs?" His own works now fill up the vacancy. The entrance of the Apollo, the Dying Gladiator, and other great works from Rome, at the end of the year, was celebrated by a procession of the two Councils, the Artists, by bands of music, and appropriate incriptions, by the rehearsing of a long dithyramdic poem and the chaunting of Horace's *Carmen Seculare*, through the streets of Paris: so oddly do they mix up new and old! Is not this *mélange* to be accounted for from the spirit of the Catholic Religion?

miracles might here look down pleased and satisfied to see the
pure homage paid to them, not out of courtesy or as a condescension
of greatness, but as due to them of right as the " salt of the earth."
The load that killed Correggio here first fell off, and Raphael
might smile at having missed a Cardinal's hat. Art, no longer a
bondswoman, was seated on a throne, and her sons were kings.
The spirit of man walked erect, and found its true level in the
triumph of real over factitious claims. Whoever felt the sense of
beauty or the yearning after excellence haunt his breast, was
amply avenged on the injustice of fortune, and might boldly answer those who asked what there was but birth and title in the
world that was not base and sordid—" Look around ! These are
my inheritance; this is the class to which I belong !" He who
had the hope, nay, but the earnest wish to achieve any thing like
the immortal works before him, rose in imagination and in the
scale of true desert above principalities and powers. All that it
had entered into his mind to conceive, ·his thought in tangled
forests, his vision of the night, was here perfected and accomplished, was acknowledged for the fair and good, honored with
the epithet of *divine*, spoke an intelligible language, thundered
over Europe, and received the bended knee of the universe.
Those masterpieces were the true handwriting on the wall, which
told the great and mighty of the earth that their empire was
passed away—that empire of arrogance and frivolity which assumed all superiority to itself, and scoffed at every thing that
could give a title to it. They might be considered as naturalized
and at home in this their adopted country, which set an exclusive
value on what could contribute to the public ornament or the public use, and had disallowed all claims to distinction that could insult
or interfere with those of truth, nature, and genius. The Louvre
was therefore " a great moral lesson ;" a school and discipline of
humanity ! Buonaparte has explained his views on this point in
a letter publicly addressed to Oriani, the celebrated mathematician, where he assures him that all men of genius, all who had
distinguished themselves in the republic of letters, were to be accounted natives of France, whatever might be the actual place of
their birth. "Hitherto," he says, "the learned in Italy did not
enjoy the consideration to which they were entitled—they lived

retired in their laboratories and libraries, too happy if they could escape the notice, and consequently the persecution of kings and priests. It is now no longer thus—there is no longer religious inquisition nor despotic power. Thought is free in Italy. I invite the literary and scientific persons to consult together, and propose to me their ideas on the subject of giving new life and vigor to the fine arts and sciences. All who desire to visit France will be received with distinction by the Government. The people of France have more pride in enrolling among their citizens a skilful mathematician, a painter of reputation, a distinguished man in any class of letters, than in adding to their territories a large and wealthy city." This is the true spirit of Jacobinism; and not the turning the Thuilleries into a potatoe-garden.—Once more, as to the charge of plunder and robbery, all the collections in Europe answer it, for they are composed of works by the same masters. If these works were heir-looms, and sacred to the soil where they grew, they could not be removed. What is subject of barter and sale in time of peace, may be reckoned among the spoils of war. The Cartoons, the Elgin Marbles answer it. That these pictures were received in lieu of other contributions is proved by this, that £80,000 were offered for the restoration of the St. Jerome, and refused. If the army agents had had their way, we should have heard nothing about the robbery, because we ourselves should have liked to have pocketed the same sum. We who transfer whole people and bombard peaceful towns, talk at our ease about rapine and sacrilege committed on statues and pictures, because they offer no temptation to our cupidity.

The population of Parma, was 40,000 souls. Its citadel was in bad repair. The duchies of Parma, Placenza, and Guastalla belonged to the Farnese family. Elizabeth, wife of Philip V. brought them into the house of Spain. Don Carlos, his son, possessed them in 1714; who being afterwards called to the throne of Naples, these duchies passed to the House of Austria in 1748, by the treaty of Aix-la-Chapelle: the Infant Don Philip was invested with them, whose son Ferdinand succeeded him in 1762. He was Condillac's famous pupil, and died in 1802. He inhabited the castle of Colorno, surrounded with monks, and occupied with the most minute and rigid observance of religious duties.

# CHAPTER X.

## CAMPAIGN IN ITALY CONTINUED.

ON the 10th of May the French army marched from Casar-Pusterlengo on Lodi, where Beaulieu had effected his junction with Sebottendorf's and Roselmini's divisions, and had directed Colli and Wukassowich northwards on Milan and Cassano. Napoleon's object was to intercept these last troops, if possible, before they could reach their destination; but on the Lodi road he met with a strong rear-guard of Austrian grenadiers, who made a most obstinate resistance, but were at last thrown into disorder, and pursued hotly by the French, who entered the town pell-mell with them, the enemy in vain endeavoring to close the gates. The fugitives rallied on the other side of the bridge, outside the town, where Beaulieu was posted with 12,000 infantry and 4000 cavalry, and between twenty and thirty pieces of cannon. Napoleon, in hopes of still cutting off the division (10,000 strong) which was marching on Cassano, resolved to pass the bridge over the Adda the same day under the enemy's fire, and to astonish them by so daring an operation. Accordingly, after a few hours' rest in the town, about five o'clock in the evening, he ordered General Beaumont with some cavalry to cross the Adda at a ford half a league above the town, and to open a fire on the enemy's right. At the same time he placed at the entrance of the bridge and near it, all the disposable artillery of the army, to answer the fire of the enemy's guns, which were ranged on the other side. In the thickest of the cannonade, he himself stepped forward to point two of the guns in such a manner as to render it impossible for any one to approach in order to undermine or blow up the bridge. He had drawn up the grenadiers in close column behind the rampart of the town, on the edge of the Adda, where they were in fact nearer the enemy's guns than the line of the Austrian infantry itself, the latter having withdrawn behind a rising ground at some distance to shelter itself from the balls of the French batteries. As soon as Buonaparte perceived the fire of the Austrian artillery slacken, and that General Beaumont had made good his landing on the other side, he ordered the charge to sound; and the head of the column of grenadiers, by a sudden wheel to the left, reached the bridge, which it crossed at a running pace in a few seconds, and instantly seized the enemy's cannon. The column had been exposed to the greatest danger at the moment of wheeling to the left to reach the bridge. From the tremendous fire they had to encounter, there was for an instant some hesitation, but Lannes, Berthier, and D'Allemagne. heading the column, hurried them on, so that they soon reached the opposite side of the bridge without any sensible loss, fell upon the Austrian line before they had time to rally, broke it, and forced them to retreat on Crema in the greatest disorder, with the loss their artillery, several stand of colors, and 2500 prisoners. ..s operation, conducted in such dangerous circumstances with so much boldness and presence of mind, has always been referred to as one of Buonaparte's most brilliant exploits. It was on this occasion, in compliment to the personal bravery he had shown, that the soldiers gave him the title of the *Little Corporal*. The French did not lose above 200 men.* Colli and Wukassowich had however crossed the Adda at Cassano, and made their escape by the Brescia road, which determined the French to march on Pizzighettone, and secure that fortress before it could be repaired or victualled. Napoleon in his nightly rounds here fell in with

---

* This account has been criticised as inconsistent with his own expression in the original bulletin, where he speaks of the "terrible passage of the bridge of Lodi." But there is no inconsistency, for he speaks in the same place of the smallness of their loss. "*If we have lost few men,*" he says "we owe it to the promptitude of the execution, and to the sudden effect produced on the enemy by the mass and formidable fire of this intrepid column." Some one having read at St. Helena an account of the battle of Lodi, in which it was said Buonaparte displayed great courage in crossing the bridge, and that Lannes passed it after him—"Before me!" cried Buonaparte, with much warmth; "Lannes passed first, and I only followed him. It is necessary to correct that on the spot!" And the correction was accordingly made in the margin of the book.

a party of prisoners, in which was an old garrulous Hungarian officer, whom he asked how matters went with them? The old captain could not deny but that they went on badly enough: " but," added he, " there is no understanding it at all; we have to do with a young General, who is this moment before us, the next behind us, then again on our flanks; one does not know where to place one's-self. This manner of making war is insufferable, and against all rule and custom."

No French troops had yet entered Milan, although that capital was several days' march in the rear of the army, which had posts at Cremona. But the Austrian authorities, with the Archduke and Duchess, had abandoned it. The municipality and the States of Lombardy sent a deputation, with Melzi at its head, to make a protest of their submission and to implore the clemency of the victor. It was in memory of this mission that the King of Italy afterwards created the duchy of Lodi in favor of Melzi. On the 15th of May Buonaparte made his entrance into Milan under triumphal arch, amidst an immense population and the nume. National Guard of the city, clothed in the three colors, green, red, and white. At the head of the corps was the Duke of Serbelloni, whom the members had chosen for their commander. Augereau retrograded to occupy Pavia; Serrurier occupied Lodi and Cremona; and Laharpe's division Como, Cassano, Lucca, and Pizzighettone, which last place was armed and victualled. Napoleon addressed the following order of the day to his men: "Soldiers, you have rushed like a torrent from the top of the Apennines; you have overthrown and sca'tered all that opposed your march. Piedmont, delivered from Austrian tyranny, indulges her natural sentiments of peace and friendship towards France. Milan is yours, and the Republican flag waves throughout Lombardy. The Dukes of Parma and Modena owe their political existence to your generosity alone. The army which so proudly threatened you can find no barrier to protect it against your courage: neither the Po, the Ticino, nor the Adda could stop you for a single day. These vaunted bulwarks of Italy opposed you in vain; you passed them as rapidly as the Apennines. These great successes have filled the heart of your country with joy; your Representatives have ordered a festival to commemo-

rate your victories, which has been held in every district of the
Republic. There your fathers, your mothers, your wives, sisters,
and mistresses rejoiced in your good fortune, and proudly boasted
of belonging to you. Yes, Soldiers, you have done much—but
remains there nothing more to do? Shall it be said of us that we
knew how to conquer, but not how to make use of victory? Shall
posterity reproach us with having found Capua in Lombardy?
But I see you already hasten to arms. An effeminate repose is
tedious to you: the days which are lost to glory are lost to your
happiness. Well then, let us set forth! We have still forced
marches to make, enemies to subdue, laurels to gather, injuries
to revenge. Let those who have sharpened the daggers of civil
war in France, who have basely murdered our ministers and
burnt our ships at Toulon, tremble! The hour of vengeance has
struck; but let the people of all countries be free from apprehension; we are the friends of the people everywhere, and more particularly of the descendants of Brutus and Scipio, and those great
men whom we have taken for our models. To restore the Capitol, to replace the statues of the heroes who rendered it illustrious,
to rouse the Roman people, stupefied by several ages of slavery—
such will be the fruit of our victories; they will form an era for
posterity; you will have the immortal glory of changing the face
of the finest part of Europe. The French people, free and respected by the whole world, will give to Europe a glorious peace,
which will indemnify them for the sacrifices of every kind which
for the last six years they have been making. You will then return to your homes, and your countrymen will say as they point
you out, *He belonged to the Army of Italy!*"

The army rested six days at Milan, improving its condition and
completing its trains of artillery. Piedmont and the Parmesan had
afforded great resources; but those found in Lombardy were even
more considerable, and furnished the means of discharging the
arrears of pay, supplying the wants of the troops, and establishing regularity in the different branches of the service. The
whole of the plain of Lombardy, extending from the Alps to the
Apennines and from the Mediterranean to the Adriatic, is one entire garden, in which there is scarcely so much as an acre of
ground either waste or not cultivated, planted, and watered in

the highest degree. On the approach of the French, the Duke of Modena, Reggio, and Mirandola sent his natural brother, the Commander of Este, to conclude an armistice; he paid ten millions of francs, gave horses and provisions of all kinds, and a certain number of works of art. He was a covetous old man, and fled to Venice to preserve his treasure, where he died in 1798. He was the last of the house of Este, so famous in the middle ages, and celebrated with such pomp and elegance by Tasso and Ariosto. His daughter, the Princess Beatrice, was the mother of the Empress of Austria, who died in 1816.

Milan was founded by the Gauls of Autun 580 years before Christ. Its population, latterly, amounted to 120,000 souls; it had ten gates, one hundred and forty convents of men and women, and a hundred confraternities. An hospital, the Ambrosian library, and a great number of fine palaces and beautiful walks adorn this city. The cathedral is the most admired in Italy, after St. Peter's; it is Gothic, faced with white marble, of the most elaborate and costly workmanship, was begun by Galeazzo in 1300, and finished by Napoleon in 1810. Under the Roman Empire, Milan was the capital of Cisalpine Gaul; and in the middle ages was the strong-hold of the Guelphs, as Pavia was the chief seat of the Ghibelline faction. In the beginning of the French Revolution, it found strong partisans here, and excited the warmest enthusiasm, as in most of the other capitals of Europe; but the scenes acted during the reign of terror had thrown a damp on this feeling. The Austrian Government was however far from being popular, and was accused of conniving at all sorts of exactions and depredations. The citadel was in a good state of defence; Beaulieu had left 2500 men in it. General Despinois was entrusted with the command of Milan and the blockade of the citadel. Not long after, the revolt of Pavia broke out. The peasants of that province had risen to the number of several thousand, and surprised the citadel of the town, which was in the hands of the French. Buonaparte sent the Archbishop of Milan to appease them, whose remonstrances had no effect. The insurgents of Pavia, who were to have been seconded by the garrison of Milan, pushed a vanguard of 800 men as far as Binasco, where they were met by Lannes, who repulsed them, took the village, pillaged and set fire to it. It was hoped that the conflagration, which was visible from the walls of Pavia, would over-awe that city. But this was not the case. Napoleon made haste there with 1500 men and six field-pieces. These hardly seemed enough to storm a city containing 30,000 souls in a state of insurrection : but the circumstances were critical ; the tocsin was sounding throughout the adjacent country ; the least check might have proved fatal to the French, and Napoleon risked the attack. The field-pieces dislodged the peasants from the ramparts, where they did all they could to annoy the troops; and the soldiers with their axes then broke down the gates. They entered the town and stationed themselves in the houses at the tops of the streets. The peasantry got alarmed, fled the city, and gained the fields, where the cavalry pursued them and put a great number to the sword. The 300 French who had been taken prisoners in the citadel liberated themselves, and made their appearance without arms and in a bad plight. The General's first impulse was to have the garrison decimated : "Cowards," he exclaimed, "I entrusted you with a post essential to the safety of the army, and you have abandoned it to a mob of wretched peasants, without offering the least resistance." The captain attempted to justify himself by an order from General Haquin, whom the insurgents had stopped while changing horses on his way from Paris, and presented a pistol to his breast, threatened to shoot him unless he caused the citadel to surrender. His conduct did not excuse the commander of the fort, who was not under his orders ; and even if he had been, should have ceased to obey the moment the other was taken prisoner. He was delivered over to a council of war and shot. The confusion in the city was extreme; but the pillage, which was afterwards much exaggerated, was confined chiefly to the goldsmiths' shops. The suppression of this revolt was a salutary lesson to the rest of Italy. Hostages were also taken from the principal families of Lombardy, who were recommended to visit France, and came back with a favorable impression. The insurrection was immediately owing to an extraordinary contribution of a million sterling, which had been just laid on, and to some individual instances of oppression. If France could have maintained her own armies, it would have been no difficult task to have made friends of the Italians; but they did not understand taking their money from them and giving them liberty in exchange. It was wonderful how Napoleon managed so well as he did, placed in such circumstances.

In the mean time, the French army continued its march on the Oglio under the command of Berthier who had succeeded Laharpe: the General-in-chief rejoined it at Soncino, and on the 28th marched with it into Brescia, one of the largest towns of the Venetian Terra Firma; the inhabitants of which were discontented with the government of the Venetian nobles. It had submitted to the Republic of Venice in 1426. Its inhabitants amount to 50,000; those of the whole province to 500,000, some living in the mountains, others cultivating rich plains. The following proclamation was posted: "It is to deliver the finest country in Europe from the iron yoke of the proud House of Austria, that the French army has braved the most formidable obstacles. Victory, siding with justice, has crowned its efforts with success, the wreck of the enemy's army has retreated behind the Mincio. In order to pursue them, the French Army enters the territory of the Republic of Venice; but it will not forget that the two Republics are united by ancient friendship. Religion, government, and customs shall be respected. Let the people be free from apprehension, the severest discipline will be kept up; whatever the army is supplied with shall be punctually paid for in money. The General-in-Chief invites the officers of the Republic of Venice, the magistrates, and priests to make known his sentiments to the people, in order that the friendship which has so long subsisted between the two nations may be cemented by confidence. Faithful in the path of honor as in that of victory, the French soldier is terrible only to the enemies of his liberty and his government."

The Senate sent Proveditores to meet the army and make protestations of its neutrality. It was agreed that the Senate should supply all ordinary provisions to be afterwards paid for. Beaulieu had received strong reinforcements on the Mincio, which river runs from the Lake of Garda into the Po by Mantua. Disregarding the remonstrances of the Venetians, he had forced the gates of the fortress of Peschiera on the Lake, and made that place the support of his right, which was commanded by General Liptay; his centre was at Valeggio and Borghetto with Pittony's division; Sebottendorf and Colli were at Pozzuolo and Goito; the reserve under Melas, 15,000 strong, was encamped at Villa-Franca, in the rear or between the Mincio and the Adige. On the 29th of May, the French army was posted at Dezenzano, Montechiaro, and Castiglione, leaving Mantua to its right. On the 30th at day-break, it marched on Borghetto, after having led the enemy to suppose it would pass the Mincio at Peschiera and drawn his reserve to that place. Near Borghetto, the French vanguard fell in with 3000 Austrian and Neapolitan cavalry in the plain: they were attacked by General Murat, who obtained an important success in this action, together with a number of cannon and prisoners, among whom was the Prince of Cuto, who commanded the Neapolitan cavalry. This was the first time that the French cavalry had measured its strength to advantage with the Austrian, and from that time forward it emulated the infantry. Colonel Gardane at the head of the Grenadiers charged into Borghetto; the enemy burnt the bridge, which could not be restored under the fire from the neighboring heights of Valeggio. Gardane threw himself into the river: the Austrians were struck with the recollection of the terrible column of Lodi and beat a retreat: Valeggio was carried. The bridge was reconstructed by noon, and the French army passed the Mincio; Augereau advancing up the left bank on Peschiera, and Serrurier pursuing the Austrian troops who were retiring on Villa-Franca. The General-in-Chief accompanied this division as long as the enemy was in sight; but as they avoided an engagement, he returned back to Valeggio, where he narrowly escaped being taken prisoner through an accident. Massena's division, appointed to guard Valeggio, was preparing dinner on the right bank of the river, not having yet passed the bridge. Sebottendorf's division, having heard the cannonnade at Valeggio, had begun its march up the left bank of the river, and their scouts having approached quite near without meeting any one, they entered the town and had proceeded as far as the lodgings where the General-in-Chief was: his piquet guard had barely time to shut the carriage gateway and cry *To arms*, which afforded him an opportunity of mounting

his horse and escaping through the gardens behind the house.
Massena's soldiers, hearing the alarm, overturned their soup-ket-
tles and passed the bridge. The sound of the drums put the
Austrian hussars to flight.

The danger which Napoleon had incurred convinced him of
the necessity of having a guard of picked men trained to the service and especially charged to watch over his personal safety.
He formed a corps to which he gave the name of *Guides :* Major
Bessieres had the charge of it. This corps thenceforth wore the
uniform which was afterwards worn by the Chasseurs of the
Guard, of which it was the germ. It was composed of picked
men who had been in the army ten years at least, and had rendered eminent services in the field. Thirty or forty of these
resolute fellows, opportunely set on, often produced the most unexpected results. The Guides had the same effect in a battle as
the squadrons on duty afterwards had under the Emperor : both
were under his immediate eye, and he ordered them on at critical
junctures. Bessieres, who was a native of Languedoc, and had
served originally in the Army of the Eastern Pyrenees, possessed
a cool species of bravery, calm and undisturbed amidst the enemy's fire ; his sight was quick, and he was much accustomed to
cavalry movements. He and Murat were the best cavalry-offi-
cers in the army, but of very opposite qualities. Murat was a
good vanguard officer, adventurous, impetuous ; Bessieres was
better adapted for a reserve, being full of vigor, but prudent and
circumspect. From the period of the enrolment of the Guides,
he was exclusively entrusted with the duty of guarding the General-in-Chief and the head-quarters. He was afterwards Duke
of Istria and a Marshal of the Empire.

In order to cover Italy and the siege of Mantua (which was
Napoleon's present object) it was necessary to occupy the line of
the Adige, and to gain possession of the bridges of Verona and
Legnago over it. The Adige runs only a short distance between
the Lake of Garda, the mountains, and the sea on the north-east-
ern side of Italy ; and consequently limited the approach of the
Austrian army to a narrow interval and a few difficult points.
All the insinuations of the Proveditore Foscarelli against marching on Verona were therefore of no avail. On the 3d of June,

Massena took possession of that fine city, which contains not less than 60,000 inhabitants; its walls extend to both sides of the river. The great object of the march of the French was thus attained: the tri-colored flag waved on the passes of the Tyrol. It was now time to force Mantua and tear that shield from Austria. Hopes were entertained in the French camp of accomplishing this event before the arrival of the new Austrian army; but what battles, what obstacles, what dangers were to be encountered first! Mantua is situated between three lakes formed by the waters of the Mincio, which runs from the Lake of Garda by this city to discharge itself into the Po near Governolo. It is accessible by five dykes or causeways, of which that of La Favorite or Roverbella is the only one defended by a citadel; the rest are without any defence, so that a handful of men placed at the extremity of each of these causeways could blockade the garrison. Since then, indeed, in the time of the Kingdom of Italy, there being an intention to complete this grand fortress, it was a preliminary step to occupy all the outlets of the dykes with fortifications. Thus, after forcing the heads of the four dykes and taking the *fauxbourg* of St. Georges (which happened on the 4th of June, under the direction of the General-in-Chief, who was near entering the city at the same time), Serrurier, who was left in command with an army of 8000 soldiers, actually blockaded a garrison containing 14,000 effective troops. A dozen gun-boats, manned with French seamen, cruised on the lakes. It was just at this period that the King of Naples sent to propose an armistice, by which 2500 horse would be withdrawn from the Austrian force. He could also send 60,000 troops into the field, which, in the approaching contest, must have made an important diversion in favor of the enemy. Beaulieu, after all these disasters, fell into disgrace with his court; he was recalled, and Melas took the command in his stead, till Marshal Wurmser could arrive from the army of the Upper Rhine. The Directory, on the other hand, intoxicated with such repeated and unexpected success, wanted to ruin every thing by sending Napoleon on with half the army to revolutionize Rome and Naples, and leaving the command of the remainder to Kellermann. Buonaparte, foreseeing the utter destruction that must follow on the execution of this scheme, indignantly resigned: the Directory became sensible of their error, and from that time meddled no farther with the Army of Italy than to approve of all that Napoleon did or suggested.

In the mean time, the citadel of Milan held out longer than was expected or convenient, as the cannon were wanted for the siege of Mantua : Gerola, the Austrian minister at Genoa, excited the Imperial Fiefs to insurrection, and organized companies of disbanded soldiers and freebooters to intercept the reinforcements of the French army ; the Court of Rome was preparing for war ; and a number of English troops were collected in Corsica, ready to embark for Leghorn.   Marshal Wurmser, who had quitted the Rhine with 30,000 choice troops, was marching on Italy, where, however, he could not arrive before the middle of July.   It was now the beginning of June.   There was therefore an interval of thirty or forty days, during which the necessary detachments might be spared to correct the partial grievances complained of, so as to return to the Adige by the middle of July.   Napoleon then repaired to Milan, where he saw the trenches opened before the citadel ; proceeded thence to Tortona, and directed a column of 1200 men, commanded by Colonel Lannes, to march into the Imperial Fiefs.   Lannes entered Arquata after an obstinate resistance ; shot the banditti who had slaughtered 150 French, and demolished the *château* of the Marquis de Spinola, the principal instigator of these disturbances.   At the same time, Murat proceeded to Genoa, and being introduced into the Senate by the Minister of the Republic Faypoult, demanded and obtained the dismission of the Governor of Novi, the expulsion of the Austrian agents, of the ambassador Gerola, and the establishment of columns of Genoese troops at the different halting-places to escort the French convoys and to keep the communication open.   General Augereau passed the Po on the 14th of ·June at Borgo-Forte, reached Bologna and Ferrara in four marches, and took possession of these two legations, which belonged to the Pope.   General Vaubois collected a brigade of 4000 men and 700 horse at Modena.   Napoleon left Tortona, passed through Placenza, Parma, and Reggio, and on the 19th arrived at Modena.   His presence produced an electrical effect on the people, who called loudly for liberty.   He did all he could to allay the ferment and to ensure obedience to the Regency. The old Duke had already fled with his treasures to Venice.   The road from Modena to Bologna runs along under the glacis of Fort Urbino, belonging to the Pope: it was armed, victualled, and defended by a strong garrison. Augereau's division had passed by it the preceding day without stopping to summon it. Colonel Vignoles advanced against it with 200 Guides, and made the Garrison surrender as prisoners of war. This fort was lined with sixty pieces of cannon, half of which were forwarded to Borgo-Forte. In the citadel of Ferrara a hundred and twelve guns had been taken, forty of which were also sent to Borgo-Forte.

At Bologna, Augereau's division found a Cardinal at the head of 400 men, whom he took prisoners. The Cardinal obtained leave to go to Rome on his parole; behaving very ill, and being desired to return, he sent a very specious answer that he was released from his parole by a brief from his Holiness, which caused a good deal of laughing in the army. Bologna is surnamed the *Learned*. It is situated at the foot of the Apennines, and contains 50,000 or 60,000 inhabitants. Its noble streets are adorned with porticos formed into arcades for the convenience of foot-passengers: its Academy is the most renowned in Italy. The people were dissatisfied with the Papal government, and complained of being subjected to a set of priests, men devoted to celibacy, and who sacrificed every thing to the interests of their order. The entrance of the army was a triumph. Caprara, Marescalchi, and Aldini did the honors to the victor, and brought their *Golden Book* to show him the names of his ancestors inscribed among the list of their senators. There were three or four hundred Spanish Jesuits at Bologna at this period; they were much alarmed, but no disrespect was shown them. In the course of the few days that Napoleon remained here, the appearance of the city was entirely changed. All but the priests assumed the military dress and sword; and even a great number of ecclesiastics were drawn in by the spirit that animated the people. The French General showed himself constantly in public, and went to the theatre every night, escorted only by the Bolognese. The Vatican now felt alarm, and the Spanish Minister, Azara, was despatched with full powers to grant an armistice till peace could be concluded, according to which Bologna and Ferrara were to remain in possession of the French, who were to garrison

Ancona ; and the Pope was to pay the value of twenty-one millions in money, horses, and provisions, and to give up one hundred works of art for the Museum at Paris. The philosophers and enemies of the Holy See were by no means pleased with this suspension of hostilities ; and the people of Bologna, more particularly, were apprehensive of returning under the Papal jurisdiction. Having made this arrangement, which secured the flanks of the army from molestation, and tended to conciliate the minds of the faithful, Napoleon passed the Apennines, and on the 26th of June joined Vaubois' division at Pistoia. He was here waited on by Manfredini, Prime Minister of the Grand Duke of Tuscany, who was assured of the friendly disposition of the French, and that they only wished to pass on to Siena. On the 30th, Murat, who led the vanguard, turned short from Firenzuola on Leghorn, hoping to surprise a hundred English ships which were laden in the port ; but they received timely notice and set sail for Corsica. The English were driven from Corsica in the month of October following, as Sir Gilbert Elliot, the Viceroy, had not sufficient strength to resist the attacks of the insurgents and refugees who flocked over under Gentili. The English merchandize seized at Leghorn brought twelve millions of francs into the army-chest. Vaubois was left here with a garrison of 2000 men ; the rest returned to the Adige. Napoleon crossed over from Leghorn to Florence on an invitation from the Grand Duke. He was without any escort, was much pleased with his reception by the Grand Duke, and visited every object of interest or curiosity in this ancient and renowned capital. While at dinner with the Grand Duke, Napoleon received the news of the taking of the citadel of Milan, which had capitulated on the 29th. Manfredini, his Prime Minister, had been preceptor to this Prince, as well as to the Archduke Charles ; he was an enlightened and liberal man, attached to the philosophical principles of the French Revolution, though he blamed its excesses, and a zealous friend to the independence of Italy. On his arrival at Bologna, Napoleon found that Lugo had revolted. The Bishop of Imola, afterwards Pius VII., in whose diocess the insurrection had broken out, published a mandate to open the eyes of the peasants, who had committed several excesses, and submitted only to force. It was on his journey across the country to Pistoia that Buonaparte stopped with his military staff at San Miniato, at the house of his uncle, an old canon, who amused them by insisting on the canonization of one Father Bonaventura Buonaparte, a Capuchin friar and a member of the family, who had worked miracles a century before. Pope Pius VII., as has already been mentioned, was solicitous to add this saint to the Calendar.

On Napoleon's return to Mantua, an attempt was made to surprise the place, but failed. Colonel Andreossy collected a number of boats on the lake, in which a hundred grenadiers were embarked : they were to land at two in the morning under the battery and bastion of the palace ; to seize the postern-gate and let down the drawbridges of the causeway of St. Georges, by which the army were to enter the city. But the Po having fallen considerably, and the waters of the lake having run off with great rapidity, there was not sufficient water for the boats, which were obliged to get among the reeds to avoid being perceived from the walls ; they grounded there during the night, and it was impossible to get them off. The next night the waters abated still more, and the attempt was altogether abandoned. On the 18th of July, all the natural obstacles to the approach of the fortress were removed : on the 22d, General Chasseloup (of the engineers) opened the trenches round the town, and the siege became an ordinary one. Napoleon's mind being made easy on the subject, and an understanding being established with the Count de St. Marsan, the King of Sardinia's agent at Milan, an intelligent and able man, he prepared to meet the storm that was ready to burst over the Tyrol.

# CHAPTER XI.

### THE TAKING OF MANTUA.

MASTERLY as were the manœuvres in the former battles of this campaign, those which followed were no less so. The comprehension of the whole, the attention to the details, the previous calculations, the sudden expedients, the clearness of head and boldness of hand were alike conspicuous and admirable. Buonaparte, instead of being discouraged by partial reverses or straitened resources, turned the former to advantage, and made up by unabated and indefatigable activity for the narrowness of his means. Instead of reposing on immediate success, he made one victory serve as a stepping-stone to another. It is the fault of most generals that after a great battle gained, they are at a loss what to do, as if confounded by their own good luck, and unwilling to push their advantage to the utmost. They make a sort of truce with fortune, and indulge in a holiday of self-congratulation and triumphant retrospect to the escape they have had, before they trust the slippery Goddess again. Buonaparte had none of this timidity or doubt of her plenary and unbounded favors. He thought nothing done while any thing remained to do, and redoubled his blows (never thinking any attempt or any success too great) till he had fairly laid his adversary prostrate at his feet, and disabled him from farther resistance. He did not interpose either through indolence or irresolution a single moment's delay, or the scruple of a doubt between the first prospect of victory and its final completion. The real clue to his brilliant ascendancy over others, and almost over fortune, was a high-spirited and heroic daring that looked danger in the face, and ran to meet it wherever it showed itself most formidable, thus by one decisive blow striking at the superiority and staggering the confidence of the enemy at first; whereas by a contrary and more cautious method he would have exhausted his strength in gaining trifling advantages, and have had to encounter the principal difficulties at last with diminished means and jaded ardor. Wherever his presence was most wanted, thither he was attracted by the irresistible impulse of conscious power to contend with an occasion worthy of it ; and his spirit flamed in every part of the theatre of war, as the lightning illumines the thunder-cloud. A question has been idly raised of Buonaparte's personal courage, and many instances have been cited in proof of it. He himself considered these things as *bagatelles ;* for he was sensible of possessing that highest mental courage, that strength of purpose and self-confidence which constitutes the definition of the hero or great leader, and which consists in attempting the utmost that is possible, with the utmost of your power and without the smallest loss of time.

The Court of Vienna being informed of the arrival of the French in the neighborhood of the Tyrol, ordered Marshal Wurmser, at the head of 30,000 men taken from the Army of the Upper Rhine, into Italy. This detachment, added to Beaulieu's army, which had been recruiting for some time, and to the garrison of Mantua, raised the Austrian force to 80,000 men. The French General with all his efforts could not muster more than 30,000 men actually under arms ; yet with this handful of tried troops he was to contend with the principal army of the House of Austria. He wrote to the Directory, requiring either that reinforcements should be sent to him, or that the armies of the Rhine should take the field without delay, since two months had elapsed beyond the time fixed for their doing so, and they were not yet out of winter quarters. The partisans of Austria began to behave in a haughty and insolent manner towards the French, and confidently asserted that this year the proverb would again be verified, that *Italy was their tomb.* The French troops were scattered between the Lakes of Idro and Garda, intercepting the road between Trent and Brescia ; to the east of the Lake of Garda, at Verona, and along the Adige by Legnago ; and at Peschiera, where six armed galleys kept possession of the lake. The head-quarters were at Castel-Nuovo. Wurmser had fixed his at Trent, above the Lake of Garda, on the Adige, and had assembled his whole army round him. He had divided it into three corps, two of which were to proceed down different sides of the Adige to the east of the Lake, and attack the French in front on the Verona side ; the third was to pass along the western side of the Lake of Garda, advance on Brescia, and turn the rear of the whole French army, which being thus separated from Milan, would have its retreat cut off and be entirely destroyed. Wurmser, proud of his great superiority of force, meditated not how to conquer, but how to take advantage of his supposed victory, and render it decisive and fatal to the enemy. Napoleon was at Milan when he heard of the movements in the Tyrol ; he repaired with all possible speed to Castel-Nuovo, a little town, where he was within equal reach of the mountains, Montebaldo, and Verona. News came in the course of the day and night of the 29th of July, that Corona and Brescia had been attacked ; that the valleys on both sides of the Lake, that of the Adige and that of Chiesa, swarmed with Austrian troops, and that one of the routes to Milan had been cut off.

Wurmser's plan was now unmasked ; he had taken the lead in moving, and hoped to keep it. He considered his adversary as fixed about Mantua, and imagined that by surrounding this fixed point he should surround the French army. In order to counteract his schemes, it was necessary for the French commander himself to take the lead, to render the army moveable by raising the siege of Mantua, abandoning the trenches and the besieging train (a dreadful sacrifice) for the purpose of advancing rapidly, with the whole army in junction, upon one of the enemy's corps, and afterwards against the other two in succession. The Austrians had the advantage in numbers, in the proportion of five to two ; but if the three corps could be attacked separately by the whole French army, the latter would be superior in number on the field of battle The enemy's right under Quasdanowich, which had debouched on Brescia by the Chiesa, was the farthest advanced ; Napoleon therefore determined to march against this corps first. Serrurier's division burned the carriages of their besieging train and their platforms, threw their powder into the water, buried their shot, spiked their cannon, and raised the siege of Mantua on the night of the 31st of July. Augereau's division proceeded from Legnago (where it had been stationed) to Bor.

ghetto on the Mincio; Massena's troops defended the heights between the Adige and the Lake of Garda during the whole of the 30th, to prevent Wurmser from advancing on that side. D'Allemagne's brigade directed its march from the Adige on Lonato. Soret was ordered to fall back on Salo, in order to disengage General Guieux, who had been left in a disadvantageous position there; nevertheless, he fought with a whole division of the enemy's troops for forty-eight hours, and repulsed them five times. Soret came up when they were making a final attack, fell on their flanks, and totally defeated them. At the same time General Ocskay's Austrian division had advanced from Gavardo on Lonato to effect its junction with Wurmser, but was driven back by D'Allemagne's brigade, which Napoleon led in person.—Wurmser had now passed the Adige, and occupied the country between that and the Lake of Garda. He placed one of his divisions at Peschiera; directed two others on Borghetto to seize the bridge over the Mincio, and establish a communication with his right; and with two other divisions marched on Mantua to force the French to raise the siege of that place, but it had already been raised twenty-four hours, and the whole camp left in a state of disorder, which indicated a precipitate flight rather than a deliberate retreat. Massena, having kept the enemy in check throughout the 30th, pushed forward in the night for Brescia. Pigeon, who brought up Massena's rearguard, had orders to dispute the passage of the Mincio with the Austrians as long as he could, and when forced, to fall back on Lonato. Augereau set out for Brescia, leaving a rearguard to line the right of this river, with orders to fall back on Castiglione when it could defend it no longer. Napoleon marched the whole night of the 31st of July with Augereau's and Massena's divisions on Brescia, which he reached at ten o'clock in the morning. The Austrian division under Quasdanowich and Ocskay, learning that the French army was debouching upon it by all the roads, hastily retreated. General Despinois and Adjutant-General Herbin went in pursuit of the enemy towards St. Ozetto and the passes of the Chiesa; while Buonaparte returned by a rapid counter-march to the Mincio, with Augereau's and Massena's two divisions, to rejoin their rearguards which had been left there, and which by this counter-

march became their vanguards.　On the 2d of August Augereau
was on the right at Montechiaro ; Massena had charge of the
centre at Ponte di San Marco, connecting his line with Soret, who
was on the left between Salo and Dezenzano, to watch the right
of the Austrian army.　The two rearguards left on the Mincio
had retreated before the enemy, who had forced that river as had
been expected.　That of Augereau, which had orders to join at
Castiglione, quitted its post too soon and in disorder (for which its
General, Valette, was cashiered before the troops,) and thus enabled the enemy to take possession of Castiglione.　General
Pigeon, with Massena's rearguard, reached Lonato in good order,
and established himself there.　On the 3d the battle of Lonato
took place with the two Austrian divisions (Liptay's being one)
that had passed at Borghetto, and that of Bayalitsch, which had
been left at Peschiera, amounting, with the cavalry, to 30,000
men on one side, against 20,000 or 22,000 French on the other.
Neither Wurmser, who had proceeded with two divisions of infantry and his cavalry to Mantua, nor Quasdanowich, who was
still retreating, could be present at this battle.　In consequence
of this separation of the Austrian forces, the victory was scarcely
doubtful.

At day-break the enemy advanced on Lonato, and commenced
a vigorous attack, intending to effect his junction with his right,
concerning which he now began to feel anxious.　Massena's vanguard was overthrown, and Lonato was taken.　The General-in-
Chief, who was at Ponte di San Marco, placed himself at the head
of the troops.　The Austrian General having extended his line
too far to his right, in hopes of opening a communication with
Salo, his centre was broken ; Lonato was retaken by assault, and
the enemy's line intersected.　One part fell back on the Mincio,
and the other attempted to throw themselves into Salo; but the
latter being taken in front by General Soret, whom they met,
and in the rear by General St. Hilaire, and turned on every side,
were obliged to lay down their arms.　The French had been attacked in the centre ; on the right they were assailants.　Augereau encountered Liptay's division before Castiglione, broke it
after an obstinate action, and forced it to retreat on Mantua,
where some reinforcements reached it too late.　Augereau's divi-

sion lost many brave men in this hard-fought action, among others
General Beyrand and Colonel Pourrailles, highly meritorious
officers.

During the night, Quasdanowich was informed of the result of
the battle of Lonato. He had heard the cannon all day, but
could do nothing to extricate himself: he thought he was surrounded in all directions. Wurmser had sent part of his troops
from Mantua towards Marcaria in pursuit of Serrurier, and had
now to recal them to Castiglione. On the 4th he was not ready
for action. Napoleon, about two or three o'clock in the afternoon, reconnoitred the Austrian line of battle, which he found to
be formidable, as it still presented from 25,000 to 30,000 combatants. He ordered Castiglione to be entrenched, rectified the
position taken up by Augereau, and set out for Lonato to superintend the movements of all the troops, which it became of the
utmost importance to assemble in the course of the night round
Castiglione. Throughout the day, Soret and Herbin on the
one side, and D'Allemagne and St. Hilaire on the other, had followed the march of the enemy's right and of those cut off from the
centre at Lonato, and had taken many prisoners : whole battalions
laid down their arms at Ozetto and at Gavardo, others were still
wandering in the neighboring valleys. Four or five thousand
men having been told by the peasants that there were only 1200
French in Lonato, marched thither in hopes of opening a road
towards Mantua. It was five o'clock in the evening. Napoleon
was entering Lonato at the same time, coming from Castiglione :
a flag of truce was brought to him summoning the town to surrender. But as he was still master of Salo and Gavardo, it was
evident that these could be only straggling columns that wanted
to clear themselves a passage. He ordered his numerous staff
to mount, had the officer who came with the flag of truce brought
in, and ordered the bandage to be taken off his eyes in the midst of
all the bustle of the head-quarters of a Commander-in-Chief. "Go
and tell your General," said he, "that I give him eight minutes
to lay down his arms ; he is in the midst of the French army ;
after that time, there are no hopes for him." These four or five
thousand men who had been strolling about for three days uncertain of their fate, believing they had been deceived by the peas-

ants, laid down their arms. This circumstance may convey
some idea of the confusion and disorder that prevailed among
these columns which had been cut off from the main body of the
Austrian army. The rest of the 4th and the whole night were
spent in rallying the troops and concentrating them on Castiglione.

Before day-break on the 5th the French army, 20,000 strong,
occupied the heights of Castiglione, an excellent position. Serrurier's division of 5000 men had received orders to set out
from Marcaria, to march all night, and to attack Wurmser s
left in the rear at day-light: the firing of this division was
to be the signal for the battle. A great deal was expected
from this unlooked-for attack; and in order to give it greater
effect, the French army made a feint of falling back; but on
the report of the first cannon fired by Serrurier's division (who
being ill, his place was supplied by General Fiorella) the
troops wheeled suddenly round and faced the enemy, whose confidence was already shaken. The hill of Medole, in the midst of
the plain, supported the enemy's left; Verdier and Marmont
were ordered to attack it, and this post after a time was carried. Massena attacked the right, Augereau the centre, and Fiorella took the left in rear. The light cavalry surprised the Austrian head-quarters and were very near taking Wurmser. The
enemy retreated from every point. Nothing but the excessive
fatigue of the French troops could have saved Wurmser's army,
which reached the left bank of the Mincio in great disorder,
hoping to rally and make a stand there. But in this he was
mistaken: the French retook all their former positions on the
Adige: General St. Hilaire drove Quasdanowich from the valley
of the Idro and took Lodrone and Rocca d'Anfo, and Wurmser
was compelled to return to Trent and Roveredo. The French
were glad to take some repose. The Austrians were still 40,000
strong, but their confidence of success had wholly abandoned
them since the commencement of the campaign. Wurmser had
indeed relieved and re-victualled Mantua, but he had lost half his
army. This failure was to be attributed, not merely to the activity
and presence of mind of Napoleon, but to an original defect in
the plan of the Austrian General in making corps, which had

no means of communication with each other, act separately in the face of an army which was centrically situated, and whose communications were easy. A second error consisted in subdividing the corps of the right; one went to Brescia where it found nobody, and the other reached Lonato in an evil hour. The troops that came from the Rhine with Wurmser were excellent and in high spirits; but the wreck of Beaulieu's army was much disheartened by its previous defeats. In the different battles and skirmishes from the 29th July to 12th August, the French army took 15,000 prisoners, seventy pieces of cannon, nine stand of colors, and killed and wounded 25,000 men; their own loss was about 7000 men.

The garrison of Mantua employed the first few days after the raising of the siege in destroying the works and getting in the stores and guns which the besiegers had abandoned; but the French were soon before the place again. The loss of their artillery, however, left them no means of resuming the siege, which was turned into a blockade, under the direction of General Sahuguet. Had Napoleon brought together a new train of artillery to attack the fortress, he might have lost it again on the arrival of a new army before the place had surrendered. The French troops employed in the blockade suffered greatly from the ravages of disease. On the first rumors of the reverses of the French, the Italians of the different states discovered their real inclinations. The Milanese showed great firmness and attachment to their new allies, and Buonaparte addressed a proclamation to them, expressive of his satisfaction. At Rome the French were insulted in the streets and the armistice broken; and Cardinal Mattei incited the people to revolt at Ferrara, and hoisted the colors of the Church in the citadel. Afterwards, when brought before the Commander-in-Chief, and interrogated as to the motives of his conduct, the old man answered only by the word *Peccavi*, which disarmed the victor, who merely confined him for three months in a religious seminary. After the death of Pius VI. great interest was made by Austria to get him elected Pope; but Chiaramonti, Bishop of Imola, gained the election, and took the name of Pius VII. It was to reward Augereau's good conduct at the battle of Lonato, where he commanded

the right and was ordered to attack Castiglione, that he was afterwards made a Duke with that title. That day was the most glorious of General Augereau's life, nor did Napoleon ever forget it.
He himself, it seems, did. His character, as drawn by Buonaparte, forms a striking contrast to that of Massena. Both were
men of low origin, and had the same courage and skill in battle;
but the one never despaired, and the other always did. Massena
fought on under the most disadvantageous circumstances, and
after losing a battle began again as if nothing had happened;
Augereau, after the most brilliant success, despaired of the events
of the next day. The one was as sanguine and obstinate as the
other was irresolute and desponding. Massena was as fond of
money as Augereau was of meddling in politics.

The armies of the Sambre and Meuse and of the Rhine and
Moselle, belonging to France, had at length passed the Rhine and
were advancing rapidly into the heart of Germany. Wurmser,
recruited with 20,000 men, was in the Tyrol: he was preparing
to march with 30,000 men to the relief of Mantua by the Lower
Adige, leaving Davidowich with 25,000 in charge of the Tyrol.

Napoleon, anxious to prevent his detaching any troops against
the Army of the Rhine, resolved instantly to resume the offensive, and if possible to complete the destruction of the Austrian
army. Kilmaine, with a corps of 2500 or 3000 soldiers of all
weapons, guarded the Adige, covering the blockade of Mantua;
the wall of Verona on the left bank of the Adige had been restored and put in a state of defence. In the instructions given to
Kilmaine for his conduct, all the circumstances which afterwards
took place were provided for.

On the 1st of September, Wurmser still had his head quarters
at Trent; Davidowich was at Roveredo, covering the Tyrol with
Wukassowich's and Reuss's divisions; the three divisions and the
cavalry with which Wurmser wished to operate on the Adige
were on their march between Trent and Barsano. On the 1st of
September, Vaubois' division, forming the left of the French
army, marched up the Chiesa from Lodrone on Trent. Massena's division, and soon after Augereau's, setting out from Verona,
marched up the left bank of the Adige in the same direction, towards the head of the Lake of Garda. General St. Hilaire, who

commanded the vanguard of Vaubois' division, came up with the
Prince of Reuss at the bridge of Sarca, attacked him furiously,
carried the bridge at the point of the bayonet, and drove him
back on his camp at Mori.   General Pigeon, with Massena's vanguard, overthrew Wukassowich at Serravalle and pursued him to
the camp of St. Mark.   The two armies came in sight on the 4th
of September at day-break, on each side of the Adige.   The attack was desperate; the resistance obstinate.   As soon as Napoleon perceived some hesitation in the Austrian line, he made General Dubois charge with 500 horse; the charge was successful,
but the brave officer who made it received three bullets and fell
dead on the spot.   The French troops entered Roveredo inter-
mixed with the enemy, who were unable to rally till they reached
the defile before Calliano, where the Adige is enclosed between two
steep mountains.   The entrance is narrow and defended by fortifications: General Davidowich was posted there with a reserve.
While the skirmishers engaged on the sides of the mountain, nine
battalions in close column rusned into the defile, attacked and
overthrew the enemy; the artillery, cavalry, and infantry were
all thrown into confusion.   Several pieces of cannon and some
hundred prisoners were taken by the French.   General Vaubois
on the right side of the river forced the camp at Mori, and pushed
briskly on in the direction of Trent.   An aid-de-camp of the
General-in-Chief, Le Marrois, had been grievously wounded in a
daring and brilliant charge at Roveredo.   He came from the department of La Manche, and was of a very ardent temperament.
On the 5th, at day-break the army entered Trent.   In the evening,
Vaubois' division took up a position three leagues beyond Trent
on the Avisio; behind which river the wrecks of Davidowich's
army were.   Napoleon ordered the general of the cavalry with
three squadrons to ford the river a little above, and to take the
enemy's troops which defended it in rear, whilst he caused them
to be charged in front.   The success of this manœuvre was complete; Davidowich hastily abandoned his position, and Vaubois
established himself on both banks of the Avisio.

  The loss of the battle of Roveredo, instead of stopping Wurmser's movement on Bassano, accelerated it; indeed, being cut off
from Trent and the Tyrol, it was necessary for him to get out of

the defiles, and reach Bassano and the Frioul as fast as possible.
But he had also another motive, which was that he had suffered
himself to be persuaded that Buonaparte's intention was to march
on Inspruck to join the Army of the Rhine, which had just then
arrived in Bavaria; and on this false supposition he ordered
Mezaros's division forward to Mantua. In the night of the 5th
of September, Napoleon heard that this division was approaching
Verona; he instantly conceived the idea of hemming in Wurmser between the Brenta and the Adige; or if he should not do
that, at least of surrounding and taking Mezaros's division, which
was already compromised. Before leaving Trent, he addressed
a proclamation to the Tyrolese, in which he roundly taxed the
Emperor's ministers with being purchased by English gold to betray their master. This had sufficient truth and might have some
effect. · On the 6th at day-break, Napoleon commenced his march
with Augereau's and Massena's divisions and the reserve (Vaubois' division having been left on the Avisio) to proceed on Bassano with all possible speed. It was necessary to perform a
march of twenty leagues over a difficult road in two days at the
utmost. In the evening, the head quarters were at Borgo-Val-
Sugagna. On the 7th he recommenced his march; his van soon
fell in with part of Wurmser's army behind Primolano, in an
almost impregnable position; but the fifth light infantry, supported by three battalions of the fourth of the line in three close
columns, broke the double line of the Austrians. The fifth
dragoons, commanded by Colonel Milhaud, cut off the road. Most
of the enemy's vanguard laid down their arms; the artillery,
colors, and baggage were taken. The little fort of Covolo, which
in vain attempted to hold out, was turned and taken. At night the
French army bivouacked in the village of Cismone, where Napoleon took up his head-quarters without attendants or baggage, and
passed the night, half dead with hunger and fatigue. A soldier
(who afterwards reminded him of the circumstance at the camp
of Boulogne in 1805 when he was Emperor) shared his ration
of bread with him. The same evening, Mezaros's division had
attacked Verona, but without success. Kilmaine expected Mezaros, and showered grape-shot on the Austrian General, so that he
was repulsed with loss and sent to Wurmser for reinforcements,

who in his turn being surprised and menaced at Bassano, ordered him to fall back and join him with all possible expedition.   He was, however, too late.   Mezaros's division did not reach Monte-bello (less than half way) till the 8th, the day on which the battle of Bassano was fought.

On the 8th of September before day-light, the French general was at the advanced posts; at six o'clock, the vanguard attacked and overthrew six Austrian battalions stationed in the passes on the two banks of the Brenta.   Their remaining force fell back on the line of battle, about 20,000 strong, but made only a feeble re-sistance.   Augereau attacked the left, Massena the right; the enemy was broken and driven back on the town of Bassano. The fourth of the line in a close column crossed the bridge as at Lodi.   At three o'clock the army entered Bassano, and took a great number of prisoners and a great quantity of stores and ammunition of all kinds.   Wurmser, cut off from the Piave, retreated to Vicenza, where he rallied Mezaros's division, and whence, having lost the line of his communica-tion with Austria, he was forced to proceed to Mantua.   Quas-danowich with 3000 men, not being able to reach Bassano, fell oack on the Frioul.   Wurmser himself out of an army of 60,000 men had now not more than 16,000 in junction under him. Never was there a more critical situation.   He himself was alarmed, and the French were every hour in hopes of seeing him lay down his arms.   Of these 16,000 troops, 6000 were cavalry, fresh, and of good quality : these horsemen scoured the country to discover a passage across the Adige.   Two squadrons of them passed to the right bank of the ferry of Albaredo, to reconnoitre, but it was impossible for the whole army to pass, closely watched as it was by the French.   Wurmser's position was become desperate, when the French evacuated Legnago without destroying the bridge; which error, committed by a lieutenant-colonel who had been led to suppose that the whole Austrian army had passed at Albaredo and were about to cut off his retreat, saved them.   Na-poleon, who was at Arcole, on receiving this vexatious intelligence, proceeded to Ronco, sent Massena over to the right bank, and or-dered Augereau to march from Padua on Legnago, still enter-taining hopes of surrounding the Marshal at last by reaching the

Molinella before him.  Wurmser on hearing that Augereau was
at Montagnana, set out for Mantua by the high road through
Cerea and Sanguinetto.  He was stopped at Cerea by Murat and
Pigeon, coming from Ronco, who drew up in a line behind the
rivulet to intercept him.  He was compelled to engage his whole
army, forced a passage, broke through the French vanguard,
and continued his march on Sanguinetto.  It was during the conflict at Cerea that the General-in-Chief, having galloped up to the
village just as his vanguard was routed, had only time enough to
turn round, clap spurs to his horse, and get clear off.  Wurmser
came up a few minutes after to the very spot where he had been;
and learning the circumstance from an old woman, sent in pursuit of
him in every direction, particularly recommending that he should
be brought in alive.  After reaching Sanguinetto, Wurmser
marched all night.  Understanding that Sahuguet's and Kilmaine's reserves were waiting for him at the Molinella, he turned
off from the high road to Villa-Impieta, where General Charl-
ton with 500 men from the army before Mantua, was left dead on
the field and his detachment surrendered.  These and other slight
successes encouraged Wurmser to keep the field.  The garrison
of Mantua came out to meet him, and he encamped his army between St. Georges and the citadel.  He had now 33,000 men
under his command.  The French army which had come up
from different quarters amounted to 24,000.  The two armies
were nearly equal, except in confidence.  On the 19th General
Bon, commanding Augereau's division, commenced the attack on
St. Georges, but was repulsed and forced to give ground.  Sahuguet engaged on the right; the enemy thought the whole line
was in action, when Massena debouched in column on the centre,
and carried disorder into the Austrian army, which retreated precipitately into the town, after having lost 3000 prisoners, among
whom was a regiment of cuirassiers completely mounted, with
their standards and eleven pieces of cannon.  After the battle of
St. Georges, Wurmser spread his troops through the Seraglio,
threw a bridge over the Po, and got provisions into the place.
At length, on the 1st of October, Kilmaine completely blockaded
the place.  From the 1st of June to the 18th of September, the
Austrians lost 27,000 men, of whom 18,000 were taken prisoners,

**3000** killed, and 6000 wounded: 10,000 men of the army escaped into the Tyrol and Frioul under Davidowich and Quasdanowich. The loss of the French amounted to 1400 prisoners, 1800 killed, and 4300 wounded.

The army stood in need of repose, and had at present no enemy before them. Vaubois was at Trent, Massena at Bassano, Augereau at Verona, Kilmaine blockaded Mantua. The garrison made several ineffectual sorties; reverses and sickness had abated its ardor. The Regency of Modena, which was hostile to the French, had sent in convoys of provisions, which put the place in a condition to hold out longer than had been expected. Contrary to all probability, and to the opinion of all Italy, the French army was yet to gain more sanguinary and arduous victories, and Austria was yet to levy and to lose two armies, before this bulwark of Italy was destined to fall.

It will be proper here to turn aside to give some account of the operations of the campaign in Germany.

Prussia had concluded a peace with the Republic in April, 1795. During the summer of that year, the Austrians had two armies acting on the Rhine: that of the Lower Rhine under the command of Field-Marshal Clairfayt, and that of the Upper Rhine (nearer Switzerland) under the command of Marshal Wurmser. To the former the French opposed the Army of the Sambre and Meuse under General Jourdan, and to the latter the Army of the Rhine under Pichegru, who occupied lines of circumvallation round Mentz. Notwithstanding the defection of Prussia, the campaign ended favorably for the Austrians. In October they forced the lines of circumvallation at Mentz, took a great number of field-pieces, and drove Pichegru into the lines of Weissemburg. Hostilities were terminated by an armistice signed the 23d of September, 1795, in consequence of which Jourdan took up his winter-quarters in the Hundsruck, Pichegru his at Strasburg, Clairfayt his at Mentz, and Wurmser his at Manheim. During the winter France and Austria omitted nothing that was necessary for the purpose of recruiting and clothing their armies, and putting them in the best possible state. The success of the last campaign had inspired the Cabinet of Vienna with fresh hopes. Prince Charles was appointed to succeed Clairfayt in the command of the army.

Pichegru caused the French government much anxiety; the operations which had led to the disasters at the end of the campaign being so unaccountable, that they were ascribed to treachery, of which, however, the Directory had no proofs. They nevertheless seized the first opportunity of removing this General from the army, and appointed him ambassador to Sweden. Pichegru declined this diplomatic mission, and retired to his estate. Moreau was appointed General-in-Chief of the Army of the Rhine in his stead, of which he took the command on the 23d of May, 1796.

In the mean time, the campaign had opened in Italy in the month of April; and the battles of Montenotte, Millesimo, and Mondovi had determined the King of Sardinia to sign the armistice of Cherasco and abandon the Coalition. The more the Aulic Council had relied on the talents and reputation of General Beaulieu, the greater was its disappointment at this news. The Archduke was immediately ordered to notify the recommencement of hostilities, and to begin operations on the Rhine, either to hinder the French from reinforcing their army beyond the Alps, or to effect a diversion in the minds of the people, and withdraw their attention from the disasters of Italy. When Napoleon left Paris in the beginning of March, he received a positive assurance that the armies on the frontier of Germany should open the campaign in the course of the month of April; yet they still remained in their winter-quarters at the end of May. Every victory gained by the Army of Italy, every step it advanced, rendered the necessity that the French armies of the Rhine should enter the field more sensible and urgent. The moment was, however, deferred under various pretexts, till at length the imprudence of the enemy did what the French government had not had the wisdom to enforce. Moreau, who was at Paris, had only just time enough to reach Strasburg. All the troops cantoned on the Moselle, the Sarre, and the Meuse put themselves in motion, and hostilities were renewed on the 1st of June. In consequence of the fresh victories gained by Napoleon, Wurmser was detached with 30,000 men from the army of the Upper Rhine, to act as a reserve to Beaulieu's army, which was repairing its losses in the Tyrol, in Carinthia, and Carniola, and if possible to stop the progress of the victor. The Emperor at the same time united the two armies of the Upper and Lower Rhine under the command of the Archduke Charles with instructions to let the armistice continue. But this order came too late, that is to say, only two hours before hostilities commenced.

The Archduke, weakened by detaching Wurmser, gave up his plans of invasion, and confined himself to defending the passage of the Rhine and guarding Germany. He had under his command, first, the army of the Lower Rhine, of which Wartensleben was second in command, consisting of 71,000 infantry and 22,000 cavalry; secondly, the army of the Upper Rhine, under the Artillery General Latour, and the Marshals Starray, Froelich, Reuss, the Prince of Condé, &c. It originally consisted of 65,000 infantry and 18,000 cavalry, in all 176,000 fighting men; but this included Wurmser's 30,000, and their absence reduced its total amount to less than 150,000 troops. The French army also consisted of about 150,000 combatants, the army of the Sambre and Meuse, and that of the Rhine and the Moselle being pretty nearly divided. The first was divided into three corps; the left, under Kleber, was on the right bank of the Rhine at Dusseldorf, General Jourdan in the Hundsruck commanded the centre, and General Marceau the right. The Army of the Rhine and the Moselle was in like manner divided into three corps; Desaix commanded the left, St. Cyr the centre, Ferino the right, and General Bourcier the reserve of cavalry.

On the 1st of June Kleber marched from Dusseldorf with his *corps d'armée*, and on the 4th attacked and beat the Prince of Wurtemburg at Altenkirchen. Jourdan also passed the Rhine at Neuwied and joined him on the Lahn, and Marceau advanced before Mentz. But Prince Charles having marched with a detachment of 8000 men from the Upper Rhine, and attacked and defeated one of Kleber's divisions on the 15th, he relinquished his plan of giving battle on the 17th, and retired behind the Danube, directing Kleber on Dusseldorf, who regained his position after a smart action without any considerable loss. At the same time, Desaix and St. Cyr by Moreau's order attacked an Austrian vanguard which Wurmser had left at the little town of Franckenthal, and compelled it to retreat with considerable loss behind the *teté-de-pont* of Manheim; but this advantage did not compensate for the check sustained by the Army of the Sambre and Meuse. At length Moreau, whose manœuvres on the left bank of the Rhine were found to be of no use, was ordered to pass the river. On the 24th of June, at two o'clock in the morning, Desaix with 25,000 men took possession of the Isle of Erlhen-Rhin, carried Kehl, taking 800 men and twelve pieces of cannon, and in the course of the night constructed a bridge, over which 40,000 troops passed the next day to the right bank. General St. Cyr with two divisions remained on the left bank opposite Manheim, and one of Ferino's divisions was stationed on the other side. The Austrian general Starray with Condé's army and the Suabian contingent was posted between Switzerland and Rastadt, and Latour from Rastadt to Manheim on the German side. On the approach of Ferino, the enemy evacuated two little camps at Wilstect and Offemburg. At the same time Desaix advanced on the Renchen, where General Starray was in position with 10,000 men, attacked him, and drove him with a loss of men and cannon as far as Rastadt, where Latour had just arrived from Manheim with 25,000 men, and taken a position behind the Murg river. But St. Cyr was no sooner informed of the Austrian general's movement up the right bank of the Rhine, than he followed him on the left, passed the bridge of Kehl, and having forced the passage of the Murg, compelled General Latour to fall back on the Alb, after a severe action which lasted the whole day (July 5th,) and with the loss of 1000 men. The French head quarters were removed to Rastadt while Ferino took possession of the Kintzig ; and as he proceeded up the Rhine, the brigades which were on the left side crossed over and joined his forces. The Archduke, as soon as he heard of the passage of the Rhine at Kehl on the 24th and 25th of June, marched at the head of twenty-four battalions and two squadrons to the aid of the army of the Upper Rhine, leaving Wartensleben with 36,000 men to observe Jourdan, and 26,000 at the entrenched camp of Hechtzheim to cover Mentz. He intended to attack the French army with all his force on the 10th of July and drive it into the Rhine, but Moreau had anticipated him. On the 9th St. Cyr forced the Rottensol, routed his left under General Keim, and drove the Saxons on the Necker. The Archduke thus disappointed directed his centre and his right against Desaix, who maintained his ground by dint of courage during the greater part of the day, and only retreated to a position a little in his rear in the evening. This unexpected resistance damped the enemy; and fearful of being cut off by General St. Cyr, who was already at Nauenburg, they beat a retreat on Forzheim on the 10th, and on the following day reached Stutgard on the Necker. In the mean time Ferino had crossed the Black Forest and arrived at Willingen; the enemy evacuated the mountains, and the Forest-towns received French garrisons.

General Kleber, finding that the Army of the Sambre and Meuse had effected its passage at Kehl, again set out from Dusseldorf on the 29th of June. He was joined by Grenier's division, which crossed the Rhine at Cologne, and by the General-in-Chief, Jourdan, with the rest of the army, by the bridge c Neuwied. They passed the Lahn in three columns, and pressed General Wartensleben, who took up a position near Frankfort, which place surrendered, with all its stores and ammunition, after a delay of a few days; but this gave the enemy time to reach the Upper Mein. The fort of Kœningstein, on the road to Cologne surrendered on the 21st of July, with ninety-three pieces of cannon and a garrison of 500 men. Jourdan, according to the instructions of the Government, left Marceau with 30,000 men before the fortresses on the frontier, and advanced into the heart of Germany with only 50,000 troops. He skirted the borders of the mountains of Thuringia on the confines of Saxony, and thus left the Danube behind him. On the 21st of July, his vanguard entered Schweinfurt; and Wurtzburg and its citadel, with three thousand of the Prince-Bishop's troops, capitulated on the 3d of August. Wartensleben retreated on Bamberg without offering any resistance. The Army of the Sambre and Meuse followed him, passed the Rednitz at Bamberg, and defeated him at Forsheim on the 6th of August. On the 15th the French marched on Salzbach and Amberg; and after a severe action, the enemy retired to Schwartzenfeld, still farther from the Archduke's army; the French passed the Wils, and Bernadotte was detached to Neumarck on the road between Ratisbon and Nuremberg. The two French armies now commanded the left bank of the Danube, and might be almost considered as in junction. The movements

of the Army of the Rhine had at first been slow, which induced
Prince Charles to think that it was not yet destined to act in ear-
nest beyond the Necker: but on the 23d of July, Desaix having
arrived at Gmund, came to action at Aalen, and St. Cyr reached
Heidenheim on the Brentz the same day. There were various
skirmishes on the 5th and 8th of August; and at this period the
Saxon contingent abandoned the Austrian army and returned into
Saxony.

Prince Charles, however, considering that the French armies
of the Sambre and Meuse and of the Rhine were only three
days' march apart, and were about to effect a junction on the Alt-
muhl, determined to risk a battle to prevent it. He turned short
round; his rear became his van, and suffered some loss in an action at Eglingen. On the 11th, at day-break, the whole Austrian Army debouched in eight columns. The French were in
advance of Neresheim, occupying a front of eight leagues with
45,000 men. Two of the three columns of the Archduke's left
debouched by Dischingen and Dillingen, attacked Duhesme, who
with 6000 men formed the right both in front and rear, separated
him from the centre, and forced him one march back; while the
third column, under General Froelich, passed the Danube at Ulm
and took the French army in the rear. The French head-quarters, the parks, and the civil lists being driven from Heidenheim,
fled to Aalem. Thus at the very beginning of the battle the
French army was turned and cut, deprived of its line of operations, and its parks and reserves thrown into confusion. The
three columns which were employed to produce this result were,
however, carried too far to take any share in the action. The
three columns of the centre which made the principal attack were
directed by the Archduke in person. They debouched from
Aufhausen, and overthrew St. Cyr's posts, who did not expect so
abrupt an attack, and was still where he was the preceding evening after the action of Eglingen. He rallied on the heights of
Dunstelkingen; and throughout the remainder of the day all the
Archduke's efforts to force him from his position were unavailing.
The loss on each side in this gallantly fought action was upwards
of 6000 men. At night the Archduke drew back his right on
the road between Nordlingen and Donawerth, and his left to Dil-

lingen on the Danube. His centre passed the night in the field;
but the line of communication of the French army with its reserve having been restored, Moreau was induced to remain on the
field of battle to collect his wounded, prepare for his retreat, or
march forward, according to the intelligence he should receive.
This was favorable; he learned that the Army of the Sambre
and Meuse had already passed the Rednitz and appeared to direct its march by Amberg on Ratisbon. It was some marches in
advance of Prince Charles, who, not having been able in the action of the 11th to overthrow the French Army and drive it into
the defiles of the mountains of the Alb, had not now a moment to
lose to avoid being surrounded. He made his retreat in the
course of the night, considering the junction of the two armies
as effected, and relinquishing all thoughts of opposing it, for he
abandoned to them the left bank of the Danube, the Warnitz,
and the Altmulh, and repassed the Danube and the Lech: the
Austrians seemed to have lost the campaign.

But Moreau, instead of following up his advantage, remained
for some days on the field of battle; at length he advanced on
Donawerth, but still did not attempt, by sending forward a part
of his cavalry, to effect his junction with Jourdan. This hesitation and want of precaution encouraged the Archduke to oppose
the junction of the two armies, which he had despaired of being
able to do. Having left General Latour to watch and keep the
Army of the Rhine in check, he passed the Danube and ad
vanced on the Nuremberg road with 30,000 troops. On the
22d he attacked Bernadotte before Neumarck, and forced him to
fall back on Forsheim. General Wartensleben immediately re
passed the Naab. The Army of the Sambre and Meuse retreated
on Amberg and Salzbach; but being attacked in this position, in
front by Wartensleben, and in flank and rear by a detachment
from Prince Charles's army, its General did not think it expedient to risk a serious affair. His retreat became exceedingly
difficult; and he did not reach Schweinfurth, constantly pursued
by the Archduke, and then by forcing a passage at the point of
the bayonet, till the 31st. In this town the troops halted as they
needed rest. Jourdan took advantage of the scattered state of the
enemy's army, and resolved to open himself a way to Wurtzburg,

which was occupied by General Hotze. On the 2d of September, in the forenoon, he recommenced his march and attacked Prince Charles on the following day; but Kray and Wartensleben came up with 40,000 infantry and 12,000 cavalry during the fight, and he lost the battle. Lefebvre's division was left at Schweinfurth; he himself reached Arnstein on the Lahn with much difficulty on the 11th. Here Moreau joined him with 10,000 men from Holland, and he might still have retrieved his affairs and changed the fortune of the campaign. But though he formed a just conception of what was fit to be done, he was wanting in activity and resolution to put it in practice. He suffered himself to be anticipated on the Lahn and driven beyond the Rhine. The brave Marceau was killed in an action at Altenkirchen; Kleber and Collaud were dismissed for insubordination. Jourdan himself was soon after superseded by Beurnonville, who was scarcely capable of manœuvring a battalion. The Archduke quitted the banks of the Lahn with 12,000 men to advance against the Army of the Rhine and Moselle, leaving General Werneck with 50,000 men to observe the army of the Sambre and Meuse.

On the 23d of August, twelve days after the battle of Nerescheim, Moreau passed the Danube and marched on the Lech. On the 24th General Ferino, who, having crossed the Black Forest and taken Lindau and Bregentz on the Lake of Constance, had returned by the Tyrol and Memmingen, forced the passage of the Lech at the ford of Hanstetten; St. Cyr passed at the ford of Lech-Hausen before Augsburg, and Desaix at the ford of Langweid. The bridges of Augsburg were repaired; and after a brave resistance, General Latour was driven from the fine positions of Friedburg, leaving seventeen pieces of cannon and 1500 prisoners in the hands of the victor. After the passage of the Lech, the right of the French army advanced on Dachau, near Munich, with its vanguard under the walls of that city; the centre on Geissenfeld, with a corps of observation on Ingoldstadt. The Austrian General removed his head-quarters to Landshut on the Iser, where he assembled his principal forces. Condé's corps occupied Munich, where he waited several days for the movement of the enemy; and finding that he made none, suspected that he had gone in search of the Archduke's army. He accordingly set out in pursuit of him, but was soon repulsed and found that he had not stirred. On the 7th of September, Moreau determined, without any particular object, to move forward. On the 8th he reached Neustadt, and it was expected he would advance on Ratisbon; but on the 10th he returned, in order to resume his old positions, and detached Desaix with 12,000 men to seek for the Army of the Sambre and Meuse, which was then eighty leagues distant from him. On the 16th, hearing what had passed, he rejoined the army on the Danube.

The Archduke on reaching the Lahn immediately detached General Petrasch with nine battalions for Manheim and Philipsburg, to get possession of Kehl and Huninguen. General Scherb, who was at Bruchsal, having received notice from deserters, got to Kehl time enough to defend it against this attack with the help of the National Guard of Strasburg. Moreau, alarmed at this attempt, which had nearly intercepted his communication with France, felt the necessity of approaching the Rhine, and commenced his celebrated retreat, which he effected after several obstinate actions and narrow escapes, by passing through Ulm, which was fortunately occupied by a detachment under Montrichard; by Biberach, where he obtained a victory over the enemy, taking some standards and 4000 or 5000 prisoners; and by the terrible defiles of the Black Valley, which the army passed on the 13th, 14th, and 15th, and entered France over the bridges of New Brisach and Huninguen. Thus Moreau lost all the advantages of the campaign that must have resulted from his junction with Jourdan, by not striking while the iron was hot, or by waiting to do that at the rebound which should have been done at once; so that nothing remained in the hands of the French on the right bank of the Rhine but the fortress of Dusseldorf and the *têtes-de-pont* of Kehl and Huninguen. Dusseldorf was too far north to give the Austrians much uneasiness; but the fortress of Kehl and that of Huninguen enabled the French army to winter on the left bank and to harass Germany; they therefore resolved to take possession of these two points. They accordingly invested them with 40,000 men; and after immense preparations for their defence and immense sacrifices on the part of the besiegers, at

14*

length carried them in the beginning of January. General Abba-
tucci, a young officer of great bravery and promise fell mortally
wounded in a sortie at the head of the garrison of Huninguen. The
success of these two operations enabled Prince Charles to take up
his winter-quarters on the right bank of the Rhine in Brisgau and
the country of Baden, and to detach powerful succors to the
army which was assembling behind the Piave, and of which he
took the command in February. This army was intended to
avenge Beaulieu, Wurmser, and Alvinzi, and to reconquer Mantua, Lombardy and Italy.—To return.

All the couriers which reached Vienna with news of Prince
Charles's successes, were followed by couriers from Wurmser,
bringing accounts of his disasters. The Court passed the whole
of the month of September in these alternations of joy and sorrow.
The satisfaction derived from its triumphs did not compensate for
the consternation caused by its defeats. Germany was saved,
but Italy was lost : the army which guarded that frontier had
disappeared. Its remains, with its veteran General at its head,
had only been able to find temporary safety by shutting themselves up in Mantua, which place was reduced to the last extremity. The Aulic Council felt the necessity of doing something.
It assembled two armies, one in the Frioul, the other in the
Tyrol ; appointed Marshal Alvinzi to the command, and ordered
him to march to save Mantua and deliver Wurmser. The Directory, on their part, promised much, but performed little ; they
sent, however, twelve battalions drafted from the Army of La
Vendée, which reached Milan in the course of September and
October ; as care was taken to make them march in twelve columns, the notion was spread abroad that each of these columns
was a regiment, and had its full compliment of men, which would
have been a very considerable reinforcement. It is true, the
French soldiers did not need encouragement ; they were in excellent condition and spirits, and were full of confidence in themselves and their chief. Public opinion was also decidedly in their
favor. The popular feeling in the states beyond the Po, Bologna,
Modena, and Reggio, was such that they might be depended on
for repulsing the Pope's army themselves, should it enter their
territories according to the threat held out.

In the beginning of October, Marshal Alvinzi was still with his army before the Isonzo; but at the end of that month he removed his head-quarters to Conegliano behind the Piave. Massena was watching his movements at Bassano. Davidowich had assembled a corps of 18,000 men in the Tyrol including the Tyrolese militia. Vaubois covered Trent with 12,000 men; Augereau's division, the reserve of cavalry, and the head-quarters of the French army were at Verona. Alvinzi's plan was, to be joined by Davidowich in Verona, and to march thence on Mantua. On the 1st of November, he threw two bridges over the Piave, and marched towards the Brenta. Massena, finding that his army amounted to upwards of 40,000 men, raised his camp at Bassano, and approached Vicenza, where Napoleon joined him with Augereau's division and the reserve, and on the 6th, at daybreak, advanced to give battle to Alvinzi, who had followed Massena's movement. After an action of several hours, Massena drove back the van under General Liptay and Provera's division to the left bank of the river, killing a great number of men, and making many prisoners. Napoleon advanced against Quasdanowich, and drove him from Lenove upon Bassano. It was four o'clock in the afternoon; he considered the passage of the bridge and the taking of the town on this day as of the utmost importance; but having ordered up the reserve for this purpose, a battalion of 900 Croats, which had been previously cut off, threw themselves into a village on the high road; and as the head of the reserve appeared to cross the village, fired upon them. It became necessary to bring up howitzers; the village was taken, and the Croats shot; but a delay of two hours had taken place, and it was impossible to reach the bridge that night.

Vaubois had received orders to attack the enemy's positions on the right bank of the Avisio. He did so, and failed. He was himself attacked in turn, and obliged to abandon Trent; nor could he make good the position he had taken up at Calliano, but was outflanked by Landon with his Tyrolese, who appeared to be advancing on Montebaldo and Rivoli. This news reached the French head-quarters at two in the morning. There was now no room for hesitation; it was indispensably necessary to hasten back to Verona. Colonel Vignoles, a confidential officer, was

dispatched to collect all the troops he could muster there, and
march with them on La Corona and Rivoli. He found a battalion of the 40th just arrived from La Vendée; the next day
Joubert reached the same important position with the 4th light
demi-brigade, brought from the blockade of Mantua. At the
same time, Vaubois returned to the right bank of the Adige, and
occupied La Corona and Rivoli in force. From the Brenta the
French army filed through Vicenza during the whole of the 7th.
The inhabitants, who had witnessed the victory of the day before,
could not account for this retreat. Alvinzi, who was preparing
to pass the Piave, no sooner heard the intelligence than he returned to the Brenta, and passed that river, in order to follow his an-
tagonist's movement.

Napoleon had Vaubois' division assembled on the plain of
Rivoli, and addressed them thus: "Soldiers, I am not satisfied
with you; you have shown neither bravery, discipline, nor perseverance; no position could rally you: you abandoned yourselves to a panic-terror; you suffered yourselves to be driven
from situations where a handful of brave men might have stopped
an army. Soldiers of the 39th and 85th, you are not French
soldiers. Quartermaster-general, let it be inscribed on their colors, *They no longer form part of the Army of Italy!*" This
harangue, pronounced in a severe tone, drew tears from these old
soldiers; the rules of discipline could not restrain their grief;
several genadiers, who had received honorary arms, cried out,
"General, we have been calumniated; place us in the van, and
you shall see whether the 39th and 85th belong to the Army of
Italy." Napoleon having produced the effect he wished, then addressed a few words of consolation to them. These two regiments a few days after highly distinguished themselves.

Alvinzi was posted on the heights of Caldiero, to the left of
Villa-Nuova, on the road to Vicenza. Napoleon determined to
attack him there; and on the 11th, at two in the afternoon, the
army passed the bridges of Verona for that purpose. Verdier's
brigade, which was at the head, overthrew the enemy's van,
made a number of prisoners, and encamped at night at the foot
of Caldiero. The fires of the bivouacs, as well as the reports of
spies and prisoners, left no doubt that Alvinzi meant to receive

battle, and had fixed himself firmly in these fine positions, resting his left on the marsh of Arcole and his right on Mount Olivetto and the village of Colognola. At day-break Massena received orders to take possession of a hill which outflanked the enemy's right, and which the latter had neglected to occupy. Brigadier-General Launay intrepidly climbed the acclivity at the head of a corps of skirmishers ; but having advanced too far, was repulsed and taken prisoner. In the mean time, the whole line had engaged, and the fire was maintained throughout the day. The rain fell in torrents ; the ground was so completely soaked, that the French artillery could not move, whilst that of the Austrians, being advantageously placed, produced its full effect. The loss in this affair was pretty equal on both sides ; the enemy, not without reason, claimed the victory, as its advanced posts approached St. Michael's, and the situation of the French was become truly hazardous. The General-in-Chief judged it expedient to return into his camp before Verona.

Vaubois had suffered considerable loss in this last battle, and had not now above 8000 men left. The other two divisions, after having fought valiantly on the Brenta, and failed in their attempt on Caldiero, did not amount to more than 13,000 men under arms. The idea of the superior strength of the enemy pervaded every mind. Vaubois' soldiers, in excuse for their retreat, declared that the Austrians were three to one against them. The enemy too had counted the small number of the French at his ease ; and had no longer any doubt of the deliverance of Mantua or of the conquest of Italy. The garrison of Mantua made frequent sorties on the besiegers. The French knew not which way to turn themselves ; they were checked on one side by the position of Caldiero and on the other by the defiles of the Tyrol. A great number of the bravest men had been wounded two or three times in different battles since the army entered Italy. Discontent began to show itself. "We cannot,' said the men, "do every body's duty. Alvinzi's army, now present, is the same that the Armies of the Rhine and of the Sambre and Meuse retreated before, and they are now idle : why are we to perform their work ? If we are beaten, we must make for the Alps as fugitives and without honor : if, on the contrary we conquer, what will be the result? We shall be opposed by another army like that of Alvinzi, as Alvinzi himself succeeded Wurmser, and as Wurmser succeeded Beaulieu; and in this unequal contest we must be overwhelmed at last." To these murmurs Napoleon caused the following answer to be given: "We have but one more effort to make, and Italy is our own. The enemy is, no doubt, more numerous than we are, but half his troops are recruits; when he is beaten Mantua must fall, and we shall remain masters of all; our labors will be at an end; for not only Italy, but a general peace is in Mantua. You talk of returning to the Alps, but you are no longer capable of doing so. From the dry and frozen bivouacs of those sterile rocks, you could very well conquer the delicious plains of Lombardy; but from the smiling flowery bivouacs of Italy you cannot return to the Alpine snows. Succors have reached us; there are more on the road; let not those who are unwilling to fight seek vain pretences; for only beat Alvinzi, and I will answer for your future welfare." These words, repeated from mouth to mouth, revived the spirits of the troops, and brought them over to an opposite way of thinking. Those who before talked of retreating, were now eager to advance. "Shall the soldiers of Italy," they said, "patiently endure the taunts and provocations of these slaves?" When it became known at Brescia, Bergamo, Milan, Cremona, Lodi, Pavia, and Boiogna, that the army had sustained a check, the wounded and sick left the hospitals before they were well cured to resume their stations in the ranks; the wounds of many of these brave men were still bleeding. This affecting sight filled the army with the most lively emotions. From this situation of doubt and danger, Napoleon extricated them by one of those unforeseen movements which stamp him for a consummate master of his art.

At length on the 14th of November, at nightfall, the camp of Verona got under arms. Three columns began their march in the deepest silence, crossed the city, passed the Adige by the three bridges, and formed on the right bank. The hour of departure, the direction taken, the silence observed in the order of the day, contrary to the invariable custom of announcing an engagement when it is to take place, the state of affairs, every thing, in short indicated that the army was retreating. The first

step in retreat would necessarily be followed by the raising of
the siege of Mantua, and foreboded the loss of Italy. Those
amongst the inhabitants who placed the hopes of their future lot
in the success of the French, followed with anxious and aching
hearts the movement of this army, which was depriving them of
every hope. But the army, instead of keeping the Peschiera
road, suddenly turned to the left, marched down the Adige, and
arrived before day-light at Ronco, where Andreossy had been
ordered to construct a bridge. By the first rays of the sun, the
troops were astonished to find themselves, by merely facing
about, on the opposite shore. The officers and soldiers who had
traversed this country before when in pursuit of Wurmser, now
began to guess the General's plan: he intended to turn Caldiero, which he had not been able to carry by an attack in front.
He could not, with 13,000 men, withstand 40,000 in the plain,
and was removing his field of battle to roads surrounded by vast
marshes, where numbers would be unavailing, but where the
courage of the heads of the columns would decide every thing.
The hopes of victory now animated every breast, and every man
vowed to surpass himself in order to second so fine and daring a
plan. Kilmaine had remained in Verona with 1500 men of all
arms, with the gates closed, and all communication strictly prohibited; the enemy was therefore completely ignorant of this
movement. The bridge of Ronco was constructed on the right
of the Alpon, about a quarter of a league from its mouth; which
situation has been censured by ill-informed military men. In
fact, if (as has been proposed) the bridge had been carried to the
left bank opposite Albaredo, all the advantages which were
ensured would have been lost. Three roads branch out from the
bridge of Ronco; the first on the left hand goes up the Adige
towards Verona, passes the villages of Bionde and Porcil, where
it opens into a plain, and where Alvinzi's head-quarters were;
the second and centre one leads to Villa-Nuova, and runs
through the village of Arcole, crossing the Alpon by a little
stone-bridge; the third to the right runs down the Adige and
leads to Albaredo.

Three columns entered upon these three roads; the left one
marched up the Adige as far as the extremity of the marshes at

the village of Porcil, whence the soldiers perceived the steeples
of Verona : it was thenceforth impossible for the Austrians to
march upon that city.   The centre column proceeded to Arcole,
where the French skirmishers got as far as the bridge unperceived.  Two battalions of Croats with two pieces of cannon, had
bivouacs there for the purpose of guarding the rear of the army
and watching any parties which the garrison of Legnago (only
three leagues off) might send in that direction.   The ground between Arcole and the Adige was not guarded, Alvinzi having
contented himself with ordering out patroles of hussars, who visited the dykes thrice every day.   The Croats were stationed on
the opposite bank of the little river Alpon, along which the French
had to pass before reaching the bridge, which turns at right an-
gles into Arcole.   By firing in front they therefore took the
column which was advancing on Arcole in flank : the soldiers
fell back precipitately as far as the point in the road, where they
ceased to be exposed to this dangerous fire.  Augereau, indignant
at this retrograde movement of his troops, rushed towards the
bridge at the head of two battalions of grenadiers, but was received by a brisk flank fire, and driven back on his division.  Alvinzi being informed of this attack, could not at first comprehend
it ; but he was soon after enabled to observe the movements of
the French from the neighboring steeples : he then plainly saw
that they had passed the Adige, and were in his rear.   But he
still believed it impossible that a whole army could have been
thus thrown into impassable marshes ; and that it could be only
some light troops which had been sent in this direction to alarm
him and to mask a real attack on the Verona side.  His reconnoitring parties however, having brought him word that all was quiet
towards Verona, he thought it important to drive these light troops
from the marshes.  He therefore ordered a division commanded
by Metrouski on the dyke of Arcole, and another commanded by
Provera on the left dyke.   Towards nine o'clock in the morning,
they attacked with impetuosity.  Massena, who was entrusted
with the defence of the left dyke, having allowed the enemy to
get fairly upon it, made a desperate charge, broke his columns,
repulsed him with great loss, and took a number of prisoners.
The same thing happened on the dyke of Arcole.  As soon as

the enemy had passed the elbow of the road, he was charged and
routed by Augereau, leaving prisoners and cannon in the victor's
hands : the marsh was covered with dead. It became of the utmost importance to gain possession of Arcole ; for by debouching
thence in the enemy's rear, the French would be able to seize
the bridge of Villa-Nuova over the Alpon, that was his only retreat. But Arcole withstood several attacks. Napoleon resolved
to try a last effort in person : he seized a flag, rushed on the
bridge, and there planted it : the column he commanded had
reached the middle of the bridge, when the flanking fire and the
arrival of a division of the enemy frustrated the attack. The
grenadiers at the head of the columns, finding themselves abandoned by the rear, hesitated at first ; but being hurried away in
the confusion, they still persisted in keeping possession of their
General. They seized him by his arms and clothes, and dragged
him along with them amidst the dead, the dying, and the smoke ;
he was precipitated into a morass, in which he sunk up to the
middle, surrounded by the enemy. The grenadiers perceiving
the danger of their General, a cry was raised, " *Forward, soldiers, to save the General!*" They immediately turned back,
rushed upon the enemy, drove him beyond the bridge, and Napoleon was rescued. This was a day filled with examples of military devotedness. Lannes, who had been wounded at Governolo,
had hastened from Milan, though still suffering ; he threw himself between the enemy and Napoleon, covering him with his
body, and received three wounds, determined never to abandon
him. Muiron, his aid-de-camp, fell dead at his feet in attempting
to cover his General with his own body. Belliard and Vignoles
were wounded in rallying the troops forward ; General Robert
was killed ; he was a soldier who never shrunk from the enemy's fire.

General Guieux having passed the Adige with a brigade at the
ferry of Albaredo, Arcole was taken in the rear. In the mean
time, Alvinzi had become fully sensible of the danger of his situation : he had abandoned Caldiero hastily, destroyed his batteries,
and made all his parks of artillery and his reserves repass the
bridge. From the top of the steeple of Ronco, the French saw
this fine booty escape them : and it was only by witnessing the

disorderly movements of the enemy that the whole extent and
consequences of Napoleon's plan could be comprehended. General Guieux was not able to reach Arcole till near four o'clock;
the village was carried without striking a blow; but it was now
of little importance, Arcole being at present only an intermediate
post between the fronts of the two armies, whereas in the morning it had been in the rear of the enemy. The day was however crowned with the most important results. Caldiero was
evacuated; Verona was no longer in danger; two divisions of Alvinzi's army had been defeated with considerable loss; numerous
columns of prisoners and a great number of trophies filed off
through the camp, and filled the officers and soldiers with enthusiasm; the troops regained their spirits and their confidence of
victory.

In the mean time Davidowich with the Tyrolese corps had attacked and taken Corona, and was at Rivoli. Vaubois was at Bussolengo in considerable peril: if he should be attacked and beaten,
the French would be obliged to raise the siege of Mantua, and the
retreat of the head-quarters and of the army would be cut off. To
prevent the possibility of this result, Buonaparte determined to
march at day-break and attack Davidowich, in case he should
have advanced from Rivoli towards Mantua. He therefore evacuated Arcole and fell back to the right bank of the Adige, leaving fires lighted all night to deceive the enemy. But Alvinzi,
apprised of the retrograde movement of the French, followed
them; they had to cross the bridge of Ronco again, and a severe
action ensued which lasted the whole day. The General-in-Chief
learned that Davidowich had not stirred the preceding evening.
Alvinzi, deceived by a spy, who assured him that the French
were in full march upon Mantua, again debouched from his
camp before dawn. The same thing happened as on the day
before. The two armies met half-way up the dykes leading
from Ronco; the action was obstinate and at one time doubtful the 75th having been broken. The French General placed
the 32d in ambush, lying on their faces in a little wood of wil-
lows near the bridge; they rose at the proper moment, fired a
volley, charged with the bayonet, and overthrew into the morass
a close column of 3000 Croats, who perished there. Massena on

the left, after experiencing some vicissitudes, placed himself at
the head of his troops, with his hat at the end of his sword, by
way of standard, and made dreadful carnage of the division opposed to him. In the afternoon the General-in-Chief conceived
that the decisive moment had arrived for attacking the enemy in
the plain and repulsing him beyond Villa-Nuova. He had the prisoners carefully counted, and calculated the number of the slain ;
and he found that the enemy did not exceed his own troops by
above a third. Their ranks were not only thinned, but their confidence was abated by these three days' battles. At two o'clock
the French drew up in line between Arcole and the road to
Porto-Legnago, with the Austrians in front. Adjutant-General
Lorset had come out of Legnago with 600 or 700 men, some
cavalry, and four pieces of cannon, in order to turn the enemy's
left in the marshes. Major Hercule was at the same time ordered
to proceed with twenty-five Guides and four trumpets across the
reeds, and to charge the extreme left of the enemy as soon as the
garrison of Legnago should begin to cannonade in the rear.
This manœuvre was ably executed, and contributed mainly to
the success of the day. The line was broken, and the enemy retreated with considerable loss. The next day when it was doubtful what course the army would have to take, the Austrians were
seen at day-break in retreat upon Vicenza, and were pursued beyond Villa-Nuova.

In the course of the day, the General-in-Chief had entered the
convent of St. Boniface, the church of which had served for an
hospital ; between 400 and 500 wounded had been crowded into
it, the greater part of whom were dead. A cadaverous smell
issued from the place. Napoleon was retiring, struck with horror, when he heard himself called by name. Two unfortunate
soldiers had been left three days among the dead, without having
had their wounds dressed ; they had despaired of relief, and were
recalled to life at the sight of their General. Every assistance
was afforded them.

Having ascertained by the reports that the enemy was in the
utmost confusion, was making no stand in any direction, and had
already got beyond Montebello, Napoleon faced to the left, and
proceeded by Verona to attack the army of the Tyrol. The

scouts captured a staff-officer sent to Alvinzi by Davidowich, who
was ignorant of all that had happened.  Alvinzi in the last three
days had lost 18,000 men, of whom 6000 were prisoners.  The
French army re-entered Verona in triumph by the Venice gate,
three days after having quitted that city almost clandestinely by
the Milan gate.  It would be difficult to describe the astonishment
and enthusiasm of the inhabitants.  The army, however, made
no stay there; but passed the Adige, and advanced on Davidowich, who had attacked Bussolengo on the 17th, and driven Vaubois on Castel-Nuovo.  Massena marched thither, joined Vaubois
and attacked Rivoli, while Augereau proceeded to Dolce on the
left bank of the Adige, and gained some capital advantages.  The
Austrians stood in need of repose.  It was to be expected that
Mantua would open its gates before the Austrian General could
collect another army : the garrison were reduced to half rations,
desertion became frequent, and diseases daily swept off more men
than would have sufficed to win a great battle.

While the animosity of the Senate of Venice against the French
hourly increased, and the negociations with Rome were broken
off from a conviction that nothing was to be done with that court
but by an armed force, Alvinzi was receiving daily reinforcements.  Austria employed the two months which elapsed after
the battle of Arcole, in bringing into the Frioul divisions drafted
from the banks of the Rhine, where the French armies were in
winter-quarters.  Several battalions of excellent sharp-shooters
were raised in the Tyrol.  A powerful impulse had been given
to the whole monarchy.  The successes in Germany encouraged,
while the defeats in Italy irritated them.  The large towns offered
battalions of volunteers.  Vienna raised four battalions, who
received their colors from the Empress, embroidered with her own
hands: they lost them, but not without a struggle.  At the beginning of January, the Austrian army in Italy amounted to 65,000
or 70,000 fighting men, besides 6000 Tyrolese and the garrison
of Mantua.  The French army had been reinforced by two demi-
brigades of infantry from the coast of Provence and by a regiment of cavalry, that is, by 7000 men ; and was formed in five
divisions, amounting to 45,000 men.  Joubert had covered La
Corona with entrenchments; the other fortresses were in a good

state of defence, and the Lakes of Garda, Como, Lugano, and Maggiore were manned by French gun-boats.

The two former plans under Wurmser and Alvinzi having failed, the Court of Vienna adopted a new one in concert with Rome; and ordered two grand attacks to be made, one by Monte-Baldo, the other by the Lower Adige: both armies were to meet under the walls of Mantua. A very intelligent secret agent sent from Vienna to Mantua was arrested by a sentinel as he was passing the last post of the blockading army. He was forced to give up his dispatches, though he had swallowed them: they were enclosed in a ball of sealing-wax, and consisted of a small letter written in a very minute hand, and signed by the Emperor Francis. He informed Wurmser that he would be relieved without delay; at all events he charged him not to capitulate, but rather to evacuate the place, pass the Po, and proceed into the Pope's territories, and there take the command of the army of the Holy See.

Alvinzi commanded the principal attack on the Tyrolese side at the head of 50,000 men, and advanced his head-quarters from Bassano to Roveredo. General Provera took the command of the army on the Lower Adige, which was 20,000 strong: its head-quarters were at Padua. A great many troops appeared on different points, and some spirited actions also took place in the course of the 12th and 13th; but the enemy had not fully unmasked his plans, so that the moment for adopting a decisive course had not yet arrived. On the 13th it rained very heavily, and Napoleon had not resolved in what direction to march, whether up or down the Adige. At ten in the evening, the accounts from Joubert at La Corona determined him. It was plain that the Austrians were operating with two independent corps, the principal attack being intended against Monte-Baldo, the minor one on the Lower Adige. Augereau's division appeared sufficient to dispute the passage of the river with Provera; but on the Monte-Baldo side the danger was imminent. There was not a moment to lose; for the enemy was about to effect a junction with his artillery and cavalry, by taking possession of the level of Rivoli; and if he could be attacked before he could gain that important point, he would be obliged to fight without artillery or cavalry. All the troops were therefore put in motion from the head-quar ters at Verona to reach Rivoli before day-break: the General-in-Chief proceeded to the same point, and arrived there at two in the morning.

The weather had cleared up; the moon shone brilliantly: the General ascended several heights, and observed the lines of the enemy's fires, which filled the whole country between the Adige and the Lake of Garda, and reddened the atmosphere. He clearly distinguished five camps, each composed of a column which had marched from different routes the preceding day, and were still dispersed at some distance from each other and from the place of destination. The Austrians amounted to 40,000 or 45,000 men: the French could not bring more than 22,000 into action; but then they had the advantage of sixty pieces of cannon and several regiments of cavalry.

From the position of the different bivouacs it seemed evident that Alvinzi could not unite his forces before ten o'clock. On this presumption, Napoleon ordered Joubert, who had evacuated St. Mark's chapel on Monte Magnone, and who now occupied the level of Rivoli only with a rearguard, to resume the offensive forthwith, to regain possession of the chapel without waiting for day-light, and to drive back the fourth column (that under D'Ocskay) as far as possible. Ten Croats having been informed of the evacuation of St. Mark's by a prisoner, had just entered the chapel, when Joubert sent General Vial up to it about four o'clock in the morning, and retook it. The firing began with a regiment of Croats, and successively with the whole of D'Ocskay's column, which before day-light was repulsed as far as the middle of the ridge of Monte Magnone. The third Austrian column, that of Koblos, then hastened its march, and reached the heights on the left of the level of Rivoli a little before nine o'clock, but without artillery. The 14th and 85th French demi-brigades, which were in line in this position, had each a battery. The 14th, which occupied the right, repulsed the enemy's attacks; the 85th was outflanked and broken. The General-in-Chief hastened to Massena's division, which having marched all night, was taking a little rest in the village of Rivoli, led it against the enemy, and in less than half an hour this column was beaten and put to flight. Liptay's column came up to the aid of that of

Koblos. Quasdanowich, who was at the bottom of the valley, perceiving that Joubert had left no troops in St. Mark's chapel in the heat of his pursuit of Ocskay, detached three battalions to climb the heights of the chapel ; but Joubert, aware of this movement and its great importance, ordered his men to run back, who reached the chapel before those of the enemy, and repulsed them to the bottom of the valley. The French battery of fifteen pieces of cannon, placed on the edge of the level of Rivoli, overwhelmed all who offered to come within its reach. Colonel Leclerc and Major Lasalle by a brilliant charge with 300 horse in platoons and 200 hussars contributed greatly to the success of the day. The Austrians were thrown into the ravine. The two columns of Quasdanowich and Wukassowich had not been able to come up in time or to join in the battle. One half of Lusignan's column was coming up on the road behind the level of Rivoli, and thought they had turned the French army ; but scarcely had they arrived at the heights when they witnessed the rout of Ocskay, Koblos, and Liptay ; and foresaw the fate which unavoidably awaited them. They were first cannonaded by fifteen twelve-pounders, and immediately afterwards attacked and taken. The other half of this column left at Dezenzano was pursued and dispersed. It was two o'clock in the afternoon, when the enemy was everywhere overthrown and the battle won. La Scaliera was the only retreat open to the Austrians, who lost 7000 prisoners and twelve pieces of cannon coming by way of Incanole. This day the French General-in-Chief was wounded more than once, and had several horses killed under him.

On the same day Provera constructed a bridge at Anghiari near Legnago, passed the river, and marched on Mantua, leaving a reserve to guard the bridge. Augereau attacked this guard the next day, defeated them, and burned the pontoons. Napoleon hearing at two o'clock in the afternoon of the 14th in the midst of the battle of Rivoli what Provera was doing, immediately foresaw what was about to take place. He left the task of pursuing Alvinzi on the following day to Massena, Murat, and Joubert, and instantly marched with four regiments to station himself before Mantua. He had thirteen leagues to go. He entered Rover-bella as Provera arrived before St. Georges. Hohenzollern with the vanguard had presented himself on the 16th at break of day at the gate of St. Georges, at the head of a regiment wearing white cloaks: he knew that this suburb was merely covered by a simple line of circumvallation, and was in hopes to surprise it. Miolis, who commanded there, had no guard except toward the city: he knew that a French division was on the Adige, and was not dreaming of the enemy. Hohenzollern's hussars resembled those of the 1st French hussar regiment. But an old serjeant of the garrison of St. Georges, who was gathering wood about two hundred yards from the walls, observed this cavalry and conceived doubts which he communicated to a drummer who was with him. It seemed to them that the white cloaks were too new for Berchini's regiment. In this uncertainty these sturdy fellows threw themselves into St. Georges, crying " *To arms !*" and shut the barrier: Hohenzollern galloped up, but was too late; he was recognized, and fired upon with grape. The troops speedily manned the parapets; at noon Provera surrounded the place; but Miolis with 15,000 men defended himself all day, which gave time for the succors from Rivoli to arrive.

Provera communicated with Mantua by means of a boat which crossed the lake, and concerted operations for the following day. On the 16th as soon as it was day, Wurmser made a sortie with the garrison, and took up a position at La Favorite. At one o'clock in the morning Napoleon stationed General Victor and the four regiments he had brought with him between La Favorite and St. Georges, to prevent the garrison of Mantua from joining the succoring army. Serrurier at the head of the troops conducting the blockade attacked the garrison : Victor attacked the army of succor. It was in this battle that the 57th earned the title of *Terrible*. They attacked the Austrian line, and overthrew every thing in their way. By two o'clock in the afternoon the garrison was driven back into the place, and Provera capitulated and laid down his arms. In the mean time, a rearguard which Provera had left at Molinella, was attacked by General Point of Augereau's division, defeated and taken. Of all Provera's troops, only 2000 who had remained beyond the Adige escaped; the rest were taken or killed. This action was called the battle of La

Favorite from the name of a palace belonging to the Dukes of Mantua situated near the field of battle.

Joubert chased Alvinzi throughout the 15th, and reached the Scaliera (ladder path) of Brentino so suddenly that 3000 men were intercepted and taken. Murat, with two battalions of light troops, embarked on the Lake of Garda and turned La Corona, so that it was with difficulty Alvinzi escaped. Joubert marched on Trent, and the army occupied the same positions as before the battle of Arcole. The Austrian troops had great difficulty in crossing the passes of the Tyrol, which were blocked up by the snow. Their loss in the course of January had been 25,000 prisoners, twenty-five standards, and sixty pieces of cannon. Bessieres carried the colors to Paris. It was in acknowledgment of the services rendered in so many battles by General Massena, that the Emperor afterwards made him Duke of Rivoli.

The garrison of Mantua had long subsisted on half rations; the horses had been eaten. Wurmser was informed of the result of the battle of Rivoli. He had no longer any thing to hope for. He was summoned to surrender, but proudly answered that he had provisions for a twelvemonth. A few days after, Klenau, his first aid-de-camp, came to head-quarters with certain proposals. Serrurier replied that he would take the orders of his General-in-Chief on the subject. Napoleon went to Roverbella; and remained *incognito*, wrapped up in his cloak, while the conversation between the officers was going on. Klenau employed all the customary artifices, expatiating at length on the great resources Wurmser still possessed. Buonaparte approached the table, took a pen, and spent nearly half an hour in writing his decisions in the margin of Wurmser's proposals, whilst the discussion was going on. When it was over, " If Wurmser," said he to Klenau, " had but provisions for eighteen or twenty days, and talked of surrendering, he would not deserve an honorable capitulation; but I respect the Marshal's age, his bravery, and his misfortunes. If he delays a fortnight, a month, or two, he shall still have the same conditions; he may therefore hold out to his last morsel of bread. I am about to pass the Po, and I shall march on Rome. You know my intentions; go and communicate them to your General." Klenau, who had been quite at a loss to comprehend the first words, soon discovered who it was that addressed him. He examined the conditions, the perusal of which filled him with gratitude for such generous and unexpected treatment. Dissimulation was become useless; he acknowledged that they had not provisions for more than three days. Wurmser sent to request the French General, as he was to cross the Po, to pass it at Mantua, which would save him much circuitous travelling over bad roads. He also wrote to him to express his obligations; and a few days after dispatched an aid-de-camp to Napoleon at Bologna to apprise him of a conspiracy to poison him, which was to be carried into effect in Romagna. This notice proved seasonable. General Serrurier presided at the ceremony of the surrender of Mantua, and saw the old Marshal and the staff of his army file off before him; Napoleon being by that time in Romagna. The indifference with which he withdrew himself from the very flattering spectacle of a Marshal of great reputation, Generalissimo of the Austrian forces in Italy, delivering up his sword at the head of his staff, was remarked throughout Europe. The garrison of Mantua still amounted to 20,000, of whom 12,000 were capable of service. In the three blockades since the month of June, 27,000 soldiers had died in the hospitals or been killed in the different actions.

Joubert, who was born in the department of the Aisne, had studied for the bar; but at the Revolution he was induced to adopt the profession of arms. He was tall and thin, and naturally of a weak constitution; but he had strengthened his frame amidst fatigue, camps, and mountain warfare. He was intrepid, vigilant, and active. In November, 1796, he was made a General of division to succeed Vaubois. He was much attached to Napoleon, who sent him to the Directory in November, 1797, with the colors taken by the Army of Italy. In 1799 he engaged in the intrigues of Paris, and was appointed General-in-Chief of the Army of Italy. He married the daughter of the Senator Semonville. He fell gloriously at the battle of Novi. He was still young, and had not acquired all the experience necessary; but his talents were such that he might have attained great military renown.

# CHAPTER XII.

CARDINAL BUSCA had succeeded Cardinal Zelada in the situation of Secretary of State at Rome. ˙ He was avowedly hostile to
the French, and wished to keep on the war by kindling the religious fanaticism of the Italians. A courier from the Cardinal
to Monsignor Albani, the Roman *chargé d'affaires* at Vienna, was
intercepted near La Mezzola on the 10th of January, 1797, from
whose dispatches the whole policy of the Vatican was disclosed.
It appeared that the Pope was determined to break off the nego-
tiations with France, that he had entered into a league with Austria, and that the Emperor had impowered General Colli to take the
command of the troops that his Holiness was levying in Romagna.
A courier was instantly dispatched to Cacault, the French minister,
with orders to quit Rome. At the same time General Victor passed
the Po at Borgo-Forte at the head of 4000 infantry and 600 horse ;
and joined the Italian division of 4000 men, commanded by Gen
eral Lahoz at Bologna. Napoleon arrived here a few days after,
and issued a manifesto, in which he accused the Papal Government of having violated the conditions of the armistice concluded
at Bologna the preceding summer, and of having entered into an
offensive alliance with the Court of Vienna. The intercepted
letters of Cardinal Busca were published in support of this manifesto. They were also sent to Cardinal Mattei, who, after having
been confined three months in a seminary at Brescia, had returned
to Rome, and who kept up a correspondence with the General-in-
Chief. Through his means these papers were communicated to
the Sacred College, who were thrown into some confusion by a
perusal of them.

On the 2d of February, head-quarters were fixed at the Bishop's palace at Imola, belonging to Chiaramonte, afterwards Pius

VII.   On the 3d the French troops reached Castel-Bolognese, and found the Pope's army on the opposite bank of the Senio, intending to dispute the passage of the bridge.   This army consisted of about 6000 or 7000 men, including regular soldiers and peasants, collected by the ringing of the tocsin, commanded by monks, and wrought up to fanatical enthusiasm by preachers and missionaries. They had eight pieces of cannon.   The French had had a fatiguing day's march.   As they were stationing their guard, a flag of truce came up and declared in a pompous manner on the part of his eminence the Lord Cardinal as Commander-in-Chief, that *if the French army continued to advance, he would fire upon it.* This threat excited much laughter among the French soldiers, who replied that *they did not wish to expose themselves to the Cardinal's thunders, and that they were going to take up their quarters for the night.*   Cardinal Busca's hopes had, however, been fulfilled.   All Romagna was in a flame ; a holy war had been begun ; the tocsin had been sounding incessantly for three days, and the lowest class of the people was thrown into a state of delirium and frenzy.   Prayers of forty hours, missions in public places, indulgences, and even miracles—every engine, in short, had been set at work with success.   Martyrs were bleeding in one place ; Madonnas weeping in another ; and every thing foreboded a scene of tumult and confusion.   Cardinal Busca had boasted to the French minister that he would make a *La Vendée* of Romagna, of the mountains of Liguria, nay, of all Italy.   The following proclamation was on this occasion posted at Imola.   " The French army is about to enter the territories of the Pope.   It will be faithful to the maxims it professes, and will protect religion and the people.   The French soldier bears in one hand the bayonet, the sure harbinger of victory ; in the other, the olive-branch, the symbol of peace and the pledge of his protection.   Woe to those who may be seduced by men of finished hypocrisy to draw upon their homes the vengeance of an army which has in six months made prisoners of 100,000 of the Emperor's best troops, taken 400 pieces of cannon, and 110 standards, and destroyed five armies." There was perhaps a little too much of a tone of gasconade in the latter part of this address for the occasion.

At four o'clock on the following morning, General Lannes with the van of the little French army marched a league and a half up the bank of the Senio; crossed it at a ford at day-break; and drew up in line in the rear of the Pope's army, cutting it off from Faenza. General Lahoz, supported by a battery and covered by a cloud of skirmishers, passed the bridge in close column. The armed mob of the enemy was routed in an instant; artillery, baggage, and every thing was taken. Four or five hundred men were put to the sword, a few monks (mostly mendicants) perished with their crucifixes in their hands, but the Cardinal-General escaped. The loss of the French was very trifling; they arrived before Faenza the same day. They found the gates shut; the tocsin sounded; the ramparts were lined with a few pieces of cannon; and the enraged populace assailed the besiegers with all sorts of abuse. When summoned to open the gates, they gave an insolent answer; and it became necessary to enter the town by main force. "This is the same thing that happened at Pavia," cried the soldiers, by way of demanding the pillage of the place. "No," replied Napoleon; "at Pavia they had revolted after taking an oath, and they wanted to massacre our soldiers who were their guests. These are only misled people, who must be subdued by clemency." In fact, a few convents only were attacked. The town was thus saved from devastation, and the next object was to calm the agitation and apprehension of the people. The prisoners taken at the action of the Senio were collected at Faenza in a garden belonging to one of the convents. Their first terror had not yet subsided. At the approach of Napoleon they threw themselves on their knees, crying out for mercy. He addressed them in Italian in these words: "I am the friend of all the nations of Italy, and particularly of the people of Rome. You are free: return to your families, and tell them that the French are the friends of religion, of order, and of the poor." The consternation of the prisoners now gave way to joy, and they abandoned themselves to the expression of their gratitude with all the liveliness that belongs to the Italian character. From the garden of the monastery Napoleon proceeded to the refectory, where he had caused the officers to be assembled; they amounted to several hundreds, and some of them belonged to the best families of Rome. He conversed with them a long time ; talked of the liberty of Italy, the abuses of the Papal power, and the uselessness of resistance, and permitted them to go back to their homes, only requiring them in return for his lenity to make known his sentiments in favor of their countrymen. The prisoners proceeded to disperse themselves in the States of the Pope, loudly declaring the generous treatment they had met with, and carrying with them proclamations, which thus reached .he remotest castles of the Apennines. The army in consequence found the people much more amicably disposed. Even the monks (with the exception of the mendicant friars) began to consider how much more they had to lose than to gain by resistance.

The French proceeded to overrun Romagna. Colli, who commanded the Pope's troops, had taken up a good position on the heights before Ancona with the 3000 men he had left, but retired to Loretto as soon as the French army came in sight. General Victor sent a flag of truce to invite the enemy to surrender. During the parley, his troops outflanked them both on the right and the left, surrounded and took them prisoners, and entered the citadel of Loretto without firing a shot. The prisoners taken on this occasion were treated in the same manner as the former ones, that is, sent home with proclamations and a favorable report of the behavior of the General-in-Chief towards them, which prepared the way for the reception of the French army. Ancona, though the only sea-port between Venice and Brindisi, the extreme point of the eastern coast of Italy, had been much neglected; even frigates could not enter it. It was at this period that Napoleon perceived what was necessary for the improvement of the fortifications and the repairs of the harbor, which were afterwards executed during the Kingdom of Italy, so that at present the port receives ships of all kinds, even three-deckers. The Jews, who were numerous at Ancona, as well as the Mahometans from Albania and Greece, had been subjected to humiliating customs and oppressive restraints, from which it was one of Napoleon's first cares to relieve them. In the meanwhile, the town's-people were running in crowds to prostrate themselves at the feet of a Madonna that was supposed to shed tears in abundance for the disasters of the country. Monge was sent to inquire into the circumstance, and the Madonna was brought to head-quarters, when it was found to be an optical illusion, ingeniously managed by means of a glass. The following day the Madonna was restored to its place in the church, but without the glass, and consequently without performing any wonders. One of the chaplains was arrested as the contriver of this imposture, which was considered as an insult to the army, and an offence against religion.

On the 10th the French army encamped at Loretto. This is a bishopric, and contains a magnificent convent. The church and buildings are sumptuous; and there are vast and well furnished apartments for the treasures of the Madonna, and for the accommodation of the abbots, the chapter, and the pilgrims. In the church is the celebrated *Casa Santa*, the pretended residence of the Virgin at Nazareth, and said to be the very place in which she received the visit of the angel Gabriel. It is a little cabin ten or twelve yards square, in which is a Madonna placed on a tabernacle. The legend states that the angels carried it from Nazareth into Dalmatia, at the time when the infidels conquered Syria; and from thence across the Adriatic to the heights of Loretto. From all parts of Christendom pilgrims flocked to see the Madonna. Presents, diamonds, and jewels sent from every quarter formed her treasures, which amounted to several millions in value. The Court of Rome, on learning the approach of the French army, had the treasures of Loretto carefully packed up and placed in safety: property in gold and silver was, notwithstanding, left to the value of upwards of a million. The Madonna, or Lady of Loretto, was forwarded to Paris. It is a wooden statue clumsily carved, which is so far a proof of its antiquity. It was to be seen for some years at the National Library. The First Consul restored it to the Pope at the time of the *Concordat;* and it has been since replaced in the *Casa Santa*.

It is to be remarked here that several thousand French priests, exiled from their country, had taken refuge in Italy. As the French Army advanced in the Peninsula, they fled into the Roman States, but they now found themselves without an asylum. Some had retired in time into Germany; Naples refused them shelter. The heads of the different convents in the States of the Pope, who were anxious to get rid of the burthen of feeding and maintaining them, made a pretext of the arrival of the army to

turn their unfortunate guests out of doors, affecting to be apprehensive that their presence would draw down the vengeance of
the victor on their heads.   Napoleon published a proclamation,
encouraging the priests, and ordering the convents, bishops, and
different chapters to receive them and furnish them with every
thing necessary for their subsistence and comfort.   He also commanded the army to look upon them as friends and fellow-countrymen, and to behave to them accordingly.   As the army fell
into the same sentiment, many interesting scenes were the consequence.   Some of the soldiers found their former pastors again;
and these unfortunate old men, banished many hundred miles
from their native soil, received for the first time tokens of
respect and affection from their countrymen, by whom they expected to be treated with the utmost harshness and indignity.
Buonaparte, in reverting to this measure, speaks of it with considerable triumph, as exciting much talk in Europe, and as approved of by the Directory.   If he was proud of it, on reflection,
as an act of humanity and generosity towards those who were the
objects of it, he was right; but if he speaks of it as a first step towards a reconciliation with men alike incapable of reason or
gratitude, and as relying on any return from them, it was the
commencement of "an Iliad of woes."   It was a mistaken view
of the nature of men and things.   As well might he hold a parley
with the sea, or take the sting out of the adder by a show of courtesy.   As men, and for the moment, they may be touched by
suffering or compassion; but the Church is an abstraction that
knows no mortifying vicissitudes, that sheds no tears and owns no
worldly obligations; nor are her votaries slow to throw away the
crutch of humility which sustained them, and exchange it for the
staff of power and spiritual dominion, which they grasp with redoubled rancor and cunning.   See what this poor, persecuted,
and compassionated race of men are doing at present in France;
see what they do in Spain.   You cannot cozen men out of purple
pride and access to the ear of kings, by beggarly donations of
rags and pity!

The greatest consternation now reigned in the Vatican.   Disastrous news arrived every hour.   The vanguard of the French army
was already on the summit of the Apennines.   The officers and

soldiers who had been taken prisoners and allowed to return home, gave a very different account of things from what had been expected ; so that the friends of liberty ventured once more to show themselves, even within the walls of the city. The members of the Sacred College began to think of providing for their own safety, and the horses were already put to the court-carriages to proceed to Naples, when the General of the Camaldolites arrived at the Vatican, and prostrated himself at the feet of the Holy Father. Napoleon in passing through Cesena had noticed this ecclesiastic, and knowing that Pius VI. reposed great confidence in him, he had charged him to assure his Holiness that no harm was intended to him personally ; that he might remain in Rome with safety, and had only to change his ministers and send plenipotentiaries to Tolentino to conclude a peace with the Republic. The Pope agreed to these terms ; dismissed Busca, countermanded his departure from Rome, and entrusted the direction of his cabinet and the conclusion of a peace to Cardinal Doria, who had been long distinguished for the liberality of his opinions. The instructions from the Directory were, it is true, against any negociation with Rome. They thought that an end should be put to the temporal power of the Pope, from whom neither moderation nor good faith could be expected, and that there could not be a better opportunity than the present ; but the General-in-Chief was of opinion that this could not be done without at the same time overturning the throne of Naples, for which purpose an army of 20,000 or 25,000 men would be requisite ; and the measure was therefore laid aside as inconsistent with Buonaparte's favorite project of dictating peace under the walls of Vienna.

The head-quarters of the French army were at Tolentino on the 13th of February, and the van was within three days' march of Rome. The Pope's Ministers-plenipotentiary, Cardinal Mattei, Monsignor Galeppi, the Duke of Braschi, and the Marquis Massini arrived the same day, and the conferences began on the 14th. The basis having been settled, the treaty was soon concluded ; the principal articles were, that the Pope renounced every offensive and defensive alliance with the powers at war with France ; that he ceded the legations of Bologna, Ferrara, and Romagna to the Republic, allowing Ancona to be occupied by a French gar

15*

rison till a general peace ; that he was to cause his Minister at Paris to disavow the murder of Basseville ; to re-establish the French school of art at Rome as before the Revolution ; to make good all the indemnifications agreed upon in the armistice of Bologna, and to furnish an additional contribution of money and horses to the army.    Buonaparte wished that the Court of Rome should undertake to suppress the Inquisition.    But this point was given up as a particular favor to the Pope.    It was represented that the Inquisition was no longer what it was, that it was little more than a tribunal of police, and that *auto-da-fés* no longer took place.    But if it was at present reduced to a nonentity, why attach so much importance to it ?    If it was only a shadow, it was a terrible one, from which the mind shrunk with hatred and fear ; why then keep up the forms of an obsolete power but as a receptacle for the spirit in case it should ever revive, or as a tacit justification and indirect avowal of all the horrors that had been committed under its sanction ?    The very name of the Inquisition is in itself an insult to common sense and humanity, from which all good and honest minds revolt.    But by keeping up the outward form, the imagination is familiarized with it, is taught to look upon it as harmless ; the tendency, the pretensions of bigotry and fanaticism are still virtually acknowledged and kept in view by their adherents, and by always having the name ready, opportunity may not be wanting to restore the *thing !*    Hence the tenaciousness with which its advocates uniformly adhere to every relic of arbitrary power, and hence the determination with which all such claims, grounded on their apparent insignificance, should be resisted.    The whole science and study of social improvement may be reduced to watching the secret aim and rooted purpose of power, and in opposing it step by step and in exact proportion to the obstinacy of its struggles for existence.    On the principle already stated, the French General did not accede to the wishes of the more sanguine patriots of the new Italian Republic to include Urbino and Macerata in its acquisitions, or extend its boundary to the frontiers of Naples, lest it should embroil the two governments in a war.    Such were the apprehensions entertained by this Court on the subject, that Pignatelli, its minister, followed the French staff from Bologna, resorting to the most contemptible expedients to satisfy his curiosity, and even playing the part of an eaves-dropper at the door of council-chambers to gain secret information.

After the signature of the treaty of Tolentino, the General-in-Chief left the superintendence of its execution to General Victor: and dispatching Colonel Junot with a respectful letter to the Pope, returned to Mantua, which had now been a month in the power of the Republic, and was full of Austrian sick. While here, he eyed the fine frescoes of the War of the Titans by Titian in the palace *del T.* with admiration; but their removal was impossible. He had the fortifications repaired, and set out for Milan, where he found the public spirit highly favorable to his plans. At length the Directory, roused from its apathy, had sent six regiments of infantry and two of cavalry, under Bernadotte, from the army of the Sambre and Meuse, and an equal force from the Army of the Rhine, under General Delmas, to reinforce the Army of Italy. They had only just reached the foot of the Alps at the time of the battles of Rivoli and La Favorite and the surrender of Mantua; and it was not till his return from Tolentino that Napoleon reviewed these new troops. They were estimated at 30,000 men, but their actual strength did not exceed 10,000, in good condition and well disciplined. The Army of Italy was henceforth equal to any enterprise, and to the enemy opposed to it.

# CHAPTER XIII.

THE Archduke Charles, who had lately acquired the highest renown in Germany, took the command of the Austrian armies of Italy, and advanced his head-quarters to Inspruck on the 6th of February 1797, whence he soon transferred them successively to Villach and Goritz. In the course of February his engineers visited the passes of the Julian and Noric Alps. They planned fortifications, which they were to construct as soon as the snow melted. Napoleon was impatient to anticipate them, and ardently hoped to attack the Archduke and chase him out of Italy before the arrival of a body of 40,000 men, whom the Aulic Council (feeling secure on that side) had detached from the armies on the Rhine, and who were marching through Germany to reinforce him.

Napoleon's army was composed of eight divisions of infantry and a reserve of cavalry, consisting of 53,000 infantry, 3000 artillery-men, serving 120 guns, and 5000 cavalry. The King of Sardinia was to have furnished a contingent of 10,000 troops; but the Directory, by refusing to ratify the armistice of Bologna, deprived the French General of this resource; and the Venetians, with whom he had been in treaty for a similar aid, showed so hostile a disposition that he was obliged to leave 10,000 men in reserve on the Adige to watch their motions. He had also hoped that the armies of the Sambre and Meuse and of the Rhine would have been united in one army of 120,000 men; and proceeding from Strasburg through Bavaria would have joined the Army of Italy, which, crossing the Tagliamento and the Julian Alps, would direct its march on the Simering, and both together, forming a body of near 200,000 men, enter Vienna, while an army of observation of 60,000 men defended Holland and blockaded

Ehrenbretstein and the fortresses on the Rhine.   But the Directory had no such thoughts in their head, and persisted, in spite of
the experience of the last campaign, either from narrowness of
mind or a mean jealousy, in keeping the armies separate.

There are three high roads from Italy to Vienna; the first,
through the Tyrol by Trent, the pass of the Brenner, Saltzburg,
and the Danube; the second, by Treviso, the Tagliamento, the Carnic Alps, Carinthia, and the Simering: the third through Carniola,
Styria, and Gratz, joins the Carinthian road at Bruck.   The
Tyrolese communicates with the Carinthian road by five cross-
roads, and the Carinthian with that of Carniola by three.

In the beginning of March, the Archduke's army was 50,000
strong; it was behind the Piave, covering Friuli, except 15,000,
who were in the Tyrol.   This army was to be joined in the
course of April by the six divisions on their march from Germany, which would make it upwards of 90,000 men.   So great
a superiority of numbers, justified the sanguine hopes of the
Cabinet of Vienna.   The French army at the same period was
stationed as follows: three divisions, amounting to 17,000 men,
were in the Tyrol under Joubert; Massena's, Augereau's, and
Bernadotte's divisions, with General Dugua's division of cavalry,
were in junction in the Bassanese and Trevisan countries, having
advanced posts along the right bank of the Piave; Victor was
still in the Apennines, but was expected to reach the Adige in
the beginning of April with a *corps d'armée* and reinforcements,
amounting to 20,000 men.   When it was found that the Archduke had arrived at Inspruck on the 6th of February, it was concluded that he would collect his chief forces in the Tyrol, by
which means the detachments from the Rhine would have been
enabled to join the army twenty days earlier.   Joubert received
orders on this conjecture to take up some strong position and keep
the enemy in check as long as he could, so as to give time to the
other divisions to take the Archduke's army in flank by the gorges
of the Brenta.   But the Archduke, adhering to the plan laid
down for him by the Aulic Council, threw himself into the Friuli,
at a distance from his reinforcements, and thus gave the French General an opportunity of attacking him before the arrival of the
divisions of the Rhine, which were still twenty days' march be-

hind.　Napoleon in consequence fixed his head-quarters at Bassano on the 9th of March, whence he addressed the following
order of the day to the army : " Soldiers ! the taking of Mantua
has now put an end to the war of Italy, and given you lasting
claims to the gratitude of your country.　You have been victorious in fourteen pitched battles and seventy actions : you have
taken 100,000 prisoners, 500 field-pieces, 2000 heavy cannon,
and four pontoon-trains.　The contributions laid on the countries
you have conquered have fed, maintained, and paid the army ;
besides which, you have sent thirty millions to the Minister of
Finance for the use of the public treasury.　You have enriched
the Museum at Paris with three hundred master-pieces of the arts
of ancient and modern Italy which it required thirty centuries to
produce.　You have conquered the finest countries in Europe.
The Transpadan and Cispadan Republics are indebted to you for
their existence.　The French flag waves for the first time on the
shores of the Adriatic, opposite the native country of Alexander,
and within twenty-four hours' sail of it.　The Kings of Sardinia
and Naples, the Pope, and the Duke of Parma are separated from
the Coalition.　You have expelled the English from Leghorn,
Genoa, and Corsica.　Yet higher destinies await you : you will
prove yourself worthy of them !　Of all the foes who conspired
to stifle the Republic in its birth, the Emperor alone remains before you.　He has now no other policy or will than those of that
perfidious Cabinet, which, unacquainted with the horrors of war,
smiles with satisfaction at the woes of the Continent.　The Executive Directory has spared no effort to give peace to Europe ; and
the moderation of its proposals was uninfluenced by the strength
of its armies.　It has not been listened to at Vienna : there is
therefore no hope of obtaining peace but by seeking it in the heart
of the Hereditary States.　You will there find a brave people.
You will respect their religion and manners, and protect their
property.　It is liberty that you carry to the brave Hungarian
nation."

It was necessary to pass the Piave and the Tagliamento in the
presence of the Austrian army, and to turn its right, in order to
anticipate it at the gorges of Ponteba.　Massena marched from
Bassano, passed the Piave in the mountains, beat Lusignan's di-

vision, taking himself prisoner, and drove the wreck of his troops
beyond the Tagliamento, taking Feltre, Cadore, and Belluno.
Serrurier marched in the morning of the 12th of March on Conegliano, where the Austrian head-quarters were; and by this
diversion enabled Guieux's division to effect the passage of the
Piave in the afternoon at Ospedaletto before Treviso. The river
is deep here, but the eagerness of the soldiers disregarded every
difficulty. A drummer was the only person in danger, who was
saved by a woman that swam after him. Bernadotte with his
division coming from Padua, joined the head quarters at Conegliano on the following day. The enemy had chosen the plains of
the Tagliamento for his field of battle, which were favorable to
his excellent and numerous cavalry. On the 16th, at 9 o'clock
in the morning, the two armies met near Valvasone on the two
banks of the river; the French being drawn up on the right bank,
and the Austrian army, in nearly equal force, on the opposite
side. This position of the Archduke did not cover the Ponteba
road, which was left open to Massena. Perhaps the Archduke
thought that a division of grenadiers on its march from the Rhine,
and which had reached Klagenfurth, would be in time to reinforce
Oeskay's division and to oppose Massena.

The cannonade began from one bank of the Tagliamento to the
other; the light cavalry making several attempts to pass the
stream. But the French troops, seeing the enemy so well prepared, ceased firing, set up the bivouacs, and prepared their mess.
The Archduke deceived by this appearance, thought as they had
marched all night, they were taking up a position. He fell back,
and returned into his camp. Two hours afterwards, when all
was quiet, the French soldiers suddenly got under arms. Duphot
at the head of the 27th light demi-brigade, being Guieux's van,
and Murat with the 15th light demi-brigade, Bernadotte's van,
each supported by its division, each regiment with its second battalion deployed, and its first and third in column by divisions at
platoon distance, rushed into the river. The enemy flew to arms:
but the whole of this first line had already passed in the finest
order, and was drawn up in line of battle on the left bank. The
cannonade and musketry began in all directions. General Dugua's division of cavalry of reserve and Serrurier's division

formed the second line, and passed the river as soon as the first line had advanced two hundred yards from the shore. After some hours' fighting, and several charges of infantry and cavalry, the enemy having been repulsed in the attacks on the villages of Gradisca and Codroipo, and finding themselves turned in a successful charge made by Dugua's division, beat a retreat, abandoned eight pieces of cannon and some prisoners to the victors.

In the mean while, Massena had effected his passage at San Danieli: he met with little resistance, and occupied Osopo, the key of the Ponteba road, which the enemy had neglected. He was thus master of the gorges of the Ponteba, and forced the remains of Ocskay's division to retreat on Tarwis. The Archduke being now unable to retreat by way of Carinthia, because Massena occupied Ponteba, resolved to regain that road by Udine, Cividale, Caporetto, and Tarwis. Marching with the rest of his army by Palma-Nuova and Gradisca, he sent forward three divisions and his parks under General Bayalitsch in that direction; but Massena was only two days' march from the pass of Tarwis, and Bayalitsch was six. The Archduke soon perceived the danger in which the latter was, hastened in person to Klagenfurth on the other side of the Alps, placing himself at the head of the division of grenadiers which he found just arrived there, and returned to take up a position before Tarwis to oppose Massena's progress. Massena who had pushed forward after some delay, found the Archduke's forces formed in a line, consisting of the remains of Ocskay's troops and the fine division of grenadiers from the Rhine. The action was obstinate, the importance of victory being felt on both sides: the Austrians knew that if Massena made himself master of the pass of Tarwis, the three Austrian divisions on their march through the valley of the Isonzo were lost. The Prince exposed himself to the greatest dangers, and was repeatedly on the point of being taken by the French skirmishers. General Brune behaved on this occasion with distinguished bravery. The Austrians were at length broken, but not until they had engaged their very last battalion in the action: they could operate no retreat, but the remains of their force made for Villach beyond the Drave in order to rally there. Massena being in possession of Tarwis waited there for the approach of

the divisions which had been ordered to take this route from the
field of battle of the Tagliamento.

The day after this battle, the Austrian head-quarters had entered Palma-Nuova, a fortress belonging to the Venetians, but
quitted it immediately.   The French who were in the rear, left
a garrison there.   Bernadotte's division appeared before Gradisca,
intending to pass the Isonzo, but found the gates shut, and the
Governor refused a parley.   This General attempted to take the
place by assault and lost upwards of 400 men, an imprudence for
which the only excuse was the eagerness of the troops of the
Sambre and Meuse to distinguish themselves and enter Gradisca
before the old troops of the Army of Italy.   The General-in-
Chief had at the same time proceeded with Serrurier's division to
the left bank of the Isonzo by the Montefalcone road.   There not
being time to construct a bridge, Colonel Andreossy threw himself in first to sound the depth, and the soldiers followed his example up to the middle in water, under a brisk fire of two battalions of Croats.   As soon as the Governor of Gradisca perceived Serrurier on the heights overlooking the town, he surrendered a prisoner of war with 3000 men, two standards, and twenty
field pieces with their teams.   Head-quarters were at Goritz the
next day.   Bernadotte's division marched on Laybach.   General
Dugua with 1000 horse took possession of Trieste, where the
English merchandize was confiscated, and quicksilver to the value
of several millions of francs was found in the Imperial warehouses
from the mine of Idria.   Serrurier marched from Goritz up the
Isonzo through Caporetto and the Austrian Chiusa to support
General Guieux, who had followed Bayalitsch's divisions, and had
greatly annoyed his rear.   On his reaching Chiusa di Pieta, the
Austrians thought themselves safe; for they did not know that Massena had been two days in possession of Tarwis.   They were attacked in front by Massena and in the rear by Guieux.   The position of Chiusa, though strong, could not withstand the 4th of the
line, called the *Impetuous*.   This demi-brigade climbed the mountain that commands the left, and thus turning this important post,
left Bayalitsch no resource but to lay down his arms.   His baggage, guns, and colors were all taken.   The prisoners however
did not amount to more than 5000, as great numbers of soldiers,

natives of Carniola and Croatia, had disbanded themselves in the passes when they found all was lost, and endeavored to reach their respective villages.

Head-quarters were successively fixed at Caporetto, Tarwis, Villach, and Klagenfurth.  The army passed the Drave over Villach bridge, which the enemy had not time to burn.  It was now in the valley of the Drave in Germany, having passed the Carnic and Julian Alps.  The language, manners, climate, soil, and state of cultivation were all different from those of Italy.  The soldiers were pleased with the hospitality and simplicity of the peasants.  The abundance of vegetables and quantities of waggons and horses were also very useful.  In Italy there were only carts drawn by oxen, whose slow and clumsy pace did not suit the vivacity and impatience of the French.  The army occupied the castles of Goritz, Trieste, and Laybach.  The two divisions from the Rhine under Kaim and Mercantin, which had now reached Klagenfurth, endeavored to defend that place, but were repulsed with loss.  Klagenfurth was surrounded with a bastioned wall, which had for ages been neglected.  The engineer-officers filled the ditches with water, repaired the parapets, demolished the houses built on the ramparts, and established hospitals and magazines of every kind in the place.  As a *point d'appui*, at the entrance of the mountains, it seemed to be important.  A proclamation was distributed here in French, German, and Italian, addressed to the inhabitants of Carinthia, Carniola, and Istria, laying the blame of the war on English gold and the treachery of the Austrian Cabinet, and offering them the good-will and protection of the General-in-Chief, which had some effect in calming the minds of the people.

Ten days had elapsed since the opening of the campaign in Friuli, while in the Tyrol both armies had remained inactive.  The Austrian general Kerpen was hourly expecting the arrival of the two divisions from the Rhine : Joubert on his part had received no orders to attack, but only to keep the enemy in check on the Avisio.  But immediately after the battle of the Tagliamento, when Napoleon had resolved to penetrate by the Carinthian road with his whole army into Germany, he dispatched orders to General Joubert to beat the enemy to whom he was superior,

drive him beyond the Brenner, and then march by facing to
the right by the Pusterthal along the road that runs by the side
of the Drave to join the army at Spital in Carinthia. Buonaparte
ordered him to leave a brigade to defend the Avisio, and to fall
back in case of need on Montebaldo; though he knew that when
the French army should arrive victorious on the Simering, mena-
cing Vienna, all that might occur in the Lower Tyrol would be
of secondary importance. General Joubert executed these orders
with promptitude and ability. On the 20th of March, he commenced his movement. He passed the Avisio at Segonzano,
while Delmas and Baraguay d'Hilliers passed it over Lavis
bridge, and directing their march in concert toward St. Michael
attacked General Kerpen, and routed him with the loss of half
his men, while Landon's corps, separated from him by the Adige,
stood idly looking on. Joubert then advanced directly on Neumarck, took that place after some resistance, and passing the
bridge defeated and dispersed the troops under General Landon,
who could not make a stand against him. Bolzano, a rich trading town, full of stores, fell into the hands of the French. In the
mean time, the first Austrian division of the Rhine under General
Sporck had reached Clausen. Kerpen rallied the remains of his
corps in the rear of this division; and stationed in a position
which he deemed impregnable, waited for the victor. The obstacles presented by the nature of the ground were indeed immense; but the heroism and intrepidity of the French troops prevailed over them. Kerpen now retreated on Mittenwald, thus
leaving the Pusterthal road leading into Carinthia open to Joubert; but he did not choose to avail himself of it with the enemy
so close in his rear. He therefore followed him, and in an action on the 28th of March, in which a charge of cavalry by
General Dumas contributed greatly to the success of the day, defeated him for the third time, and forced him to evacuate Sterzing,
and retreat on the Brenner. The alarm spread to Inspruck, as it
was thought he was marching on that place to effect his junction
with the Army of the Rhine; a step that would have been sufficiently fatal. But there being now no obstacle to prevent him
from fulfilling his orders, he began his march by the Pusterthal
road, calling in all his posts from the Tyrol, except a reserve of

1200 ; and shortly after joined the General-in-Chief with 12,000 men.   Thus in less than twenty days the Archduke's army had been defeated in two pitched battles and several actions, and driven beyond the Brenner, the Julian Alps, and the Isonzo : Trieste and Fiume, the only two sea-ports of the monarchy, were in possession of the enemy. · The French head-quarters were in Germany, not more than sixty leagues from Vienna.   Every thing seemed to indicate that in the course of May the victorious armies would be in possession of that capital ; for Austria had not above 80,000 men left, while the French armies of the Sambre and Meuse and of the Rhine amounted alone to above 130,000 men.

The news of these events succeeding each other, struck the inhabitants of Vienna with dismay.   The capital was menaced, and was destitute of all effectual means of resistance.   The most valuable effects and important papers were packed up.   The Danube was covered with boats, which were transporting goods into Hungary, whither also the young Archdukes and Archduchesses were sent.   Among these was the Archduchess Maria Louisa, then five years and a half old.   The people complained that the ministry did not think of making peace, though they had no means of stopping the progress of the French arms.   The Armies of the Rhine and Moselle and of the Sambre and Meuse were by agreement to have opened the campaign, and passed the Rhine on the same day that the Army of Italy passed the Piave, and were to advance as speedily as possible into Germany.   When Napoleon sent home an account of the battle of the Tagliamento, he announced that he should pass the Julian Alps in a few days, and enter the heart of Germany ; that between the 1st and 10th of April he should be at Klagenfurth, the capital of Carinthia, that is to say, within sixty leagues of Vienna ; and before the 20th of April, on the top of the Simering, twenty-five leagues from Vienna ; that it was therefore of importance that the armies of the Rhine should put themselves in motion, and that he should be apprised of their march.   The Government on the 23d of March wrote to him in answer, complimenting him on the victory of the Tagliamento, stating reasons why the Armies of the Rhine had not taken the field, and assuring him that they would march forthwith : when, three days after, the Ministers wrote to say that Mo-

reau's army could not take the field, that it was in want of boats
to effect the passage of the Rhine, and that the Army of Italy
was not to reckon on the co-operation of the Armies of Germany,
but on itself alone.    These dispatches, which reached Klagenfurth
on the 31st of March, gave rise to many conjectures.    Was the
Directory apprehensive that these three armies comprising all the
forces of the Republic, might, if united under one commander,
render him too powerful?    Were they intimidated by the reverses
which the Army of the Rhine had suffered the year before?    Was
this strange pusillanimity to be ascribed to a want of vigor and
resolution in the Generals?    That was impossible.    Or was there
an intention to sacrifice the Army of Italy, as had been attempted
in June 1796, by sending one-half of it against Naples?    It is
not wonderful that Buonaparte, in ruminating over his disappointment, should have formed designs of getting rid of this knot of
drivellers and marplots, who would not do any thing themselves
nor let others, and who prejudiced the public cause, out of a mean
jealousy that it might redound to the credit or influence of those
who were capable of advancing it in the noblest manner.    It is so
far the misfortune of republican institutions, that those who are
placed at the head of them cannot repose on mere external dignity, independently of merit or services; and are therefore more
disposed to look with jaundiced eyes on talents or exertions that
eclipse their own, and to which of course they ought in justice to
yield the precedence.    An hereditary pre-eminence, not founded
on worth or capacity, cannot be supposed to be jealous of it, or to
suffer in the comparison with pretensions that are quite foreign to
its own.    The danger on this side is not from a spirit of rivalry
of popular pretensions, but from a total ignorance and contempt
for them!—As Napoleon could no longer calculate on the assistance of these two armies, he was obliged to relinquish all thoughts
of making his entrance into Vienna: he had not sufficient cavalry to descend into the plain of the Danube; but he thought he
might safely advance to the summit of the Simering, and that
the most advantageous use he could make of his present position
was to conclude a peace, which was the general wish of all
France.

Within twelve hours from the receipt of the dispatches of the

Directory, Buonaparte wrote to Prince Charles in these terms:
" While brave soldiers carry on war, they wish for peace. Has
not this war already lasted six years? Have we not killed men
enough, and inflicted sufficient sufferings on the human race?
Humanity calls loudly upon us. Europe has laid down the arms
she took up against the French Republic. Your nation alone
perseveres; yet blood is to flow more copiously than ever. Fatal
omens attend the opening of this campaign. But whatever be
its issue, we shall kill some thousands of men on both sides; and
after all we must come to an understanding, since all things have
an end, not excepting vindictive passions. The Executive
Directory of the French Republic communicated to his Majesty
the Emperor its wish to put an end to the war which afflicts both
nations. The intervention of the Court of London defeated this
measure. Is there no hope of arrangement? And must we, on
account of the passions and interests of a people which is a
stranger to the horrors of the war, continue to slaughter each
other? You, General, whose birth places you so near the throne,
and above those petty passions which often actuate ministers and
governments, are you disposed to merit the title of a benefactor
to the whole human race, and the saviour of Germany? Do not
imagine, Sir, that I mean to deny that it may be possible to save
Germany by force of arms; but even supposing the chances of
war should become favorable to you, the country would nevertheless be ravaged. For my part, General, if the overture I have
the honor to make to you should only save the life of a single
man, I should feel more proud of the civic crown I should think
I thereby merited than of all the melancholy glory that the most
distinguished military successes can afford."

On the 2d of April, Prince Charles replied as follows: " Most
certainly, General, whilst I carry on war in obedience to the
call of honor and duty, I am desirous, as you are, of peace, for
the sake of the people and of humanity. Nevertheless, as it
does not belong to me in the functions with which I am entrusted
to inquire into or terminate the quarrel of the belligerent nations,
and as I am not furnished with any powers to treat on the part
of his Majesty the Emperor, you will not consider it extraordinary
that I do not enter into any negociation with you and that I wait

for superior orders on this important subject, which is not essentially within my province.   But whatever may be the future
chances of war, or whatever hopes of peace may exist, I beg
you to rest convinced, General, of my esteem and particular consideration."

In order to second this overture for negociation, it was important to march forward and approach Vienna.   On the 1st of
April at break of day, Massena advanced on Freisach.   In front
of the castle, he met with the enemy's rearguard ; he attacked
them briskly, and entered the town pell-mell with them continu-
ing the pursuit almost as far as Neumarck, where he found the
Archduke with four battalions from the Rhine and the remains
of his old armies, drawn up to defend the gorges of Neumarck.
The General-in-Chief immediately ordered Massena, with all his
division, to join on the left of the high road : placed Guieux's
division on the heights to the right, and Serrurier's in reserve
At three in the afternoon, the second light infantry charged the
enemy's first line, and performed wonders.   These troops came
from the Rhine, and had been called in contempt the *contingent*
in allusion to the troops furnished by the German princes, which
were supposed to be none of the best.   Piqued by this appellation, they challenged the old soldiers of the Army of Italy to go
as fast and as far as they did.   Prince Charles on this occasion
exposed himself to the greatest personal danger, but in vain ; he
was driven from all his positions and lost 3000 men.   At night
the French troops entered Neumarck.   Scheiffling was still
twelve leagues off, where, it was hoped by the Archduke, General Kerpen might join by the third cross-road leading from the
Tyrol ; and to gain time, he proposed a suspension of arms for
twenty-four hours, but Berthier replied that they might fight
and negociate at the same time.   Napoleon sent forward strong
reconnoitring parties, and went in person to meet Kerpen ; but
that corps had fallen back, and its rearguard under Sporck was
only slightly harassed.   On the 4th and 5th the head-quarters
remained at Scheiffling, a castle situated on the banks of the
Muer.   From Scheiffling to Knittenfield the road runs along the
Muer, through formidable defiles.   Positions which might have
stopped the French army were to be found at every step.   On

the 3d the van had a furious engagement with the enemy in the
defiles of Unzmarkt. The loss of the Austrians was considerable ; Colonel Carrère, a distinguished and brave officer commanding the artillery of the French vanguard, was killed ; his death
was much regretted. One of the frigates taken at Venice was
named after him ; and it was one of those with which Napoleon
sailed from Egypt, when he returned to France and landed at
Frejus.

After the action at Unzmarkt, the army met with no further
resistance, and reached Leoben on the 7th. Lieutenant-General
Bellegarde, the Archduke's adjutant, and Major-General Merfeld
presented themselves at this place under a flag of truce, with a
note from the Emperor, offering a suspension of arms to treat
for a definitive peace. Napoleon the same day gave answer,
that though a suspension of arms was wholly prejudical to the
French army, yet as a step towards that desirable object he was
willing to agree to it. The armistice was accordingly signed
in the evening of the 7th, and was to last five days. The whole
country, as far as the Simering, was to be occupied by the French.
Gratz, one of the largest towns of the Austrian monarchy, was
surrendered with its citadel. General Berthier, at dinner, asked
the Austrian commissioners where they supposed Bernadotte's
division to be ? " About Laybach," was the reply. " And Joubert's ?" " Between Brixen and Mulbach." " No," answered
he ; " they are all in echelons ; the most distant is only a day's
march behind." At this they were much surprised. General
Leclerc, an intrepid officer and skilful negociator, was sent
to Paris to acquaint the Government with the signature of the
armistice.

The French General-in-Chief had sent his aide-de-camp Lavalette at the head of a party of cavalry from Klagenfurth, on the
30th of March, to meet General Joubert, who was still detained
in the Tyrol. Lavalette proceeded as far as Lienz, where the
town's-people, perceiving that the French were but sixty men,
took up arms against them, and the detachment was with difficulty saved by the coolness and intrepidity of its commander ;
one dragoon only was assassinated. The inhabitants were afterwards punished for this violence. On the 8th of April, Joubert

arrived at Spital near Nillach, so as to form the left of the army. He had his prisoners, which were very numerous, immediately removed into the rear. Bernadotte, having received orders to join the army at Leoben, left General Friand with a column of 1500 men to cover Fiume and keep Carniola in awe. On the 6th of April this column was attacked by a body of 6000 Croats, and was obliged to fall back on Materia near Trieste. This event, exaggerated like those which had occurred in the Tyrol, was eagerly caught hold of at Venice, and was one chief cause of the hostility and commotions which produced the downfal of that state. The armistice expired on the 13th ; but at nine in the morning Count Merfeld, accompanied by the Marquis de Gallo, ambassador from Naples to Vienna, arrived with full powers to negociate and sign preliminaries of peace. A farther armistice was concluded till the 20th. On the 16th three plans were agreed upon and sent to Vienna ; and the next day, the answer of the Cabinet of Vienna was brought by Baron Vincent, the Emperor's aide-de-camp. General Clarke had been furnished with full powers on the part of the French government, but he was then at Turin. As it required time for him to reach head-quarters, Napoleon took the responsibility upon himself, and signed the treaty. General Clarke arrived a few days after. The Austrian plenipotentiaries had set down as the first article, that the Emperor acknowledged the French Republic. "Strike that out," said Napoleon : "the Republic is like the sun which shines by its own light ; none but the blind can fail to see it." Buonaparte gives as a politic reason for what appears only a natural burst of romantic enthusiasm, that in case the French people had afterwards wished to establish a monarchy, the Emperor might have objected that he had only acknowledged the Republic. This was prying narrowly into futurity for difficulties, and looks too much like a deep-laid scheme to extinguish that light which was said to shine so bright ! It was stipulated by the preliminaries that the definitive treaty should be settled at Berne, and the peace of the Empire referred to another Congress to be held in a German city. The limits of the Rhine were guaranteed to France. The Oglio was to divide the States of the house of Austria in Italy from the Cisalpine Republic. Mantua was to be restored to

the Emperor, while the Republic gained Venice, with the legations of Ferrara, Bologna, and Romagna annexed to it, as a com-
pensation for the loss of its possessions on the Terra Firma.  By
this arrangement the French armies communicated with Venice
by Milan, and could at any time take possession of it when it
suited their convenience.   This blow was suspended over Venice
in retaliation of the spirit which had just broken out there, and
of the murders committed in the rear of the army, of which accounts had been transmitted by General Kilmaine.   An insurrectionary cockade was displayed at Venice, and the English
Minister wore it in triumph, having also the Lion of St. Mark on
his gondola.

On the 27th of April the Marquis de Gallow presented the preliminaries, ratified by the Emperor, to the French General-in-
Chief at Gratz.   While waiting for the ratification of the Executive Directory, several overtures were made by the Emperor's plenipotentiaries, and the aide-de-camp Lemarrois carried
the answers to Vienna.   He was well received ; and this was the
first time that the tri-colored cockade had been seen in that capital.   It was in a conference at Gratz that one of the plenipotentiaries, authorized by an autograph letter of the Emperor, is
said to have offered Napoleon, on the conclusion of a peace, a
sovereignty of 250,000 souls for himself and family in Germany,
in order to place him beyond the reach of republican ingratitude.   The General smiled, and having desired the plenipotentiary to thank the Emperor for this proof of the interest he took in
his welfare, said he wished for no greatness or wealth unless conferred on him by the French people, adding—"And with that
support, believe me, Sir, my ambition will be satisfied."*   Adjutant-General Dessolles was dispatched to Paris with the news of
the opening of the negociations ; and Massena, who had contributed so much to it by the share he had in almost every victory,
carried the preliminary treaty of peace to the Directory.

* The Commander of Este, brother to the Duke of Modena, wanted to
purchase the friendship of the French General by placing four chests, containing a million of francs each, at his disposal.  "Not for four millions,"
replied Napoleon, "will I put myself in the power of the Commander of
Este."  The Venetians tried the same thing.

Hoche had just been promoted to the command of the Army of the Sambre and Meuse. He was a young man full of talent, bravery, and ambition; he had an army of 80,000 men under his command, and his heart swelled with impatience at the news of every victory that arrived from the Army of Italy. He importuned the Directory to allow him to enter Germany. On the 18th of April he passed the Rhine at the bridge of Neuwied, whilst Championnet, who had marched from Desseldorf, reached Uckerath and Altenkirchen. Kray commanded the Austrian army. Hoche attacked him at Hedersdorf, took a great number of prisoners, and forced him to fall back on the Maine. On the 22d, he arrived before Frankfort, when General Kray's staff transmitted to him dispatches from Berthier, informing him of the signature of the treaty of Leoben, and he immediately concluded an armistice. Moreau was at Paris, soliciting the paltry sum of 30,000 or 40,000 crowns to pay for pontoons to pass the Rhine at Strasburg; but as soon as Desaix, who commanded the Army of the Rhine in his absence, learned that Hoche was engaged with the enemy, he constructed a bridge on the 20th at the village of Kilstett, several leagues below Strasburg. On the 21st, at two in the morning, the army passed the Rhine. Moreau, who had posted with all possible speed from Paris, found himself at the head of the army, just as Starray, who had collected 20,000 men and twenty pieces of cannon, was attacking it. The Austrians were routed, and left a number of prisoners and their cannon in the power of the conquerors. Among other booty taken was Kinglin's waggon, containing Pichegru's correspondence with the Prince of Condé, which Moreau kept secret for four months without communicating it to the Government. After this victory, the Army marched up the Rhine, and took Kehl. The van had proceeded beyond Offenbach in the valley of Kintzig, when a courier arriving from Leoben, Moreau put a stop to hostilities, and concluded an armistice with Starray. Thus the zeal and efforts of the armies were rendered fruitless. But the war was conducted on a bad system, without energy or concert. By one of the clauses of the Constitution of the year 3, the treasury was made independent of the Government—an error which was alone sufficient to endanger the existenc of the Republic.

During the months of May and June, the French head-quarters
were fixed at Montebello, a castle situated a few leagues from
Milan, on a hill which commands a view of the whole plain of
Lombardy.  The daily assemblage here of the principal ladies of
Milan to pay their court to Josephine, the wife of the General-in-
Chief; the presence of the Ministers of Austria, the Pope, the
Kings of Naples and Sardinia, the Republics of Genoa and Venice, the Duke of Parma, the Swiss Cantons, and of several of
the German Princes; the attendants of all the Generals, of the
authorities of the Cisalpine Republic, and the deputies of the
towns; the great number of couriers going and returning every
hour to and from Paris, Rome, Naples, Vienna, Florence, Venice,
Turin, and Genoa, and the style of living at this fine castle induced the Italians to call it the *Court of Montebello*.  The mind
takes pleasure in reverting to this short period of gaity and romance, followed by such mighty achievements and such sad reverses.  It was in fact a brilliant scene.  The negociations for
peace with the emperor, the political affairs of Germany, and the
fate of the King of Sardinia, of Switzerland, Venice, and Genoa
were here suspended in the balance.  The Court of Montebello
made several excursions to the Lago Maggiore, the Borronean
Isles, and the Lake of Como ; taking up its temporary residence
in the several country-houses which surround these beautiful
spots.  Every town and village was eager to testify its homage and
respect to him whom they then considered, and still consider, as
the *Liberator of Italy*.  These circumstances altogether made a
strong impression on the Diplomatic Body.  General Serrurier
carried the last colors taken from the Archduke to the Directory,
with a highly commendatory letter from Buonaparte, in which he
characterized him as one who was severe to himself and sometimes
to others.  He took a journey into his native department of the
Aisne; and though of very moderate revolutionary principles,
he returned to the army a warm and decided supporter of the Republic, having been highly incensed at the spirit of disaffection
and vacillation he had observed in Paris.

The exchange of the ratifications of the preliminaries of Leoben took place at Montebello on the 24th of May between Napoleon and the Marquis de Gallo.  A question of etiquette arose for

the first time : the Emperors of Germany did not give the Kings
of France the alternative ; the Cabinet of Vienna was somewhat
apprehensive that the Republic would not acknowledge this custom, and that the other powers of Europe, following the example
of the French, would oblige the Holy Roman Empire to descend
from that sort of supremacy it had enjoyed ever since the time of
Charlemagne.    It was in the first ecstacies of the Austrian Minister at the acquiescence of France in the customary etiquette,
that he renounced the idea of the Congress of Berne, and agreed
to the following as the basis of a definitive treaty :    1. The boundary of the Rhine for France ;  2. Venice and the boundary of
the Adige for the Emperor ;  3. Mantua and the boundary of the
Adige for the Cisalpine Republic.    Clarke, who was associated
with Napoleon on this critical emergency, had been a captain in
the Orleans dragoons when the Revolution broke out.    From
1789 he attached himself to the Orleans party.    In 1795 he was
placed by the Committee of Public Safety at the head of the Topographical Department.    Being patronized by Carnot, he was
chosen by the Directory in 1796 to make overtures of peace to
the Emperor, for which purpose he went to Milan.    But the real
object of his mission was less to open a negociation than to act as
a secret agent of the Directory at head-quarters, and to watch the
General, whose victories already began to give umbrage.    Napoleon was aware of this ; but being convinced that it is necessary
for governments to have information, was glad they had entrusted
this task to a man of known ability rather than to one of those
subaltern agents who pick up the most absurd reports in anti-
chambers and taverns.    He therefore encouraged Clarke, and
employed him in several negociations with Sardinia and the Princes of Italy.    Clarke's genius was not military ; he was an official man, exact and upright in business, and a great enemy to
knaves.    He was descended from one of the Irish families that
accompanied the Stuarts in their misfortunes.    His foible was that
of priding himself on his ancestry, and he rendered himself ridiculous in the Imperial reign by genealogical researches, which
were strangely at variance with the opinions he had professed,
the course of his life, and the circumstances of the times    In the
time of the Empire, Clarke rendered important services by the

integrity of his administration ; and it has been remarked as the greatest blot upon his memory that towards the end of his career he belonged to a ministry that made France pass under the *Caudine Forks*, by consenting to the disbanding of an army that had for twenty-five years been its country's glory, and by giving up to astonished Europe her still invincible fortresses.

Count Merfeld arrived at Montebello on the 19th of June. By him the Cabinet of Vienna disavowed the Marquis de Gallo's concessions, and refused to treat, except in the Congress of Berne. There was an evident change of plan. Was this owing to a new Coalition, to the advance of the Russian armies, to the effects of Pichegru's conspiracy, or to the civil war which ravaged the departments of the West, and which, it was hoped, might soon spread over all France, and put the supreme power into the hands of the insurgents? The Austrian plenipotentiaries had nothing to reply when Napoleon observed that England and Russia would never consent to give up Venice to the Emperor, and that it was a vain pretext to wait to treat in conjunction with them. Thugut sent new instructions and agreed to a separate negociation. Buonaparte withdrew from this doubtful negociation, leaving Clarke to manage it, and passed all July and August at Milan. Austria was watching to see the result of the troubles in France. The events of the 18th of Fructidor baffled all her hopes. Count Cobentzel then hastened to Udine, invested with full powers by the Emperor, whose entire confidence he possessed. Napoleon proceeded to Passeriano ; Clarke having been recalled, he was now the only plenipotentiary on the part of France. The conferences were held alternately at Udine and at Passeriano. The four Austrian plenipotentiaries sat on one side of a rectangular table ; at the two ends were the Secretaries of Legation ; and on the other side was the French plenipotentiary. When the conferences were held at Passeriano, the dinner was given by Napoleon ; when at Udine, it was given by Count Cobentzel. In the first conference the Count disclaimed all that his colleagues had been saying for four months, urging the most extravagant pretensions. With a man of this sort there was but one method of proceeding, which was to go as far beyond the true medium in the opposite direction as he did. This time the Austrian Cabinet was

sincere in its desire for peace ; but it was now the turn of the
Directory.    The affair of the 18th of Fructidor had led them to
trust too much to their own strength, and they refused to yield
either Venice or the line of the Adige to the Emperor—a refusal
that was equivalent to a declaration of war.

Napoleon in this dilemma did not know how to act.    With respect to military operations he had fixed principles as to the degree
of obedience the government had a right to exact.    If he did not
approve of the orders that were issued to him, he would have considered it criminal to undertake the execution of an injudicious
plan, and in that case would have thought himself obliged to offer
his resignation, as he had done on one occasion.    But he was not
so clear as to the degree of obedience due from him as a plenipotentiary.    Besides, his functions here were complicated.    Was
he to renounce his mission in the midst of a negociation, or to declare war as a plenipotentiary, and at the same time to give up
his command as a general, thus doubly involving his country in
difficulties ?    The Minister for Foreign Affairs extricated him
from this uncertainty.    In one of his dispatches he informed him
that the Directory had thought he could enforce their *ultimatum ;*
but if not, that the war or peace rested in his hands.    He determined to abide by the terms settled at Montebello on the 6th of
May.    His principal reasons for being unwilling to prolong the
war were, that it was too late in the season to advance farther into
Germany ; that the command of the Army of the Rhine was entrusted to Augereau, whose violent political opinions would prevent a proper harmony and understanding between the armies ;
that the reinforcement of 12,000 foot and 4000 horse which he
had required had been refused ; and that the Directory had resolved not to ratify the treaty with the King of Sardinia, thus
creating a new enemy in their rear.    The Directory indeed soon
after sent word that they would furnish an army of 6000 men and
ratify the treaty with Sardinia ; but the treaty of Campo-Formio
had been signed three days before the writing of these dispatches,
which did not reach Passeriano till twelve days after the signature
of the peace.

It was Napoleon's interest to conclude peace.    The republican
party at home already manifested a certain ,ealousy of him, and

began to hint that so much **glory** was incompatible with liberty.
If he had recommenced hostilities and the French army had occupied Vienna, the Directory would have been desirous to revolutionize Germany, which would have involved France in a new
war with the rest of Europe.    **Had Napoleon** broken off the negociations, **the blame** would have rested with him; but by giving
peace at this time, he added to the glory of conquest that of ter-
minating the war, and of being the founder of two republics.
Thus crowned with laurels and with the olive-branch in his hand,
he thought he should return safely into private life, like the great
men of antiquity ; the first act of his political career would be
honorably concluded, circumstances and the interests of his country would **regulate** the remainder of it.    France was anxious for
peace.    The quarrel of the Allied Kings with the Republic was
a **conflict of principles** and a struggle on her part for existence,
which had ended **favorably** for her.    The General-in-Chief had
conceived the project of changing **this state of the** question, which
left France opposed singly to them all, and of throwing **an apple**
of discord among the Allies, **by** creating a **diversion** of other interests and passions.    **Vain and** mistaken policy, to suppose that
any other object could distract their attention, while the great and
paramount one of their sovereign power and existence by divine
imprescriptible right remained unprovided for ; which blinded him
**from first to last, and ruined him** in the end by preventing him
**from seeing the** abyss over which with every shifting breath of
fortune he hung suspended !    To make Austria odious by giving
**her up Venice was perhaps** more feasible, and might serve as a
**warning to the lesser powers;** but was not France also, whatever
**might be her provocations,** a party to the wrong ?    Venice, after
twelve hundred years of **freedom,** by passing under a foreign yoke
for a while, might be **better** prepared to merge her individual and
lofty pretensions in the general incorporation of Italy, an object
on which Buonaparte was always intent, and which he was about
to **have proclaimed** fifteen **years** afterwards, as soon as he had a
second son born to him.    Austria, it is true, received but a barren
equivalent for **Lombardy and** Belgium in Styria, Carinthia and
Hungary ; but these **provinces were near** and conveniently placed,
and her situation was critical.    Still the Austrian negociator,

Count Cobentzel, held out strenuously to the last.   He insisted
on "the Adda as a boundary, or nothing.   If the Emperor, my
master," he said, " were to give you the keys of Mentz, the strongest fortress in the world, without changing them for the keys of
Mantua, it would be a degrading act."   Neither party would
yield.   At length, on the 16th of October, the conferences were
held at Udine, where Buonaparte recapitulated the different arguments, and Count Cobentzel replied at great length, and concluded
with saying that he should depart that night, at the same time
throwing the blame on the French negociator, who would be responsible for all the blood that should be shed in the ensuing contest.   Upon this the latter, with great seeming coolness, although
he was much irritated at this attack, arose, and took from the
mantel-piece a little porcelain vase, which Count Cobentzel prized
as a present from the Empress Catharine.   "Well," said Napoleon, "the truce is at an end, and war is declared; but remember,
that before the end of autumn, I will shatter your monarchy as I
shatter this porcelain."   Saying so, he dashed it furiously down,
and the carpet was instantly covered with the fragments.   He
then saluted the Congress and retired.   The Austrian plenipotentiaries were struck dumb.   A few moments afterwards, they
found that as Napoleon got into his carriage, he had dispatched an
officer to the Archduke Charles to inform him that the negociations
were broken off, and that hostilities would recommence in twenty-
four hours.   Count Cobentzel, seriously alarmed, sent the Marquis de Gallo to Passeriano with a written declaration that he consented to the *ultimatum* of France.   The treaty was signed the
following day, and was dated from Campo-Formio, a small village
between Passeriano and Udine, which had been neutralized for
that purpose by the Secretaries of Legation, though it was not
thought necessary to remove thither, as there was no suitable
house in the place for the accommodation of the plenipotentiaries.

By this treaty, in addition to the particulars already stated,
France was to have the Valteline, and Austria ceded Brisgaw,
which placed a greater distance between the Hereditary States
and the French frontier.   Mentz was to be given up at a general
Congress that was to meet at Rastadt.   The Princes of the Empire dispossessed on the left bank of the Rhine were to be indemni-

fied out of the Ecclesiastical States. Corfu, Zante, Cephalonia, Santa Maura, and Cerigo were ceded to France, in exchange for two millions of souls added to the Austrian dominions on the left bank of the Adige. By a special article of the treaty, the property which the Archduke Charles possessed in Belgium as the heir of the Archduchess Christina, was secured to him. Napoleon afterwards, when Emperor, purchased the mansion of Lacken, near Brussels, for a million of francs. This stipulation was intended as a mark of respect on the part of the French plenipotentiary to the General he had been fighting with. Buonaparte prided himself on his talent for making peace as much as on his talent for making war, and was always anxious (with reason) to repel the imputation of being a mere military man. He was more willing to admit an equality with himself in the field than in the cabinet, and thought he had overcome greater difficulties and accomplished more improbable things in the one than in the other. There is something chivalrous in his mode of negociation; and the same appearance of firmness, promptitude, clearness, and determination to leave nothing unattempted by art or force in both.

During the conferences at Passeriano, General Desaix came from the Army of the Rhine to visit the fields of battle which the Army of Italy had rendered so famous. Napoleon received him at head-quarters, and thought to surprise him by imparting to him the light which the discovery of D'Entraigues' portfolio threw on Pichegru's conduct. "We have long known," said Desaix, smiling, "that Pichegru was a traitor. Moreau found proofs of the fact in Kinglin's papers, with all the particulars of the bribes he had received, and the concerted motives of his military manœuvres. Moreau, Regnier, and myself are the only persons in the secret. I wished Moreau to inform Government of it immediately, but he would not. Pichegru," added he, "is perhaps the only General who ever got himself purposely beaten." He alluded to the manœuvre by which Pichegru had intentionally moved his principal force up the Rhine, in order to prevent the success of the operations before Mentz. Desaix visited the camps, and was received with the greatest respect in all of them. This was the commencement of the friendship between him and Napoleon. He loved glory for glory's sake, and his country above every thing.

He was of an unsophisticated pleasing character, and possessed extensive information.   He had thoroughly studied the theatre of the war along the Rhine.   The victor of Marengo shed tears for his death.

Hoche about this time died suddenly at Mentz.   This young General distinguished himself at the lines of Weissemburg in 1794, and for a short time pacified La Vendée.   He marched his troops on Paris at the crisis of the 18th of Fructidor.   He is famous for having landed the expedition in Ireland.   Enthusiastic, brave, and restless, he knew not how to wait for opportunities, but exposed himself to failure by premature enterprises.   He on all occasions expressed a high regard for Napoleon.   By his death and the disgrace of Moreau, the command of the armies both of the Sambre and Meuse and of the Rhine became vacant. The directory united them into one, and gave the command to Augereau.

Berthier took the treaty of Campo-Formio to Paris ; and Buonaparte, as a mark of his respect for the sciences and of his personal esteem, sent Monge along with him.   The General-in-Chief was fond of the conversation of this great geometrician, who loved the French people as his own family, and liberty and equality as the result of a mathematical demonstration.   At the time of the invasion of France by the Prussians in 1792, he offered to give his two daughters in marriage to the first volunteers who should lose a limb in the defence of their native soil ; and this offer, however extravagant it may sound was in him sincere. and heart-felt.   He accompanied Napoleon into Egypt ; and always remained faithful to him.   Immediately after the signature of the treaty, Buonaparte returned to Milan, when he took leave of the Italians in an energetic and flattering address, and issued the following order of the day to the army : " Soldiers, I set out to-morrow for Germany.   Separated from the army, I shall sigh for the moment of my rejoining it, and braving fresh dangers. Whatever post government may assign to the soldiers of the Army of Italy, they will always be the worthy supporters of liberty and of the glory of the French name.   Soldiers, when you talk of the princes you have conquered, of the nations you have

set free, and the battles you have fought in two campaigns, say—
*In the next two we shall do still more !"*

Napoleon proceeded to Turin, where he alighted at Guingené's,
the French minister's, on the 17th of November.  The King of
Sardinia desired to see him and to express his obligations in a
public manner; but circumstances were already such that he
did not think it expedient to indulge in court-entertainments.
He continued his journey to Rastadt across Mount Cenis.  At
Geneva he was received as he might have expected to be, had it
been a French town.  On his entering the Pays de Vaud, three
parties of handsome young girls came to compliment him at the
head of the inhabitants : one party was clothed in white, another
in red, and a third in blue.  These maidens presented him with a
crown, on which was inscribed the famous sentence which proclaimed the liberty of the Valteline and so dear to the hearts of
the Vaudois, that *one nation cannot be subject to another.*  He
passed through several Swiss towns, Berne among others, and
crossed the Rhine at Bale, proceeding towards Rastadt.  He here
found Treilhard and Bonnier, appointed by the Directory, and
who had arrived before him.  Old Count Metternich represented
the Emperor as head of the Germanic Confederation ; Count
Cobentzel as head of the House of Austria.  The greatest opposition arose as to the first article, the delivering up of Mentz.
All the German princes complained loudly against it.  They said
that Mentz did not belong to Austria, and they did not scruple to
accuse the Emperor of having betrayed Germany for the sake
of his interests in Italy.  Count Lerbach, as deputy for the Circle of Austria, had to answer all these protestations, of which
task he acquitted himself with all the energy, arrogance, and su-
perciliousness which marked his character.  Sweden also appeared at Rastadt as a mediatrix, and as one of the powers which
had guaranteed the treaty of Westphalia.  This claim was somewhat obsolete.  The Court had moreover sent Baron Fersen as
its representative to the Congress, whose appointment, from the
favor he had enjoyed at the Court of Versailles,* his intrigues in

* He was a favorite of the Queen's, and in disguise drove the carriage in
which the King set out to Varennes.  See p. 120.

the time of the Constituent Assembly, and the hatred he had on all occasions expressed against France, might be regarded as an insult to the Republic.  On his first interview Napoleon told him that he could not acknowledge any mediator ; and as his known opinions particularly disqualified him from coming forward in that capacity between the Republic and the Emperor of Germany, he could receive him no more.  Baron Fersen, disconcerted by this reception which was much talked of, left Rastadt the following day.

Immediately after the surrender of Mentz to the French troops, Buonaparte finding affairs grow more complicated every day, and already dissatisfied with the foreign policy of the Directory, determined to meddle no farther in a negociation that seemed to promise no probable end.  In the heated and unsettled state of parties in France, the same motives which had induced him to shun the civilities of the Court of Sardinia, led him to withdraw himself from the flattering marks of attention which the German princes lavished upon him.  During his short stay at the Congress, he procured the French plenipotentiaries, who had been previously very much neglected, the respect and consideration to which they were entitled as the representatives of a great nation ; and he also persuaded the Government to increase the allowance of the negociators, so as to enable them to appear on a footing of equality with the ambassadors of foreign courts.  It ought not to be passed over in this place, that Napoleon among other conditions of the treaty of Campo-Formio, had procured the liberation of La Fayette and his unfortunate companions, who had been confined for four years in the dungeons of Olmutz ; and it should be known, in justice to all parties, that this article cost him more trouble than all the rest.  Napoleon left Rastadt, travelled through France *incognito*, reached Paris without stopping on the road, and alighted at his small house in the Chaussée d'Antin, Rue Chantereine.  The different public bodies vied with each other in expressing the gratitude of the nation towards him.  A committee of the Council of Ancients drew up an act for settling the estate of Chambord and a mansion in the capital upon him ; but this proposal was in some way defeated by the Directory.

The name of the Rue de la Victoire was given to the Rue Chantereine. It is needless to add that it no longer bears that name ; but victory and defeat and a thousand other recollections will remain forever engraved upon it in all the bright and solemn obscurity of a dream

# CHAPTER XIV.

## NEGOCIATIONS IN 1797.

GREAT and important changes had taken place in the course of the five months that elapsed between the ratification of the preliminaries of Leoben and the signing of the treaty of Campo-Formio, on which they had a considerable influence. It is necessary to turn back to them here. The events of the 18th of Fructidor, which also belongs to this interval, will be treated of in a subsequent chapter.

Venice was founded in the fifth century by the inhabitants of the neighboring shores who sought refuge there from the incursions of the barbarians. In the earliest times Padua gave laws to the Venetians. In 697 they first named a Doge of their own. King Pepin constructed a flotilla at Ravenna, and compelled the Venetians to retire from Grado and Heraclea to Rialto and the surrounding isles, which is the present situation of Venice. In 830 the body of St. Mark the Evangelist having been, according to tradition, transported thither from Egypt, he became the patron-saint of the Republic. In 960 the Venetians were masters of Istria and the Adriatic; and in 1250, in conjunction with the French, took Constantinople. They were in possession of the Morea and Candia till the middle of the seventeenth century; and amidst all the revolutions and change of masters to which Italy has been subject, Venice still remained independent and free, having never submitted to a foreign yoke. It is the best-situated commercial port in all Italy. Before the discovery of the Cape of Good Hope, Venice carried on the trade with India by Alexandria and the Red Sea; and afterwards maintained a long struggle for the priority with the Portuguese. After the abolition of the democracy in 1200, the sovereignty resided in the aristocracy of several hundred families whose names were inscribed in the

Golden Book, and who were entitled to vote in the Grand Council. The population of the States of the Republic was composed
chiefly of three millions of inhabitants dispersed in the Terra
Firma, Istria, Dalmatia, and the Ionian Isles. The Venetian territory is bounded to the north by the upper ridge of the Julian Alps,
over which there are only three outlets into Germany. At the
time of the breaking out of the French Revolution, Venice was
but the shadow of its former self. Three generations had passed
away without engaging in war; during which time they had submitted to the insults of the Austrians, French, and Spaniards without
offering the least resistance. The navy consisted of twelve sixty-
four gun ships, as many frigates, with smaller vessels, sufficient
to keep the Barbarians in awe; and their army, 14,000 strong,
was made up of regiments raised in the Terra Firma or of Sclavonian recruits. None but the families inscribed in the Golden
Book had any right to share in the government. This rendered
the nobles of the Terra Firma, among whom were many rich,
old, and powerful families, whose ancestors had long fought
against Venice, discontented, and sowed the seeds of dissension
and a desire of change amongst them.

In 1792 the Combined Powers invited Venice to take part in
the war; but the Republic thought itself too distant to feel any
but a very languid interest in the affairs of France, and even
when the Count de Lille (Louis XVIII.) took refuge in Verona,
the Senate did not grant him permission to remain there, till it
had obtained the acquiescence of the Committee of Public Safety.
When in 1794 the French troops marched towards Oneglia, it
was thought that Italy was menaced with invasion, and several
powers held a congress at Milan. Venice refused to appear there,
not because she approved of French principles, but as fearing to
place herself at the mercy of Austria, and unwilling to depart
from that tame and enervated policy which she had so long pursued. But when Napoleon arrived at Milan and Beaulieu fled in
consternation beyond the Mincio, occupying Peschiera, great anxiety and alarm prevailed in the Senate. The wide space which
had hitherto separated Venice from the struggle that was going
on between the old and new forms of government had now been
traversed; the blow had fallen like a thunder-bolt at her feet;

and stormy discussions arose in the councils, in which three different opinions were contended for. The young and hot-headed members of the oligarchy wished for an armed neutrality: they advised that strong garrisons should be thrown into Peschiera, Brescia, Porto Legnago, and Verona; that the army should be increased to 60,000 men, the coasts put in a state of defence, and protected with gun-boats; and that in this formidable attitude the Republic should declare war against the first power that violated its neutrality. The partizans of the old policy still maintained on the other hand that it would be best to take no decisive measures, but to temporize, give way, and watch the course of events. The encroachments of Austria and the principles of France were both to be dreaded, but these evils were but temporary; the French were of a placable disposition, easily won by attention and caresses; the Venetian capital was fortunately placed out of the reach of insult; and patience, moderation, and time would do the rest. The third party, at the head of whom was Battaglia, proposed in the extremity to which they were reduced to augment the Golden Book, so as to obtain the good-will and adherence of the inhabitants of the Terra Firma; to offer the French General an offensive and defensive alliance, and thus secure the foundations of the constitution and their independence from the power of Austria. This advice gained but few suffrages, and aristocratical prejudices prevailed over the interests of the Republic.

The proveditore Mocenigo at Brescia received Napoleon in a style of great magnificence; splendid fêtes were given, and an intimacy was studiously cemented between the officers of the army and the principal families of the town. At Verona, the proveditore Foscarelli pretended to do the same thing; but he was of too proud and violent a character to disguise his ill-will to the French. On Napoleon's arrival at Peschiera, he endeavored to dissuade him from marching on Verona, and even refused to deliver up the keys of the city. "It is too late," said the General-in-Chief; "neutrality consists in having the same weight and measure for all parties. If you are not my enemies, you must grant me what you have granted, or at least tolerated in my enemies." With the advance of the French, a considerable agitation spread through the Terra Firma. The ancient animosity en-

tertained against the oligarchy was strengthened by an attachment
to the new opinions. " What right has Venice," said the inhabitants, " to govern our cities ? Are we less brave, enlightened,
opulent, or noble than the Venetians ?" Every thing announced
the approach of a violent catastrophe. Buonaparte did all in his
power to moderate this popular impulse. On his return from
Tolentino, and before marching on Vienna, he thought it high
time to settle the affairs of this country, and sent for Pesaro, who
at that time managed the concerns of the Republic, to urge upon
him the acceptance of Battaglia's plan of accommodation. Pesaro set out for Venice, undertaking to employ his good offices.
In the mean time, Bergamo and Brescia had openly revolted, and
repulsed the Venetian troops who were sent against them. Pesaro,
on returning to head-quarters, found them at Goritz. The Archduke had been defeated at the Tagliamento, and the French flag
waved on the summit of the Julian Alps. " Have I kept my
word ?" said Napoleon; "or does the Republic accept my alliance ?" " Venice," replied Pesaro, " rejoices in your triumphs ;
she knows that she cannot exist but by means of France ; but
faithful to her ancient and wise policy, she wishes to remain
neutral." Napoleon made a last effort, but failed. On Pesaro's
taking leave, he said to him : " I am marching on Vienna. Things
that I might have forgiven when I was in Italy, would be unpardonable crimes when I am in Germany. Should my soldiers be
assassinated, my convoys harassed, and my communications intercepted in the Venetian territories, your Republic will have
ceased to exist."

After the movement of Joubert to join the army in Carinthia,
Laudon, who was left to guard the Tyrol, increased his force by
10,000 Tyrolese militia, beat General Serviez's little corps of
observation, and compelled them to retreat on Montebaldo, occupying Trent. Being master of the Tyrol, he inundated Italy
with proclamations, filled with the most absurd reports of the defeat of the French armies, the brilliant victories of the Archduke
Charles, and his own advance with 60,000 men to cut off the retreat of the wreck of the Army of Italy. On this intelligence
the Venetian oligarchy no longer kept any terms. It was in
vain that the French Minister alleged the falsehood of these state-

ments, and endeavored to convince the Senate that it was digging
a pit for itself. Pesaro, who ruled its decisions, was too desirous
of the defeat of the French not to credit these communications;
and Austria was busy at work in fomenting insurrections in the
rear of the invading army. Order was maintained by the prudence of Mocenigo in Friuli, which was nearer the scene of
operations; but in the Veronese more than 30,000 peasants had
been secretly furnished with arms, and only waited the signal for
slaughter. The proveditore Emili concerted measures with
Laudon, apprising him of the weakness of the garrison of Verona; and on the 17th of April (Tuesday in Easter week) after
vespers the tocsin sounded. The insurrection broke out at the
same time in the city and country; the French were massacred
on all sides, and four hundred sick were murdered in the hospitals. General Balland shut himself up in the castles with the
garrison. The fire of the forts, which he directed against the
city, induced the Veronese authorities to hold a parley, but the
rage of the multitude interrupted it; and emboldened by the arrival of 2000 Sclavonians from Vicenza, and the approach of the
Austrian General Nieperg, they revenged the mischief done by
the bombardment of the city, by slaughtering the garrison of
Chiusa, which had been obliged to surrender to the levy in mass
of the mountaineers.

General Kilmaine, who was entrusted with the chief command
of Lombardy, sent to the relief of General Balland as soon as
he heard of the insurrection at Verona. On the 21st of April
his first columns appeared before its gates; and Generals Cha-
bran, Lahoz, and Chevalier came up on the day following. On
the 23d the signature of the preliminaries of peace became known
to the insurgents, with the news that Victor's division was on its
march from Treviso. They were now seized with consternation,
and their fear being equal to their former fury, accepted on their
knees the conditions which General Balland imposed on them.
The French were entitled to make severe reprisals; but only
three of the inhabitants were delivered up to the tribunals; a
general disarming was effected, and the peasants were sent home
to their villages.

The Venetians, equally infatuated, also suffered the crew of a

French privateer, which being pursued by an Austrian frigate
had taken shelter under the batteries of the Lido (where it was
entitled to protection) to be murdered before their eyes; and when
the French Minister demanded redress for this outrage, the Senate
both laughed at his threats and remonstrances, and rewarded such
of its satellites as had participated in the murder of Captain **Laugier** and his men. It is thus that the old governments, whenever
they had an opportunity, have treated the French people as a set
of outlaws, with whom no faith was to be kept nor any mercy
shown to them, at the same time lifting up their hands and eyes
at every infringement of the nicest punctilio on their parts, as an
unheard-of and wanton aggression on all lawful authority.\* As
soon as Napoleon heard of these events, he sent Junot to Venice,
charging him to present a letter to the Senate, in which he reproached them with their treachery and duplicity. That officer
fulfilled his mission with the plain bluntness of a soldier. Terror
prevailed in the Government. The Senate humbled itself and
endeavored to find excuses, and sent a deputation to the General-
in-Chief at Gratz to offer every reparation he might require, and
to bribe all those who had any credit with him. This method
succeeded better at Paris than in the Army; and the Directory
showed themselves favorable to the Senate in the orders they sent.
But Napoleon, by means of some intercepted dispatches, had in
his hands the proofs of the intrigue that had been carried on, and
he annulled, of his own authority, all that had been done. On
the 23d of May he issued from his camp at Palma-Nuova the
following declaration of war against the Republic of Venice.

" Whilst the French army is in the defiles of Styria, having
left Italy and its principal establishments far behind, where only
a few battalions remained, this is the line of conduct pursued by
the Government of Venice. It takes the opportunity of Passion-

---

\* On this principle the captain of an English seventy-four attacked the
French frigate Modeste in the port of Genoa, then at peace with France,
desiring him to hoist the white flag, and saying he did not know what the
tri-colored flag meant. The crew of the Modeste, to escape the fire of the
seventy-four, threw themselves into the water, and were pursued and killed
or wounded by the English boats. This happened in October, 1793, and
would at that time be considered as a fine trait of our contempt for the enemy, and consequent superiority over them.

week to arm 40,000 peasants, adds ten regiments of Sclavonians to that force, forms them into several corps, and posts them at different points to intercept the communications of the army. Extraordinary commissions, muskets, ammunition of all kinds, and artillery are sent from the city of Venice to complete the organization of the different corps. All who received the French in a friendly manner in the Terra Firma are arrested; while those who are distinguished by an outrageous hatred of the French name obtain the favors and entire confidence of the Government; and especially the fourteen conspirators of Verona, whom the proveditore Priuli had caused to be arrested three months ago as convicted of having plotted the slaughter of the French. In the squares, coffee-houses, and other public places at Venice, the French are insulted, called Jacobins, regicides, and atheists; and at length are expelled the city with a prohibition ever to return. The people of Padua, Vicenza, and Verona are ordered to take up arms, to second the different bodies of troops, and in short to begin these new Sicilian Vespers. It is ours, say the Venetian officers, to verify the proverb, that *Italy is the tomb of the French.* The priests from their pulpits preach a crusade; and in the States of Venice, priests never utter any thing but what is dictated by the Government. Pamphlets, perfidious proclamations, and anonymous letters are printed in various towns, and begin to work upon the minds of the people; and in a state in which liberty of the press is not allowed—in a government not less dreaded than secretly abhorred—authors and printers only write and publish what is approved by the Senate.

" At first every thing seems to favor the treacherous designs of the Government; French blood flows in all directions. On every road the convoys, couriers, and all belonging to the army are intercepted. At Padua a chief of battalion and two other Frenchmen are murdered; at Castiglione di Mori several soldiers are disarmed and murdered; on the high-roads from Mantua to Legnago and from Cassano to Verona, upwards of 200 French are murdered. Two battalions on their way to join the army, are met at Chiari by a Venetian division, which opposes their progress. An obstinate action commences; and our brave soldiers force a passage over the bodies of their enemies. At

Valeggio there is another engagement; and at Dezenzano they
are again obliged to fight. The French are in all these cases
few in number, but they are accustomed to disregard the numbers of their enemies. On the second holiday of Easter, at the
ringing of the bell, all the French in Verona are murdered; the
assassins spare neither the sick in the hospitals nor those who are
convalescent and walking in the streets: the last was thrown into
the Adige, after receiving a thousand stabs with stilettoes. Upwards of 400 soldiers are thus massacred. During eight days
the Venetian army besieges the three castles of Verona; the
cannon it plants against them are taken by the French at the
point of the bayonet; the city is set on fire; and the corps of
observation, which comes up during these transactions, completely
routs these cowards, taking 3000 prisoners with several Generals.
The house of the French Consul at Zante is burnt down. In
Dalmatia, a Venetian man-of-war takes an Austrian convoy
under its protection, and fires several shots at the sloop La Brune.
The Republican ship Le Libérateur d'Italie, carrying only three
or four small guns, is sunk in the port of Venice by order of the
Government. The young and lamented Lieutenant Laugier, her
commander, finding himself attacked both by the fire of the fort
and that of the Admiral's galley, being within pistol-shot of both,
orders his crew under hatches. He alone mounts on deck amidst
a shower of grape-shot, and endeavors to disarm the fury of these
assassins by addressing them; but he falls dead on the spot.
His crew betake themselves to swimming, and are pursued by
six boats manned by troops in the pay of the Republic of Venice,
who killed several of the French with axes as they are endeavoring
to save their lives by swimming towards the sea. A boatswain,
wounded in several places, weakened and bleeding profusely, is
fortunate enough to make the shore, and clings to a piece of timber projecting from the harbor castle; but the commandant himself chops off his hand with an axe.

"Considering the above-mentioned grievances, and authorized
by title XII, article 328, of the Constitution of the Republic, and
seeing the urgency of the occasion, the General-in-Chief requires
the Minister of France to the Republic of Venice to depart from
the said city; orders the different agents of the Venetian Repub-

lic in Lombardy and the Venetian Terra Firma to depart within twenty-four hours; orders the different Generals of division to treat the troops of the Republic of Venice as enemies; and to pull down the Lion of St. Mark in every town of the Terra Firma. To-morrow in the order of the day, each of them will receive particular instructions respecting further military proceedings."

On reading this manifesto the weapons fell from the hands of the oligarchy, who no longer thought of defending themselves. The Grand Council of the state dissolved itself, and a municipal body was entrusted with the supreme power. Thus this haughty aristocracy fell without a struggle. In its last agonies it in vain supplicated the Court of Austria to be included in the general peace; but that court turned a deaf ear to its entreaties, having opposite views of its own. On the 11th of May, Baraguay d'Hilliers entered Venice at the call of the inhabitants, who were in dread of the Sclavonian troops. The tri-colored flag was hoisted in St. Mark's Place, and the popular Constitution was declared by the partisans of freedom, who chose Dandolo for their head. The Lion of St. Mark and the Corinthian horses on the gates of the Doge's palace were removed to Paris. The Venetian fleet was manned and sent to Toulon. General Gentili, the same who had driven the English out of Corsica, proceeded to Corfu and took possession of this place, the key to the Adriatic, and of the other Ionian islands. Pesaro was overwhelmed by the general reprobation and escaped to Vienna. Battaglia deeply regretted the fall of his country, and did not long survive it. The Doge Manini suddenly fell down dead, while taking the oath to Austria, administered by Morosini, who afterwards became the Emperor's commissioner. On the receipt of the order of the day, declaring war against Venice, the whole Terra Firma revolted, and adopted the principles of the French Revolution, abolishing convents and suppressing feudal tenures. Notwithstanding the care of Napoleon to prevent abuses and peculation, more disorders were committed on this occasion than during any other period of the war. The bank at Verona was plundered of property to the amount of seven or eight millions of francs. Bouquet, a commissary, and Andrieux, a colonel of hussars, were accused of being concerned in

this robbery, and compelled to refund all that was found upon
them.   Bernadotte presented the colors taken from the Venetians
and other trophies to the Directory a few days before the 18th of
Fructidor—a sort of ceremony very useful to the Government
at that period ; for the disaffected were overawed and silenced
by these frequent displays of the spirit and success of the armies.

At the moment of the entrance of the French troops into Venice,
one of the persons who escaped from that city was the Count
d'Entraigues.   He was arrested on the Brenta by Bernadotte's
division, and sent to the head-quarters at Milan.   Count d'Estrai-
gues was a native of the Vivarais, was a deputy from the noblesse
to the Constituent Assembly, and at first an ardent assertor of
liberty ; but soon after changed sides, emigrated, and became one
of the principal agents of the foreign party.   He had been two
years at Venice in this capacity, and was suspected of having
had an important share in the massacre at Verona.   In consequence of papers found upon him, he was ordered to be tried by
a military commission ; but in the interim he applied to Napoleon, to whom he made unreserved communications, discovered
all the intrigues of the time, and compromised his party more
than it was necessary to do.   He received permission to reside
in the city on his parole and without a guard.   Some time after
he made his escape into Switzerland, where he published and circulated with great industry a pamphlet against his benefactor,
describing the horrible dungeon in which he had been immured,
the tortures he had suffered, the boldness he had displayed, and
the dangers he had braved in making his escape.   This excited
a great deal of indignation at Milan, where he had been seen in
the public walks and theatres enjoying the utmost liberty—an instance among so many others of the gratitude of those slaves of
power who think that to lie is a court privilege, and that to disregard every common obligation of truth or justice is the distinguishing characteristic of a gentleman and a man of honor,
and the most acceptable compliment they can pay to their superiors !

Genoa came in for its share in the negociations carried on in
the summer of 1797 at Montebello.   This little Republic had
been engaged in continual wars and struggles, both with Corsica

and other states, during the whole of the last century, and kept
up its spirit and energy much better than the Republic of Venice
had done during that time. The Genoese aristocracy had accordingly faced the storm that for some time threatened them,
and suffered neither the Allied Powers nor France nor the popular party among themselves to intimidate them. The Republic
had maintained the Constitution which Andrew Doria had given
it in the sixteenth century in its original integrity. But the proclamation of the independence of the Cispadan and Transpadan
Republics, the abdication of the aristocracy of Venice, and the
enthusiasm which the victories of the French excited, gave such
a preponderance to the popular party, that a change in the Government became unavoidable. Yet France wished the Genoese to
bring this about themselves without appearing in it. Faypoult,
the French minister, was a man of moderation and prudence,
which favored this object. The Morandi club, on the other hand,
impatient of the slow progress of the revolution, wished to precipitate matters, and drew up a petition to the Doge to proclaim
the triumph of liberty, who did not seem averse to the measure,
as he appointed a junta of nine persons, four of them being of
the plebeian class, to propose alterations in the Constitution to
him.

The three state-inquisitors or supreme censors, who were the
leaders of the oligarchy and the enemies of France, beheld this
turn of affairs with dissatisfaction. Being convinced that the
aristocracy could not subsist many months longer if they permitted events to take their obvious course, they called in the aid of
fanaticism, and excited the enthusiasm of the colliers and porters
by the usual artifices of preaching, of miracles, the elevation of
the host, and prayers of forty hours. The Morandists, on their
part, were not idle, but incensed the people against the priests
and nobles by every expedient, and made a great number of pro-
selytes. Thinking things ripe for the attempt, on the 22d of May,
at ten o'clock in the morning, they seized on the gates of the ar
senal, St. Thomas, and the port. The terrified Inquisitors gave
the signal to the colliers and porters, who in a few hours assembled at the armory, with shouts of *Viva Maria*, to the amount of
10,000. The patriots in despair mounted the French cockade,

which enraged the populace, and nearly proved fatal to the French
families settled in Genoa and to the minister Faypoult. Several
persons were massacred. The naval commissioner, Menard, a
retired and inoffensive man, was dragged by the hair of his head
as far as the light-house fort; the Consul La Chaise had his
house plundered and escaped with difficulty. In the midst of the
tumult Admiral Bruyes, returning from Corsica with two men-
of-war and two frigates, came in sight of the port, but Faypoult
had the weakness to send him orders not to land but to make for
Toulon.

The oligarchy had been persuaded that Napoleon would con-
nive at these disorders, but no sooner was he informed of the
events which had taken place and of the shedding of French
blood, than he dispatched Lavalette to Genoa, and required of the
Doge that all the French should be set at liberty, their property
protected, the colliers disarmed, and that the French minister
should repair to Tortona with such of the French families as chose
to follow him. Though the French were immediately released
on the arrival of Lavalette, the answer of the Senate was not satisfactory; but as soon as they found that Faypoult demanded his
passport, they met again, and resolved that a deputation of Cam-
biaso the Doge, Serra, and Carbonari should proceed directly to
Montebello; that the colliers should be disarmed, and the three
Inquisitors put in a state of arrest. On the 6th of June the depu-
ies from the Senate signed a convention at Montebello which put
an end to the power of the oligarchy, and established a democrat-
ical constitution at Genoa.

The people, intoxicated with the news, committed several excesses, burnt the Golden Book, and broke the statue of Doria in
pieces. Buonaparte was much displeased at this outrage on the
memory of a great man, the real benefactor of his country, which
showed the blindness of the multitude who look neither before
nor behind them; and required the Provisional Government to
repair the statue. The exclusionists, however, got the upper
hand, and every thing was subjected to their influence; by which
means the priests were rendered discontented and the nobles
highly exasperated, being shut out from all offices in the state.
The Constitution was to be submitted to the approbation of the

people on the 11th of September ; it was printed and posted in all the communes.   Several of the country cantons declared against it ; and insurrections broke out in the valleys of Polcevera and the Bisagno, which General Duphot was compelled to put down by an armed force.   Tranquillity was thus restored, and the peasants were disarmed.   This news was a disappointment to Napoleon.   He was then much occupied by the negociation with Austria, but he had strongly recommended that the priests should be conciliated and the nobles admitted to public offices ; since to exclude them would be the same glaring piece of injustice towards them that had been made the subject of such loud complaints against them.   The Constitution was afterwards modified according to this suggestion, and carried into effect with general approbation.   Not a single French soldier passed beyond Tortona during this change, which 'was owing to the influence of the Third Estate.   The advice given by Napoleon to the Genoese Republic was also intended for the French Government, who were then debating on the motion of Siéyes to expel all the nobles from France and give them the value of their estates in manufactured goods. They took the hint, and this violent measure was no more talked of.

Immediately after the refusal of the Court of Vienna to ratify the convention signed at Montebello by the Marquis de Gallo, Napoleon united the Cispadan and Transpadan Republics into one, under the title of the Cisalpine Republic.   Some persons objected to this title, and would have had it called the Transalpine Republic, making Paris the centre of every thing : but the Italians had fixed their eyes on Rome, and this appellation flattered their hopes and was dictated by the soundest policy.   The people on the two banks of the Po, the inhabitants of Reggio, Modena, Bologna, and Ferrara, from old antipathies and local prejudices, had a great aversion to uniting into one government ; and nothing could well have overcome this repugnance but the secret hope held out to them that it was but the prelude to the union of all the nations of the Peninsula under a single head.   By the treaty of Campo-Formio the Cisalpine Republic obtained the addition of that part of the states of Venice which was situated on the right bank of the Adige, which, together with the acquisition of the Valteline,

gave it a population of 3,600,000 souls.    These provinces, without doubt the richest and finest in Europe, formed ten departments, extending from the mountains of Switzerland to the Tus-
can and Roman Apennines, and from the Ticino to the Adriatic.

Napoleon would willingly have given the Cisalpine State a
constitution different from that of France ; and with this view desired to have some celebrated publicist, such as Siéyes, sent to him
at Milan : but the Directory would not hear of any alteration in
this respect.    A general federation of the National Guards and
the authorities of the new Republic took place at the Lazaretto
of Milan.    On the 14th of July 30,000 National Guards, with
the deputies from the departments, took an oath of fraternity, and
swore to use their utmost efforts to revive the liberty of Italy and
make her once more a nation.    The keys of Milan and of the
fortresses were delivered by the French to the Cisalpine officers.
The army left the states of the Republic, and went into canton-
ments in the territory of Venice.    From this period may be dated
the first formation of the Italian army, which afterwards acquired
so great a share of glory.    The manners of the Italians under-
went a striking change.    The cassock, the fashionable dress for
youth, gave place to regimentals : instead of passing their time
at the feet of women, the young Italians now frequented the rid-
ing and fencing-schools and places of exercise : the children no
longer played at *chapel*, but had regiments armed with tin guns,
and mimicked the occurrences of war in their favorite games.
In their comedies and street-farces, there had always been an
Italian, who was represented as a very cowardly though witty
fellow, and a kind of bullying captain, sometimes a Frenchman,
but more frequently a German, a very powerful, brave, and brutal character, who never failed to conclude with caning the Italian, to the great satisfaction and applause of the spectators.    But
such allusions were now no longer endured by the populace, who
insisted on seeing valiant Italians introduced on the stage, putting
foreigners to flight and defending themselves with resolution and
boldness.    A national spirit had arisen ; Italy had her patriotic
and warlike songs ; and the women contemptuously repulsed
those suitors who affected effeminate manners in order to please
them.

The Valteline, which was incorporated with the Cisalpine Republic, is composed of three valleys, the Valteline properly so called, the Bormio, and the Chiavenna : its population is 160,000 souls ; and the inhabitants profess the Roman Catholic religion, and speak Italian. It belongs geographically to Italy ; it borders the Adda down to its discharge into the Lake of Como, and is separated from Germany by the Higher Alps, being eighteen leagues in length and six in breadth. Chiavenna, its capital, is two leagues from the lake of Como, and fourteen from Coire in Switzerland. The Valteline was anciently part of the Milanese. Barnabas Visconti, Archbishop and Duke of Milan, in 1404 gave these three valleys to the church of Coire. In 1512 the Grison Leagues were invested with the sovereignty by Sforza upon certain conditional statutes which the Dukes of Milan were to guarantee. The people of the Valteline thus found themselves subject to the three Leagues, the inhabitants of which were separated from them by religion, language, and situation.

There is no condition more dreadful than that of a nation which is subject to another nation. It was thus that the Lower Valais was subject to the Upper Valais, and the Pays de Vaud to the canton of Berne. The unfortunate people of the Valteline had long complained of the oppressions under which they groaned. The Grisons, poor and ignorant, came to enrich themselves in the Valteline. The lowest peasant of the Leagues considered himself as much superior to the richest inhabitant of the Valteline, as a sovereign is to his subjects. In the course of May, 1797, the people of the three valleys revolted, unfurled the tri-colored flag, published a manifesto setting forth their grievances and the rights of which they had been deprived, and sent the deputies Juidiconni, Planta, and Paribelli to Montebello to claim the execution of their statutes, which had been violated by the Grisons in every point. Napoleon was reluctant to interfere in questions which might affect Switzerland ; but being called upon by both parties, and finding on examination into the archives of Milan that the Milanese government was invested with the right of guaranteeing the statutes, he accepted the office of mediator. Napoleon previously to giving any decision, invited both parties to come to an amicable arrangement, and proposed as a mode of accommodation, that

the Valteline should form a fourth League upon a footing of
equality with the three former. This suggestion deeply wounded
the pride of the Grisons. How could it be imagined, they said,
that a peasant who drinks the water of the Adda could be the
equal of one who drinks the water of the Rhine ? They therefore rejected with disdain so unreasonable a proposal as that of
equalizing Catholic peasants who spoke Italian and were rich and
well informed, with Protestant peasants who spoke German and
were poor and ignorant. The leading characters among them did
not share these prejudices, but were misled by avarice. They
declined measures of accommodation, and sent no deputies at the
time appointed for hearing the different claims, though they had
before agreed to do so. Buonaparte accordingly gave judgment
by default against the Leagues, and in a decision pronounced the
10th of October, 1797, gave the people of the Valteline liberty to
unite themselves with the Cisalpine Republic. The Grisons,
frantic with rage and mortification, immediately after this award
wrote word to Napoleon that their deputies were setting out to
appear before him; but he answered that it was too late. In
speaking of this event afterwards Buonaparte gives himself great
credit for the decision he had made. "The principles," he ob-
serves, "on which this sentence was founded echoed through all
Europe, and aimed a mortal blow at the usurpation of the Swiss
cantons, which held more than one people in subjection. It
might have been expected that the aristocracy of Venice would
have been sufficiently warned by this example, to feel that the
moment for making some concessions to the enlightened state of
the age, to the influence of France and to justice had arrived.
But prejudice and pride never listen to the voice of reason, nature,
or religion. An oligarchy yields to nothing but force." It may
be asked here, was Napoleon sincere in these principles on which
he seems to lay so much stress, and to which he often adhered so
little in practice ? There is no need to doubt it : every one is
sincere in the condemnation of wrong, till it comes to be his own
turn to inflict it.

The treaties with Rome, Naples, and Sardinia had been formally ratified in the course of these negociations : but the materials of which they were composed were of too frail and discordant

a nature to promise a lasting union. The Piedmontese in particular loudly called for a revolution, and the Court of Turin already
looked to Sardinia as a place of refuge. Rome vacillated and
lost itself between contradictory and ill-judged counsels, keeping
up the sense of self-importance after its authority was gone—too
feeble to assert its claims, too obstinate to forego them. Naples
placed at a distance from the storm might have escaped, but for
the disorderly and violent passions of the Queen, who ruled every
thing but herself. The treaty of peace in October 1796 made no
alteration in the conduct of this cabinet, which continued to levy
troops and excite alarm during the whole of the year 1797; yet
the treaty was an exceedingly favorable one. At the time that
Napoleon was in the Marches threatening Rome, Prince Belmonte
Pignatelli, the Neapolitan Minister, who was at head-quarters,
showed him in confidence a letter from the Queen, informing him
that she was about to order 30,000 men to march to the relief of
Rome. "I thank you for this confidential communication," said
the General, "and in return I will make you a similar one."
He rang for his secretary, ordered him to bring the papers relating to Naples, took out a dispatch which he had written to the
Directory in the month of November 1796 before the taking of
Mantua, and read as follows: "The difficulties arising from Alvinzi's approach would not prevent me from sending 6000 Lom-
bards and Poles to punish the Court of Rome; but as it is probable that the King of Naples might send 30,000 men to defend the
Holy See, I shall not march on Rome, until Mantua shall have
fallen, and the reinforcements you announce shall have arrived;
in order that in case the Court of Naples should violate the treaty
of Paris, I might have 25,000 men disposable to occupy its capital and compel it to take refuge in Sicily." In the course of the
night, Prince Pignatelli dispatched an extraordinary courier,
doubtless for the purpose of informing the Queen of the manner
in which her insinuation had been received.

# CHAPTER XV.

### THE EIGHTEENTH OF FRUCTIDOR.

AFTER the battles and sieges, defeats and victories with which we have been lately occupied, it is with some reluctance I return to take up the internal affairs of the Revolution once more. In war one is only answerable for the event ; in politics one is concerned not only with what takes place, but with what ought to take place, and which seldom actually does so. In a campaign, the plan, the execution, the details, the success and alternate vicissitudes are every thing, the merits of the case are for the moment laid aside ; in government, fortune and justice are constantly at issue, at every step our prejudices are shocked, our reason taken to task, our hopes disappointed or overturned. If in religion, where we have to conform our own actions to a certain standard, conscience is the great tormentor of the human breast ; in philosophy, when we come to refine and speculate on what is best for the whole, the moral sense is the great poisoner of reflection and troubler of the peace and happiness of human life.

"At the time* that the Directory were first installed in the Luxembourg," says M. Bailleul, "there was hardly a single article of furniture in it. In a small room, round a little broken table, one of the legs of which had given way from age, on which table they had deposited a quire of letter-paper, and a writing desk *à calamet*, which luckily they had had the precaution to bring with them from the Committee of Public Safety, seated on four rush-bottomed chairs, in front of some logs of wood ill-lighted, the whole borrowed from the porter Dupont ; who would believe that it was in this deplorable condition that the members of the new government, after having examined all the difficulties, nay, let me add, all the horrors of their situation, resolved to confront

* October 27, 1795.

all obstacles, and that they would either deliver France from the abyss in which she was plunged or perish in the attempt ? They drew up on a sheet of letter-paper the act by which they declared themselves constituted, and immediately forwarded it to the Legislative Bodies."

The Directors divided the different functions amongst themselves according to their respective inclinations and the qualities for which they had been chosen.   Rewbell, a man of business and of great activity of mind and body, undertook the departments of finance, justice, and foreign affairs.   Barras, indolent, with few resources, but bold, intriguing, and well acquainted or connected with all parties, with the nobles by birth, with the revolutionists by habit, had the management of the police.   He also did the honors of the Directory, and held a kind of court (not the most respectable) at the Luxembourg.   The modest and well-meaning Lepaux took charge of the arts, manufactures, and public instruction.   Carnot was appointed to the war-department, in which he introduced great improvements and met with great success; and Letourneur superintended the marine and the colonies.   Thus all parties labored, each in his province, and with a perfect good understanding, to benefit and restore the State.   They had quite enough on their hands.   An alarming scarcity prevailed in Paris; and it was necessary to resort to extraordinary measures to avert the calamities of absolute famine; but at the end of a month this difficulty had been so far overcome that the capital was supplied with provisions by the ordinary channels.   The finances were in a deplorable state : there was no money in the public treasury, so that even the couriers were sometimes stopped for want of the trifling sum necessary to pay their expenses on the road.   The Convention had supplied the armies and the people with bread by means of requisitions and the *maximum ;* but when this forced system came to an end, things fell into a worse state than ever. The paper-money was totally depreciated, so as to be quite worthless : nobody would sell, for nobody could buy, and commerce and industry were almost at a stand for want of credit.   The Directory at first attempted to remedy this distress by a forced loan and by a new issue of paper-money, secured on the sale of the national domains, but with very little success.   By degrees, however, affairs began to wear a better aspect. The fever and the violence of the Revolution being over, the intense activity it had called forth seemed to turn to the benefit of the State. A great number of the people quitted the clubs and public places to return to the fields or to their work-shops: and it was at this period that the advantages of a change of government which had destroyed exclusive corporations, parcelled out the land, abolished vexatious privileges, and augmented the means of civilization, were strikingly felt. The Directory seconded this favorable tendency by salutary measures. It established public prizes for industry and improved upon the system of education decreed by the Convention. The National Institute, and the primary and central schools were so many nurseries and shrines of arts and science and of republican sentiments. A mild and benevolent tone pervaded their addresses to the nation, which must have done much to inspire confidence and to conciliate good-will. "All will be well," they said in one of these, "when by your zeal and steadiness that sincere love of freedom, which consecrated the dawn of the Revolution, shall return to animate the breasts of all Frenchmen. The colors of liberty waving over your houses, the republican device inscribed on your doors, undoubtedly present a sight sufficiently interesting. Do not rest contented with this; hasten the day when the sacred name of the Republic shall be voluntarily engraven in all hearts." The D rector Reveillere-Lepaux, as entrusted with the moral administration of the government, wished to found the sect of Theo-philanthropists, which soon fell into contempt and disuse, as equally opposed to the prejudices of the Catholics and the sceptical opinions of the philosophers. All attempts at compromise or holding the balance between extreme and hostile sects and parties necessarily meet with the same fate. The only way to succeed is either to strengthen power and opinion, or to overturn it. Every middle course is fallacious.

The situation of the armies was by no means brilliant. Insubordination prevailed among the troops;, defection among the Generals. That of Pichegru had been nearly fatal to the Republic, though all its circumstances were not as yet known. The Directory found the frontier of the Rhine uncovered, the war rekindled in La Vendée, and Holland menaced with a descent

from England; and lastly, the Army of Italy in want of everything was reduced to the defensive under Scherer and Kellermann.
Hoche succeeded in pacifying La Vendée; and Buonaparte, appointed through the influence of Barras and Carnot to the command of the Army of Italy in the following spring (1796), repaired every disaster, and gave to France an arm of steel.

It was thus that the Directory contended at the commencement
of its career with the difficulties it had to overcome as to its internal administration and foreign hostilities. It had yet another
enemy to encounter, which was faction, as this was composed of
the two extremes of republicanism and royalism. The democrats,
uneasy under the new government from which they were exclu-
ded and which did not give sufficient scope to the violence of their
opinions and passions, still regretted the death of Robespierre and
the termination of the reign of terror as of evil augury. Not
being able to take their full swing, and give every wild thought
its instant effect, they considered themselves as "cooped, confined, and cabined in" by narrow forms and legal sophisms.
They held a club at the Pantheon, which the Directory tolerated
for some time, and of which Gracchus Baboeuf was at the head,
who called himself the *Tribune of the People*. He appears to
have been a decided political fanatic, an honest but misled man,
with considerable influence over his immediate associates, for all
enthusiasm is infectious; or rather perhaps there is a certain sort
of minds that are always inoculated with it and ready to break
out. His conspiracy furnishes a striking example among so many
others of the manner in which with persons of this sanguine and
self opinionated cast the strength of the imagination and passions
predominates over sober sense and reason, and makes them firmly
persuaded they have only to grasp at the most extravagant chi-
meras in order to convert them into triumphant realities. Their
brains are heated by their internal impressions, which they mistake for external power and a certainty of success. All reformers, all speculative reasoners, it is to be observed, belong to the
class of those, in whom imagination or the belief and hope of *what
is not* bears sway over *what is*, and are more or less tinctured with
this weakness. The honestest among them are not the least so;
though on the other hand it is true that men of much speculative

refinement in general are not inclined to action, and for the most part confine their extravagance and credulity to words and theories, with which they would have others as well satisfied as they are. It is men of coarser minds and more bustling habits, who when suddenly inspired and intoxicated with some new and dazzling light, cannot be restrained by any consideration of prudence from putting their theories into practice, and rush blindfold upon destruction.

Baboeuf was one of the latter class; he prepared the way, as he said in a sort of journal that he set up, for *the reign of the common good*. The Society of the Pantheon became more numerous from day to day, as well as more alarming to the Directory, who strove at first to circumscribe it within certain bounds. But presently the sittings were prolonged into the night; the democrats met together armed, and talked of nothing less than marching against the Directory and the Councils. On this the Directory shut up their place of meeting in February, 1796, and apprised the legislative body by a message of the step they had taken. The party, thus deprived of their place of rendezvous, had recourse to other expedients; they gained over the soldiers of the *Legion of Police*, who were disarmed in consequence by the Government. They next formed an *Insurrectionary Committee of Public Safety*, which was in intelligence with the lowest of the Parisian rabble. Besides Baboeuf, among the members of this committee were Vadier, Amar, Choudieu, Ricord, Drouet, who belonged to the violent party in the Convention, with the former generals of the decemviral committee, Rossignol, Parrein, Fyon, Lami. A number of displaced officers, patriots driven from the Departments, and the old leaven of the Jacobin Club, formed the strength of this faction. Its chiefs often met at a place which they called the *Temple of Reason:* here they chaunted their lamentations over the fall of Robespierre, and deplored the servitude of the people. They wanted to establish an understanding with the troops of the camp of Grenelle; and with this view admitted among them a Captain belonging to the camp, of the name of Grisel, of whom they thought themselves sure, and concerted the mode of attack with him. Their plan was arranged for purging the commonwealth: it consisted in a community of goods, the calling a convention composed of sixty-eight surviving members of the old Mountain, with the addition of a pure republican from each department: the motto of one of their flags was to be, *Those who usurp the sovereignty ought to be put to death by free men;* every thing was ready, the proclamation printed, the day fixed, when they were betrayed by Grisel, as it commonly happens in the greater number of such conspiracies.

On the 21st of Floreal (May, 1796), the evening before this scheme was to be put in execution, the conspirators were seized in their place of rendezvous. The plan and all the proofs of the conspiracy were found on Babœuf. Considerable alarm was excited by the discovery of the plot. Babœuf, though a prisoner, had the hardihood to propose terms of accommodation to the Directory; and that dismissing him as the chief of a rival faction, they should declare that there had been no conspiracy. The Directory published his letter and sent his accomplices before the high court of Vendôme. Their partisans made one more desperate attempt. In the middle of the night of the 23d of Fructidor they marched in a body of 600 or 700 men, armed with sabres and pistols, against the Directory; but they were stopped by the guard. They then turned their steps to the camp at Grenelle, which they hoped to gain over in consequence of an understanding they still kept up there. The camp was asleep when they arrived. To the challenge of the sentinels, they replied, *Long live the Republic and the Constitution of* 93! The sentinels at this immediately gave the alarm. The assailants, reckoning on the assistance of a battalion which had been displaced, proceeded to the tent of the commandant Malo, who sounded the charge, and made his dragoons mount half-naked on horseback. The conspirators, not prepared for such a reception, made but a feeble resistance: they were sabred by the dragoons and put to flight, after leaving a great number of dead as well as prisoners on the field of battle. This unsuccessful attempt was the death-blow of the party. Besides their loss at the time, a military commission condemned thirty-one of the insurgents to death, thirty more to transportation, and twenty-five to imprisonment.

Shortly after the high court of Vendôme tried Babœuf and his accomplices, among whom were Amar, Vadier, and Darthé, formerly secretary to Joseph Lebon. They did not belie their pre tensions, neither the one or the other; but spoke as men who neither feared to avow their purpose nor to die in defence of their cause. At the commencement and at the end of each examination they struck up the Marseillois. This well-known song of victory, with their stedfast countenance, filled the spectators with awe, and seemed to render them still formidable. Their wives were present in the court. Babœuf, in closing his defence, turned towards them, and said that "they should accompany them even to Calvary, since there was nothing in the cause for which they suffered to make them blush." Babœuf and Darthé were condemned to death; and on hearing their sentence, stabbed themselves. There is something truly affecting in this scene, and it is highly characteristic of the spirit that prevailed in the French Revolution. It shows in the midst of errors, of crimes, and anguish, that ardent zeal for liberty and truth which nothing but death could damp or extinguish; which burnt like a flame on the altar of their country and ascended in loud Hosannas with their latest breath, proclaiming peace on earth, good-will to men. Be it that liberty and truth are but a dream, that men mistake both the means and the end; yet the belief in good and a willingness to die for it will not remain a less proud distinction of those who cherish this "fine madness" as their ruling passion and their final hope, and should preserve their names alike from oblivion and from the tooth of calumny!—In the interval between the attack on Grenelle and the condemnation of Babœuf, the royalists also had their conspiracy. The secret movers of this party hoped (for they too are credulous like all who have strong passions in which they have been disappointed) to find auxiliaries in the troops of the camp of Grenelle, who had repulsed the Babœuf faction. On this idle presumption they employed three men without influence and without name, the Abbé Brothier, an advocate in the old parliament, Lavilheurnois, and a sort of adventurer, one Dunan, to go to the chief commander Malo, and request him simply to give them up the camp of Grenelle and thus enable them to bring back the ancient *régime*. Malo informed the Directory of their application, who delivered them over to the civil tribunals; where, under the influence of the counter-revolutionary spirit which at this time was the fashion, they were treated with

great lenity and escaped with a short imprisonment as their only
punishment.   These men were martyrs and confessors in their
way ; yet I cannot bring myself to write their panegyric.   Romantic generosity suits but ill with servility of spirit ; and he
who shows himself a hero in order to become a slave or make
others so, can hope for little disinterested sympathy.   There is a
want of keeping and of consequent effect.

Buonaparte severely criticises the government of the Directory ; and this is but natural in him, as he must wish to find reasons for having finally stripped them of their authority.   The
Republican calendar had divided the year into twelve equal
months of thirty days, and the months into *décades ;* Sunday
was abolished, and the *décadi,* or tenth day, had been appointed
as the day of rest.   The Directory, not satisfied with this idle
and fanciful measure, went, he says, still farther, and prohibited
the people under regular penalties from working on the *décadi*
and from resting on the Sunday, employing the peace-officers,
*gensdarmes,* and others, to enforce the execution of these absurd
regulations.   The people were thus tormented and exposed to
persecution and vexation for matters with which the state had
nothing to do, and all this in the name of liberty and the rights
of man.   Nothing renders a government unpopular or excites
hatred and contempt sooner than a disposition to interfere in trifles,
and without any reason but the itch of governing.   The new
system of weights and measures was another grievance complained of.   The want of uniformity in French weights and measures
was an inconvenience that had been long felt ; and it was expected among other things that the Revolution would have corrected this evil.   The remedy was in fact simple and at hand ; it
was to render the system of weights and measures used in the
city of Paris, and which had been also employed by the Government and artists for centuries, common throughout all the provinces.   Instead of this, the Government, who at that time did
every thing upon a grand scale of abstraction, consulted the alge-
braists and geometricians upon a question of practical utility
who soon hit upon a system which neither agreed with the regulations of the public administration, with the tables of dimensions
used in all arts, nor with those of any of the existing machines.

Nor would other nations have agreed to this, which was meant to
be an universal benefit to the world. What would the English,
for instance, have said to it? The new system not only was at
variance with common sense and custom, and required all the
calculations of the arts and sciences to be reversed, but was in
itself impracticable and unintelligible. It converted the commonest
affairs of life into an abstruse mathematical calculation. Thus a
soldier's ration is expressed by twenty-four ounces in the old nomenclature; this is a very simple process; but when translated
into the new one, it becomes seven hundred and thirty-four
grammes and two hundred and fifty-nine thousandths. All the
dimensions and lines that compose architectural works, all the
tools and measures used in clock-making, jewellery, paper-
making, and the other mechanic arts, had been invented and calculated according to the ancient nomenclature, and were expressed by simple numbers, which must now be represented by
five or six figures. Another disadvantage was, that the *savans*
introduced Greek roots, which farther multiplied difficulties; for
these denominations, though they might be useful to the learned,
only perplexed the common people. But the Directory made the
weights and measures one of the principal affairs of Government.
Instead of leaving it to time to work the change, and merely en-
couraging the new system by the power of example and fashion,
they made compulsory laws and had them rigorously executed.
Merchants and artisans found themselves harassed about matters
in themselves indifferent; and this increased the unpopularity of
a government which placed itself above the wants and the reach
of the people, infringing on their habits and usages with all the
violence that might be expected from a Tartar conqueror. It is
always bad policy in a government to meddle more than it can
help with the concerns of private life, which individuals understand so much better than mere theorists, thus subjecting itself at
once to the charge of meanness and incapacity.

Another thing which gave no small degree of umbrage, was
the favor shown to the sect of Theophilanthropists and the dis-
countenancing of the Catholic priests. Many were hurt and
scandalized at this preference, which in some cases took the
shape of intolerance. The Directory had all voted for the death

of the King. It was therefore thought they would favor such of their colleagues in the Convention as had been re-elected to the Councils. But the contrary was the case. The Title of a *Conventional* had become a term of reproach; and the Directory, by shunning all intercourse with them, sought to avoid the disgrace that might be reflected back upon themselves. The men of 1793 were at first disposed to attach themselves to the new order of things, but were repelled and chilled by a number of ungracious acts; and being driven to extremities, they conspired together to deliver themselves from the yoke of the *Five Gentlemen of the Luxembourg*, as the Directors were called in derision. On the other hand, the Government affected to gain partisans in the privileged classes, but, as might be expected, without success. These could feel little respect for persons who had not the advantages of birth and rank on their side, who had not distinguished themselves by any signal services, and who, with the exception of Carnot, were not men of very decided or prominent character. There is something fluttering and unsteady in the French character, which must either be awed by fear or shackled by prejudice or dazzled by success. The Directory were placed at the head of the Government on none of these grounds, but merely because being men of good intentions and of active habits they maintained the tranquillity and equipoise of the Republic—the very reason which induced the plotting and restless spirits who could not live without violence and change, to wish to get rid of them. In this manner the two extreme parties were brought forward again; the Republicans from being discountenanced, the privileged classes from being courted. The Jacobins had tried their fortune, and had been foiled. It was now the turn of the Royalists.

The elections of the year 5 (May 1797) were favorable to this party. They had possessed a minority of some consequence in the preceding legislative bodies, having at its head such men as Barbé-Marbois, Pastoret, Dumas, Portalis, Simeon, Vaublanc. Fronçon-Ducoudray, Dupont de Nemours, and others; but they waited for the succor they expected from the new third (the choice of which they influenced by every method of intimidation and intrigue) before they commenced an open attack on the government. From the first opening of the new Chambers, the spirit which animated them was pretty evident. Pichegru, who was called by his party the French General Monk, was elected president of the Council of Five Hundred; and Barbé-Marbois with the same intention president of the Council of Ancients. The legislative body then proceeded to the nomination of a Director to replace Letourneur, who went out by rote, and the choice fell upon Barthelemy, ambassador to Switzerland; whose views coincided with those of the party who, now that the Revolution had done all the mischief, wished to prevent all the good it might do, and to heal the wounds of their country by throwing themselves with insane gratitude and fawning submission into the arms of those who had deliberately caused them. This strange and voluntary bias of a large proportion of a people to return to a slavery that had bowed them down for centuries, and to escape from which had cost oceans of blood and indignities unparalleled, is one of those phenomena in the history of modern times, which would be wholly unaccountable but for the fascination and despotic influence which power in the abstract (and the older and more corrupt the more it is an object of veneration) exercises over the imagination of the thoughtless, the cowardly, and the selfish, who feel pride only in having a master, ease and security, in chains!

This band of parasites and renegades proceeded systematically and artfully to their end. They reproached the Directory with the continuance of the war, as if the foreign cabinets only waited a nod from them to put an end to it; with the disorder of the finances, as if regularity and neatness were the properties of a volcano; they insisted on the unrestrained liberty of the press, in order that venal journalists might strike at the root of all liberty, and invoke tyranny as their tutelary saint; they recommended peace, as a preliminary step to disarming the Republic, economy as a means of crippling her armies. The nation, willing to listen to reason and too ready to trust to fair appearances, shared in these professed demands, but not in their secret intention. They longed for peace, but not to purchase it at the expense of all the objects for which they had contended, and which they had obtained. They had repelled the Bourbons by force of

arms and by efforts of heroic courage; they did not wish tamely,
for mere mental cowardice and in a fit of mawkish sentimen-
tality (won over by elegiac strains or high-flown rhapsodies) to
bow their necks to the yoke of the vanquished. They had been
provoked by foreign aggression and internal discord to commit
acts of violence and outrage, and had been condemned to endure
and inflict much evil in the arduous struggle ; but they did not
choose to set the seal to their own infamy, and by not only dis-
avowing the excesses, but by abandoning the principles of the
Revolution, to give those all the credit and the triumph of this
dereliction of common sense and natural feeling, who had, by
making war on its principles, given rise to its excesses, and had
constantly fomented the calamities of the country in order to lead
to such a deplorable relapse. They might wish to forget their
sufferings and wipe out the stain of their errors or their passions,
but they would best do this by making a good use of the advan-
tagés they had gained, and by consolidating the elements of freedom, which had hitherto stood the shock of all opposition, and not
by running from the extremes of licentiousness into those of servility, thus leaving themselves without a shadow of excuse in the
strength of their attachment to the principles of liberty, and
showing that their loyalty was equally a sudden mechanical impulse, the whim of the moment, without object or consistency.
They would thus indeed deservedly become the bye-word of Europe, and would earn the insulting appellation of *half-tiger, half-
monkey,* which had been set upon them. If they had in moments
of frenzy outraged humanity, that was no reason why they should
deliberately betray it. They would in that case have more reason to blush for the tardy reparation than for the original wrong.
They did not wish the priests to be imprisoned or banished in a
body, on the ground of their religion or on mere suspicion of disaffection ; but neither did it seem equitable that under pretence
of liberality and toleration, they should have exclusive distinctions granted them, or be exempted from the common oath of allegiance to the state, that so they might preach sedition with impunity, sow the seeds of dissension and massacres, and when they
themselves became the sufferers by the hostility they had provoked, turn with pleading hands and a countenance of meek, in-

jured innocence, to the patrons of religion and social order, and help to scatter fire-brands and kindle a Holy War throughout Europe! Carnot, one of the firmest and most upright characters of the Revolution, was led away by this change in opinion, and being uneasy at the reproaches cast upon him as a member of the Committee of Public Safety, was willing to efface the recollection by associating himself with the *preux chevaliers* or equivocal patriots, who met at the Clichy Club. This was a weakness; but his subsequent conduct proved, that though he sought to escape odium and have the good word of this knot of intriguers and busybodies, he did not at all enter into their views or principles. Or he might tamper with the proposals and allurements of power when he saw no prospect of their being realized, which, when it came to the push and his country was in danger, he resisted with all his might. Such persons may be said to repent *before the fact* of their desertion of principle, as others of weaker minds do *after it*, when it is too late.

Camille-Jordan, the deputy from Lyons, a young man of considerable eloquence and spirit, but vain and extravagant, distinguished himself by a pompous panegyric on the refractory clergy, and by a proposal to restore the use of bells as peculiar to the Catholic worship. There is in this a common reaction of opinion, by means of which, as new fashions become old and the old ones new, so the petulance and egotism of the young and giddy are piqued in affecting a superiority to the prevailing tone and established maxims, and antiquated prejudices and exploded mummery are revived as brilliant and adventurous paradoxes, which show a manly and independent way of thinking. Thus Chateaubriand afterwards published an eulogy on Christianity, not out of conviction, but thinking it would strike as a singularity, for I cannot help supposing there was a vast difference between his belief in Christianity and Fenelon's; and borrowed from Sir Robert Filmer the old story of passive obedience and non-resistance, which he gave out as a startling light and compunctious visitation of his own conscience. Camille-Jordan's first and lively sally in this retrograde path of philosophical discovery did not meet with the same success. *His* quackery was not backed by five hundred thousand bayonets. He got himself the nickname of *Jordan*

*Carillon* (Jordan of the Chimes.) His motion to render the priests independent of the state and of all political obligations, was negatived in the Council of Five Hundred, who sanctioned the civic oath with acclamations of *Vive la Republic!*

Every thing seemed to announce a crisis. The refractory priests and emigrants returned in crowds. Reprisals were common in the departments against the most noted revolutionists and the holders of the national domains. The attacks of the Councils on the Directory became more frequent and undisguised, which, however, lost them the confidence of the mass of the people, who were not disposed to any serious change. The army joined enthusiastically in expressing their sentiments of fidelity; and the Government made Hoche advance with several regiments of the Army of the Sambre and Meuse near Paris, passing the constitutional barrier—a violation of the law of which the Councils complained loudly, and of which the Directory excused themselves by pretending ignorance. Carnot in vain attempted a reconciliation between the two opposite parties. He had attached himself to Barthelemy, with whom he formed a minority in the Directory against Barras, Rewbell, and La Reveillère. These were inclined to try a *coup d'état* against the Councils, while Carnot (through a timidity, the result of previous over-daring) was bent upon adhering to the letter of the law. The Councils next endeavored to introduce their party into the Government by proposing a change of ministry; but instead of attending to their recommendation, the Directory displaced only those whom they wished to keep in, and Benezech was succeeded by François de Neufchâteau as Minister of the Interior, Petiet by Hoche and soon after by Sherer as Minister at war, and Cochon de l'Apparent by Lenoir Laroche, and Laroche by Sotin, as Minister of Police. Talleyrand also crept into the bosom of the Government on this occasion, which he afterwards stung to death. The struggle drew nearer and nearer, and the Directory was anxious to put it off till another year, when the new elections would in all probability have decided its fate and that of the Republic. They encouraged violent addresses against the Legislative Body from the armies. Augereau brought that from the Army of Italy, by Buonaparte's desire; and had the 18th of Fructidor turned out differently, he

himself was prepared to follow with 15,000 men, expel the royalists, and place himself at the head of the popular party.    This
address ran thus :—" Tremble, Royalists !   From the Adige to
the Seine there is but one step.    Tremble !   Your iniquities are
counted, and you will find that their reward is at the end of our
bayonets."   " It is with indignation," said the address of the
état-major, " that we have seen the cause of liberty menaced by
the intrigues of royalists.    We have sworn, by the names of the
heroes who have died for their country, implacable enmity to royalists and royalty.    Such are our sentiments, such are yours,"
(to the Directory,) "such are those of all good patriots.    Let the
royalists show themselves, and they will have ceased to live !"
The Councils remonstrated, but to no purpose, against the interference of the army.    General Richepanse, who commanded the
troops that had arrived from the frontier, stationed them at Versailles, Meudon, and Vincennes.

The Councils meantime increased the powers of the Commission of Inspectors of the Hall, to which Willot and Pichegru belonged.    On the 17th of Fructidor, the Legislative Body voted
the formation of a National Guard and the removal of the regular troops ; and the following day Willott proposed that if these
measures were not complied with, they should decree the arrest
of Barras, Rewbell, and La Reveillère, march against the Directory with Pichegru at their head, and overturn the Government.
It is said that Pichegru hesitated, and thus lost the game he had
been so long playing for.    This was not the case with the Directory.    They determined to aim an instant blow at Carnot, Barthelemy, and the majority of the Legislature.    The morning of
the following day (September 4th) was fixed upon for the execution of their plan.    During the night the troops encamped
round Paris entered the city, under the command of Augereau.
The intention of the triumvirate was to make the soldiers occupy the Thuilleries before the meeting of the Legislative Body,
in order to avoid the scandal of a violent expulsion ; to convoke
the Councils in the neighborhood of the Luxembourg, after having arrested their principal agitators, and to accomplish, by an
official measure, what had been begun by force.    They were in intelligence with the Minority of the Councils, and hoped for the

approbation of the mass. At one in the morning the troops arrived at the Hôtel-de-Ville, and dispersed themselves along the quays, on the bridges, in the Champs-Elysées, and shortly 12,000 men and forty pieces of cannon surrounded the Thuilleries. At four o'clock the alarm-gun was fired; and General Augereau presented himself at the grate of the Pont-Tournant.

The guard of the Legislative Body was under arms. The Inspectors of the Hall, apprised over-night of the intended movement, had gone to the Thuilleries to block up the entrance. Ramel, the Commander of the Guard, was devoted to the Councils, and had placed his eight hundred grenadiers in the divers avenues of the garden which was closed by iron gates. But it was not with so small and uncertain a force that Pichegru, Willot, and Ramel could offer an effectual resistance to the Directory. Augereau had not even occasion to force the passage of the Pont-Tournant; he was no sooner in sight of the grenadiers than he called out to them, " Are you Republicans ?" and these, lowering their arms, replied, " *Long live Augereau! Long live the Directory!*"—and immediately joined him. Augereau then crossed the Garden of the Thuilleries, reached the Hall of the Councils, arrested Pichegru, Willot, Ramel, all the Inspectors, and had them conveyed to the Temple. The members of the Councils, called together in haste, repaired in crowds to the place of their sittings, but were arrested or conducted back by the armed force. Augereau informed them that the Directory, urged by the necessity of defending the Republic against conspirators sitting in the midst of them, had designated the Odeon and the School of Medicine as the places of their meeting. The greater number of the deputies present exclaimed against military violence and the usurpation of the Directory; but they were compelled to yield.

At six in the morning the enterprise was completed. The Parisians, when they awoke, found the troops still under arms, and the walls placarded with proclamations which announced the detection of a formidable conspiracy. The people were invited to maintain order and tranquillity. As soon as the Councils were assembled at the Odeon and the School of Medicine in sufficient numbers to deliberate, they declared themselves permanent. A message from the Directory acquainted them with the motives of

the steps it had just taken. It was to this effect : "Citizen Legislators, if the Directory had waited a day longer, the Republic
would have been delivered up into the power of its enemies.
The very place of your sittings was the point of communication
between the conspirators ; it was from thence that they distributed
money and tickets for the delivery of arms ; it is from thence that
they corresponded during this night with their accomplices ; it is
from thence, or in the neighborhood, that they yet strive to collect seditious and clandestine assemblages of their partisans, which
the police are at this moment employed in dispersing. It would
have been to compromise the public safety and that of the Deputies who continued faithful to their trust, to have suffered them to
remain confounded with the enemies of the country in a den of
conspirators." A commission, composed of Siéyes, Poulain-
Grandpré, Villars, Chazal, and Boulay de la Meurthe, was ordered by the Council of Five Hundred to present a law of public
safety on the occasion. By this law two of the Directors were
sentenced to banishment, with fifty-two Deputies, and one hundred
and forty-eight private individuals, journalists and others; the
elections of several departments were annulled, new measures of
public security were decreed, the nomination of Carnot and Barthelemy to the Executive Directory was set aside, and they were
replaced by Merlin and François de Neufchâteau. Most of those
who were included in this sweeping condemnation were sent to
Cayenne, but several went no farther than the Isle of Rhé.
Carnot, who had warning given him the night preceding, escaped
to Geneva. Thus the scheme of the Royalist party was defeated
by a vigor beyond the law, but scarcely beyond the occasion.
The plan, at least of those who were in the true secret of the
plot, had been to discredit and weaken the Directory, to fill it
with their creatures, and then to proclaim a counter-revolution,
as the only remedy for the calamities which afflicted the country.
Buonaparte finds fault with the severity and precipitation used
by the Directory at this juncture, and their conduct appears in
some instances to have been rash and ill-judged. They would
not, or could not, discriminate between accidental aberrations and
rooted hostility and lukewarmness. He himself afterwards tried
the opposite scheme of forbearance and lenity, and composed an

administration of neutrals and reclaimed renegades. The event was answerable; for by giving power to your adversaries, you do not make them your friends : nor do personal favors alter the sentiments of individuals, except by corrupting their principles, which is a bad ground of confidence and attachment.

The public was at first equally astonished and incredulous as to the measures of the 18th and 19th of Fructidor. It was suspected that D'Entraigue's papers and Duverne's discoveries (the evidence to which the Directory had hitherto appealed) were forged ; but all doubt ceased and men's minds were satisfied when the following proclamation appeared, addressed by Moreau to his army, and dated from his head-quarters at Strasburg, 23d of Fructidor (September 9, 1797) :—"Soldiers, I have this instant received the proclamation of the Executive Directory, dated the 18th of this month, informing France that Pichegru has rendered himself unworthy of the confidence with which he has so long inspired the whole Republic and the armies in particular. I have also been informed that several military men, too confident in the patriotism of that representative, and considering the services he had rendered to the state, doubted this assertion. I owe it to my brethren in arms and fellow-citizens to declare the truth. It is but too true that Pichegru has betrayed the confidence of all France. On the 17th of this month I informed one of the members of the Directory that a correspondence with Condé and other agents of the Pretender had fallen into my hands, which left no doubt of these treasonable acts. The Directory has summoned me to Paris, requiring, no doubt, more complete information respecting this correspondence. Soldiers, be calm, and dismiss all anxiety respecting the state of affairs at home ; depend upon it that the Government will keep down the royalists, and vigilantly maintain the republican constitution which you have sworn to defend."

On the 24th (September 10) Moreau wrote as follows to the Directory :—"I did not receive your order to set out for Paris till a very late hour on the 22d, when I was ten leagues from Strasburg. Some hours were necessary for me to make arrangements for my departure, to secure the tranquillity of the army, and to apprehend several persons compromised in an interesting correspondence which I shall myself deliver to you. I send you subjoined a proclamation which I have issued, which has had the effect of convincing many incredulous persons; and I confess I find it difficult to believe that a man who had done his country such important services, and had no interest in betraying it, could have been guilty of such infamous conduct. I was thought to be a friend of Pichegrú; but I have long ceased to esteem him. You will see that no one was in greater danger than myself, for the whole scheme was founded on the expected reverses of the army which I commanded: its courage has saved the Republic."

There is an extremely conscious exculpatory tone in all this, which, coupled with subsequent transactions and the tardy exposure of Pichegru's plot, throws a very suspicious light on Moreau's character and intentions even at this early period. The letter which he alludes to as having been addressed to Barthelemy (a very safe depository for such a letter in case the plan had not been defeated) was as follows: "Citizen Director—You will recollect, no doubt, that on my last visit to Bâle, I informed you that at the passage of the Rhine we took a waggon from General Kinglin, containing two or three hundred letters of his correspondence; those of Wittersbach formed part of them, but were the least important. Many of these letters are in cypher, but we have found out the key to them: the whole are now decyphering, which occupies much time. No person is called by his real name in these letters, so that many Frenchmen who are in correspondence with Kinglin, Condé, Wickham, D'Enghien, and others, are not easily discovered. We have nevertheless such indications, that several are already known. I had determined not to give publicity to this correspondence, since, as peace might be presumed at hand, there seemed to be no danger to the Republic: besides, these papers could have afforded proofs against but few persons, as no one is named in them. But seeing at the head of the parties which are now doing so much mischief to our country, and in possession of an eminent situation of the highest confidence, a man deeply implicated in this correspondence and intended to act an important part in the recal of the Pretender (the object to which it relates), I have thought it my duty to apprise you of the circumstance, that you may not be duped by his pretended republicanism; that you may watch over his proceedings, and oppose his fatal projects against our country, since nothing but a civil war can be the object of his schemes. I confess, Citizen Director, that it is with deep regret that I inform you of this treason, and the more so, because the man I denounce to you was once my friend, and would certainly have continued so still, had I not detected him. I speak of the representative of the people, Pichegru. He has been too prudent to commit any thing to writing; he only communicated verbally with those who were entrusted with this correspondence, who carried his proposals and received his answers. He is designated under several names, that of Baptiste among others. A Brigadier-General, named Badouville, was attached to him, and is mentioned by the name of *Coco.* He was one of the couriers whom Pichegru and the other correspondents employed; you must have seen him frequently at Bâle. Their grand movement was to have taken place at the beginning of the campaign of the year IV. They reckoned on the probable occurrence of some disasters on my taking the command of the army: which, as they expected, discontented at its defeat, would call for its old commander, who in that case was to have acted according to circumstances and the instructions he would have received. He was to have 900 louis-d'ors for the journey which he took to Paris at the time of his discharge; which accounts in a natural way for his refusing the Swedish embassy. I suspect the Lajolais family of being concerned in this plot. The confidence which I have in your patriotism and prudence alone determined me to give you this intelligence. The proofs are as clear as day; but I doubt whether they are judicial. I entreat you, Citizen Director, to have the goodness to assist me with your advice on this perplexing occasion. You know me well enough to conceive how dear this disclosure costs me; nothing less than the danger which threatened my country could have induced me to make it. The secret is confined to five persons; General Desaix, General Regnier, one of my aides-de camp, and an officer engaged in the secret service of the army, who is constantly employed in pursuing the clue of information afforded by the decyphered letters."

The letters found in Kinglin's waggon were soon after pub-

lished ; proofs of Pichegru's treachery came pouring in from all
sides ; and he became the object of general detestation.    When
Napoleon heard of the result of the 18th of Fructidor, he expressed great dissatisfaction with the conduct of the Directory.
They had included in the same unsparing proscription persons
who were concerned in plotting the destruction of the Republic,
and who were known to be in correspondence with its enemies,
and those of whose guilt there was either no proof, or who were
in the main, notwithstanding any minor differences of opinion or
momentary disgusts, among its staunchest and warmest friends.
He would have had Pichegru, Willot, Imbert Colomés, and two
or three more of that stamp, brought to trial, and condemned to
expiate on the scaffold the crimes which they had committed, and
of which Government possessed the proofs ; and he would have
had those who were suspected to have listened to or not revealed
their intrigues, deprived of their functions and placed under inspection in the interior, as a measure of necessary precaution ;
but here he would have stopped.    He was shocked to see men of
great talents, who had done much for the Revolution, and of whose
defection there was no proof but conjecture or hearsay, condemned to perish, without trial or evidence, in the marshes of
Sinnamari.    So far he was right in this discrimination of classes
and degrees of delinquency, and in making some entire exceptions ; but whether he was right in calling the most dissatisfied
and lukewarm of this band of negative patriots to some of the
chief offices of the state afterwards, is a question that admits of
great doubt, and the measure was hardly justified by the event.

In October, 1796, the English Government had consented to
treat for peace with the French Republic, and sent Lord Malmesbury over to Paris for that purpose ; but the cession of Belgium
to Austria was a stumbling-block in the way, and the negociations
were broken off.    It was on this occasion that Mr. Burke wrote
his celebrated pamphlet against a *Regicide Peace*.    The preliminary treaty of Leoben, by which the Emperor relinquished Belgium, induced the English to renew the proposal, and Lord Malmesbury repaired to Lisle.    A favorable issue was expected, and a
treaty was on the point of being concluded on terms more advantageous to France than those of the peace of Amiens ; when the

events of the 18th of Fructidor taking place, the Directory, elated
with success, raised their demands; the conferences were broken
off; and Lord Malmesbury wrote over from London to say that
the English Cabinet would send no more plenipotentiaries till
it was better convinced of the sincerity of the French Government, or of the stability and reasonableness of its views and engagements.

# CHAPTER XVI.

### BUONAPARTE'S RETURN TO PARIS IN 1797.

NAPOLEON, during the two years of his campaigns in Italy, had filled all Europe with the renown of his arms, which gave the first stunning blow to the Coalition. Fame, after having slept a thousand years, seemed to have seized her ancient trump ; and, as in the early periods of Greece and Rome, freedom smiled on victory. Those who ever felt the dawn of a brighter day, that spring-time of hope and glow of exultation, animate their breasts, cannot easily be taught to forget it, either in the dazzling glare or cheerless gloom that was to succeed it. But it is perhaps, enough for great actions to *have been*, and still to be remembered when they have ceased to be ; and thus to stir the mind in after-ages with mingled awe, admiration, and regret.

On Napoleon's arrival in Paris, the leaders of the different parties were eager to call upon him, and to make him different offers, to which he paid little seeming attention. The streets and squares through which he was expected to pass were constantly crowded with people, curious to see the gainer of so many battles, who but seldom showed himself. The Institute having chosen him one of its members, he adopted its costume. He had no regular visitors, except a few men of science, such as Monge, Berthollet, Borda, Laplace, Prony, and Lagrange ; Generals Berthier, Desaix, Lefebvre, Caffarelli Dufalga, Kleber, and a very few deputies. He had a public audience given him by the Directory, who had scaffoldings erected in the Place du Luxembourg for the ceremony, the ostensible reason for which was the delivery of the treaty of Campo-Formio. In his address to the Directory, he made use of the following expressions, which were considered as remarkable at the time, and which did not become less so in their application to subsequent events. " In order to

attain freedom, the French people had to fight with the Allied
Kings; and to obtain a constitution founded on reason, they had
to combat the prejudices of eighteen centuries. Superstition, the
feudal system, and despotism have successively governed Europe
for twenty ages; but the era of representative governments may
be dated from the peace which you have just concluded. You
have accomplished the organization of the Great Nation, whose
vast territories are bounded only by the limits which nature herself has set to them. I present you the treaty of Campo-Formio,
ratified by the Emperor. This peace secures the liberty, prosperity, and glory of the Republic. When the happiness of the
French people shall be established upon the best-founded laws,
the whole of Europe will become free."

The same reflection almost unavoidably occurs here as that suggested in the line in Hamlet—"Methinks the lady doth profess too
much." But as Buonaparte's power and reputation hitherto had
been connected with the triumph of the broad principles of the
Revolution, they would naturally still predominate in his mind,
whatever designs might lurk there pointing to a different conclusion. The floating visions of ambition and power had not yet acquired solidity or consistency enough to afford a practical counterpoise to the world of opinion and feeling around him. Men
take their hue from surrounding objects and circumstances, till
they can mould them in their turn; and scarcely acknowledge or
bestow a glance of approbation on their own projects of aggrandizement or selfish policy, till they are ripe for execution, and seem
by the near prospect of success to justify the attempt. Generals
Joubert and Andreossy on this occasion carried the standard
which the Legislative Body had presented to the Army of Italy,
with the chief actions which it had performed inscribed in letters
of gold. The Directory, the Legislative Body, and the Minister
for Foreign Affairs gave entertainments to Napoleon. He appeared at them, but only for a short time. At the house of Talleyrand, a celebrated woman (Madame de Stael) wishing to enter
the lists with the Conqueror of Italy, addressed him in the
midst of a numerous circle, desiring to know who in his opinion
was the greatest woman in the world, dead or alive? "*She who
has borne the greatest number of children*," was the answer. This

was the commencement of a long and galling rivalry between the
wit and the future statesman.   People thronged to the sittings of
the Institute for the purpose of seeing Napoleon, who usually took
his place there between Laplace and Lagrange, the latter of whom
was sincerely attached to him.   He never attended the theatre
except in a private box ;  and declined a proposal from the man-
agers of the Opera, who wished to give a grand representation in
honor of him.   When he afterwards appeared in public on his return from Egypt, his person was still unknown to the inhabitants
of Paris, who flocked eagerly to see him.   This shyness was not,
as it may be thought, affected or the result of policy, but natural.
It was the coming forward that was forced or like assuming a
part.   His temper was in itself reserved, and all his habits plain
and simple.   Besides, true glory always shrinks from the public
gaze and admiration, except on rare and appropriate occasions ;
it has " that within which passes show ;"  and mere personal appearance or external homage can but ill correspond with and but
imperfectly express the great things it has performed, or the
greater which it meditates.   It was well for Napoleon when he
had, in the decline of his fortune, to show himself at the loop-holes
of the Thuilleries on " some raw and gusty day," in answer to
the cries of a few idle boys who shouted " Vive l'Empereur!" under his window, that he could recal a time when he had withdrawn from the tumultuous and extravagant demonstrations of
popular applause, and only submitted to it as a state necessity, or
when the course of public events forced it upon him.

The Directory kept up an appearance of the greatest cordiality.
When they thought proper to consult him, they used to send one
of the Ministers to request him to assist at the Council, where he
took his seat between two of them, and delivered his opinion on
the matters in question.   At the same time, the troops as they returned to France extolled him to the skies in their songs and in
their talk ; declaring that it was time to turn the lawyers out, and
make him king.   The Directory carried the affectation of candor
so far as to show him the secret reports which were made by the
police on the subject, though they could not conceal the jealousy
and mortification which all this popularity excited in their minds.
Napoleon was aware of the delicacy and difficulty of his situation.

There was evidently something behind the Government greater than the Government itself. The proceedings of the administration were by no means popular, and many persons turned their eyes on the conqueror of Italy. The Directory proposed to him to return to Rastadt; but he refused to do so, on the ground that his mission into Italy had terminated at Campo-Formio, and it no longer became him to wield both the pen and the sword. Soon after this he consented to accept the command of the Army of England, as a cover to the design and preparations for the expedition into Egypt. The troops composing this army were quartered in Normandy, Picardy, and Belgium. Their new General visited every point, but chose to travel *incognito* through the Departments. His public reputation did not yet come up to his idea of himself. These secret journeys contributed to increase the anxiety of the British Government, and to mask the preparations making in the South of France. It was at this period that he visited Antwerp, and conceived the plan of the important naval establishments which he carried into execution under the Empire. It was also in one of these journeys that he perceived the great advantages which St. Quentin would derive from the canal which was opened under the Consulate; and gave the preference to Boulogne over Calais, from the circumstance of the tide, for the purpose of attempting a descent upon England in boats. Nothing can be more shallow or unjust than the imputation so often thrown out against Buonaparte that he was a mere soldier, and was compelled to go to war because he had no talents for or resources in peace. He had a mind and eye at all times alive and intent on whatever objects could aggrandize or adorn his country, either in peace or war, and, as he said of himself, "there was not an understanding in all France more essentially *civil* than his." His only fault was, that as he had a great capacity for business of every kind and an indefatigable activity, he wished to extend his influence too far beyond what is consistent with human ability or the nature of human affairs, and sunk under the attempt to subject every thing to his control, as if he possessed a kind of omnipresence.

He had about this period several subjects of difference with the Directory, in few of which his advice prevailed. The first was the line of conduct to be observed towards Switzerland. France had serious grounds of complaint against the canton of Berne and the Swiss aristocracy; all the foreign agents who had been employed to raise disturbances in France, had constantly made Berne their chief place of rendezvous. A fit occasion had now arrived for destroying the preponderance of this aristocracy, by means of the great influence which the Republic had lately acquired in Europe. Buonaparte approved highly of the resentment of the Directory at the intrigues and machinations carried on against France, and was for seizing this opportunity for putting an end to them; but he did not think it necessary for that purpose to overturn every thing in the country. The proper course appeared to him to be, for the French Ambassador to present a note to the Helvetic Diet, supported by two camps, one in Savoy, the other in Franche-Comté; and to declare by this note that France and Italy considered it essential to their policy, their safety, and the tranquillity of all parties, that the Pays-de-Vaud, Argau, and the Italian bailiwicks should become free and independent cantons, on an equal footing with the other cantons; that they had reason to complain of the aristocracy of certain families of Berne, Soleure, and Fribourg; but that they would consign all these causes of discontent to oblivion, provided the peasants of those cantons and of the Italian Bailiwicks were reinstated in their original rights. These moderate changes might have been effected without difficulty, and without resorting to arms; but Rewbell, over-persuaded, by some zealous Swiss patriot, had got a different system in his head; and the Directory, without paying the least attention to the manners, religion, or local peculiarities of the different cantons, resolved upon giving Switzerland a constitution exactly similar to that of France. The small cantons were enraged at the loss of their liberty; the rest took up arms in defence of their immunities, and much blood was shed in appeasing a fruitless and unnecessary quarrel. This was furnishing a handle to the fears and jealousy of the continental powers; and violating (without any adequate motive) an asylum long held sacred to liberty. Switzerland was *rhetorical* ground: and in a war of names and prejudices, ought not in prudence to have been meddled with. Buonaparté himself fell into the same snare afterwards, tempted by the same bait, the love of power and interference. The inde-pendence of Switzerland thenceforth became one of the watch-words of the Allied Sovereigns, and a standing common-place in the list of phrases of their hireling declaimers. It is curious to see Napoleon, not only remonstrating against the conduct of the Directory beforehand, but inveighing against it with bitterness and derision even after he himself had been led to imitate the weak and unsound part of it. He should have taken warning, and let Switzerland alone ; his not doing it was making war upon the name and language of liberty, often of more consequence than the thing itself!

Not satisfied with waking the echoes of ancient liberty in the rocks and valleys of Switzerland, the Directory were determined to bring all the owls and bats about their ears that were likely to be dislodged from the crumbling ruins of papal superstition. The court of Rome even after the treaty of Tolentino, urged on by its disappointments and disregarding its engagements, still chose to persist in its hostility against the French name, quarrelled with the Cisalpine Republic, again placed an Austrian General (Provera) at the head of its troops, and excited a popular tumult ; in attempting to quell which Duphot, a young General of the greatest promise, and who happened to be at this time at Rome on his travels, was murdered at the gate of the French Ambassa-dor's palace. The latter withdrew to Florence. Napoleon when consulted replied that " *Events ought not to govern policy, but policy events ;* that however wrong the court of Rome might be, the object was not to punish its folly or presumption, but to pre-vent the recurrence of similar accidents in future ; that for this purpose it would be best not to overturn the Holy See, but to require that it should make an example of the guilty, send away Provera, compose its ministry of the most moderate prelates, and conclude a Concordat with the Cisalpine Republic, which might prepare men's minds for something like a similar arrangement at a future period with the French Republic." But all this, except the last, had been tried before and failed. The Directory there-fore (this time led by Lepaux) determined to give the rein to their resentment and revolutionary zeal, to march against the Pope, and dethrone that idol of slavish superstition. They

thought that the words *Roman Republic* would act as a talisman
and kindle all Italy into a flame. They did not at all approve
of the half-measures suggested and pursued by Napoleon, his
neutralizing the spirit of liberty and tampering with the remains
of antiquated bigotry ; and threw out shrewd hints that he might
have his private views in all this caution and moderation, and
that not only by his considerate behavior to the Pope, but by his
zealous anxiety for the exiled priests, he wished to gain friends
(and indeed had done so) among those who were not the friends
of the Revolution. The idea that the attack on Rome might
bring on a war with Naples they treated as altogether chimerical. Berthier accordingly received orders to march an army on
Rome, and to re-establish the old Roman Republic, which was done
without delay. The Capitol once more beheld Consuls, a Senate, and a Tribunate. Fourteen Cardinals went in procession to
St. Peter's to sing *Te Deum* in commemoration of the restoration
of the Roman Republic, and the destruction of the throne of St.
Peter. Really in reading over such accounts as these, one is not
surprised at Mr. Burke's expression of "the grand carnival and
masquerade of this our age," applied to the freaks and absurdities of the French Revolution, though no one contributed more
to them than he did by impeding its natural and salutary course
with the rubbish of mouldering prejudices and venal sophistry.
One would suppose from the scene acted on this occasion that
states were built up and Republics manufactured on the same
principle that children build houses with packs of cards. But
revolutions must be accomplished, like other things, according to
nature. The fabric of society must grow up from a solid foundation, and its improvements be effected by the wide-spread and
gradual triumph of general principles, and not by the sudden
changes of scenery or preposterous assumptions of character, that
are met with in a pantomime. Power and authority has its date ;
and different systems and maxims prevail at different periods of
the world, and sweep away all traces of those which went before
them ; but to suppose that we can disarm inveterate bigotry and
crimson pride by a few cant-phrases, that we can decompose the
texture of men's minds and the inmost passions of their souls by
infusing into them our own opinions of yesterday, or that we can

get the very props and pillars of an ancient edifice of superstition to become accessary to their own condemnation and to walk in the pageant of their own disgrace, is contrary to all we know of history or human nature.   To make an adversary an accomplice in the triumph over him, is a cruel mockery : those on the other hand who suppose that others are sincere converts to a cause that takes all their power and self-consequence from them, or thrusts them out from being installed as the oracles of truth or the vice-gerents of God upon earth, to be a bye-word and a laughing-stock to the world or to depend upon the shout and caprice of a mob, who before scarcely breathed but through their nostrils, are grossly deceived, and will in the end be both the dupes and victims of their own egotism and blindfold presumption.  Scenes of a very scandalous and disorderly kind followed this farcical establishment of a republic, without one element of feeling or conviction to cement it ; the hand that formerly restrained rapine and violence, and that seemed to say to the excesses of each party, " Hitherto shalt thou come and no further !" was removed, and it was not till after some time that the ferment subsided.   There is no occasion to suppose that it was fomented by the intrigues of foreign agents, though they might be very ready to lend a helping hand to it ; but the thing could hardly happen otherwise.

Bernadotte had been sent ambassador to Vienna—a choice which Napoleon objected to ; both as a soldier is a bad envoy to an enemy who has been often beaten, and on account of the violence of his character.   Bernadotte suffered his temper to get the better of his judgment, and committed several imprudences.   One day, he thought proper to hoist the tri-colored flag at the top of his Hotel, without any apparent reason for so doing.   The populace immediately rose, tore down the flag, and insulted Bernadotte.   The Directory in the ebullition of its resentment sent for Napoleon, in order to obtain the sanction of his opinion.   They communicated to him a message to the Councils, declaring war against Austria, and a decree investing him with the command of the Army of Germany ; but he strenuously dissuaded them from this step.   " If you had intended war," he said, " you should have prepared for it independently of what has happened to Bernadotte, who has been materially to blame.   In declaring war, you are only playing the game of **England**. It would indicate very little knowledge of the policy of the Cabinet of Vienna to imagine that if it had wished for **war**, it would have insulted you ; on the contrary, it would have flattered you and lulled your suspicions, whilst it was putting its troops in motion, and **you** would have learnt its real intentions only by the first cannon-shot. Depend upon it, Austria will give you every satisfaction.   To be thus hurried away by every event is to have no political system at all."   These assurances of Napoleon calmed the irritation of the Directory ; the conferences at Seltz took place, and as he had predicted, the Emperor gave satisfaction.   Yet it may be doubted whether this political reasoning is not spun too fine, and whether **Austria was** not more actuated by soreness at the recent defeats and by former ill-blood, which broke out in spite of its attempts at keeping up appearances, than by the dictates of sound policy. Buonaparte judging from himself (though he too not unfrequently resembled an angry chess-player) allowed too much to cool calculation and too little to passion in the motives and conduct of courts.   The Cabinet of Vienna could, under any circumstances, ill brook the neighborhood of the French Government, and was always ready to come to blows with it.   It is certain that war did break out soon after ; that Austria did nourish the hope and wish for it in her bosom, though restrained by the presence of the victor, whose back was no sooner turned than she threw off the mask, broke up the negociations, and the first intimation the Republic received of it was by the murder of its ambassadors.   It was with an enemy, with a host of enemies like this, that Napoleon always insists on keeping terms of moderation and temper ; and perhaps with the iron bit that he held in their mouths, such might be the wisest policy ; but for any one else, the advice was madness.

Buonaparte, in the mean time, who had at first given into the plan of the expedition to Egypt with great ardor, began to cool in his eagerness for it—whether he suspected that this expedition had been originally devised merely to get rid of him, or that he found more difficulties in the enterprise than **he at first** thought of, or that the plot and texture of affairs began to thicken around him, and to promise scope and food for his activity and ambition at home. He stated his opinion to the Directory. "Europe," he observed, "is any thing but tranquil; the Congress at Rastadt does not come to a close; you require a force in the interior and to keep the Western Departments in awe. Would it not be advisable to countermand the expedition, and wait for a more favorable opportunity?"

The Directory, alarmed at this apparent hesitation, urged the scheme more warmly than ever. They represented the affairs of the Republic as in a most prosperous condition, though they were on the brink of a precipice. The present moment, according to them, was the most propitious that had ever occurred for attacking England through Ireland and the East. Napoleon then offered to leave Desaix and Kleber, whose talents might prove serviceable to France in case of any emergency. The Directory, who knew not their value, refused, and said, "they were more likely to want soldiers than generals." Though a party was not at this time wanting to offer to come forward and place Napoleon at the head of the Government, he declined; he was not as yet popular enough to stand alone, and had he come forward now, he must have conformed and subjected himself to the views and maxims of others on the nature and ends of government, with whom he did not agree. He could not have stamped his own character on the state. He determined on these considerations to sail for Egypt, intending to return as soon as circumstances should be sufficiently ripe to call for his re-appearance on the stage. To give him the ascendency over others, it was necessary that disasters should happen in his absence, that France should deplore the want of his powerful aid, and that victory should return to her standards with him. In alluding to this part of his life, he remarks that he had peculiar ideas of the nature of government, and that the time was not come for putting them to the trial. What these peculiar ideas were, is pretty apparent. He thought of taking the command of the state into his own hands, as he took the command of an army. He was equally fitted for one or the other; but in neither case was he to have control or competitor. He would have his council of state as he had his council of war —to suggest and advise; but he was to determine, and the people were to obey. He vaulted into the empty seat of government

as a wild Arab throws himself on the back of a horse without a
rider, " to turn and wind a fiery Pegasus," that answers both to
the bit and the spur. A popular government was to him as chimerical an idea as a herd of centaurs; and he hated what he had
no faith in. It was so far a disadvantage to Buonaparte that he
began his career as a military man; for many had thus got a
notion of his taking the helm of government as unprofessional
and a sort of imposture and quackery. The world never resign
without reluctance the idea they first conceive of a man; and
because they had not given him credit for various talents till he
displayed them, think he could not have had them till they knew
of them, though they must have existed equally before any proofs
of them appeared. Hence half the obloquy, abuse, and misre-
presentation poured upon his astonishing career. Men's little-
ness, envy, and incredulity must be bribed a long way beforehand to admit lofty and opposite pretensions, so that it is only
when an individual is born to a throne that they conclude without hesitation or grudging that he must possess the abilities to fit
him for it!

The Government at this time (January 1798) celebrated the
anniversary of the death of Louis XVI.; and it was a great
point in dispute whether Napoleon should be invited to attend the
ceremony. On the one hand it was feared that if he did not go,
it would tend to render the festival unpopular; and on the other,
that if he went, the Directory would be neglected, and he alone
would be the object of public attention. He would have declined
appearing at this fête altogether, as he did not approve of the occasion of it, and he enumerated his objections to the minister,
who was sent to request his attendance, in the following manner :—" That he had no public functions; that he had personally
nothing to do with this pretended fête, which from its very nature
was agreeable but to few people; that it was a very impolitic
one, the event it commemorated being a tragedy and a national
calamity; that he very well understood why the 14th of July
was observed, being the period when the people had recovered
their rights; but that it might have recovered them and established a republic without polluting itself with the slaughter of a
prince who had been declared inviolable and irresponsible by the

Constitution itself;* that he did not undertake to determine whether that measure had been useful or injurious, but maintained that
it was a melancholy event; that national fêtes were held in celebration of victories, but that the victims left on the field of battle
were lamented; that to keep the anniversary of a man's death
ought never to be the act of a government, although it might suit
a faction or a sanguinary club; that he could not comprehend
how the Directory, who had shut up the meetings of the Jacobins
and the Revolutionary Clubs, could fail to perceive that this ceremony created the Republic many more enemies than friends;
that it estranged, instead of conciliating, irritated, instead of
calming; and shook the foundations of government, instead of
adding to their strength." The minister employed by the Directory brought his classical parallels into play in answer to all
this. He said that " Athens had always solemnized the anniversary of the death of Pisistratus, and Rome the fall of the Decem-
virs; that it was the custom for all countries, and especially republics, to celebrate the fall of absolute power and the overthrow
of tyrants as a triumph; that it was moreover a law of the
country; and lastly, that the influence of the General of the
Army of Italy over public opinion was such, that it was incumbent on him to appear at this ceremony, as his absence might be
prejudicial to the interests of the commonwealth." A truer answer seems to be, that if the death of Louis XVI. was unjustifiable and contrary to every feeling that should animate the Republic, the best thing would have been for the French people to
go into mourning on the occasion, and to recal the Count de
Lille, as the best reparation they could make for the injury.
But as long as all Europe made war upon the French Government to avenge and compel them to acknowledge this wrong and

* Which constitution, be it remembered, he was in league with other
princes of the like inviolable and irresponsible class to overturn by the
slaughter, if needful, of millions of his people. Buonaparte afterwards pol-
luted himself with the slaughter of another prince of the same house without a warrant from the strict letter of law or treaties, but with a very good
one from the laws of self-preservation and dictates of common sense. Those
who take it upon them to execute summary justice, and "cut the Gordian
knot of policy" in that way, ought not to cavil about legal forms of proceeding.

as they stood upon the defensive, refusing to give up the rights
and privileges which devolved to them from the headless monarchy, repelling scorn with scorn and force with force, in God's
name let them take heart of grace on the occasion, and not blush
or grow pale at an idle show in commemoration of an act when
they stood up to their knees in blood to defend it! The *backing
out* of the Revolution in this manner was turning every drop of
blood shed in its defence into a wanton waste of life, and every
particle of spirit that was required to maintain it in time of need
into cold water. Unfortunately the effect was but too plainly
perceived afterwards. If Buonaparte was there, in the place
which was assigned him, to make good this act of national justice, this grave and imposing example to prove that one man was
not of more worth than a whole people, and to keep out all im-
pugners of this great principle at issue between the race of mankind and the race of kings, whether he was the leader of those
armies bright that once defied all opposition, or sat enthroned in
mock-regal state, but still to the exclusion and in bitter derision
of their pretensions, it was well—but if it was not so and for this
purpose, he had no business where he was, first or last!

A middle course was pitched upon after several consultations.
The Institute attended this ceremony; and it was settled that
Napoleon should walk among the members in the class to which
he belonged, thus performing as a duty attached to a public body
an act which he did not consider voluntary. This arrangement
of the matter was very agreeable to the Directory. But when
the Institute entered the church of St. Sulpice, some one who
recognized Napoleon having pointed him out, he instantly became
the object of general attention. As the Directory had been apprehensive, they were totally eclipsed. At the conclusion of the
ceremony, the multitude suffered the Directory to walk out by
themselves, and rent the air with shouts of "*Long live the
General of the Army of Italy!*" This trifling circumstance did
not serve to allay the displeasure of the rulers of the state against
him.

Another circumstance which happened about this time placed
Napoleon under the necessity of loudly condemning the conduct
of the Directory. At the Garchi coffee-house, two young men,

on account of the manner in which they wore their hair in tresses (which was considered as a political distinction) were insulted, attacked, and killed on the spot.   This murder had been conducted, as it was supposed, under the orders of the Minister of Police, and was executed by some of its agents.   Napoleon, even with a view to his own safety, found it necessary to keep a vigilant eye upon events of this nature.   He gave a loose to his indignation. The Directory were alarmed, and were weak enough to send one of their emissaries to him to gloss over this outrage, but without making any impression on Buonaparte, who persisted in the most unqualified and pointed reprobation of it.   It was also at this period that Sir Sidney Smith, who was confined as a close prisoner in the Temple, applied to Buonaparte to use his influence with the Directory to allow him his freedom ; but he made answer that he could do nothing, as they were determined to carry things with a high hand.   It is a singular example of the effect of personal character and of a spirit of generosity and bravery when it shines through the whole air and deportment of a man, that Sir Sidney Smith, during the two years he remained in the Temple, obtained such influence over the gaoler, and the latter reposed such confidence in his bare word of honor, that he often let him out on his parole, and accompanied him to coffee-houses, the theatres, or even went out hunting with him in the woods of Echoen near Paris, at the very time when he was supposed to be *au secret.*   Such is the ascendant which courage and frankness of spirit exercise over the honest and humane mind.

A considerable change had taken place in Buonaparte's situation and manner of living since his return to Paris this time.   He lived in a style of affluence, and was (whether he encouraged it or not) an object of public attention.   Two years before, he had lived in great frugality as well as obscurity, and had often passed whole mornings at a little reading-room in the Palais-Royal, where seeing him cold and tired, the wife of the master of the shop would sometimes invite him to take a basin of soup with her, applying to him the familiar epithet of her Little Corsican (*Petit Corsico*). As a recompence for this kindness and hospitality, Buonaparte, when First Consul, gave her husband the employment of making the Abridgment of the Moniteurs, which was a considerable ad-

vantage to him.   When afterwards it became a question how to
restrict the liberty of the press, and some one proposed to Buonaparte to strike at the grievance complained of at once by putting
down the reading-rooms, he replied, " No, he would never do that
—he had known too well the comfort of having a place of that
kind to go to, where he could always find a fire and the newspaper or pamphlet of the day to amuse him, ever to deprive others
who might be in his situation of the same resource."*

   * He used at this time to frequent the Chaffé Corazza in the Palais-Royal.

# APPENDIX.

## No. I.

### THE SUPPER OF BEAUCAIRE.

I WAS at Beaucaire, on the last day of the fair, and happened to have for company at supper two merchants of Marseilles, an inhabitant of Nimes, and a manufacturer of Montpellier. In the space of a few minutes, which were passed in becoming acquainted, they learned that I came from Avignon, and that I was an officer. The attention of my company, which had all the week before been fixed on the course of trade, which increases wealth, was at that moment turned to the issue of the present contest, upon which depends its preservation. They wished to know my opinion, in order that, by comparing it with their own, they might be the better enabled to form probable conjectures respecting the future, which affected us in different ways. The Marseillais, in particular, appeared to be less petulant; the evacuation of Avignon had taught them to doubt of every thing, and they manifested great solicitude about their future fate. Confidence soon made us communicative, and we began a conversation nearly in the following terms :—

#### THE NIMOIS.

"Is Cartaux's army strong? It is said to have sustained a heavy loss in the attack; but if it be true that it has been repulsed, why have the Marseillais evacuated Avignon?"

#### THE OFFICER.

"The army was four thousand strong when it attacked Avignon, and is now six thousand, and in four days more it will be ten thousand : it lost five killed and four wounded; it was not repulsed, since it made no regular attack; it hovered about the place, it strove to force the gates by attaching petards to them; it fired a few cannon-shot to try the temper of the garrison; it afterwards retired into its camp to combine its attack for the following night. The Marseillais were three thousand six hundred strong; they had a heavier and more numerous artillery, and yet they were obliged to retreat across the Durance. You are much astonished at this; but the fact is, that none but veteran troops can contend with the vicissitudes of a siege; we were masters of the Rhone, of Villeneuve, and of the country; we should have interrupted all their communications. They were obliged to evacuate the town; the cavalry pursued them in their retreat; they lost a great many prisoners, and two pieces of cannon."

### THE MARSEILLAIS.

" We have received a different account: I will not dispute yours, since you were present, but you must own that all that will lead to nothing; our army is at Aix; three good generals are come in place of the former ones; they are raising fresh battalions at Marseilles; we have a fresh train of artillery, including several twenty-four-pounders; in a few days we shall be in a posture to retake Avignon, or at least we shall remain masters of the Durance."

### THE OFFICER.

" All this has been told you in order to lead you to the brink of the abyss, which is deepening every moment, and which will perhaps ingulf the finest city in France, that which has deserved the most of the patriots. But you were also told that you should traverse France, that you should sway the Republic, and yet your very first steps have been checked; you were told that Avignon could resist for a long time a force of 20,000 men, and yet a single column of the army, without a battering-train, got possession of it in twenty-four hours; you were told that the South had risen, and yet you found yourselves alone; you were told that the cavalry of Nimes was about to crush the Allobroges, and yet the latter were at Saint-Esprit and at Villeneuve; you were told that 4000 Lyonnais were marching to your aid, and yet the Lyonnais were negociating an accommodation for themselves. Acknowledge, then, that you are deceived, see the incompetence of your directors, and distrust their calculations; self-love is the most dangerous of counsellors; you are naturally impetuous, they are leading you to your destruction by the same means which has ruined so many nations, by inflaming your vanity. You have considerable wealth and population, and their amount is exaggerated to you; you have rendered signal services to liberty, and you are reminded of them, without at the same time pointing out to you that the genius of the Republic was with you then, whereas it has now abandoned you. Your army, say you, is at Aix, with a large train of artillery and good generals; well, do what it may, I assure you that it will be beaten. You had 3600 men, of which a full half is dispersed; Marseilles, and a few refugees from the department, may furnish you 4000 men at the most; you will then have 5000 or 6000 men, without unity, without order, without discipline. You say you have good generals; as I do not know them, I cannot dispute their ability, but they will be entirely occupied in the details: their exertions will not be seconded by the

subalterns, they cannot do any thing to maintain the reputation which they
may have acquired; for it would take two months to organize their army
tolerably, and in four days Cartaux will have passed the Durance, and with
what soldiers?  With the excellent light troops of the Allobroges, the old
regiment of Burgundy, a good regiment of cavalry, the brave battalion of
the Côte d'Or, which has been victorious in a hundred combats, and six or
seven other veteran corps, encouraged by their successes on the frontiers
and against your army.  You have eighteen and twenty-four-pounders, and
you think yourselves impregnable; therein you follow the vulgar notion,
but professional men will tell you, and fatal experience will shortly demonstrate to you, that good four and eight-pounders are as effective in the field,
and are preferable on many accounts to pieces of heavy calibre.  You have
cannoneers newly raised, and your adversaries have gunners from the regiments of the line, the best masters of their art in Europe.  What will your
army do if it concentrates itself at Aix?  It is lost; it is an axiom in the
military art, that the army which remains in its intrenchments is beaten;
theory and experience entirely agree on this point; and the walls of Aix
are not equal to the worst field-intrenchment, especially if we consider their
extent, and the houses which surround them exteriorly, within pistol-shot.
Be assured then, that this course, which seems to you the best, is the worst;
besides, how can you supply the town in so short a time with every kind
of provision which it wants?  Will your army go and meet the enemy?  It
is less numerous, its artillery is less adapted to the field, it would be broken
and defeated without resource, for the cavalry would prevent it from rallying.  Expect, then, to have the war carried into the territory of Marseilles;
there a very numerous party is for the Republic, and that will be the moment for it to declare itself; the junction will be made, and that city, the
centre of the commerce of the Levant, the emporium of the South of Europe,
is ruined.  Remember the recent example of Lisle,* and the barbarous
laws of war.  What infatuation has all at once possessed your people? what
fatal blindness is leading them to their destruction?  How can they think
of resisting the entire Republic?  Suppose they could oblige its army to
fall back upon Avignon, can they doubt that in a few days fresh combatants
would come to supply the places of the former?  Will the Republic, which
gives the law to Europe, receive it from Marseilles?

"United with Bourdeaux, Lyons, Montpellier, Nîmes, Grenoble, the
Jura, the Eure, the Calvados, you undertook a revolution, and you had
some probability of success; your instigators might be ill-intentioned, but
you had an imposing mass of strength.  But now that Lyons, Nîmes, Montpellier, Bourdeaux, the Jura, the Eure, Grenoble, Caen, have received the
Constitution; now that Avignon, Tarascon, Arles, have submitted, confess
that there is madness in your obstinacy.  It is because you are influenced by
persons who, having nothing more to lose, would involve you in their ruin.

* Lisle, a small town of the department of Vaucluse, four leagues east of Avignon, hav
ing resisted the army of Cartaux, was taken by assault on the 26th of July, 1798

'Your army will be composed of all the wealthiest portion of your city, for the *sans-culottes* might very easily turn against you. You are going, then, to risk the flower of your young men, accustomed to hold the commercial balance of the Mediterranean, and to enrich you by their economy and their speculations, against veteran soldiers who have so often bathed their hands in the blood of the furious Aristocrat, the ferocious Prussian.

"Let poor countries fight to the last extremity; the inhabitant of the Vivarais, of the Cévènnes, or of Corsica, exposes himself without fear to the issue of a combat; if he is victorious, he gains his object—if he is beaten, he finds himself as before, at liberty to make peace, and in the same position. But you—lose a battle and the fruits of a thousand years of industry, economy, and prosperity become the prey of the soldier. Such, however, are the risks which you are induced so inconsiderately to run."

### THE MARSEILLAIS.

"You get on fast, and you alarm me. I agree with you that the circumstances are critical; perhaps it is true that the position in which we at present stand is not sufficiently considered; but you must acknowledge that we still have immense resources to oppose to you.

"You have persuaded me that we cannot resist at Aix; your observation respecting the want of provisions for a siege of long duration is perhaps unanswerable; but do you think that all Provence can long witness calmly the investment of Aix? It will rise spontaneously; and your army, hemmed in on every side, will be fortunate if it can repass the Durance."

### THE OFFICER.

"How little knowledge this displays of the spirit of men and that of the time! Everywhere there are two parties; the moment you are besieged, the Sectionary party will be put down in all the country places. The example of Tarascon, of Orgon, of Arles should convince you of this; where twenty dragoons have sufficed to re-establish the old authorities, and put the others to the rout.

"Henceforward any great movement in your favor is impossible in your department; it might have taken place when the army was beyond the Durance, and you were unbroken. At Toulon men's minds are much divided; and the Sectionaries have not the same superiority there as at Marseilles, so that they must remain in the town to repress their adversaries. As for the department of the Lower Alps, you know that nearly the whole of it has accepted the Constitution."

### THE MARSEILLAIS.

"We will attack Cartaux in our mountains, where his cavalry will be of no use to him."

### THE OFFICER.

"As if an army protecting a town could choose the point of attack. Besides, it is not true that there are any mountains near Marseilles sufficiently impracticable to render cavalry ineffective ; your olive-grounds, indeed, are sufficiently steep to render the management of artillery more difficult, and thereby give your enemies a great advantage; for it is on broken ground that, by the celerity of his movements, the exactness in serving his guns, and the accuracy of his elevations, the expert cannoneer has the greatest superiority."

## THE MARSEILLAIS.

"You think, then, that we are without resources. Can it possibly be the fate of that city which resisted the Romans, and preserved a part of its laws under the despots who succeeded them, to become the prey of a few brigands ? What! shall the Allobroges, laden with the spoils of Lisle, give law to Marseille ? What, shall Dubois de Crancé and Albitte reign uncontrolled ? shall those blood-thirsty men, in whose hands the calamities of the time have placed the guidance of affairs, be absolute masters ? What a melancholy prospect you present to me ; our property, under different pretexts, would be invaded ; we should continually be made the victims of a soldiery whom plunder unites under the same banners ; our best citizens would be imprisoned and would perish by violence. The Club would again lift its monstrous head to execute its infernal projects! Nothing can be worse than this horrible idea ; it is better to leave ourselves a chance of victory, than to become victims without any alternative."

## THE OFFICER.

"Such is civil war. men go on in mutual defamation, abhorrence, and slaughter, without knowing one another. The Allobroges—what do you think they are ? Africans ? inhabitants of Siberia ? Not at all; they are your fellow-countrymen, Provençaux, Dauphinois, Savoyards. You think them barbarous because their name is strange. If your phalanx were called the Phocæan phalanx, people would give credit to every species of fable respecting it.

"It is true that you have reminded me of one fact, the case of Lisle. I do not justify it, but I will explain it. The people of Lisle killed the trumpeter who was sent to them ; they resisted without hope of success; their town was taken by assault; the soldiers entered it amidst fire and slaughter, it was not possible to restrain them ; and indignation did the rest.

"Those soldiers whom you call brigands are our best troops, and most disciplined battalions ; their reputation is above calumny.

"Dubois-Crancé and Albitte, constant friends of the people, have never deviated from the straight line ; they are villains in the eyes of the bad. But Condorcet, Brissot, Barbaroux, were also villains while they were consistent; it will always be the lot of the good to be spoken ill of by the bad. You think they show you no mercy, and yet they are treating you like wayward children. Do you think that if they had chosen to detain it, the Marseillais could have withdrawn the merchandize which they had at Beau caire; they could have sequestrated it until the issue of the war; they did not wish to do so; and you owe it to them that you can return quietly to your homes.

"You call Cartaux an assassin; but know, that that General takes the greatest care to preserve order and discipline; witness his conduct at Saint Esprit and at Avignon, where not a pin's worth was taken. He imprisoned a serjeant who ventured to seize the person of a Marseillais of your army who had remained in one of the houses, because he had violated the asylum of a citizen without an express order. Some people of Avignon were punished for pointing out a house as aristocratical. One soldier is under prosecution on a charge of theft. Your army, on the contrary, has killed, assassinated more than thirty persons, has violated the retreats of families, and filled the prisons with citizens on the vague pretext that they were robbers.

"Do not be afraid of the army; it esteems Marseilles, because it knows that no town has made so many sacrifices to the common weal; you have eighteen thousand men on the frontier; you have not spared yourselves on any occasion. Throw off the yoke of the few aristocrats who govern you return to sounder principles, and you will have no truer friend than the soldier."

### THE MARSEILLAIS.

"Ah! you soldiers have greatly degenerated from the army of 1789; that army would not take up arms against the nation; yours should imitate so noble an example, and not turn their arms against their fellow-citizens."

### THE OFFICER.

"Had those principles been followed, La Vendée would ere now have planted the white flag on the walls of the re-erected Bastille, and the camp of Jalès would have been ruling at Marseilles."

### THE MARSEILLAIS.

"La Vendée desires a king, a counter-revolution; the war of La Vendée, of the camp of Jalès is that of fanaticism; ours, on the contrary, is that of true republicanism, friends of the laws and of order, enemies of anarchy and of bad men. Have we not the tri-colored flag? And what interest should we have in wishing to be slaves?"

### THE OFFICER.

"I am well aware that the people of Marseilles differ widely from those of La Vendée with respect to a counter-revolution. The appetite of the people of La Vendée is strong and healthy; that of the people of Marseilles weak and sickly; the pill must be sugared in order to make them swallow it, to establish the new doctrine among them they must be deceived, but in the course of four years of revolution, in such a number of stratagems, plots, and conspiracies, all the perversity of human nature has been developed under different aspects, and men have perfected their natural subtlety; so true is this, that in spite of the departmental coalition, in spite of the ability of the leaders, and the numerous resources of all **the enemies of the Revolution, the people everywhere awoke at the moment they were thought to be spell-bound.**

"You say you have the tri-colored flag; Paoli also hoisted it **in Corsica to** have time to deceive the people, to crush the true friends of liberty, to lead his fellow-countrymen to concur in his ambitious and criminal projects; he hoisted the tri-colored flag, and **yet he** fired **upon the vessels** of the Republic, and he drove our troops from the fortresses, and he disarmed those which remained there, **and** he assembled forces **to expel those which** were in the **island, and he plundered the magazines, selling at a low** price all **their contents to get money to carry on** his revolt, **and he ravaged and confiscated the property of the wealthiest families because they were attached to the** unity of the Republic, and he got **himself** appointed generalissimo, and he declared all those who should remain in our army enemies to their country; he had previously caused the failure of the Sardinian expedition, and yet he had the shamelessness to call himself the friend of France and a good Republican, and yet he deceived the Convention, which passed its decree of deprivation; **in short he acted** in such a manner, that when at length he **was unmasked by** his own letters found at Calvi, **it was too late, the enemy's** fleets already intercepted all our communications.

"We must no longer rely upon words; we must examine **actions; and** you must acknowledge that in estimating yours, it is **easy to show that you** are counter-revolutionists. What effect has **the movement which you have** made produced on the Republic? You have brought it to the brink of ruin; you have retarded the operations of our armies. I know not whether you are paid by the Spaniard and the Austrian; but certainly they could not desire more powerful diversions. What more could **you do if you were so** paid? **Your** success has been an object of solicitude **to all the known aristocrats; you have placed declared aristocrats** at the head of your sections **and of** your armies, as one Latourette, formerly **a colonel, one** Soumise, formerly a lieutenant-colonel of engineers, who abandoned their corps at the breaking out of the war that they might not fight for the liberty of nations; your battalions are full of such men, and your cause **would not** be theirs if it were that of the **Republic."**

### THE MARSEILLAIS.

"But Brissot, Barbaroux, Condorcet, Buzot, Vergniaux, **are they too** aristocrats? Who founded the Republic? who overthrew the tyrant? who supported their country at the perilous period of the last campaign?

### THE OFFICER.

"I will not examine whether those men who had deserved well of the **nation on many occasions did** really conspire against it; it is sufficient for me to know that the Mountain, through public or through party spirit, having proceeded to the last extremities against them, having denounced, imprisoned, and, if you will have it so, calumniated them, the Brissotins were lost, unless a civil war should enable them to give the law to their enemies. It was then to them that your war was really useful; had they merited their former reputation, they would have laid down their arms on beholding the Constitution, they would have sacrificed their interests to the public good; but it is easier to cite the example of Decius than to imitate him; they have now become guilty of the greatest of all crimes—they have by their conduct justified their denouncement; the blood which they have caused to flow has effaced the real services they had rendered."

### THE MANUFACTURER OF MONTPELLIER.

"You have considered the question in the point of view most favorable to those gentlemen; for it seems to be proved that the Brissotins were really guilty; but guilty or not, the days are gone by when men fought for personal interests. England shed torrents of blood for the families of York and Lancaster, France for those of Lorraine and Bourbon; but do we live in those times of barbarism?"

### THE NIMOIS.

"So we abandoned the Marseillais as soon as we perceived that they wished for the counter-revolution, and that they fought in private quarrels. The mask fell when they refused to publish the Constitution, and we then pardoned some irregularities in the Mountain. We forgot Rabaud and his Jeremaids in contemplating the infant Republic, surrounded by the most monstrous of coalitions, threatening to stifle it in its cradle—in contemplating the joy of the aristocrats and the armed hostility of Europe."

### THE MARSEILLAIS.

"You meanly abandoned us after inciting us by ephemeral deputations."

### THE NIMOIS.

"We were sincere, but you were double-dealing; we desired the Republic, we could not but accept a Republican Constitution. You were dissatisfied with the Mountain, and with the 31st of May; you then should also have accepted the Constitution in order to get rid of it, and terminate its mission."

### THE MARSEILLAIS.

"We too wish for the Republic, but we wish our Constitution to be formed by representatives free in their operations; we wish for liberty, but we wish to receive it from representatives whom we esteem, we do not wish that our Constitution should protect plunder and anarchy. Our first condition is, that there shall be no Clubs, none of those frequent primary assemblies, that property shall be respected."

### THE MANUFACTURER OF MONTPELLIER.

"It is clear to every reflecting person, that a part of Marseilles is for the counter-revolution: they profess to wish for the Republic, but this is only a curtain which they would every day render more transparent, until they accustomed you to contemplate the counter-revolution undisguised ; the veil which covers it is already but a flimsy one; your people are well disposed, but in time the mass of them would be perverted but for the genius of the Revolution which watches over them.

"Our troops have deserved well of their country for having taken up arms against you with so much energy; it was not their duty to imitate the army of 1789, since you are not the nation. The centre of unity is the Convention; that is the true sovereign, especially when the people are divided.

" You have overturned every law, every decent form. By what right did you cashier your Department? Had it been formed at Marseilles? By what right does the battalion of your town traverse the districts ? By what right did your National Guards pretend to enter Avignon ? The district of that town was the first constituted body since the Department was dissolved. By what right did you presume to enter the territory of the Drôme? and why do you suppose that Department has no right to call upon the public force to defend it ? You have then confounded all rights; you have established anarchy; and since you pretend to justify your operations by the right of force, you are brigands, anarchists.

" You have set up a popular government, appointed by Marseilles alone; it is contrary to every law ; it cannot be other than a tribunal of blood, since it is the tribunal of a faction; you have by force subjected to that tribunal the whole of your Department. And by what right ? You do then usurp that authority with which you unjustly reproach Paris. Your Committee of the Sections has recognized affiliations. Here then is a coalition similar to that of the clubs against which you exclaim ; your Committee has exercised acts of administration over certain communes of the Var ; this is a breach of the territorial division.

" At Avignon you have imprisoned without mandate, decree, or requisition from the administrative bodies; you have violated the retreats of families, infringed the liberty of individuals; you have in the public places murdered in cold blood; you have revived with aggravated horror the scenes which afflicted the early days of the Revolution; without examination, without trial, without other knowledge of the victims than from the designation of their enemies, you have seized them, torn them from their children, dragged them through the streets, and sabred them to death : you have sacrificed in this manner as many as thirty; you have dragged the statue of liberty through the mire; you have made a public execution of it, and have subjected it to every kind of insult from licentious youths; you have mangled it with swords; you cannot deny it; it was noon-day; more than two hundred of your party were present at this criminal profanation; the procession passed through several streets to the Place de l'Horloge, &c. &c. I must interrupt my reflections and my indignation. And is it thus that you wish for the Republic? You have retarded the march of our armies, by stopping the convoys. How can we resist the evidence of so many facts? or how call you other than enemies of your country?"

### THE OFFICER.

"There is the clearest evidence that the Marseillais have hindered the operations of our armies, and sought the destruction of liberty; but the question before us now is, whether they have any thing to hope, and what course remains for them to pursue."

### THE MARSEILLAIS.

"We have fewer resources than I thought; but there is great strength in being resolved to die; and we will rather do so than again receive the yoke of the men who governed the state; you know that a drowning man catches at every twig, and rather than suffer ourselves to be massacred, we will——. Yes, we have all taken part in this new Revolution, and we should all be sacrificed to revenge. Two months ago they had conspired to murder four thousand of our best citizens; judge then to what excesses they would proceed now. We have not forgotten that monster, who was nevertheless one of the heads of the club; he had a citizen hung on the lamp-post (*lanterne*), plundered his house, and violated his wife, after making her drink a glass of her husband's blood."

### THE OFFICER.

"How horrid!—but is that story true? I doubt it, for you know that nobody believes in violation now-a-days."

### THE MARSEILLAIS.

"Yes, rather than submit to such men we will go to the last extremity—we will give ourselves to the enemy; we will call in the Spaniards. There is no people whose character is less congenial with our own; there is no one more hateful to us. Judge, then, by the sacrifice which we make, of the wickedness of the men whom we fear."

### THE OFFICER.

"Give yourselves to the Spaniards!—we will not give you time."

### THE MARSEILLAIS.

"They are seen every day before our ports."

### THE NIMOIS.

"That threat alone is sufficient for me to decide which is for the Republic, the Mountain or the Federals. The Mountain was at one moment the weakest, and the commotion appeared general. Yet did it ever talk of calling in the enemy? Do you not know that the war between the patriots and the despots of Europe is a war unto death? If then you hope for assistance from the latter, your leaders must have good reasons to expect their favor. But I have still too good an opinion of your people, to believe that the majority of them would go with you in the execution of so base a project."

### THE OFFICER.

"Do you think that you would thereby do a great injury to the Republic, and that your threat is really alarming? Let us weigh it. The Spaniards have no troops wherewith to effect a landing, and their vessels cannot enter your port. If you were to call in the Spaniards it might be useful to those who govern you, in saving themselves and part of their property; but the indignation would be general throughout the Republic; in less than a week you would have sixty thousand men at your gates, the Spaniards would carry off from Marseilles whatever they could, and enough would still be left to enrich the conquerors.

"If the Spaniards had thirty or forty thousand men on board their fleet, all ready to disembark, your threat would be alarming; but as matters are, it is only ridiculous; it would only hasten your destruction."

### THE MANUFACTURER OF MONTPELLIER.

"If you were capable of so base an act, not one stone ought to be left upon another in your superb city. In a month from this time, it should appear to the traveller passing over its ruins as if it had been destroyed for a century."

### THE OFFICER.

"Marseillais, take my advice; throw off the yoke of the small number of bad men who would lead you to a counter-revolution, restore your constituted authorities; accept the Constitution; liberate the Representatives; let them go to Paris and intercede for you. You have been misled; it is not unusual for the people to be so by a few conspirators and intriguers; in all ages the pliancy and ignorance of the multitude have been the cause of most civil wars."

### THE MARSEILLAIS.

"Ah! Sir, who can do any good to Marseilles? Can the refugees who arrive on all sides from the Department? They are interested in acting with desperation. Can they who govern us? are not they in the same situation? Can the people? One part of them does not know its position; it is rendered blind and fanatical: the other part is disarmed, suspected, humbled. With profound affliction then I contemplate irremediable calamities."

### THE OFFICER.

"You are at last brought to reason: why should not a like revolution be effected in the minds of a great number of your fellow-citizens, who are deceived and sincere?  Then Albitte, who cannot but wish to spare French blood, will send to you some honest and able men; an understanding will be come to, and without a moment's delay, the army will be marched off to the neighborhood of Perpignan to humble the pride of the Spaniard, which a little success has elevated, and Marseilles will still be the centre of gravity to liberty, it will only be necessary to tear a few pages from its history."

This happy prognostication put us all in good humor; the Marseillais very readily paid for a few bottles of Champagne, which dissipated all our cares and anxieties.  We went to bed at two in the morning, having agreed to meet again at breakfast, where the Marseillais had many more doubts to propose, and I had many interesting truths to acquaint him with

*July 29, 1793*

# No. II.

## BUONAPARTE'S LETTER TO GENERAL PAOLI.

" GENERAL,

" I was born when my country was perishing. Thirty thousand French-men, landed on our coast, bathing the throne of liberty in streams of blood, such was the odious spectacle which first presented itself to my sight. The cries of the dying, the groans of the oppressed, the tears of despair were the companions of my infant days. You quitted our island and with you disappeared all hopes of happiness; slavery was the reward of our submission; loaded with the triple chain of the soldier, the legislator, and the tax-gatherer, our countrymen live despised—despised by those who have the command over us. Is it not the greatest pain that one who has the slightest elevation of sentiment can suffer! Can the wretched Peruvian writhing under the tortures of the avaricious Spaniard feel a greater? No! wretches, whom a desire of gain and plunder corrupts, to justify themselves, have invented calumnies against the national government and against you, Sir, in particular. Authors, confiding in their veracity, transmit them to posterity. While perusing them my heart boils with indignation, and I have resolved to dissipate these delusions, the offspring of ignorance. An early study of the French language, long observation, and the memorials to which I have had access in the portfolios of the patriots, have led me to promise myself some success. I wish to compare your government with the present one. I wish to blacken with the pencil of dishonor those who have betrayed the common cause. I wish to call before the tribunal of public opinion those who are in power, set forth their vexatious proceedings, expose their secret intrigues, and if possible interest the present virtuous minister in the deplorable situation that we are now in. If my fortune permitted me to live in the capital, I should have found out other means of making known our complaints, but being obliged to serve in the army, I find myself thus compelled to make use of this, the only means of publicity; for as to private memorials, either they would not reach the government, or, stifled by the clamor of the parties concerned, they would only occasion the ruin of the author.

" Still young, my enterprize may seem daring; but love for truth, of my country, and fellow-citizens, that enthusiasm which the prospect of an amelioration in our state always gives, bear me up. If you, General, condescend to approve of a work in which your name will so often occur, if you

19*

condescend to encourage the efforts of a young man whom you have known from infancy, and whose parents were always attached to the good cause, I shall dare to augur favorably of my success. I hoped at one time to be able to go to London to express to you the sentiments you have raised in my bosom, and to converse together on the misfortunes of our country; but the distance is an objection. Perhaps a time will come when I shall be able to overcome it. · Whatever may be the success of my undertaking, I know that it will raise against me the numerous body of Frenchmen who govern our island and whom I attack; but what matters it so as the welfare of my country is concerned! I shall hear the wicked upbraid; and if the bolt falls, I shall examine my heart and shall recollect the lawfulness of my motives, and at that moment I shall defy it.

"Permit me, General, to offer you the homage of my family—why should I not add, of my countrymen? They sigh at the recollection of a time when they had hoped for liberty. My mother, Madame Letitia, has charged me above all to recal to your remembrance the years long since passed at Corté.

"I remain with respect, General,

"Your most humble and most obedient servant,

"NAPOLEON BUONAPARTE.

"Officer in the Regiment of La Fère

"*Auxonne in Burgundy, June* 12, 1789."

# No. III.

### EXTRACT FROM THE PROCES-VERBAL OF THE NOBILITY OF THE STATES-GENERAL OF 1614.  P. 113.

" On Tuesday, 25th of November, having obtained an audience, Mon. de Senecey addressed the King thus :

"Sire,

" The goodness of our kings has always granted to their nobility the privilege of having recourse to them on all occasions, the greatness of their quality bringing them near their own persons, so that they have always been the principal executors of their royal behests.

" I should never have done, Sire, were I to recapitulate to your Majesty all that antiquity has handed down to us of the pre-eminence which birth has given to this order, and what distinction there is between it and the rest of the people, with which it can suffer no sort of comparison.  I could extend the subject, Sire, to a great length ; but a truth so glaring has need of no other testimony than that which is known to all the world——and then I speak before the King ; whom we hope to find as jealous to preserve to us that lustre which we share with him, as we should ourselves be anxious to require and intreat it of him, sorry that an extraordinary novelty opens our mouth rather to complaints than to the very humble supplications for which we are at this time assembled.

" Sire, your Majesty has been pleased to assemble the States-General of the three orders of your kingdom, orders destined and separated from each other by their functions and their rank.  The church, dedicated to the service of God and for the direction of souls, holds the first rank.  We honor the prelates and ministers as fathers and mediators for our reconciliation with God.

" The nobility, Sire, holds the second rank.  It is the right arm of justice, the support of your throne, and is the invincible defence of the state.  Under the happy auspices and by the brave conduct of our kings, at the price of their blood and by the force of their victorious arms, the public peace has been established, and by their endeavors the Commons are enabled to enjoy the conveniences which peace affords them.

" This order, Sire, which holds the third rank in the assembly, an order composed of the people, both of town and country, these last are dependants on and under the jurisdiction of the two first orders ; those of the towns, commoners, tradesmen, and some officers.  These are they who forgetting their situation and all sort of duty, without the consent of those whom they represent, wish to compare themselves to us.

"I blush, Sire, to tell you the terms which have anew offended us. They compare your state to a family composed of three brothers. They say that the ecclesiastical order is the eldest, ours the second, and *their own the youngest*. Into what a miserable condition are we fallen, if this be true! After that, what would be the use of so **many services rendered from time** immemorial, so many honors and dignities transmitted hereditarily to the nobility, and deserved by their labors and fidelity, had they really, instead of raising it, abased it, so that it should be in the most intimate sort of society with the common people, that subsists among men, namely brotherhood. And not contented with calling themselves brothers, they attribute to themselves the **restoration** of the state in which, as France well enough knows, they **had no share;** so that every one knows that they can in no manner compare themselves to us, and a pretension, with so poor a foundation, would be insupportable.

"Do justice, Sire, and by an equitable **decree** cause them to return to their duty and acknowledge **who** we are and what a difference there is between us. We humbly beseech this of your Majesty, in the name of all the French nobility, since it is in their name that we now come; that preserving their pre-eminence, they may devote, as they always have done, their lives and honor to the service of your Majesty."

## No. IV.

### CHARACTER OF MARAT, BY BRISSOT.

"I ALSO saw the experiments which Marat published on light and fire, and which had excited my curiosity. The independent character which that man, since become so noted, displayed, induced me to seek his acquaintance, and we became intimately connected. Marat related to me certain circumstances of his life, which increased my esteem for him. He held himself forth as the apostle of liberty, and had written, when in England, in 1775, a work on this subject, which was entitled 'The Chains of Slavery.' In this publication he unmasked the corruption of the court and of the administration. The work, he told me, had made a great noise in England, and that he had been rewarded by valuable presents, and by his admission into corporations, and the freedom of several cities. He spoke to me of his connexion with the celebrated Kauffman, of his prodigious success in practice, which was so great, that on his *debut* at Paris he was paid thirty-six livres every visit, and had not time sufficient for all the consultations to which he was called. Though he was very well lodged, I did not see that sort of luxury which might have been the result of the wealth that was showered on him. But I have already observed that I was habitually credulous; and it is only in going over the different circumstances of my connexion with this detestable man, in bringing into one point of view the part which he has acted in the Revolution, that I have been convinced of the quackery which through his whole life directed and veiled his actions and his writings.

" Marat told me, that having made great discoveries in natural philosophy, he quitted practice, which at Paris was the profession only of a quack, and unworthy of himself. But while he renounced his profession he sold from time to time remedies and bottles, the efficacy of which he warranted, and he was very careful to name the price. I recollect that a wart on my hand having struck his eye, he sent me a bottle of very limpid water, for which I thanked him, and asked him the price, which was twelve livres. I made no use of the remedy. Marat had given me some distrust, if not of his success, at least of his medical knowledge. He told me one day, that in order to cure himself of the cholic, he wanted to have his belly opened, but that happily for him the surgeon had not the complaisance to comply with his desire.

" Marat was so entirely full of himself, of his discoveries, and of the glory which he fancied **he deserved**, that he did not appear to me to feel the slightest impression of beauty, and he was certainly little calculated to please. Nevertheless, he had found the secret of exciting an attachment in Madame La Marquise de L——, a woman whose elegant mind rendered her conversation highly interesting. Being separated from her husband, who **was** overwhelmed with debts, and dishonored by **a** course of infamous conduct, she put herself under the care of Marat; who **did** not confine his attention to her as a physician, but was ambitious of succeeding the husband. This union for a long time astonished me. The lady was soft, amiable, and good; and there was nothing so disgusting, violent, and savage in domestic life as Marat.

"I must do him the justice to observe, that the rigor which he exercised against others, he exercised also on himself. Insensible of the pleasures of the table, and the enjoyments of life, he consecrated all his time and his money to philosophical experiments Employed night and day in repeating them, he would have been contented with bread and water, in order to have the pleasure of humbling at some future day the Academy of Sciences. This was the *ne plus ultra* of his ambition. Enraged at the academicians, who had treated his **first essays** with contempt, he thirsted with the desire of vengeance, and to overturn the first of their idols, Newton; for which purpose he employed himself wholly in experiments destined to destroy his principles of optics. To combat and overthrow the reputation of celebrated men was his ruling passion: such was the motive which dictated the first of his works—his treatise on 'The Principles of Man,' which appeared in 1775, in three volumes, and which Voltaire burlesqued in his questions on the Encyclopedia.

"The system of Helvetius was then in the greatest vogue, and it was against Helvetius that Marat wished to enter the lists. Certainly Voltaire was in the right to ridicule some of the propositions and extravagancies of Marat; but he did not do him justice in other points of view.

"The academicians, for instance, were violently exasperated against his **experiments on** light, **on fire,** and **on** electricity; and I have never seen any **of them** distinguish or acknowledge what **was new** or valuable in his experiments; nor did they wish his name even to be pronounced, so fearful **were** they of contributing even by their criticisms to his celebrity. I own that this injustice on the part of the class of experimental philosophers has **always** disgusted me; and this was what dictated a chapter in my treatise on truth, on academical prejudice, page 353, which I composed at the end of a long and warm dispute I had with the geometrician La P——, which chapter is a faithful recital of this dispute. La P—— might possibly be in the right, and I might answer with too much harshness; but I could not bear the insolence and despotism with which they treated a philosopher, because he did not, like themselves, wear a **gown.**

"I followed Marat's experiments **for** three years, and I thought that **some** esteem was due to a man who had buried himself in solitude to enlarge the bounds of science: not indeed that this was his first view; for he regarded only himself; he speculated on sciences only for his own glory, and was anxious to raise his reputation on the wreck of that of others.

"He had not failed to observe, that journalists were privileged distributors of fame; but his vanity, insolence, and arrogance had made him totally neglected by those whose good offices he sought after. He knew that I was connected with many amongst them; and I believe it is to this circumstance that I was indebted for that kind of attachment which he professed for me during so many years. He was continually sending me extracts from his works, and criticisms written on them with his own hand. I never could have conceived that any one could have had the impudence to bestow so many praises on himself; but considering him only as a person suffering under literary oppression, I exerted myself in making his works known, and I often succeeded. He never thanked me; and the reason was, that in spite of my esteem for his knowledge and his discoveries, I did not fully share in the admiration which he complaisantly felt for himself; and being sometimes in doubt as to the truth of his propositions, I undertook to soften his exaggerations, especially in the praising parts. This modesty which I felt on his account he never forgave.

"As I earnestly wished for his success, I continued to bring him new acquaintances to see his experiments. I know not by what fatality every one left his house very well pleased with his philosophical feats, and very ill satisfied with the philosopher. He expressed himself with difficulty, his ideas were confused; and as his vanity was easily awakened by the slightest opposition or the least sign of contempt or indifference, he became suddenly enraged, and his fury rose to such a height, that his ideas were disordered, and he lost his recollection. I saw one day a striking instance of this inflammability. Volta, so celebrated for his experiments on electricity, was very curious to see those which Marat announced as overturning the theory of Franklin; but scarcely had he repeated a few of them and heard one or two objections, than, suspecting Volta's incredulity, he insulted him grossly, instead of answering his objections.

"He was however conscious of his difficulty in speaking, and of his want of temper in conversation, which were the reason why he sought the acquaintance of a literary man who had abilities for speaking, and who could display his theory for him; after which he would have appeared in his temple like a God, to receive the incense of simple mortals.

"He made me this proposition several times. I objected on account of my timidity, and my ignorance in experimental philosophy. He promised to initiate me in a short time into the most abstruse mysteries of his discoveries. I constantly persisted in my refusal, because I did not wish to be any man's second; because I never had any very strong passion for that branch of knowledge; because I did not think myself sufficiently skilled in making experiments; and in fine, because my feelings led me rather to shun Marat than become more intimately connected with him. Curiosity, and

the wish to procure information **had** made me seek his acquaintance; the
desire of being useful **to** him, because he seemed oppressed, had induced me
to keep up that acquaintance; but he had never inspired me with any of
those sentiments that constitute the delight of friendship.

"It was from a sentiment of **humanity** that I procured him **the sale of his**
books, and little chests of instruments; from the **earnestness which he dis-**
covered in collecting the little profit of his works, I judged that he was **in**
distress, although he **had too** much pride to acknowledge it. Alas! this
service, which I did him gratuitously, has since furnished him matter for
treating me with the most atrocious insults in one of his numbers. So far
was I from withholding the money for his works, that I would have shared
my **purse** with him, had I then been provided for myself.

"**I have** at all **times done justice** to Marat, and I will continue to **do so,**
**though I** owe to **him a part of the** persecutions which I am now suffering.
**He was** indefatigable in labor, and had great address in making experi-
**ments; a** tribute which I heard Franklin once render him, who was en-
**chanted with** his experiments on light. I cannot say so much for those on
**fire and** electricity. Marat thought he had made **discoveries which over-**
**threw the** system of Franklin; but Franklin was not the dupe of his quackery. Le Roy, the academician, who was named commissary to examine his
discoveries on light, agreed that those which he had made on the prism
were ingenious, and that Marat had a singular talent in making them. His
report was in many respects favorable, but some of the academicians forced
him to suppress it.

"Marat was most earnestly solicitous to obtain an eulogium from the
Academy of Sciences, and this earnestness suggested the idea of a stratagem which cost him immense labor. He undertook making a new translation of Newton's Principia on optics. This was a new mode of destroying
the system; for I have no doubt but that he made alterations in translating
it. He wished the Academy to give their approbation of this translation;
**but** his name would have excited their suspicions, and led them to examine
the work with **more** severity. **In order to avoid suspicion, he proposed to**
**many of his friends to** lend him their **name; and he** succeeded with **Baus-**
**sée, the grammarian, a** weak and **easy man, who was not aware of Marat's**
**manœuvres.** With Baussée's name, the commissaries of the **Academy did**
**not hesitate to** give, without reading, their approbation and **praises to the**
**work of their** enemy. I cannot tell what advantage he reaped from it; for
this **translation is** unknown, though it is magnificently printed. Marat
made me a **present** of a copy of it on vellum paper in the beginning of the
Revolution.

"At this period Marat was poor, and lived wretchedly; and though since
**my** return from America I have not conversed with him, **I** do not think that
he has changed his principles. He is accused of venality and corruption,
but **I have** never forborne repeating, **that** he was above corruption. Marat
**had but** one single passion—that of being foremost in the career which he

was running. Anxiety for fame was his disease, for he had not that or avarice. He was of a bilious habit, and passionate in his disposition, obstinate in his sentiments, and persevering in his conduct. We may judge of his perseverance from one trait—that although he was under the greatest embarrassment in speaking, he has nevertheless exhibited himself in every tribune. He forgot every thing in pursuit of his favorite object.

" His earnestness to obtain his ends made him employ all sorts of means, lies and calumny of every kind: he was an actor in every thing. He defended the people as he defended truth in natural philosophy; not for the sake of being useful to the people, for Marat despised them, but in order to accomplish his designs. He found flattery the best mode of obtaining the suffrages of the mob, he therefore flattered them: had tyranny promised him better success, he would have preferred it, but a man must be a tribune, before he becomes a tyrant.

" All his motions were those of a mountebank. He looked like a puppet, whose head and arms were moved at the will of the puppet-show-man. Every thing was abrupt and unconnected in his discourses, as well as in his gestures, because nothing proceeded from his heart, but all from his head, and every thing was artificial.

" Marat loved no man, and had no belief in virtue. He was selfish, never bestowed praise on any writer, and seemed as if all talents and all genius were concentrated in himself. He very seriously imagined that he alone was capable of governing France, and entrusted it in confidence to some friends, who were obliged to support the party which protected him, for the chiefs of which he had the most profound contempt.

"I have said that he was daring; notwithstanding which, he was not brave. He had neither the courage of a gladiator, nor that of a philosopher; though he wanted one day to fight with Charles, because he had not spoken with respect of his experiments; and he was continually talking of blood, and challenging the whole world. This rodomontade never imposed on me, for I had seen him too nearly. He was violent, but not courageous; under despotism he was afraid of the Bastille, and since the reign of liberty he has been always in fear of prisons. I shall mention two traits on this head to show his character.

" Marat in 1780 was a candidate for the prize given by the Economical Society of Berne, on the question of the reform of the criminal law. This society delayed every year pronouncing its judgment. In 1782, I advertised my Collection of Criminal Laws in ten volumes. Marat begged me to insert the memoir which he had addressed to the Society. There was a boldness in this essay which might prove disagreeable to government. I asked Marat if he wished his name to appear. ' By no means,' answered he, ' for the Bastille is there, and I do not much like to be shut up:' and he left me to run the chance, as my name appeared at the head of the collection.

"I met him one day in the Thuilleries, in 1786 or 1787: it was a long time since I had seen him. We talked of his works; I asked him why he

was so bent on pursuing natural philosophy, when he had against him all
the academies and all the philosophers. I advised him to consecrate his labors to politics. 'It is time,' I observed to him, 'to think of overturning
despotism; join your labors to mine, and to those enlightened men who
have sworn its overthrow, and this undertaking will cover you with glory.'
Marat answered, that he would rather continue his experiments in peace,
because philosophy did not lead to the Bastille; and he made me understand very plainly, that the French people were not sufficiently ripe, nor
sufficiently courageous to support a revolution.

"When the Bastille was overthrown, Marat was no longer afraid of it,
and quitted his cave. He even pretended at this period that all the honors
of this glorious Revolution belonged to himself; and making up some sort
of story about a colonel of dragoons whom he had arrested on the Pont-
Neuf, he entreated me to print it in the Patriote Français. He bestowed so
many extravagant praises on himself in the account, that I could not carry
my complaisance so far. I therefore struck out the praises and published
the fact; which Marat never forgave. As he despaired of finding journalists who would flatter him, he undertook a journal himself, which I advertised with an eulogium, in order to get him subscribers; and in doing him
this service, which I never refused to any of my brother journalists, I thought
I did service to the public. Good God! how great was my error! and what
was my surprise, when I read some of his numbers! How was it possible
that a writer who had any respect for himself could become so degraded as
to make use of a style so vile, scandalous, and atrocious!

"I own that I thought Marat a mean writer, an inconsistent logician, incredulous as to morals, ambitious, an enemy to all men of talents; but I did
not think that he would violate every principle, every law, so far as to ca-
lumniate the most virtuous men, and preach massacre and pillage. . . .
I stop here . . . . And I finish with this reflection; Whatever injury
Marat may have done me, I forgive; but I can never forgive him for having
corrupted the morals of the people, and having inspired them with a taste
for blood; for without morals and without humanity there is no republic.

"I have thought it right to enlarge with respect to this man, because he
is better known from that part of his life preceding the Revolution than
that which followed. Since 1789 he has been constantly on stilts; before
that period, you see him at home, and more like himself.

"In spite of the provocations of Marat, I have never thought it right to
reveal to the world the circumstances which I have just related. Personal
discussions have always been disagreeable to me, and seemed to me only
fitted to serve the purposes of the enemies of the Revolution."

## No. V.

## ACCOUNT OF THE GIRONDINS, SILLERY AND LA SOURCE.

"I HAVE yet only given you a general outline of our prison; but there was one scene of calamity which myself and my family were alone doomed to witness, and in which our fellow-captives had no share. Our apartment, with two others adjoining, were separated from the public room by a little passage and a door, which the *huissiers* carefully locked at night. It happened that these apartments were then occupied by two persons, in whose society we had passed some of the most agreeable hours of our residence in France. These persons were Sillery and La Source, two of the members of the Convention, who had been long in close confinement, and who were now on the point of appearing before that sanguinary tribunal, whence, after the most shocking mockery of justice, they were inhumanly dragged to the scaffold. Sillery, on account of his infirmities, had with much difficulty obtained permission from the police for his servant to be admitted into the prison during the day, together with an old female friend, who, on the plea of his illness, had implored leave to attend him as his nurse, with that eloquence which belongs to affliction, and which sometimes even the most hardened hearts are unable to resist. While men assume over our sex so many claims to superiority, let them at least bestow on us the palm of constancy, and allow that in the fidelity of our attachments we have the right of pre-eminence. Those prisons from which men shrunk back with terror, and where they often left their friends abandoned, lest they should be involved in their fate—women, in whom the force of sensibility overcame the fears of female weakness, demanded and sometimes obtained permission to visit, in defiance of all the dangers that surrounded their gloomy walls. Sillery's friend and his servant being allowed to go in and out of his apartment, the door was not kept constantly locked, although he and La Source were closely confined, and not permitted to have any communication with the other prisoners. The second night of our abode in the Luxembourg when the prisoners had retired to their respective chambers, and the keeper had locked the outer door which enclosed our three apartments, La Source entered our room. Oh! how different was this interview from those meetings of social enjoyment that were embellished by the charms of his conversation, always distinguished by a flow of eloquence, and animated by that enthusiastic fervor which peculiarly belonged to his character! La Source

was a native of Languedoc, and united **with very** superior talents that vivid
warmth of imagination for which **the southern** provinces of France have
been renowned since the period when, **awakened** by the genial influence of
those luxuriant regions, the song of the Troubadours burst from the gloom
of Gothic barbarism.   Liberty in the soul of La Source was less a principle
than a passion, for his bosom beat high with philanthropy; and in his former
situation as **a** Protestant minister he had felt **in a** peculiar manner the oppression of the ancient system.   His sensibility was acute ; and his detestation of the crimes by which **the** Revolution had been sullied, was in proportion to his devoted attachment to its cause.   La Source was polite and
**amiable in his manners; he had a** taste for music and a powerful voice, **and
sung, as he conversed, with all** the energy of feeling.   After **the day had
passed in** the fatigue of public debates, he was glad to lay aside **the** tumult
of politics in the evening, for the conversation of some literary men whom
he met occasionally at our tea-table.   Ah, how little **did we** then foresee the
horrors of that period when we should meet him **in the gloom** of a prison, a
proscribed **victim,** with whom this melancholy **interview** was beset with
**danger!**

"We were obliged to converse in whispers, while **we kept watch** successively at the outer door, that if any step approached, he might instantly fly
to his chamber.   He had much to ask, having been three months a close
prisoner, and knowing little of what was passing in the world; and though
he seemed to forget all the horrors of his situation in the consolation he derived from these moments of confidential conversation, yet he frequently
lamented, that this last gleam of pleasure which was shed over his existence
was purchased at the price of our captivity.   In the solitude of his prison,
no voice of friendship, no accents of pity had reached his ear; and after our
arrival, he used through the lonely day to count the hours till the prison-
**gates** were closed, till all was still within its walls, and no sound was heard
**without, except,** at intervals, the hoarse cry of the sentinels, when he has-
**tened to our apartment.** The discovery of these visits would **indeed have
exposed us to the most** fatal **consequences; but our** sympathy prevailed over
**our fears; nor could** we, **whatever might be** the event, refuse our devoted
**friend this last melancholy** satisfaction.   La Source at **his** second **visit** was
accompanied by **Sillery, the** husband **of Madame de Sillery** (Genlis), whose
writings are so **well known** in England.   Sillery was **about** sixty **years of
age;** had lived freely, like most men of **his** former **rank in** France; and
from this dissipated life had more the appearance **of age than** belonged to
his years.   **His manners retained** the elegance, by **which** that class was distinguished which Mr. **Burke has denominated** "the Corinthian capital of pol-
ished society."   Sillery had a fine taste for drawing, **and** during his confinement displayed the powers of his **pencil** by tracing beautiful landscapes.
He also amused himself **by** reading history; **and** possessing considerable
talents for literature, had recorded with a rich warmth of coloring the events
**of the Revolution,** in which he had been a distinguished actor, and of which

he had treasured up details precious for history.  With keen regret he told me that he had committed several volumes of manuscript to the flames, a sad sacrifice to the Omars of the day.

"The mind of Sillery was somewhat less fortified against his approaching fate than that of La Source.  The old man often turned back on the past and wept, and sometimes inquired with an anxious look, if we believed there was any chance of his deliverance.  Alas! I have no words to paint the sensations of those moments!—To know that the days of our fellow-captives were numbered—that they were doomed to perish—that the bloody tribunal before which they were going to appear, was but the pathway to the scaffold —to have the painful task of stifling our feelings, while we endeavored to soothe the weakness of humanity by hopes which we knew were fallacious, was a species of misery almost insupportable.  There were moments, indeed, when the task became too painful to be endured.  There were moments, when, shocked by some new incident of terror, this cruel restraint gave way to uncontrolable emotion; when the tears, the sobbings of convulsive anguish, would no longer be suppressed, and our unfortunate friends were obliged to give instead of receiving consolation.

"They had in their calamity that support which is, of all others, the most effectual under misfortune.  Religion was in La Source a habit of the mind. Impressed with the most sublime ideas of the Supreme Being, although the ways of heaven never appeared more dark or intricate than in this triumph of guilt over innocence, he reposed with unbounded confidence in that Providence in whose hand are the issues of life and death.  Sillery, who had a feeling heart, found devotion the most soothing refuge of affliction.  He and La Source composed together a little hymn adapted to a sweet solemn air, which they called their evening service.  Every night before we parted they sung this simple dirge in a low tone, to prevent their being heard in the other apartments, which made it seem more plaintive.  Those mournful sounds, the knell of my departing friends, yet thrill upon my heart!

"Calme nos allarmes,
Prete nous les armes,
Source de vrai bien,
Brise nos liens!
Entends les accens
De tes enfans
Dans les tourmens;
Ils souffrent, et leurs larmes
C'est leur seul encens.

Prends notre défense,
Grand Dieu de l'innocence!
Près de toi toujours
Elle trouve son secours;
Tu connois nos cœurs,
Et les auteurs
De nos malheurs;
D'un sort qui t'offense
Détruis la rigueur.

Quand la tyrannie
Frappe notre vie,
Fiers de notre sort,
Méprisant la mort,
Nous te bénissons,
Nous triomphons,
Et nous savons
Qu'un jour, la patrie
Vengera nos noms !

"La Source often spoke of his wife with tender regret. He had been married only a week, when he was chosen a member of the Legislative Assembly, and was obliged to hasten to Paris, while his wife remained in Languedoc to take care of an aged mother. When the Legislative Assembly was dissolved, La Source was immediately elected a member of the National Convention, and could find no interval in which to visit his native spot or his wife, whom he saw no more. In his meditations on the chain of political events, he mentioned one little incident which seemed to hang on his mind with a sort of superstitious feeling. A few days after the 10th of August, he dined in the Fauxbourg St. Antoine with several members of the Legislative Assembly, who were the most distinguished for their talents and patriotism. They were exulting in the birth of the new Republic, and the glorious part they were to act as its founders, when a citizen of the Fauxbourg, who had been invited to partake of the repast, observed, that he feared a different destiny awaited them. 'As you have been the founders of the Republic,' said he, 'you will also be its victims. In a short time you will be obliged to impose restraints and duties on the people, to whom your enemies and theirs will represent you as having overthrown regal power only to establish your own. You will be accused of aristocracy; and I foresee,' he added with much seeming perturbation, 'that you will all perish on the scaffold.'

"The company smiled at his singular prediction; but during the ensuing winter, when the storm was gathering over the political horizon, La Source recalled the prophecy, and sometimes reminded Vergniaud of the man of the Fauxbourg St. Antoine. Vergniaud had little heeded the augur; but a few days previous to the 31st of May, when the Convention was for the first time besieged, La Source said again to Vergniaud, 'Well, what think you of the prophet of the Fauxbourg?' 'The prophet of the Fauxbourg,' answered Vergniaud, 'was in the right.'

"The morning now arrived when La Source and Sillery, together with nineteen other members of the Convention, were led before the revolutionary tribunal. When the guards who were to conduct them arrived, the other prisoners crowded to the public room to see them pass, and we shut ourselves up in our own apartment. They returned about five in the evening; soon after which their counsel arrived, and we had no opportunity of seeing them till midnight, when they related to us what had passed. The conduct of the judges and the aspect of the jury were calculated to banish every gleam of hope from the bosoms of the prisoners ; the former permitted with reluctance any thing to be urged in their defence, and the latter listened with impatience, casting upon their victims looks of atrocity in which they might easily read their fate; yet in spite of these unhappy omens, our friends returned from the tribunal with their minds much elevated. La Source described in his eloquent language the noble enthusiasm of liberty, the ardent love of their country, the heroical contempt of death which animated his colleagues, whom he had not seen for some time, since they had been transferred to the Conciergerie, while himself and Sillery had obtained permission to remain at the Luxembourg upon the certificates of their physicians, that they were too ill to be removed without danger. La Source declared that ancient history offered no model of public virtue beyond that which was exhibited by his friends at the tribunal, and who in their prison, blending with the fortitude of Romans the gaiety of Frenchmen, and being confined in one apartment, passed the short interval of life which was left, in conversation and cheerful repasts which were usually concluded with patriotic songs. ' You, said Vergniaud to La Source when they met at the tribunal, ' you perhaps will find something to regret in the loss of life. You have a glimpse of the gardens of the Luxembourg, which may remind you that there is something beautiful in nature; but we who live in humble shambles, who every day see fresh victims dragged to execution, we are become so familiarized with death, that we look on it with unconcern.'

" A few days before this sanguinary trial ended, the administration of the police sent orders that the English women confined in the Luxembourg should be removed the next day to a convent in the Fauxbourg St. Antoine. With what keen regret La Source and Sillery received this intelligence ! A thousand and a thousand times they thanked us for the dangers we had risked in receiving them, and for the sympathy which had soothed the last hours of their existence—a thousand times they declared, that if it were yet possible their lives might be preserved, they should consider themselves for ever bound to us by the most sacred ties of gratitude and friendship; but they felt, alas! how small was the chance that we should meet again in this world. Sillery cut off a lock of his white hairs, which he begged I would preserve for his sake, and La Source gave me the same relic. They embraced us with much emotion. They prayed that the blessing of God might be upon us; we mingled our tears together, and parted to meet no more!"—*Miss Williams's Letters from France,* vol. i. pp. 44—60.

**END OF VOLUME ONE.**